D0852999

The Drowning Summer

The Drowning Summer

CHRISTINE LYNN HERMAN

L B

LITTLE, BROWN AND COMPANY
New York Boston

Copyright © 2022 by Christine Lynn Herman

Cover art © 2022 by Carolina Rodríguez Fuenmayor. Cover design by Karina Granda. Cover copyright © 2022 by Hachette Book Group, Inc.

Hachette Book Group supports the right to free expression and the value of copyright. The purpose of copyright is to encourage writers and artists to produce the creative works that enrich our culture.

The scanning, uploading, and distribution of this book without permission is a theft of the author's intellectual property. If you would like permission to use material from the book (other than for review purposes), please contact permissions@hbgusa.com. Thank you for your support of the author's rights.

Little, Brown and Company
Hachette Book Group
1290 Avenue of the Americas, New York, NY 10104
Visit us at LBYR.com

First Edition: April 2022

Little, Brown and Company is a division of Hachette Book Group, Inc. The Little, Brown name and logo are trademarks of Hachette Book Group, Inc.

The publisher is not responsible for websites (or their content) that are not owned by the publisher.

Library of Congress Cataloging-in-Publication Data
Names: Herman, Christine Lynn, author.
Title: The drowning summer / Christine Lynn Herman.
Description: First edition. | New York ; Boston : Little, Brown and Company, 2022. | Audience: Ages 14 & up. | Summary: Sixteen-year-old fledgling mediums Mina and Evelyn navigate their growing attraction as they investigate the connection between a vengeful spirit and murders that rocked their coastal Long Island town six years ago.
Identifiers: LCCN 2021012751 | ISBN 9780759557536 (hardcover) | ISBN 9780759557802 (ebook)
Subjects: CYAC: Mediums—Fiction. | Spirits—Fiction. | Bisexuality—Fiction. | Water—Pollution—Fiction. | Ocean—Fiction. | Italian Americans—Fiction. | Long Island (N.Y.)—Fiction.
Classification: LCC PZ7.1.H4934 Dr 2022 | DDC [Fic]—dc23
LC record available at https://lccn.loc.gov/2021012751

ISBNs: 978-0-7595-5753-6 (hardcover), 978-0-7595-5780-2 (ebook)

Printed in the United States of America

LSC-C

Printing 1, 2022

For my grandmother Carmella Parrinello,
who taught me everything I know about
the Sound, Italian food, and making
the most of the time you've got.

I miss you.

Chapter One

This time, the dead came calling in the middle of the night.

Mina Zanetti had been waiting for them to reach out to her mother for hours, working on her latest dress design so she wouldn't fall asleep.

The candles burning low on Mina's windowsill cast a dim, flickering light over the discarded clothes and fabric strewn across her bedroom floor. Mina sat in the corner, staring at Regina—her mannequin—who was draped in her current tailoring project.

She hadn't expected her mother to take so long. But if she wasn't going to sleep, she might as well work.

"Almost," Mina muttered, picking out a series of basting stitches with her seam ripper. She had spent the past few days attempting to execute a pattern for a midi dress with a high neckline, but it wasn't cooperating. And it was easier to focus on her flawed design attempt than it was to consider what she was waiting for.

Because it wasn't her work that worried her right now. It was her mother's. Mina had been asking to be included in Stella's career for as long as she could remember. Not the Italian American catering business her mother ran out of their cozy bungalow in Cliffside Bay—her other job. Her *real* job.

Most of the Zanettis had a little something extra, a connection to the spirits they could either nurture or ignore. The dead called to her family, and her family answered them, guiding ghosts from this world to whatever came next. Mina had seen firsthand how this work helped both the living and the deceased, kept Mina's little corner of Long Island balanced. She wanted nothing more than to follow in her family's footsteps.

But Stella seemed to have other ideas.

Mina shifted the dress's waistline up a quarter inch, thinking about how her favorite lipstick and platform sandals would pair with the cream-colored fabric. Visualizing the finished piece soothed her as she readied herself for the negotiations she would have to go through to be included tonight.

She was determined. She was ready. She had waited long enough.

It had taken years of pleading and several artfully constructed PowerPoint presentations for Stella to even consider letting Mina join the family business. But over the last six months, she'd slowly started to relent. Mina had sat patiently through lectures about the ebb and flow of the dead alongside the tides and the moon, and the ethics of being a medium, even though she'd absorbed all of this via osmosis years ago. She'd been a model student. Her patience was rewarded in early May when Stella finally promised to take Mina along the next time she went out in the field.

But as May rolled into June, Mina had realized it was a promise her mother had no intention of keeping. Which was why she'd taken matters into her own hands.

At 1:57 AM, soft, careful footsteps sounded in front of her bedroom, paused, then continued down the hallway. Mina flung open her door and called after her mother, who froze before reluctantly turning around.

"Oh, my seashell," Stella Zanetti stage-whispered, flipping on the hall light.

She'd had Mina when she was a college senior. Sixteen years later, the two looked more like siblings than a mother and daughter: two white women with the same pointed chin, a slight gap between their front teeth, and a mole beneath each of their left eyes. But where Mina's hair was bleached blond and brittle, her mother's was dark, wavy, and improbably long, falling almost to her waist. Mina noted with grim satisfaction that her mother's familiar face, so often guarded, was twisted with guilt.

"You waited up for me, didn't you?"

"You promised to take me with you," Mina said. "But you weren't going to wake me up at all."

"Well, no, I wasn't," Stella said hesitantly. "I thought..."

She thought Mina wasn't ready. Mina's wrist twinged, an old injury, an old mistake, but she refused to flinch. That was ancient history now.

"You thought I'd forgotten the dead are impossible to ignore tonight? I learned the moon phases before I learned the alphabet."

"That's a slight exaggeration." Mina had been trying to make a joke. But her mother's response sounded careful, almost wary.

Mina had spent her whole life studying Stella's moods and habits. She was the only person in the world who understood Stella's organization system for her spice rack. Who'd held her hand while she talked to a lawyer on the phone about starting her own company. Who knew exactly how Stella's workday had been by how she'd arranged her shoes at the front door. The only thing she didn't understand about her mother was Stella's resistance to include her in this part of her life, when she'd always been included in everything else.

"Please," Mina said weakly.

When Mina had asked years ago how her mother had discovered her talents, Stella said, "A ghost called to me when I was young, and I answered. And once you start speaking to the dead, you cannot stop. It's not something you can turn on and off whenever you feel like it—it's forever."

"What if I want them to talk to me?" Mina had asked, and Stella had made a low, frightened noise and shaken her head. The look she'd had on her face then was the same one she wore now.

Mina braced herself for another rejection...but to her surprise, Stella's expression shifted, like a cloud floating away from the moon.

"You can come along," her mother said at last. "But we need to hurry up. The dead are louder than usual tonight."

A rickety flight of stairs behind their house led from the cliff to the beach below. Mina followed her mother down, her steps cautious on the flimsy wooden planks. By the time her shoes touched the shoreline, her mother had already waded into the surf. Unlike Mina, who'd opted for leggings and waterproof boots, Stella had worn a highly impractical outfit to talk to the dead—a flowing maxi dress and her favorite opal headband twined through her dark hair.

They stood in Sand Dollar Cove, a crescent moon–shaped slice of sand on Long Island's North Shore. The tide was high enough to swallow most of the coastline, leaving nothing but a thin stretch littered with rocks and broken seashells between the cliff and the open sea. The full moon shone in the sky, a large, glimmering orb that cast a thin light across the beach. It was a peaceful, idyllic sight, yet Mina couldn't suppress a shudder as she glanced behind her, where a cave opened in the rocks like an unhinged jaw. Three high school juniors had been found dead in that cave six years ago.

It had stopped most of the town from going there. But it hadn't stopped Stella Zanetti from using Sand Dollar Cove to communicate with spirits.

"There you are." Stella looked like the medium she was, standing tall and regal in the surf, as ethereal and unknowable as the spirits she guided from the earth to their final resting place. "Remember to stay on the beach. I don't want you exposed to the ocean until you're ready."

Mina choked down disappointment. Saltwater was her family's primary channel of communication with spirits—the ocean currents tended to pull ghosts to the shore the same way they washed up tangles of seaweed on the sand. If she wasn't in the sea, they wouldn't notice her.

"But I *am* ready," she said, trying to keep the desperation out of her voice.

"I need you to trust me," Stella said. "Can you do that?"

Mina's wrist ached again. She stared at the smooth, unblemished skin there, remembering the only time she'd ever let Stella down. But maybe once was enough. Maybe that was the real reason behind her mother's resistance to teach Mina how to be a medium.

So Mina backed away from the surf, swallowed her disappointment, and forced herself to smile. Because she was lucky to be on this beach at all. "Yes, I can. What now?"

Stella gestured to the beach behind her in response. "Candles—will you set them up?"

"Of course."

There were several different kinds of spirit summonings. Stella had been tight-lipped about the implications of the way each of them varied, but Mina knew that when using the ocean to communicate with ghosts, it was important to create a symbolic barrier between the world of the dead and the living. A small row of candles on the upper shoreline would work nicely. When Mina was done, she stood behind the flickering barrier and waited.

Stella thanked her gently, then reached for the scrying focus around her neck. In someone else's hands, it was just a cheap glass pendant shaped like a lavender diamond. But in hers, it was much more. The spirits had a whole ocean to communicate through. Yet all that water, all that energy, was overwhelming. Mediums needed an anchor to ground themselves, to keep their powers channeled and focused. "Now I work and you watch, all right?"

Mina nodded reluctantly. "All right."

She observed carefully from the beach as her mother pulled the pendant over her head, her fingers clasped tightly around the purple glass, and turned to face the water. When Stella opened her hand a few seconds later, the scrying focus glowed blue in her palm. She knelt and dunked the pendant in the sea. Its deep, cobalt light spread from Stella's hand and into the water, glowing like bioluminescence beneath the waves. A small path shot across the surface, and at the edge of the horizon, coming closer to them, Mina saw an answering glow. It was translucent and faint, a small, concentrated ball of blue light.

"I see it," Mina whispered, her voice soft with awe. "That's a spirit, right?"

"Yes." The unease in Stella's voice had deepened. Her mother rose to her feet, the pendant still glowing in her hand. Saltwater dripped from the ends of her hair and soaked through her dress, but she didn't seem to mind. "They're coming closer now."

Water rippled beneath the light as it moved toward them, guided by a gentle wave. The ball expanded as it drew nearer, twisting into a humanoid form that hovered over the sea. Mina felt something rising in her, humming beneath her skin. It tugged her toward the spirit's warm, calming glow.

That pull, that connection, was what Mina had come here to find. She wanted to communicate with a spirit, and since they were strongest during the full and new moons, she'd known this would be her best chance. Mina understood that some would consider talking to the dead more of a curse than a gift. But she was a Zanetti, and although this job would not be easy, it was still one she wanted.

Stella was waist-deep in the ocean now, lost in concentration.

Another surge of light bled from her scrying focus and circled through the water, coursing gently toward the spirit.

There was nobody watching Mina except the waves and the cloudy sky above them.

Nobody to tell her no.

So she stepped over the line of candles and into the surf, that pull still surging through her, and knelt.

The moment her skin made contact with the ocean, the humming in her chest intensified. She heard a soft, rustling noise, like the sound a shell made when she held it up to her ear. The water lapped gently against her hand, and a familiar blue-green glow began to spread from Mina's fingertips.

"Whoa." Mina gazed at the light as it spread away from her hand, tendrils spiraling into the water like elongated fingers. She felt awe and pride and a deep, wonderful relief.

"Mina!" Her mother's voice was sharp. "What are you doing?"

Mina jerked her head up. The spirit hovered perhaps thirty feet away now. Their glow fully illuminated the panic on Stella's face.

"I..." But Mina had no explanation, no excuse except that she'd wanted this so desperately. Surely Stella could understand that.

"Get out of the ocean." Stella started toward her, gripping her scrying focus like she wanted to shatter it. Her face was slack with fear. "Don't make me say it again."

And it was exactly at that moment that Mina felt something else. The humming grew louder, crackling beneath her skin like an electrical current. Mina smelled salt and brine with an edge of rot, so powerful she nearly gagged. The ocean surged against her knees, and the sound surged with it.

The humming unspooled into a tangle of distinct, panicked voices, like water sloshing inside her skull. There was more than one spirit in Sand Dollar Cove, far more than one, and all of them were screaming. It was an agonizing assault of noise that left Mina gasping and immobile in the surf.

She'd been wrong. She *wasn't* ready. But that no longer mattered. The voices roared as that pull through her entire body intensified, a calling, a yearning. She groaned and forced her eyes open, searching for the spirits, searching for her mother. Mina looked up just in time to see the wave crashing toward her, far higher than her kneeling body. It sent her tumbling through the surf like an errant seashell.

The wave knocked her on her back and filled her mouth with saltwater. Mina flipped over, coughing, and clawed at the rocky sand. It was harder than it should've been to crawl back to the beach, as if the ocean itself was grasping at her with a thousand tiny fingers, refusing to release her to the shore. But then Stella was in front of her, extending a hand. Mina grasped it and scrambled away from the waves. Mother and daughter wound up crouched beside the staircase that led back up to the bungalow, on that precious slice of beach that remained safe from high tide.

The wave had completely destroyed Mina's candle barrier. A dozen waterlogged tea lights scattered across the rocks, their tiny flames snuffed out.

"Oh, Mina," Stella whispered.

Their hands were still clasped together. Mina's eyes scanned the water for any trace of the spirit, but they were gone.

"Are you all right?"

"I'm fine." Mina gasped, blinking away salt. The taste of the ocean still lingered in her mouth, and her clothes were caked with sand and seaweed. Although it was nearly summer, she was shivering—the water had been cold, and the echoes of those voices were still ringing in her head. She knew the memory would stay with her for a long time. "I'm sorry, Mom. I shouldn't have—"

"It's all right." Stella squeezed her hand. "I'm just glad you're safe. This is why I didn't want you to come out here. The spirits have been growing stronger and stronger lately—even with a scrying focus, I can't always manage them. But I had no idea they'd be so dangerous tonight."

Mina turned toward the ocean, where the waves now lapped calmly against the beach. There was no evidence of the dread and horror she had felt just moments ago, and yet it still lingered inside of her, pressing against her ribcage.

"Why was it so bad tonight?"

Her mother's voice was grim. "Because someone *else* called a spirit."

Mina knew people who weren't mediums tried to talk to the dead sometimes. Most of them reached out to relatives or friends they couldn't bear the thought of never seeing again. But Stella seemed nervous about this in a way that didn't quite match up with an amateur summoning attempt.

"Another medium?" she asked.

Stella shook her head. "I'd never call that the work of a

medium. Someone summoned this spirit with the express purpose of bending them to their will."

Memories stirred in Mina's mind. A ring of salt. Candles snuffing out. A sharp scream.

There were other reasons people wanted to contact the dead. Awful reasons. Mina had spent the last six years trying to forget them.

"And you think that's what we just dealt with?"

"Absolutely." Stella pulled Mina up from the sand. "But you shouldn't worry. This work is clumsy, inexperienced. Your uncle and I will deal with it."

She started toward the stairs. Mina turned to follow her... and gasped with pain.

Her left wrist was on fire. Voices surged in her head, stronger this time, and the taste of salt rose in her throat once more. Mina gagged and doubled over on the beach, her watery eyes fixed on the mark that had appeared on her wrist. It was a bluish-green sand dollar the size of a quarter, and it hurt in a way she had only felt once before: the first time it had appeared on her arm.

Something stirred at the very bottom of her memory, like a long-dormant creature waking on the ocean floor. And suddenly she was ten again, staring at Evelyn Mackenzie over a flickering candle flame as Mina felt something course through that cave in the side of the cliff, a whispering that felt strong enough to shatter her skull. Her wrist had blazed with pain until all that remained was that same sand dollar, etched into her skin.

A mark of the spirit she and Evelyn had summoned—and what they had asked the ghost to do.

"Mina?" Her mother's voice pierced through Mina's haze of alarm. "Are you coming?"

Mina stuffed her hand in the pocket of her sweatshirt and swiveled around, struggling to keep her voice calm. "Just thought I saw something in the water."

It had been a long time since that day. Mina had assumed that Evelyn had forgotten about what they'd done, blocked their summoning out the same way she'd blocked out their entire friendship. Heat pulsed in Mina's wrist in time with the waves crashing behind her as she made herself a silent promise.

One way or another, she would ensure that Evelyn Mackenzie kept their secret.

Chapter Two

Evelyn Mackenzie didn't appreciate being called *difficult*.

Not by her father, who used the word every time Evelyn brought home a lackluster report card or wound up in detention for sleeping in class after a morning shift. Not by her sister, who always answered her phone calls with a twinge of dread in her voice.

And certainly not by Nick Slater, her boyfriend, who mumbled the word accusatorially when Evelyn showed up at his house after her disciplinary hearing with Cliffside High's academic honesty council.

"C'mon, Evie," he whined as they stood in the foyer, beneath an oil painting of Nick, his brother, and his parents—four white people with matching ice-blue eyes who looked like they'd rather be anywhere else. The portrait had probably cost more money than Evelyn's future college tuition. "Why do you have to be so difficult? It's not like they're expelling you or anything."

Evelyn hated when he whined. "It's going on my permanent academic record. Which means colleges will see it. And Cliffside High is notifying every summer internship I applied to that I cheated. I can't *believe* you didn't tell them the truth."

"It wouldn't have changed anything. They would've just punished both of us."

"But it was *your* idea." Sophomore biology was Evelyn's highest grade and her favorite subject. But Nick was pulling a C, and his dad had threatened to ground him for the entire summer if he didn't get at least a B minus in every class.

So he'd asked his girlfriend for help on the final exam.

Evelyn wasn't sure what made her more furious: that she'd been caught, that Nick had let her take the fall, or that she'd agreed to steal an answer key in the first place.

"It's done, okay?" Nick said, lowering his voice. "Let's just forget about it."

"No, this isn't finished," Evelyn said. "But we are."

And it was only later, after they were done breaking up and she'd slammed the Slaters' front door behind her with all the force of her pent-up rage, that she wondered what it even meant. Being difficult.

Maybe, she thought, choking back tears as she slid her longboard onto the pavement and clipped her helmet beneath her chin, *difficult* was just a word people used for anyone too smart, too angry, too *inconvenient*.

Cliffside Bay was the kind of Long Island suburb where the homes looked like an architect had practiced on each of them, growing more skilled as they went on. Nick lived in one of the imposing modern mansions at the top of the cliff that had given the town its name. So Evelyn let momentum take her down the entire slope until she reached the streets at the very edge of town, lined with shabby clapboard houses and brown yards. Going there straight from Nick's made her house look even shittier than usual, made the knot in her stomach double in size.

Evelyn coasted to a stop once the paved street gave way to her gravel driveway. She scooped up her longboard and stomped up the front steps, halting only to kick open the unlocked door.

Her father was busy becoming one with his recliner in the living room, staring intently at the glow of the TV screen. The blinds behind him hadn't been opened or dusted in the three years since Meredith had left for college.

"Veggie burgers for dinner?" she asked, instead of saying hello.

Greg Mackenzie blinked at her as if she were an alien. Her father was a middle-aged white guy with the prematurely sun-damaged skin of a man who'd spent most of his life outdoors. Now, the closest he got to nature was the Discovery Channel.

"Sure," he said, after a moment's hesitation. "Use less charcoal this time, though—don't want the neighbors up our asses again."

"The Kowalskis throw a rager every weekend, Dad. They can handle a few scorch marks."

"You set their fence on fire, kid. You're lucky they didn't sue us."

"Fine," Evelyn muttered. "Microwave pizza it is."

She headed up the stairs, relieved. His tone was too warm for him to have found out about the disciplinary hearing yet.

He'd been invited, of course, but she'd figured out his email password and his phone passcode years ago—he could barely work either without her help. And it wasn't like Cliffside High was going to reach out to her mom. But deleting the school's messages was only buying her time before the inevitable disappointment, because there was no way she could hide this from her dad forever.

Evelyn's room was small and cozy, with a collection of plants crowded on the windowsill, dark blue walls she'd painted herself, and a flannel-patterned bedspread. A neon sign shaped like a cloud—a birthday gift from Meredith—hung above the rumpled covers.

She dropped her helmet and backpack on the floor, then went to the cage beside her closet, where her corn snake Clara was curled up in her favorite hide.

Nick had always hated Clara. He thought the whole reptiles-as-pets thing was creepy, couldn't understand why Evelyn worked extra shifts at the Scales & Tails Pet Shop for an entire sweaty summer just to adopt her and give her the perfect enclosure.

"Should've known he was an asshole," Evelyn told her snake.

She chose to believe that Clara was lifting her yellow-and-white snout in solidarity, even though Evelyn knew her pet was probably just hungry. She was due for a feeding tomorrow.

As far as the breakup went, Evelyn knew she would be fine. Yes, Nick had been her boyfriend for the past four months, but it wasn't like she loved him. This was nothing a few cute reptile videos wouldn't solve.

The bigger problem here was her tarnished academic record.

Bile rose in Evelyn's throat as she thought of how the news of her cheating would spread around the school. She wasn't exactly popular, but she wasn't a nobody, either. Her dad's involvement in the drowning summer had given her a sort of double-edged notoriety that got her invited to parties. And dating Nick, for better or for worse, had made people remember her for something other than her last name. But she had no real friends, no support system that would stop the rumors about what had happened on the biology final... or the fact that it would have to go on her college applications.

Evelyn excavated her laptop from her unmade bed and pulled up the website for the Coastal Wildlife Conservation and Research Society of Long Island. She had applied to a bunch of summer stuff across Long Island, but this one was perfect for her: two months spent shadowing real scientists as they monitored the populations of local species in protected beachfront habitats. She'd already aced her interview and was waiting to hear back about their final decision.

But once they found out that she'd cheated on her exam, they would never hire her. And that was just the beginning.

College was her way out of Cliffside Bay for good. But after Meredith left and Evelyn took on a second job, her grades had started slipping. Pair that with a messy disciplinary record and a lack of prestigious extracurriculars, and the goals Evelyn had painstakingly worked toward for years would crumble.

She couldn't let Nick Slater take her future away.

Evelyn pushed the laptop aside and swung off the bed, rummaging through the bins shoved beneath the mattress until she found the one she was looking for. It was filled with evidence of a friendship she couldn't bear to forget—a crumbling seashell strung on a necklace, notes written back and forth on yellowed loose-leaf paper. She paused on a faded picture of two tiny white girls posing behind a sand castle. Evelyn was the one on the left, mid-yell, blurry from her decision to jump around when her father said *Hold still.* Mina Zanetti sat on the right. She dyed her hair now, but the face beneath her dark brown bangs was still unmistakably hers. Solemn. Careful.

Evelyn sighed and put the photo down, pushing away the familiar twinge of hurt. She was looking for one note in particular. It was hidden at the bottom of the bin, tucked inside an old school folder patterned with cartoon cats and puppies. The page was written in a child's handwriting, a copy of notes jotted down by someone much older.

At the beginning was a short message, underlined sharply.

Are you sure you want to try this?

After what had happened the first and only time she and Mina had talked to the dead, Evelyn had accepted that it was dangerous. That this power wasn't hers to use—instead, it belonged to the girl who'd given her that spell in the first place. A girl who would probably disapprove of her using terms like *spell* or *magic* at all.

But tonight felt different. Cliffside Bay had finally taken too much.

She had to make this go away. She would not fail. There was no other option.

Evelyn scanned the paper, her hands shaking so hard she feared it would rip.

How to Summon a Spirit to Do Your Bidding

The list of instructions was pretty short for a spell that promised to put a spirit's energy to use for any purpose. But the very first item made her pause.

Necessary location: a place of great pain for you or your target, after the sun has set, during the full or new moon. A graveyard will do, although it's rather derivative. It's an archaic fable that spirits only come out at night, but admittedly it's more likely they show up from dusk onward. And the darkness will cloak you from prying eyes that aren't the ones you seek.

"I don't know if this is a good idea," she said to Clara.

Her snake flicked her tongue out in response. Evelyn could've sworn she saw a warning in her red, unblinking eyes.

But some part of Evelyn had already made the decision the moment she pulled the bin out from under the bed. She hadn't used this spell when her mother left them, or when Meredith went away to school, because forcing someone to stay had felt too selfish. But it was *Nick's* selfishness that had gotten her here. And for the second time, Evelyn understood what it was like to need something big with the kind of intense, all-consuming fervor that overrode everything else. She knew in her bones that if she followed these instructions, she would summon a spirit again.

She shoved the rest of the items on the list into her backpack: Nick's varsity soccer sweatshirt. A lighter and three small candles. A saltshaker. A bowl.

The last item on the list was a knife. Evelyn stole her father's crimson switchblade from his hiding place in the back of his desk and tucked it carefully into her sweatshirt pocket. She wanted it close, just in case.

"I'll make dinner when I come back," she hollered at him as she raced toward the front door. He grunted in response.

Her longboard chased the setting sun toward the horizon as she looped around the bottom of the hill and coasted toward the water.

The massive slopes of brownish-tan rock that had given Cliffside Bay its name curved inward just enough to allow for occasional pockets of rocky shore and lapping waves. Sand Dollar Cove was the most picturesque of these by far, a perfect little hideaway secluded from the larger Long Island Sound. But thanks to the drowning summer, Evelyn wasn't worried about finding anyone there as she rounded the bend of the shoreline and walked in.

The tide was low, revealing the way the cliffs transitioned into a beach that was more rock than sand before finally hitting the surf. Evelyn scowled as her sneakers crunched across a broken bottle. She had spent her childhood spying on the organisms that chose to make their homes here, in the intertidal zone, where the harsh extremes of the tides and the temperatures made for hearty creatures that didn't take any bullshit. But everyone had their limits, and Evelyn wondered if tonight she'd reached hers.

She filled an empty water bottle in the surf, then headed to the cliff's base. The cave waited for her there about six feet off the ground, carved into the rock like an open eye. Behind her, the sunset bled out across the foamy water, red and orange reflections spilling onto the sand.

There were no sand dollars in Sand Dollar Cove. Actually, there were no sand dollars in Cliffside Bay at all, at least not on the beaches. Evelyn Mackenzie knew enough about what washed up on Long Island's North Shore to know sand dollars didn't—which was why this place had been called Horseshoe Crab Cove for most of Evelyn's life. The beach had gotten its new name six years ago, when three drowned teenagers were found inside that cave, laid out on the rocks with sand dollars placed neatly over their eyes.

The killer was never caught.

Evelyn had been ten when it happened. Old enough to remember the media frenzy. Old enough to remember the way the town had whispered the names of the dead, like a prayer, like a warning. Tamara Winger. Colin Maxwell.

And Jesse Slater. Nick's older brother... and her older sister Meredith's ex-boyfriend.

Enough time had passed since then for podcasts and conspiracy theorists to dissect every tiny detail of how the "Cliffside Trio" were murdered. For the occasional annoying tourist or reporter to show up with a camera and a lot of questions.

But not nearly enough time for anyone to take their kids into this cove to play.

It was a strange sight every summer, the lone deserted stretch of shoreline in a town where sunbathing spots were basically handed down from parent to child. And although no one had been charged with the murders, that didn't stop the town from meting out their own version of justice: stares and rumors and occasional vandalism. When Evelyn closed her eyes, she still saw the ugly scrawl of the letters someone had spray-painted across her father's car. The way his face had crumpled as he tried to shield her from the word.

MURDERER.

Greg Mackenzie hadn't killed anybody. Evelyn knew that. But Cliffside Bay's suspicion had cost Evelyn everything. It had made her mother leave, made her sister follow as soon as she graduated. It had destroyed Evelyn's friendship with Mina Zanetti. And it was still messing up her relationships to this day—making her feel like she owed Nick something. Like she had to help him cheat because he'd lost a brother and she still had a sister.

A place of great pain for you or your target.

Evelyn set her jaw. The cave worked for both her and Nick, which made it terrible, which made it perfect.

She clambered up the rocks and into the opening, her unease fading as she used her phone flashlight to survey the space. It wasn't so bad, really. About the size of her bedroom, with curved, craggy walls and rock formations that jutted unpredictably from the floor. If not for the overwhelming smell of brine and sulfur, it would've been almost comfortable.

Evelyn tried not to think about the last time she'd been here—with Mina Zanetti by her side, talking her through the summoning instructions. But it was hard not to remember how it had felt when that unknowable *thing* had rushed through her, and the voices of the dead had wailed in her mind. Hard not to remember her panic when she heard Mina's cry of pain and saw the sand dollar–shaped mark on her friend's wrist.

After they called that spirit, Mina got sick. Really sick. When she came back to school a week later, that sand dollar mark had disappeared…along with her and Evelyn's friendship. Evelyn had spent months bracing herself for the spirit to hurt her, too, but nothing ever happened. She'd thought it was because the magic was all Mina. Her friend was the medium, after all. Part of her still believed she'd had nothing to do with that spell, but she had to try this anyway.

"It's worth it," she told herself now. "It has to be."

Make a circle of salt, then light the candles around it.

Evelyn did as instructed, although the saltshaker's aim left much to be desired. This wasn't part of the instructions, but she remembered Mina telling her to *never* put so much as a finger inside the circle once the summoning started. It was a barrier between herself and the spirit that shouldn't be broken, ever. She put the bowl in the center of the circle, poured the salt-water inside, then piled the sweatshirt in as the sun vanished beneath the horizon.

There was only one step left now: *Supply the offering and make your request. In order to bind yourself to a spirit, you must offer part of your mortal body to them.*

Her pulse pounded in her ears as she pulled the switchblade out of her pocket and pressed it against her palm.

This was her last chance to turn back.

But Evelyn's future was what she clung to when the weather was harsh and the tides were unforgiving—and if she didn't do this, it would be gone forever.

She snarled and sliced the switchblade across the center of her palm, cutting through the skin in a sharp, perfect X. Evelyn held it over the bowl.

"I summon you," she said, panting softly as red splotches

appeared on the sweatshirt, then seeped into the saltwater. "And in return I want you to make all this cheating stuff with Nick go away—take it off my record permanently. Like it never happened at all, like I never got caught. Whoever you are. And, um—thank you."

Her words bounced off the cave walls, not quite echoes, but copies, maybe, like someone was repeating them back to her. Like someone was listening. She pulled her hand back hastily, remembering Mina's warning.

A gust of wind surged through the cave, blowing out the candles and sending her hair swirling across her face. Voices rumbled through her mind, some loud, some soft and scattered, until one drowned them all out, a roar that somehow felt both frightening and exhilarating. The smell of the ocean intensified until she nearly choked on it, and below her, waves pounded against the shoreline. Although she knew the tide was too low for the water to touch her, she could've sworn she felt the spray of saltwater on her face.

When the noise finally faded away, Evelyn knelt in the dark, her bloody hand clenched in a fist. She scrambled to turn on her phone flashlight. Nick's sweatshirt was charred and twisted now. Crimson-stained saltwater swirled around it.

Evelyn moved to stand—and gasped.

There was a smudgy handprint on the floor of the cave, outlined in salt. It had pushed outward at the edge of the circle, dragging the grains as far as it could. But the salt hadn't broken. The outmost tip of the middle finger was less than an inch from Evelyn's knees.

Evelyn bandaged her palm, her mouth as dry and salty as

if she'd swallowed the seawater in the bowl. She scanned her wrist, but there was no mark, no pain.

"I did it," Evelyn whispered. And as it all sank in, she began to weep, smudging her mascara down her cheeks.

Because the magic had found her again, just when she needed it most.

Chapter Three

It was the last week of school before summer vacation at Cliff-side High, and for the first time all year, Evelyn felt invincible as she walked through the front doors.

Because her summoning had already worked.

All the emails about Evelyn's academic dishonesty hearing had vanished from her phone sometime between leaving the beach the night before and arriving back at home. Evelyn checked her grades in her academic portal—her incomplete for biology had gone back to an A. Around eleven, she'd gotten a single text from Nick, apologizing that they'd "fought about the cheating even though they'd gotten away with it," and asking if they could get back together.

Evelyn let the text sit until the morning, then responded with a single word: no.

Nothing could lower her spirits. Not even the lackluster B she'd gotten on her French final, or the fact that Meredith hadn't answered Evelyn's texts asking if she was still planning on visiting over summer break. Not until the end of the school day, anyway, when Nick finally tracked her down in the parking lot. Evelyn cursed silently as he approached.

"Evie," he said, apologetic. "I don't know what happened last night, but I want to make it up to you."

"I don't want to date you anymore, all right? That's what happened." The cut on Evelyn's palm throbbed painfully behind its bandage. She could see a few of Nick's soccer teammates watching from the steps—nobody at Cliffside High knew how to mind their own business. She'd learned that the hard way as a kid, and again last fall, when one disastrous beach bonfire had been enough to get her whispered about for the next few months. At least dating Nick had made that stop.

Nick winced. "You don't have to be so blunt about it. I don't even understand what I did."

Evelyn lowered her voice. "You convinced me to cheat. That's not okay."

He looked at her, puzzled. "But we didn't get caught, and now I'm not getting grounded. It's a win-win."

"No, Nick. It's a win for *you*." It didn't matter that she had erased all traces of the cheating. Evelyn couldn't erase the knowledge that Nick had sold her out the moment they got caught. She knew there was more to him than the rich athlete most of the school saw, but that wasn't enough anymore.

"At least let me give you a ride to work," Nick said, gesturing toward the shiny black SUV his parents had bought him for his sixteenth birthday.

Evelyn lowered her trusty longboard to the pavement, put a warning sneaker on the tail. "You know I hate that car."

The car had been their first fight. It was impossible to care about marine ecology without also caring about rising sea levels and fossil fuels, and after an argument, Nick had told her that he'd arrange a carpool to "minimize impact." But Evelyn had known he was only doing it so that she'd stop complaining.

"I just don't think we make sense anymore. I'm not sure we ever did."

She tightened the straps of her helmet, which was black and faded and covered in stickers. And then she was off, weaving easily through the parking lot and down the sidewalk that would take her into town. She was already late to work.

Evelyn had gotten her first part-time job the week she turned fourteen. Her mother's alimony payments covered rent and most bills, but her father had struggled to find steady work since the drowning summer, and Evelyn had the acute knowledge that a single emergency could be catastrophic to their funds. Before Meredith left for college, she'd helped Evelyn set up a savings account. Evelyn had spent the last few years learning how to be responsible for her own food, her own clothes, her own future.

When she swung open the door to the Scales & Tails Pet Shop, Luisa Morales was already behind the register, piling mustard greens and bell peppers into Hal the iguana's food bowl. Luisa was a Mexican American girl in Evelyn's grade, a budding photographer with a wry sense of humor who'd taken the pet store's social media accounts to new heights. Evelyn liked their shifts together—Luisa really cared about the animals, unlike some of their coworkers, who were more interested in shirking cage-cleaning duty than making sure the aquariums' pH levels were balanced.

"What happened?" Luisa asked as she placed Hal's food bowl in his tank. Her curly brown ponytail swung behind her head as she bent down to shut his enclosure. "You're never late to work."

"Yeah. Sorry. Bad day. I broke up with my boyfriend, and he doesn't seem to get that we're done."

Luisa's brow furrowed. "That Slater guy, right? The one whose brother..." She trailed off awkwardly.

Evelyn sighed and nodded. When people thought about Nick, it was either *that trust-fund jock* or *the boy with the dead brother.* "That's him."

Hal—the unofficial mascot of Scales & Tails—gave Evelyn what felt a lot like a judging look. Luisa snapped a photo of him as he devoured a bell pepper, grinning.

"What a handsome man," she cooed. "See, this is the only kind of attention we need."

"You want us to become...the reptile equivalent of cat ladies?"

"I'm just saying," Luisa pointed out, "Hal won't text you long emotional paragraphs about how much you mean to him and then pretend he doesn't see you at lunch the next day."

"So your ex is still doing that, huh?" Evelyn had absorbed a fair bit of Luisa's life over the seven or eight months they'd been working together, though she wouldn't really call them friends. Her coworker hung out with the other art-class kids at Cliffside High, who had always been friendly but distant to Evelyn. Evelyn didn't mind. Friendly but distant was the safest kind of relationship she knew how to have. "You should just ghost him for the summer."

"I'm thinking about it," Luisa said, sighing. "But we have a best friend in common. You know how it is when friendships get all tangled—I don't want to make anyone pick sides."

Evelyn didn't know, actually, but she nodded anyway. "It gets messy."

"Exactly. Hey—I could set you up with Talia, if you want," Luisa offered. "You're bi, right? Because I really think you'd get along."

"Talia does take great selfies," Evelyn admitted. "But I think I need a little while before I date again."

Evelyn had come out on social media the year before, and for the most part, it had gone over well. But she *had* gotten an anonymous comment calling her fake once she started dating Nick. Saying she'd "claimed to be bi" only for the attention, that if she was dating a guy, she was straight. She'd deleted it right away, but the memory still stung. It was nice to talk to somebody about it who treated it like no big deal, because it wasn't, at least not to Evelyn.

She and Luisa chatted about the photography projects Luisa wanted to work on that summer as they settled into their usual rhythm at Scales & Tails. The opening employees had taken care of feeding the animals and cleaning the cages that morning, but Evelyn and Luisa still liked to check on everyone. There was always somebody who needed a little extra attention. Luisa had been thorough like that for as long as Evelyn had known her, which was a while—her mom worked at the library, a place where Evelyn had spent a lot of time as a kid.

After they were done, Luisa took a bathroom break while Evelyn waited behind the counter. She was admiring Hal's massive enclosure, which stretched almost to the ceiling, when the snake-shaped doorbell rang. She turned toward the entrance, expecting to see one of the shop regulars or perhaps even Mr. Clark, popping in to check on his employees.

Instead, she saw Mina Zanetti, wearing a perfectly tailored blue sundress she had undoubtedly sewn herself, a golden cuff bracelet on her left wrist, and a grim look of determination.

Evelyn froze.

In the year she'd worked at Scales & Tails, Mina had never come inside.

They had an unspoken agreement that usually kept them off each other's turf. Mina got the Shorewell Community Center, where her mom worked. Evelyn had Scales & Tails. School and the Basic Bean were neutral territory, but when the girls were in the same room, it was always on opposite sides. Evelyn couldn't remember the last time they had willingly spoken.

It wasn't because she hated Mina. It was because Mina had pulled away from her after what they'd done during the drowning summer.

Together, they'd summoned a spirit to clear Greg Mackenzie of the authorities' suspicion and stop him from being charged. The secret could have pulled them closer, but instead, Mina's subsequent illness and withdrawal had torn them apart.

Now, staring at Mina's bleached-blond bob and annoyingly symmetrical face, Evelyn knew that her ex–best friend's presence here the day after Evelyn had called a spirit on her own was no coincidence.

"Welcome to Scales and Tails," she said, trying to keep her voice professional. "Can I help you with something?"

Mina looked around the store, her gaze deeply unimpressed. "You can, yes. I've got some questions. About *this*."

She yanked off the cuff bracelet and extended her arm across the counter.

Evelyn's stomach sank straight to the soles of her beat-up sneakers at the sight of that all-too-familiar sand dollar. The mark practically glowed, vivid and blue green against Mina's pale wrist.

"Shit."

"Precisely." Mina slipped the cuff back on. She still spoke as mildly as if they were talking about the weather, which only unnerved Evelyn more. "Now, then, I assume this isn't a conversation you want to have in public?"

Evelyn *knew* she looked panicked—she sucked at hiding her feelings. Mina had chosen her location well. This wasn't school, where everyone would be watching them, but it wasn't home, either, where Evelyn could easily avoid her. Right now Mina was technically a customer, and Evelyn's job was to help her.

"Ugh. Fine." She scanned the store while fumbling mentally for some sort of plan. "Follow me."

She led Mina into the back-corner supply room of Scales & Tails, hoping Luisa's bathroom break was almost over. They weren't supposed to leave the register unattended, but this was an emergency. Evelyn's heart hammered a tattoo against her rib cage as she turned on the light, revealing stacks of food bags, two massive storage fridges, and enough substrate and empty cages to set up a second location.

"Make this quick," Evelyn said, before Mina could speak. "I'm not in the mood for a lecture."

"You really think I'm here to lecture you?" The light bulb

hanging above their heads emphasized Mina's perfectly applied eyeshadow. Yeah, Evelyn had avoided her for six years, but that hadn't stopped her from noticing how glamorous her old friend looked all the time. It was completely unfair.

"What else would you be here to do? Catch up?" Something about how unflappable Mina seemed only made Evelyn more agitated. "So the mark came back. That sucks. But I don't get what that has to do with me."

"It has *everything* to do with you." Mina stepped closer to her. "Because you summoned a spirit last night."

Evelyn felt cornered and exposed—a tide pool in the sun, a mollusk cowering as a predator approached. "You can't prove it."

"I don't need proof. I know it was you." Mina was less than a foot away from her now, close enough for Evelyn to see the tiny golden studs glimmering in her ears. Their height difference plus Mina's platform sandals forced Evelyn to crane her neck, squinting into the light. "You promised me you'd never do this again. You promised to keep it a secret."

"And I did." Evelyn's voice broke on the last word. "I've never told a soul."

"That doesn't matter." Mina's expression wavered at last, although she pulled it back to normal so quickly Evelyn nearly missed it. "Last time this happened, I had a fever so high I went to the hospital. I vomited every day for a week before that mark finally faded. Were you trying to hurt me?"

For the second time that afternoon, Evelyn felt guilty. "Of course not."

"Then what could have possibly been important enough to risk that again?"

Evelyn gulped. "Uh...I needed to do something about Nick."

"This was about your boyfriend? Seriously? You bent a spirit to your will for something so...silly?"

Evelyn's temper crackled to life at the other girl's patronizing tone. It had been Mina's choice to tell her that the rumors about the Zanettis were true, to summon a spirit with her. Mina had no right to treat her like this, not when Evelyn had lied for her all these years. Not when Evelyn truly hadn't realized that the consequences of this spell could happen to Mina again when she wasn't even there.

"This wasn't about being petty," she said. "Nick screwed me over. Screwed up my future, too. I had to undo it—I *had* to. I didn't know it would hurt you again."

Something in Evelyn's words must have reached the other girl, because Mina paused. "What did he—"

"I don't want to talk about it."

"All right." Mina's voice was far gentler than it had been before. "Look, even in emergencies, it's not acceptable to call spirits like that. I didn't know better when we were kids, but using a ghost to do your bidding is amoral. They're a person, not a tool."

Evelyn swallowed. She hadn't been thinking about that. Or about anything, really, except herself.

"Okay, okay, I get it," she muttered. "I'm a horrible person."

"That's not..." Mina sighed. "You didn't know better. Now you do."

Evelyn bowed her head, ashamed. "Yeah. I guess. But even if I don't do it again, you still have that mark. Is it going to make you sick?"

For the briefest of moments, Mina's voice trembled—and then it was gone again, just like the vulnerability in her expression. "I have no idea. But we need to fix this before that happens. And before anyone other than me notices what you did. This mark showed up when I was out in the field with my mom in the middle of the night. You're lucky she didn't see it."

"What happens if your family finds out I called a spirit?" Evelyn asked nervously.

"I don't know," Mina said. "My mother has been telling me my whole life that a corrupted or untrained medium is far more dangerous than the most unsettled spirit. So she and my uncle would have no choice but to punish you."

Evelyn felt cornered again, panic flickering in her like the light bulb above. But there was something off about Mina's tone. She didn't sound scared. She sounded almost...guilty. Besides, Evelyn knew Mina's mom was young and fairly cool, and when they'd been kids, Mina had absolutely adored her. She didn't seem like the kind of person who would punish a teenager for making an understandable mistake.

And then Evelyn realized what was bothering her about Mina's story.

"I summoned the ghost yesterday, right after sunset," she said slowly. "But you said your mark showed up in the middle of the night. Wouldn't those two things have happened at the same time? Why are you so sure it's my fault?"

"The mark returned when I tried to talk to a spirit for the first time since we did that summoning." Mina's right hand tugged at her wrist cuff, fingers curling around the gold. "So it must be tied to you, because if you haven't done it since either..."

The storeroom went silent, and for the first time since Mina had walked through the door of Scales & Tails, Evelyn felt like she had the upper hand.

"So you really don't have proof that this is my fault," she said, putting it all together. Why Mina was being so cagey about her mother. Why she had broken her six-year silent treatment to speak to Evelyn at all. "But you're here anyway. Which means this isn't about me—this is about you. You don't want your family to know what happened."

Mina's eyes flicked to her sandals, her fingers knotting together in front of her dress. "Mom's already resistant to me becoming a medium. If she finds out the real truth about what happened during the drowning summer, she'll never teach me anything. So I think you can agree that perhaps we need to help each other."

"I don't *need* to do anything," Evelyn said. "If this isn't my fault—"

"It is." A desperate edge crept into Mina's voice. "It has to be."

"Because you're too perfect to ever make a mistake?" Evelyn wouldn't have this blamed on her. Her father had been the town punching bag for six years—she had no interest in following in his footsteps. "Sounds to me like this is totally your problem."

"You don't understand," Mina snapped. "That spirit you summoned, Evelyn—you're messing with something you don't understand, and it's possible that this could get dangerous."

"Very convenient that you're bringing up this whole danger thing now," Evelyn said. "I'm sorry about your mark. And I won't call a spirit again. But I'm not going to let you blame me for something I didn't do."

"Fine, then, get yourself killed messing with the dead," Mina said coldly. "See if I care." She whirled around, wrenched the storeroom door open, and walked stiffly away.

Evelyn was left alone with her guilt. She leaned against an empty row of tanks and exhaled slowly, staring at a bag of substrate as she tried to process the last few minutes.

What she'd done had been selfish and dangerous. She saw that now. She'd been thinking of this as magic, and spells, but...that wasn't true. Mina had been right about one thing: A spirit was a person, not a power source, and they deserved to be treated like one.

"I'm sorry," she said aloud, feeling kind of silly. "I...I didn't mean to use you. And I'll never do anything like this again. I'm not sure how to apologize to a ghost, but I'll, uh, do my best."

A scent wafted through the room around her, salty with an edge of rot, like the beach on a sweltering summer day. A soft moaning whirled around the storeroom.

Like that feeling she'd had in the cave. Like someone was talking back.

Suddenly she regretted letting Mina leave. She felt utterly vulnerable—she had no instructions for this.

"Um," Evelyn whispered, "are you answering me?"

The noise grew louder, and Evelyn heard screams, so loud and shrill that they had to have been coming from right beside her. The cut on her palm throbbed like a tiny heartbeat. She looked frantically around the storeroom, but there was nothing, no one, and the wailing wouldn't stop.

"Evelyn!" Luisa's voice was high with terror.

Evelyn yanked the storeroom door open—and gaped.

The saltwater tanks along the right wall of the store were overflowing. Water gushed down the front of the tanks and puddled rapidly on the concrete floor. The entire store smelled of rotting fish and salt.

"Over here!" called Luisa, beckoning to her from the register. She was huddled behind the counter. Evelyn hurried over to join her, realizing as she did so that every reptile was active. Snakes writhed out of their hides, hissing, while bearded dragons pawed at the glass of their tanks.

"What the hell is happening?" Evelyn gasped, panic clawing at her throat as she knelt down beside Luisa.

"I don't know," her coworker whimpered. The fluorescent lights above their heads flickered, then shattered with a series of sharp *pop*s. Evelyn ducked her head as glass rained down on the floor. She shuddered as the plate-glass windows at the front of the store crashed to the ground.

She and Luisa stayed down until Evelyn could no longer hear breaking glass, rushing water, or those strange, distant screams. Then she raised her head and stood again, pulling Luisa up with her to survey the damage.

Her first thought was that it could have been worse. Although the animals were all agitated, none of the cages had broken. Glass from the burnt-out lights above their heads littered the floor, along with puddles of synthetic saltwater, and the front windows looked like they'd been punched in with a crowbar.

She and Luisa immediately hurried off to check on everyone. The knot in Evelyn's stomach loosened with every cage—although the property had been damaged, not a single fish or reptile was anything more than stressed, even the more delicate ones. They'd have to call in someone to check on the heating and filtration systems, but for now, at least, everything was fine. And Mr. Clark wasn't the kind of boss who would blame this on Evelyn and Luisa, or try to charge them for the damages. He knew how much both of them cared about the animals.

"Mr. Clark will definitely have to close for a little while," said Luisa nervously as they reconvened in the middle of the store. "I'm just glad we're the only ones here."

"Me too," Evelyn said weakly. "Do you want me to call him?"

"I can do it." Luisa headed toward the back of the store, giving Hal the iguana a relieved little wave along the way.

Left alone at last, Evelyn gazed at the row of fish tanks, the smell of the sea wafting over her, and tried to push down the dread in her stomach.

This was just a coincidence. This was completely explainable.

Yet as Evelyn stared at the saltwater dripping down the sides of the tank, she was overcome by that same sensation she'd had the night before. Energy buzzed beneath her skin; a sound rushed in her ears like an endless series of crashing waves. And she couldn't shake the feeling that maybe Mina had been right to warn her after all.

Chapter Four

Mina returned home from her disappointing confrontation with Evelyn to find the kitchen full of steam. Her mother stood before a giant silver pot on the stove, hands on her hips, long strands of brown hair plastered to her sweaty forehead.

"Oh, excellent, you're back," she said when Mina walked in. "I need your help cleaning the rest of these clams."

"So you went to see Uncle Dom today?" Mina eyed the brown paper bag on the counter. For most of Mina's childhood they'd lived with Uncle Dom and his son, Sergio, until her mother's business took off and they could afford their own house. Stella still visited Dom frequently, and every time she did she came home with fresh seafood from his early-morning excursions out on Long Island Sound. Although he caught less and less every year, something Mina had heard many complaints about.

"I did," Stella said. "It was *informative.*" She said the word like it was an expletive. Mina tried to hide her nerves and went to change out of her dress. She'd learned the hard way that clam juice and any outfit she cared about didn't mix.

In the privacy of her room, she inspected the sand dollar burned into her wrist. The first time it had appeared, she'd fallen ill almost immediately. But Mina had felt fine all day, aside from the anxiety and guilt that threatened to burn a hole in her stomach.

Talking to Evelyn hadn't helped. Her former friend had proven to be even more stubborn than Mina remembered, which was unfortunate, because Mina needed to get rid of the sand dollar before Stella saw it. Otherwise her mother would push her training back again—maybe forever.

When Mina returned to the kitchen, her mother had moved in front of the three windows fanned out in a half circle behind the sink. She'd slid the blinds open on each of them, revealing the sun sinking beneath the waves, and begun fanning herself with the edge of her apron.

Food was Stella's love language, and the kitchen was her workshop. It was organized clutter at its finest, wooden cabinets packed with mismatched china and mugs and a walk-in pantry that housed both their washing machine and seemingly endless mason jars filled with spices and canned goods. Dried herbs hung from the ceiling in sweet-smelling clusters, and their potted counterparts lived on a massive shelving unit—parsley, basil, oregano, mint.

Her mother's cooking had nothing to do with the supernatural, but it was good enough to feel like it. Two years ago, Stella had signed an exclusive catering contract with the Shorewell Community Center, and her ingenuity and talent had led to a completely booked summer of weddings and parties. One day, Mina wanted people to talk about her clothing designs the way they talked about her mother's olive-and-escarole bread or her marinated artichoke hearts.

"So, about Uncle Dom." Mina opened the bag of clams and shook them into a strainer. "What happened this morning?"

Stella snapped her apron back down with more force than was necessary. "The usual suspects are loud again."

Mina ran cold water over the clamshells as Stella spoke, scrubbing the sand off them one by one before putting them in a bowl. Like Stella, her uncle was also a medium. There had been many more Zanettis when Mina was younger, but they'd all drifted away from Cliffside Bay. Mina barely remembered them now, and Stella had told her that they didn't matter—their real family was the people who had stayed here.

"Aren't they always loud at the full moon?" Mina asked.

Stella's voice was grim. "Louder than usual."

Mina knew who the usual suspects were, of course. The drowning summer victims were a cautionary tale for her in more ways than one. In the six years since their murders, their spirits had lingered, unable to leave the mortal world behind. All her mother and uncle had managed to do for them was keep them relatively quiet.

Every ghost faded eventually, no matter how strong their ties to the human world—they eroded just like a rock perched at the edge of the ocean, no match for the endless pressure of the sea. Most were gone within five years, but the occasional stragglers lasted twenty, thirty, even fifty. Mina had an uncomfortable feeling that the drowning summer spirits were in the latter category, and she couldn't help but wonder if it was because she and Evelyn had summoned that ghost to close the investigation.

If it was the victims' spirits they had called upon that night. Her wrist ached, although whether it was mental or physical pain, she didn't know. She tried to focus on the cold water, on the rough clamshells scraping against her hands.

"So that amateur medium summoned one of the Cliffside Trio last night?" she asked.

"Most likely." Stella grabbed her pot holders and headed for the stove. "Your uncle checked the cave this morning on a hunch and found detritus that looks quite similar to the summoning ceremony we use."

"Huh," Mina croaked out.

"You know medium practices are highly individualized, Mina, based on the cultural influences and beliefs of the people who interact with spirits. There's incredible variance all around the world. So to see something almost identical to our own technique... well, it's quite a coincidence."

Mina gripped a clamshell a bit too tightly as she met her mother's eyes.

"It wasn't me," she said hastily. "I would never do something like that." *Again.*

Stella lifted the lid off the giant pot, releasing a cloud of steam. Mina knew what had happened to the batch of clams inside: Their shells had opened little by little until her mother could finally pry out the meat inside.

"I trust you, my seashell. And it's true that you were home all day and all evening, I told Dom as much. But I can't overlook how odd this is."

"I understand that." Mina released her clam into the strainer. Her palms were raw and aching. "And I know I shouldn't have gone into the water last night. But I promise you, I didn't go anywhere near that cave."

"We'll get to the bottom of this." Stella lowered the lid back onto the pot. "The full moon is already waning. But when the new moon comes at the end of the month..."

"I know," Mina said. The Zanettis' power was tied to the ocean, which in turn was tied to the moon and the tides. When the range of potential high and low tides was greater, the spirits were louder, like the mediums had clearer access to more channels on a radio. Mina saw it as a double-edged sword—yes, her mother could reach the dead more easily during these times, but ghosts were often frenetic. Unstable. "You're going to try talking to them. The Cliffside Trio, I mean."

"If they allow it, yes."

"I could help," Mina said, "if you taught me how to listen."

Stella hesitated. "I don't know, Mina. Things are changing in Cliffside Bay. The dead grow more dangerous every year, and after last night..."

"I apologized for that." Mina had seen these changes, too, albeit from a distance, but she'd never heard Stella admit that she was having real trouble handling spirits before. Maybe it meant she would finally let Mina in. "And I told you the truth. I had nothing to do with whoever summoned that ghost last night."

The smell of brine wafted from the pot, so strong that Mina could almost pretend she was back on the beach. Hearing those voices call to her. Watching her mother wade into the waves.

"You've always been so eager to be part of this," Stella said. "But it's important to me that you have the options I didn't. The life you truly want. Not the life you feel obligated to live."

Mina remembered all the times her mother had tried to protect her—how she'd intervened moments before Mina could
step on an upside-down horseshoe crab, how she'd rearranged
her catering shifts to help Mina study for big tests, how she'd sat
with Mina in the living room after she got stood up by Kaitlyn
Mallow and fed her garlic-Parmesan popcorn until she no longer
felt like crying.

Stella was only so worried about this because she wanted
Mina to be safe. But her mother didn't—couldn't—understand
that she was six years too late. Evelyn might not have felt like
any of the drowning summer's aftermath was her fault, but
Mina knew they were both to blame. They had made a mistake
that day in the cave. And the only way Mina could atone for it
was to help everyone she'd hurt.

"I don't want this because of you," she said. "I promise."

Maybe it was the way she'd said it. Maybe it was the look
on her face. Mina didn't know. But just like the clams slowly
cracking under the pressure of the steam, Stella's expression
softened.

"Well, your uncle and I do have an appointment with a
potential client in a little over a week," she said. "If you want to
shadow us, you can. But you must make me two promises."

"Anything," Mina said quickly, trying not to show her excite-
ment. Client meetings were a rarity these days—the rumors
about the Zanetti family had nearly faded out, and Stella and
Uncle Dom seemed uninterested in rekindling them. The few clients they worked with these days were almost all direct connections, with an aunt or a cousin who'd been helped by the Zanettis
before. She didn't want to miss this opportunity to learn.

"First, you must not interfere. Not like you did last time."

Mina nodded obediently.

"And second—you have to wear your necklace again."

"Mom. Seriously?"

"I am deathly serious, Marina Elena."

Six years ago, when Mina had stumbled home with that sand dollar on her wrist and confessed to trying to talk to the drowning summer ghosts, the mark her summoning had left behind hadn't just made her physically ill. It had plunged her into a waking nightmare where voices screamed and pleaded for her help, plaguing her at all hours of the day and night. When she finally told her mother what was happening, Stella had gone pale as a sheet.

"Those aren't nightmares," she'd told Mina. "They're ghosts, reaching out to you."

The next day, she had given Mina a warded necklace to block the spirits out.

"Until you're no longer a child," she'd said. Earlier this year, Mina had finally been allowed to take it off for more than a few hours at a time. Stella had watched her like a hawk, but the dead hadn't spoken to her again.

Until last night.

"I thought I didn't need that thing anymore," Mina protested. "You know what happened six years ago"—*well, most of it*—"and you know I can protect myself."

"Those are my conditions," her mother said firmly. "Take them or leave them."

Mina swallowed down her disappointment. She didn't want to think about what the aftermath would be if her mother realized the full extent of her and Evelyn's meddling, if she was willing to make Mina put her medium training wheels back on for something so small.

There was a place in Mina's mind where she went to feel safe. An ocean—her ocean, where the water was always calm and smooth as glass, and the bottom was so far down, no one had ever found it.

Her and Evelyn's betrayal belonged on the seafloor. She would do anything to keep it there.

"I promise," she said at last.

Stella smiled. "That's my seashell." She lifted the pot lid and reached in with a slotted spoon. A moment later, she pulled out a clam, cracked wide open. She extracted the meat effortlessly with a fork and handed it to Mina.

"Go on," she said. "Try it."

Mina was expecting it to be delicious, but instead the overwhelming taste of brine flooded her mouth. She couldn't suppress a gag.

"Sorry, Mom," she said, coughing. "It tastes like saltwater."

Stella frowned, looking disappointed, and took a bite of her own. "Are you sure? Tastes fine to me." She handed Mina another bite.

This time, the clam was buttery and perfect. But the taste of the sea lingered in Mina's mouth for the rest of the evening, her throat as dry and parched as it had been when that wave had broken over her head.

Chapter Five

Working as a barista at the Basic Bean was Evelyn's other part-time job, where she made overpriced coffee drinks, fought with the chip reader, and tried to avoid uncomfortable small talk. Perks: free pastries and caffeine. Downsides: she didn't get to work with animals, and she'd had to double her shifts over the week and a half since Scales & Tails had been forced to temporarily close.

Also...everyone in Cliffside Bay came here. Including Mina. Including Nick. Although to be fair, this time she'd invited him.

"This is a mess," mumbled Kenny Thompson, staring at the box Evelyn had pulled out of her backpack. He was the coworker she always seemed to be on shifts with, a white boy with horn-rimmed glasses and red hair who was one bad coffee spill away from disintegrating at all times. "You're giving this to him here?"

"He wants his stuff back. So I told him to come get it."

The stuff in question had been shoved into a shoebox and labeled TRASH in Evelyn's awful handwriting.

"You're going to piss off the whole soccer team," Kenny moaned, tugging at the ties of his canvas apron. "They're going to ruin your life, and then my life, because I'm basically an accomplice—"

"I'm not scared of the soccer team." They'd unfollowed her on social media after the breakup, and Evelyn had been to enough of their off-season parties over the last four months to know that would be about it in terms of social consequences. Which had stung, but Evelyn knew she'd never made an effort to get close to any of them. She'd been too scared of what they might ask her, about her dad, about her secrets. It was better to avoid getting to that point entirely.

"Easy for you to say," Kenny grumbled. "We can't all just . . . not care about things."

Evelyn smiled grimly at him. "Trust me. I care."

"What's even in there?" Kenny asked, looking curiously at the shoebox. He was incurably nosy, which Evelyn mostly found annoying. But if it would make him stop freaking out, she was happy to distract him.

Evelyn waved a hand at the scuffed-up cardboard lid. "See for yourself."

A customer walked up to the register, and Evelyn hurried off to take her order. When she'd finished filling up her iced coffee, Evelyn went to check on Kenny and found him holding a pair of pearl earrings, looking puzzled.

"Did he buy you these?" he asked. "They look real."

Evelyn sighed. "That's because they are."

Nick had that kind of money to throw around—she'd seen it on their dates. He'd drive her to a movie in that terrible SUV, hand over his dad's credit card to the employee behind the ticket counter, then spring for more overpriced popcorn than they could possibly eat. He never let her pay for anything.

"Let me treat you," he'd insisted time and time again.

The first time she and Nick had truly met was at a beach bonfire last fall, where she'd embarrassed herself by drinking too much and making a scene when someone asked about her dad. Nick had been the only one to help her at that party. He'd gotten her home safely, then messaged her the next day to make sure she was all right. He even told the soccer team to shut up when they tried to spread the story. Sometimes it felt like she'd been trying to pay him back for that ever since.

So when he'd asked her for one favor—cheating on the exam—in the face of so much kindness, saying no hadn't felt like an option.

"Huh." Kenny put the jewelry back. "Don't take this the wrong way, but you don't really strike me as a pearl earrings type of person."

"I'm not." Evelyn grabbed the lid and shoved it overtop the box's contents, before Kenny could comment on anything else.

"You know," Kenny said solemnly, "in my favorite podcast audio-drama miniseries, the—"

"*The Great Star of Dawn*, Kenny, yes, you've told me about this a million times—"

"Not this part!" Kenny looked at her indignantly. "I just think if you listened to it, you'd see that in addition to being a sci-fi epic, there are parallels to real-life situations. I swear."

Evelyn glared at him. "I don't want your advice. Or your podcast recommendations."

Kenny crossed his arms. "Well, you're missing out."

"Hello?" called another customer from the register.

Evelyn let out a soft swear and turned to deal with them, only to realize that it was Nick. Finally. She gave Kenny a *Don't say anything* look and grabbed the shoebox.

"Hey," she said, trying to sound calm.

"It's good to see you, Evie."

She forced a smile. "I'm glad you showed up."

The Basic Bean tried to pretend it wasn't a massive chain with its exposed brick walls, succulents lining the window-sills, and faux-industrial bulbs hanging from the ceiling. Evelyn could barely see anything in the dim lighting, but Nick still managed to lean against the counter at an angle that high-lighted the appealingly messy way his dark brown hair fell into his eyes. Evelyn knew how hard he worked to make it look like that, but that didn't dampen the effect as much as she wanted it to.

"Um. Well. Here's your stuff." She cleared her throat and shoved the box over the counter.

Evelyn watched him read the word on the top, braced for a sardonic remark. But instead, he just chuckled ruefully.

"You've been so hard to get ahold of. I just wish I could give you a real apology at least, maybe sometime when you're not at work...."

There was that guilt again. That after everything he'd done, she owed him a conversation. That she'd been too hasty, too mean.

"Maybe." Evelyn's phone buzzed in her apron pocket. She

pulled it out. There was an email sitting on her lock screen from her dream internship.

After weeks of waiting, they'd finally gotten back to her. Immediately her stomach began to churn. For some reason, she smelled saltwater, and for a brief moment she was crouching behind the counter back in Scales & Tails. She shuddered and pushed the memory away.

Evelyn couldn't open this email in front of Nick, but she needed to know. Right now.

"I need to go," she said quickly. "Sorry—this is important."

Thankfully, Kenny was eavesdropping on her, so when she turned around and mouthed *Cover me* he couldn't pretend not to see her.

She hurried to the bathroom, locked the door behind her, and leaned against the grungy tile wall. Her hands trembled as she opened the email.

> **Dear Ms. Mackenzie,**
>
> **Thank you so much for your application and your interview. Although we were impressed by your obvious passion for our research, we regret to inform you—**

She didn't have to read any more.

Part of her had known this was going to happen, but that didn't make it any easier to handle. Evelyn shoved her phone into her pocket as her vision blurred with tears.

It didn't matter that they hadn't heard about her academic dishonesty. She still wasn't good enough. A tiny insignificant organism in a tiny insignificant tide pool who would stay trapped there until she died.

The sound of sobbing echoed off the walls, and Evelyn tried to stifle herself before someone heard her and came to see what was wrong. She couldn't decide whose pity she wanted less: Kenny's or Nick's.

But as her crying decreased to sniffles, she realized the sobbing wasn't coming from her. She stared frantically around at the graffitied walls. Nothing. No one else.

A smell wafted through the air, not the stench of a poorly cleaned toilet, but salt. She heard the gentle crashing of waves against the shoreline as the sobbing grew louder. Something hummed beneath her skin. And then there were voices again, whispering, pleading.

Evelyn blinked back tears as the bathroom sink began to drip.

"It's all in your head," she whispered. But it took everything she had to walk toward the tap, shaking, and turn the knob until it stopped.

For a moment, everything was quiet—and then the sink roared to life, water gushing out of the faucet. The voices grew even louder, a gasping and moaning that seemed to fill the bathroom. The scent of salt was unbearable now. Something hovered between the sink and the grimy tile wall, a humanoid figure, wispy and indistinct, made of the murky greens and browns of the ocean floor. In the place where its eyes should have been were two sand dollars. It disappeared between one blink and the next, not even enough time for Evelyn to scream.

She gasped instead, backing up until she hit the door. But

just as quickly as they'd arrived, the voices faded. The scent of salt faded with them as Evelyn trembled, tears still wet on her cheeks.

Evelyn couldn't ignore it any longer—something terrible was happening to her, something that was only getting worse. And even though it would destroy her last remaining bit of pride, she needed to get help before it happened again.

Chapter Six

Mrs. Giacomo was crying. Mina watched her anxiously through the one-way glass that separated the Shorewell Community Center kitchen from the dining room. She'd told her mother she wanted to shadow this client meeting, but she hadn't realized it would mean sitting behind what felt like an interrogation window while her mom and uncle comforted a grieving woman.

The community center was perched at the very top of Cliffside Bay, a massive building with an A-frame central roof and two glass arms extending from either side like an eagle poised to take off from the cliff's edge. It had been a house at one point, but the owners donated it to the town shortly after building it, their family's last name—Shorewell—the only evidence it had ever been private property at all. Now it was used for community classes, meetings, and events. Stella's catering contract had come with unfettered access to the building, which she'd made full use of over the last few years.

"Can't believe we're up this early," Sergio Zanetti grumbled from beside Mina. "Can't Dad choose any time other than the ass-crack of dawn to do this shit?"

"It's nine in the morning."

Her cousin put his legs up on a stool slotted beneath one of the prep tables. "I rest my case."

Sergio had always been easygoing, but over the last few years, that had developed into a kind of emotional stagnation. He lived in his dad's basement rent-free, ostensibly taking college classes, but he spent most of his time playing video games and going to dive bars with his friends. When they were kids he'd been Mina's perpetual babysitter, but now she was the one he called when he needed a sober ride home.

"Why did Uncle Dom even invite you?" she asked.

"Why did Aunt Stella invite *you*?" he countered. "Shouldn't you be in school?"

"School let out last week," Mina said. It was June 25— exactly ten days since she'd tried to get Evelyn to see reason. "And I'm shadowing Mom."

Sergio looked pained. "Well, Dad said I should shadow him, too. Like it'll shake something loose. I don't know why he bothers."

Sergio resembled his father physically almost as strongly as Mina resembled her mother—they were both white men with stocky builds and wavy brown hair, although recently Dom's had grown thinner and grayer. But he didn't take after Uncle Dom in the only way the man really cared about, because no matter how many times Sergio tried to speak to the dead, they never responded.

At first, Sergio hadn't seemed to mind. But as the years went on and Uncle Dom insisted he keep "training" to become a medium, her cousin had grown more and more resentful. Mina wondered sometimes why he didn't just move out of Cliffside Bay entirely. But then she remembered how impossible it felt to even consider leaving Stella alone.

"I'm sorry," Mina said. "He shouldn't have forced you to come here."

"Eh, it's cool," Sergio said. "Someone has to be the family disappointment, and it definitely isn't you. Aunt Stella told Dad you're taking basically every AP class in school next year. Want to do my summer coursework for me?"

"No, thanks." Mina's high GPA wasn't because she liked anything about Cliffside High—it was a large, crowded place filled with near strangers. But she knew Stella was going to help with her college tuition, and now that the catering business was doing so well, Mina didn't want her mother to sacrifice all that hard-earned money on design school. Besides, Stella would use even the tiniest of excuses to prevent Mina from medium training, grades included.

"So let me guess—you're doing something fancy this summer?"

"Not exactly. Just working on the Zanetti Collection."

Mina had been trying to design an actual clothing collection for a while. It was the first piece in an elaborate plan that began with sharing her garments on social media and ended in getting the funding and interest to start her own fashion line. She was also studying for the SAT, but that was a lot less interesting.

"What about parties?" Sergio asked. "What about friends?"

"I've got you and your dad and Mom, haven't I?"

"That doesn't count," Sergio said. "Are you really happy like that? By yourself?"

"Yes," Mina said firmly.

Perhaps the prospect of having no social life whatsoever depressed Sergio, but Mina didn't mind. She had more time to study. More time to think of new clothing designs. And more time for her and Stella to watch their favorite movies for the eight hundredth time while sharing a bowl of garlic-Parmesan popcorn.

It hurt sometimes to scroll through social media and see everyone else at birthday parties and bonfires and after-school hangouts. But whenever Mina felt the sadness taking hold, Stella was there to remind her that this was really all she needed. Mina couldn't be alone when she had her family—that wasn't how it worked.

"Can we at least pay attention to what we're here for?"

"Sure," Sergio said dryly. "But it's already pretty depressing."

Mina shook her head and turned her attention back to the scene unfolding outside the kitchen, where Mrs. Giacomo, an older white woman, dabbed at her eyes with a tissue while Stella patted her shoulder. When Mina looked through the glass, she realized her uncle was waving at them both to come out.

Mina stood, her feet wobbly with nerves in her wicker sandals. She touched the warding necklace that she'd been forced to put back on, a chunky brass oval-shaped pendant with a glass heart set into the center. A compromise that would hopefully be worthwhile.

"You go," Sergio muttered as Mina headed for the door.

She turned. "You're staying?"

"I've seen them do this a dozen times. It doesn't work for me. I can watch it, but I can't hear it like they do." He hesitated, then added, "You know it's thankless, right? Being a medium? I know Dad thinks I lost out, but the truth is, I'm lucky. You could be lucky, too."

"I want this. And they need the help."

She also didn't have a choice, not the way Sergio thought she did. Stella had given up a lot to have Mina so young, put her career on hold, refocused her dreams onto both of them. Mina needed to be the kind of daughter who was worth all that sacrifice. So she pasted on her best sympathetic smile and swung open the kitchen door.

"Perfect," Stella said as Mina walked over. "I was just telling Mrs. Giacomo that you and your cousin will be joining us today."

"Sergio isn't coming," Mina said, which earned her a glower from Uncle Dom but no actual response. Mina had the distinct impression he didn't want to upset their client.

"It'll be fine," Stella said quickly, smoothing over any discomfort. "Now, Mrs. Giacomo, meet my daughter, Mina. She'll be assisting as we do our best to get in touch with your husband."

"I'm so sorry for your loss," Mina said.

"Thank you, dear." The older woman's voice quavered. "My husband Sal...well...our daughter had our first grandchild a little while ago. We were due to go visit right after his retirement. But his heart gave out last week, and now I hear him everywhere. When I turn on the sink, when I run the shower... like he's talking to me..." She trailed off nervously.

Mina understood immediately why she'd been allowed to shadow this particular case: It was a simple haunting with a clear motivation. Sal would never be able to meet his grandchild and most likely wouldn't understand why harassing his wife about it would only hurt them both more.

"It's going to be all right, Mrs. Giacomo," Mina told her, although the truth was that she had no idea what to say beyond basic platitudes. For all that her family spoke to the dead, she'd yet to lose someone she really cared about. Her grandparents had passed on when she was still a toddler, and the rest of her family had been gone for so long that she barely remembered their faces. "Uncle Dom and my mother will help you."

"And you're...like them?" Mrs. Giacomo asked, as they began to walk out of the dining room.

"I will be," Mina said proudly. Finally, she was being included.

Mina had found the pool in the Shorewell Community Center's basement years ago, while her mother was waitressing at some wedding and she'd been brought along due to lack of childcare. Nobody else on the catering staff snitched as long as Mina was quiet, so she'd learned to do her homework in the corners of the kitchen or linger by the coatroom, drawing pictures of the partygoers' dresses and suits as they bustled in and out.

The basement was a wonderland to her, wooden archways and dusty lace curtains, fake bouquets scattered across the floor like a maze. She'd crept through the mess, something inside her tugging her forward, until she'd found a door behind an ancient set of curtains. A padlock swung from a chain that was nearly rusted through. It didn't take much to break it.

When Mina had first stepped through the doorway, she'd

seen an abandoned indoor pool at the bottom of one of the building's glass arms, filled with debris and assorted garbage. Stella and Dom had since fixed the space up. The pool was filled with saltwater, something Mina still didn't understand how they'd managed to do, and the windows were clean and bright. The space around it was perpetually littered with a giant circle of salt.

It was perfect for summoning specific ghosts: not as big or unruly as a whole ocean, but not nearly as small as the bowls Stella and Dom used in emergencies.

"Please take a seat," Stella urged, showing Mrs. Giacomo to a cushioned wicker chair. "Mina, stay with her, all right? And remember what I told you."

"I remember. You can trust me." Although the sand dollar mark beneath Mina's cuff bracelet was proof that Stella couldn't.

Her mother nodded and hurried over to her brother, where they moved with the practice and ease of a routine long rehearsed. Dom sprinkled fresh salt around the pool from a bag he'd retrieved from the corner, while Stella lit perhaps thirty tea light candles around it. They bought summoning ingredients in bulk every year or so, then stored them in her uncle's basement.

Mina had asked about both of these tools years ago—if the spirits traveled through saltwater, she'd said, why could they not pass through a salt barrier? And what about the candles?

"Saltwater is a passageway," Stella had explained. "One of many potential channels away from our world. But there's something about the Sound that's different from the Atlantic Ocean. Ghosts who don't want to leave tend to linger here, halfway to their destination. Often our job is as simple a matter as guiding them across. But on land, as a safety precaution, we use salt and light as reinforcements to keep them contained and remind them where they no longer belong. To push them where they're meant to go."

Mina noticed as Stella and Dom sat beside each other, backs to the glass windows, that they didn't spill any blood into the saltwater. Not like she and Evelyn had. She'd never been brave enough to ask why the instructions she'd discovered in Stella's jewelry box included that particular step, or why her mother even had those instructions at all. That would mean admitting she'd found them, and that line of questioning led nowhere good.

Dom procured a pair of glasses from his pocket. Mrs. Giacomo stiffened—they had evidently belonged to Sal. Her uncle placed them into the pool, where they began to sink below the water. Then he pulled out his scrying focus, a glass bird, while Stella curled her fingers around her necklace.

"We summon you, Salvatore Giacomo," they said together.

"Show yourself, and we will hear your story." Dom's voice was deep and gruff.

"Show yourself, and we will help you find peace," said Stella, her melodic words bouncing off the glass walls.

"We summon you, Salvatore," they chanted, together once more. The sand dollar on Mina's wrist began to throb beneath her bracelet.

A breeze whipped through the room, and the candle flames flickered. Mrs. Giacomo gripped her arm.

"Is that him?" she whispered. "Is he coming?"

Mina patted her hand awkwardly. "I think so."

Her wrist throbbed again, stronger this time, but her hiss of pain was drowned out by the sound of rushing water as it swirled in the center of the pool. The glasses floated to the surface in the very center of the current.

"Salvatore." Dom sounded authoritative now. "We summon you."

The water began to glow, blue-green light spreading outward from the glasses. Mina could see something taking form around them: a hand. She leaned forward, gasping, and as her sand dollar continued to pulsate, her warding necklace grew warm against her skin.

"Come on," Stella murmured. "Talk to us."

The hand closed around the glasses, and a moment later a spirit rose from the center of the pool, stopping once his torso was above the water. He was translucent and bluish green, with a bashful face and a mostly bald head. Mrs. Giacomo gasped at the sight of him.

"Sal?" she whispered. He slotted the glasses onto his face and turned.

"Jenny?" he rasped. Behind him, Dom gripped his glass bird while Stella clutched at her pendant, which both glowed the same bluish green as Salvatore's spirit. Their faces were set with careful concentration.

"Oh, Sal." Mrs. Giacomo was on her feet now, yanking Mina up with her. The pendant heated up with every step Mina took toward the ghost, pulsing in time with the sand dollar. Something was wrong, but Mina didn't want to frighten this woman. She'd keep it together. She had to. "We had so much left to do."

"We did." Sal's spirit floated toward the edge of the pool,

where his wife waited for him. Mina tugged Mrs. Giacomo back from the salt circle. She could tell that, unattended, the woman would leap right into the water, no matter what instructions she'd been given beforehand. "We were going to go meet our grandchild—"

"I know," Mrs. Giacomo said, her voice shaking. "I wish you could stay. I wish we could see him together. But you're frightening me, Sal. Making the pipes shake. Making me have these awful nightmares."

"I just...I didn't want to leave you." He stretched out a hand. When it hit the edge of the salt circle below him, it was as if a barrier had drawn upward from its place on the ground. His fingertips dissolved, and he pulled them back, hissing. He'd looked so human up until that point, but for a moment something shifted, the illusion imperfect. Mina caught a glimpse of barnacles curling up his forearm, a tendril of sickly orange twined through them, before they faded away. Heat flared against her neck again, and she held back a wince. "I didn't mean to frighten you, Jenny. I just love you so much, and I wish—"

"I love you, too." Mrs. Giacomo's face was wet with tears. She clung to Mina like a lifeline. "Now and always. And I'm so sorry you'll never get to meet your grandson, but—but you can't. I need you to accept that."

For a second, Sal looked furious. But then it passed, and his expression softened, resignation clouding his features.

"Promise you'll tell him about me," he whispered. "Promise you won't let everyone forget."

"I promise," she whispered back, and Sal smiled.

Mina held back tears of her own as she watched the couple gazing at each other, one alive, one dead.

"We don't know where people go when they die," Stella always said. "Our job is to help them when they get stuck along the way. I don't care what you believe in—if you're a spirit or a living person who reaches out to me for help, I'll help. If you don't want my help, I'll leave you alone. It's that simple."

This was what her family did. They let people say goodbye, let them find peace.

Becoming a medium wouldn't be easy—but in moments like this, Mina understood exactly why it was worth it.

"Are you ready now, Sal?" Stella asked gently.

The old man nodded, and Mrs. Giacomo whimpered with relief.

And then, without warning, a glowing blue-green hand burst from the water. First one, then three, then six, grasping at Sal's legs. Dull, rusty orange spread from each place they touched him. Mina's warded necklace flared against her neck again. This time, she couldn't hold back a whimper.

"What's going on?" Mrs. Giacomo gasped.

Across the circle, Stella and Dom had stiffened. Stella gripped her scrying focus and spoke an unintelligible word that sounded like a swear; the hands faded out, but the water around where they'd been was still disturbed, coiling into tiny spirals.

Dom met Mina's eyes and jerked his head toward the exit. Mina got the message.

"Nothing out of the ordinary," she said hastily. "Sometimes, other spirits bleed through when we're only trying to talk to one. But it's important that we get you out of here. It can be very dangerous to civilians."

"I don't want to leave my husband," Mrs. Giacomo protested.

And then Salvatore Giacomo's ghost began to scream.

It was a horrible, unearthly wail, a jagged sound of terror. His form contorted and thrashed as those hands rose again, pulling him into the water. They grasped at his arms, his shoulders, until he was low enough for two of them to close around his throat. The smell of salt and rot wafted through the room, so strong it made Mina gag.

Mrs. Giacomo went limp in Mina's arms. Mina managed to catch her as she fainted, then lay her down gently by the wicker chairs with the cushioned seat as a makeshift pillow. She checked her pulse frantically and was relieved to find her still breathing.

"What do I do?" Mina called out. The ghost was still shrieking and thrashing, but the noise was muffled now. The hands around Mr. Giacomo's throat glowed vividly, and rusty tendrils spread from their grasp, eroding his face. His glasses toppled from his nose and splashed back into the pool. His shrieking cut off abruptly—he no longer had a mouth.

"Take her with you!" Stella called from the other side of the circle. "Get out of here!"

But Mina was in too much pain to move. The ward around her neck was unbearable now, scalding her flesh. She grabbed frantically at the chain and yanked it over her head.

"Mina, what the hell are you doing?" Dom growled from across the circle. "That's the only thing keeping you safe—"

"It's burning me," Mina gasped, her hand trembling as she tried to hang on to the pendant.

The pool between them writhed and boiled, the smell of a scalding summer day so strong Mina could taste it. Sal's spirit was almost gone, but three others were materializing around him, their hands extending into barely humanoid shapes. Mina recognized their outfits from the photos that had leaked from the coroner's office onto the internet. That was Tamara Winger's cardigan, Colin Maxwell's basketball jersey, both now studded with barnacles and seaweed. Bits of orange light twined through their blue-green forms, muddying their features, like silt dredged up from the seafloor.

The ghost strangling Sal turned to look at Mina, mouth opening in a horrifying, crooked smile. Jesse Slater's teeth looked like broken bits of sea glass protruding from his gums.

In the places where their eyes should have been were sand dollars.

Mina didn't remember dropping the pendant. But it fell to the floor, hitting the tile with a violent *crack*. The voices wailed and snarled, words too fragmented to make out if they even were words at all.

It was too much. She was unable to breathe, unable to think; she fell to her knees. It felt as if the sand dollar on her wrist were tugging her forward—as if it wanted her to cross that salt circle and dive into the pool. Another surge of voices rushed through her skull, and Mina couldn't take it anymore.

She fainted.

Chapter Seven

When Mina came to, she was sprawled on the tile floor, Stella crouched above her. Mina's warding pendant was back around her neck, and the pool was finally calm. The only remaining sign of the spirits was a slight disturbance in the water.

Her uncle assured Mrs. Giacomo that everything was fine and offered her a ride, while her mother helped Mina to the car. She was woozy and nauseous the entire way home.

Back at the cottage, Stella set her up on the orange velvet couch in their living room before rushing around in a frenzy. She drew the curtains across the windows, secured every dead bolt, and fussed with the tiny glass figurines placed all over the house. When they'd moved in, Mina had stood above a bowl of saltwater while her mother pricked both their fingers and let the blood fall in. Then she'd dipped the glass objects in one by one, waited until they began to glow, and pulled them out. They were wards, just like Mina's necklace.

"Mom," Mina croaked out at last. "Can we talk?"

Stella's determined expression sagged. Mina hated the moments where she could see her mother coming loose at the seams. A person was not a dress—you couldn't just rip out their seams and sew them back together when things went wrong.

"All right, my seashell," she murmured, lowering herself onto the other end of the couch. She'd bundled Mina in crocheted blankets and set a steaming mug of tea on the coffee table beside her, even though it was the end of June. She'd given Mina that same treatment during every childhood sick day. "How are you feeling? Is there anything else you need?"

Answers. Always. Mina didn't know if her mother would give them to her, but she needed to try.

"I'll be fine," she said. "But, Mom . . . what *was* that? I had no idea that ghosts could . . . well . . . attack each other."

It was rare for Mina to see her mother this shaken—shaken enough that she could *see* Stella's expression shifting as she performed the same delicate calculations she'd done for Mina's entire life. She had always thought that her mother's protectiveness around being a medium came from not wanting Mina to be sucked into a lifetime of responsibility, but after what had happened at the community center, she knew it must be more than that.

"Most spirits don't engage in such behavior," Stella said finally. "But there are . . . exceptions. Tell me, Mina—why do you think mediums are necessary at all?"

Mina had known this since she was a child, but she played along. "Because not all spirits can move on without help?"

"That's the answer I taught you." Stella drew a long fingernail over the velvet, leaving a trail of lighter orange behind it. The color reminded Mina of the corrosion that had spread across Mr. Giacomo's face. "Most living things adhere to the nature of the universe without much fuss. On some level, they understand that death is simply part of a bigger cycle. But so many humans are stubborn. They think normal rules don't apply to them. They think they're going to live forever."

After what she'd just seen, the words hit Mina hard. She was sixteen and in no particular danger of dying, but that was probably what the Cliffside Trio had thought, too.

"But we're not," she whispered.

"No, we're not," her mother said. "Making someone understand that once they're already dead can be taxing, and difficult, and occasionally quite disturbing. And sometimes, well—sometimes the spirits that reach out to your uncle and me don't do it because they need help. They do it because they're...changing."

"Are you talking about whatever was happening to Mr. Giacomo's ghost?"

The curtains ruffled behind Stella as she spoke, the breeze a quiet accompaniment to her words. "The longer a spirit remains unsettled, the more they forget the person they used to be. There's a reason spirits can only stick around for a half century. They grow tired, and their tethers to the world fade away. But over the last few decades, we've noticed that some spirits have been warping before they vanish in a way our family's never seen before."

"Warping how?" Mina clung to each tiny piece of information, filing them away in her mind. She wouldn't waste this valuable opportunity to learn as much as she could.

"Some spirits have become more violent, as you saw," Stella said. "All of them are louder, even the peaceful ones. More erratic,

too. The full moon and the new moon are when I'm most connected to the dead. That used to be a great help. But these days,
it takes all my concentration to stay afloat—that's why we chose
to meet with Mrs. Giacomo when the new moon isn't for another
few days. And, well…there is the small matter of spirits feeding
on one another."

"Excuse me?" Mina's voice cracked. "They're…eating each
other?"

Stella clutched her scrying focus. "What you witnessed was
something your uncle and I have begun to call the unraveling.
Sometimes an unsettled spirit will absorb ghosts that are ready
to move on and continue to run off the power of their souls. The
more spirits they devour, the more dangerous they become."

Mina thought again of those hands closing around Mr. Giacomo's neck. How they'd glowed more strongly as he'd begun to
disappear. Suddenly she was far too hot beneath the blankets.
She tugged them down around her waist, careful not to jostle
her bracelet.

"Dangerous how?" Ghosts could pester the living the way Mr.
Giacomo had, calling out to those they'd been close to or those
who they blamed for their death. That was what she'd warned Evelyn about. Disarming behavior, certainly, but not truly threatening.

"Well, it's impossible to say definitively," Stella said, releasing
her necklace. "What your uncle and I *do* know is that the stronger a spirit like this becomes, the greater effect they can have on
the living world. They could even ascend to a state where they
can prey on the living in addition to the dead. To demonhood."

"Demons are *real?*" The words were an indelible reminder
of just how little Mina knew about her mother's world. It was

as if her view into life as a medium had been a grimy window and Stella had finally cleared the glass, only to reveal something awful standing on the other side.

"Theoretically, yes." Stella frowned. "A word like *demon* implies evil in a way I would ordinarily find quite limiting, but I don't know what other term to use for a creature powered by the souls of others. Particularly when I believe that they could grow powerful enough to unravel living people the same way they unravel the dead."

Mina thought of those grotesque faces she'd seen, twisted in agony, and felt a fresh swell of nausea. "Wait, so . . . are you saying the drowning summer victims are demons?"

Stella jerked backward. "No! Absolutely not. A demon would be catastrophic. On par with a natural disaster. I'm saying the Cliffside Trio are some of the spirits that have been absorbed by a ghost that's trying to become a demon. They're working as an extension of whatever anchoring spirit is hiding behind them, growing its parasitic network further by finding new victims."

"How long have you known about this?" It came out like an accusation. Maybe it was.

"The spirits have been changing since before you were born, Mina. But the potential for a demon? I didn't think that was possible until six years ago. After this ghost absorbed the drowning summer victims."

Mina thought again of her and Evelyn sitting in that cave, calling out into the night and seeing who answered.

"What happens to the people those absorbed souls belonged to?" she croaked out. "Can they be saved?"

"It depends," Stella said. "The essence of a person is not easily unraveled. But if this ghost is left unchecked, those people will eventually disappear forever."

"So Mr. Giacomo..." Mina didn't have to finish her sentence. "Are you going to tell his wife the truth?"

Stella hesitated. "I don't know. I'm hoping we can stop this and free him, along with the others, before things go too far."

So, no. Her mother wasn't going to tell her client the truth. But Mina felt too ill to push her anymore.

"Your warding necklace is meant to keep ghosts from bothering you," Stella continued. "I believe it physically hurt you because this particular ghost is beginning to have an effect on the living. Well, more specifically, on mediums."

"How can you be sure it's just us?"

"Because we stand on the bridge between life and death, Mina. Which makes us quite a bit easier to reach than everyone else in town. And most important, we stand in the way of the ghost's ascension. Which is why you *must* keep your necklace on, no matter what. I don't know what this spirit is capable of, but I don't want you to find out."

Mina had dozens more questions—hundreds, maybe. But right now, only one really seemed to matter.

"So how do we stop an ascension?"

"Not *we*, Mina. Your uncle and I will handle this problem, along with the issue of the amateur medium. We're protected by our scrying focuses and a lifetime of knowledge, but if today proved nothing else, it's that you truly aren't ready to be exposed to this kind of danger."

"I'll keep my necklace on," Mina said. "I'll do whatever you want."

"What I want is for you to be safe." Stella brushed a strand of blond hair from Mina's sweaty forehead. "I've told you all of this so that you can understand why it's so important that you listen to me."

"But I can help—"

"No."

It wasn't just the word. It was the way she said it—sharp. Angry. Stella didn't believe in yelling at Mina, but this was close.

Mina knew there was nothing she could say to convince her mother that she still deserved to be included in this. She had proven herself a liability, not once but twice, and that wasn't even accounting for the secret hidden beneath her cuff bracelet. Frustration swelled in her, begging her to make her case—that she didn't want to stand idly by while a ghost tried to break the barrier between life and death. But Mina took a deep breath and forced all of it down. When she spoke again, she sounded perfectly calm.

"I understand. But would it be possible for me to get more basic training, so that I can learn some better ways to protect myself?"

Stella's expression had smoothed out into a gentle smile. "Yes, I think that's a lovely idea."

In Mina's mind, she was a sailor in a boat. A net floated behind it, scooping up bits and pieces that did not belong on the water's surface.

She took the truth about demons and Stella's *no* and her own secrets. Caught them in that net. Kept her ocean calm and gentle.

"Great," she said. "I'm looking forward to it."

It had been hours since Stella had told Mina the truth, and she still didn't know what to do. The sand dollar on her wrist hurt, and she kept fiddling with her warding necklace, wondering what horrors awaited her if she took it off. She'd decorated her room so carefully with soft colors and gentle fabrics, but none of them soothed her now. All she could do was replay the conversation with Stella again and again.

Demon. Demon. Demon.

The word wouldn't leave her alone. Not just because her mother had kept it from her. But because Mina had recognized so much of what her mother had talked about.

A being that wanted only to cause harm. Someone so distanced from their former human life, they wouldn't care about the consequences of hurting a child—or of striking again as soon as that child was foolish enough to wade into the ocean during a summoning, defenseless.

Maybe she was just being paranoid. She hoped so.

Her mother had gone to help Uncle Dom clean up the mess they'd left behind at the community center after more warnings to Mina to stay put. But Mina was filled with restless energy. She wound up on the floor again, taking a seam ripper to that same ruffled dress. She'd been stuck on it for almost two weeks—designer's block, maybe.

When her phone buzzed, she let it go. The doorbell rang, but she ignored that, too.

Until it rang again. And again. And someone started knocking, loud and impatient.

Clearly, this person wasn't going to leave on their own. Mina knew she looked a mess, her blond hair mussed from wallowing in bed, her makeup mostly gone from crying. She'd changed out of the salt-stained clothes she'd worn to the community center, so she answered the door in satin pajama pants and a rumpled T-shirt with a tiny embroidered rainbow on the pocket. The moment she swung it open, she wished she'd pulled herself together a little more. Because Evelyn Mackenzie was standing on her doorstep.

Evelyn was the kind of pretty that Mina had always wanted to be: liquid-lined eyes the color of the ocean, long brown beach-wave hair, lips always set in a slight, pouting smirk that showed off her deep dimples. Mina worked hard to look polished and put-together. But Evelyn always seemed to be utterly and effortlessly herself, as if she genuinely didn't care what anybody else thought.

There was this story that had circulated last fall, about Evelyn yelling at someone who'd insulted her dad and then throwing up at some party. That sort of attention would have made Mina want to shrivel up like a snail, but Evelyn hadn't even seemed to notice. It was a confidence Mina wished she shared.

"Fine!" Evelyn said, instead of *hello*. "Fine, Zanetti! You win!" She dropped her longboard and helmet in the front hallway, then fled dramatically to the orange velvet couch, shedding her canvas tote bag somewhere along the way.

"Shoes!" Mina said, feeling like her mother as she trailed after her. "You'll get dirt everywhere. And you could have at least asked before you invited yourself inside."

"Dirt is the least of my problems," Evelyn said, but she tugged off her sneakers anyway and tucked her mismatched socks beneath her knees, pretzel-style. "Is your mom home?"

Mina shook her head. She didn't understand how she could feel so ambushed in her own house, on her own turf. Everything about Evelyn Mackenzie was utterly destabilizing.

"Okay, good," Evelyn said. "Because we need to talk."

"I gathered that, yes." Mina eyed the dirt smudges Evelyn's sneakers had left on the pristine shag carpet as she perched on the other end of the couch. She needed a mug of tea and ten seconds to think, but she wasn't going to get it. "What brought you here so, uh, urgently?"

Evelyn frowned at her. "What the hell do you think? Spooky ghost shit, obviously."

It took every ounce of self-control Mina possessed not to say *I told you so*. Instead, she gave Evelyn her best polite smile.

"So you need my help?" she asked, trying not to sound smug.

The look Evelyn shot her told Mina she'd definitely failed. "Just tell me the spell or ritual or whatever I have to do to make this stop."

"If you want me to give you any insight, you're going to need to be a little more specific about what's happening to you."

"You want specific?" Even though Evelyn had never been to the cottage before, she looked right at home in Mina's living room, squeezed between the pile of crocheted blankets and a plushy pillow. "Something broke a window and caused a power outage at Scales and Tails. And I saw this creepy figure in the mirror today with sand dollars on its eyes, like I'm in some kind of low-budget horror movie—"

"I get the idea." Unease swirled through Mina, the same unease that had been festering all morning. "You're being haunted by whatever you summoned two weeks ago."

Evelyn blew a piece of hair out of her face and flopped backward on the couch, gazing up at the popcorn ceiling. "Wow, what a breakthrough," she drawled. "I never would've guessed."

"You don't have to be rude." Mina glared at Evelyn's mismatched socks. One was patterned with cacti, the other with smiley faces with the eyes X-ed out. "Let me finish."

"As if that's going to make this suck less," Evelyn muttered. Mina felt like she was looking anywhere but at her—apparently asking for help wasn't the other girl's specialty.

"Well, you're right about that part." Mina cleared her throat uncomfortably. "Um...I don't think you summoned a ghost to help you. Or at least, no ordinary ghost."

"Aww, you think my ghost is special?"

Mina knew it was a bad idea to tell the truth like this, but Evelyn was the only other person in the world who knew what had happened in Sand Dollar Cove six years ago. And after what she'd learned today, she *needed* to talk to someone about it. "I think your ghost is a potential demon."

Evelyn tilted her head back down, locked her gaze with Mina's. There was so much in those eyes—a maelstrom of emotions that made Mina uncomfortable even from a safe distance. She suspected this was why she found it so difficult to make friends: She knew how to handle Stella's feelings, but pretty much anyone else's were off-limits.

This also made dating virtually impossible. She'd come out as bi last year after talking it through with Stella for weeks, in an act of vulnerability that she was unsure she'd ever be capable of again. And then the one girl who she'd ever tried to ask out had stood her up, so, clearly, it wasn't even worth trying.

Evelyn's voice snapped Mina out of her thoughts. "What do you mean, a *demon*?"

Mina explained the events of that morning and the revelations that had followed. It was an unfortunate conversation, made more unfortunate by the number of questions Evelyn asked that Mina couldn't answer.

"So you're being targeted by this...thing," Evelyn said.

"You, too," Mina said weakly. "All mediums are vulnerable to this ghost."

Evelyn's voice shook. "I'm not a medium."

Mina could have argued with that, but...maybe it was true. If this was the only entity Evelyn had ever interacted with, it might be because of Mina. Banish this ghost, and it was possible Evelyn could return to her normal life.

"You still need to protect yourself," Mina said. "Can you accept that, at least?"

"Why do you think I came here, Zanetti?" Evelyn scowled. "Now tell me the magic words and I'll say them. Salt circles, water, candles. Let's do it."

"I already told you it's not that simple. But I'm willing to help you figure it out."

"Fine. But what about the drowning summer victims? How do they fit into all of this?"

"They've been trapped inside the ghost. Like a spiderweb, only the spider digests its prey extremely slowly."

Evelyn looked horrified. "We need to tell their families."

Mina remembered saying those same words to Stella just a few hours ago. She shuddered as she realized exactly why her mother had said no.

"We can't tell them about any of this," she said. "It'll only make things worse."

Evelyn stood, blazing with sudden fury. She'd had an irrepressible temper for as long as Mina had known her, an inability to hold her feelings inside that couldn't be tamped down by any bully or teacher. Mina had always considered it courageous, but now she wondered if it had merely been recklessness.

"You're not close to this like I am, Mina. My sister was in love with Jesse Slater. He was Nick's older brother, and I know we've broken up, but it still feels wrong to keep him out of this. Shouldn't they get the chance to know what really happened to him?"

"It won't help," Mina said. "These families believe their loved ones are at peace. Breaking that illusion would only cause them pain."

"That's not a choice we should get to make."

"I'm starting to wonder if making impossible choices is part of being a medium," Mina said quietly, thinking of the sand dollar beneath her bracelet. "But I have to believe my family's rules exist for a reason."

"You've broken those rules before." Evelyn was standing above Mina now. Shadows pooled beneath Evelyn's eyes, and her lips were parted in indignation. "Remember?"

Mina remembered.

It had been the day after Evelyn's dad was taken to the police station for questioning. Any other kid would have stayed home, but Evelyn had showed up at school anyway, stalking past the whispers and stares like they didn't matter. Mina would have been fooled, too, if she hadn't known her so well. So when Evelyn slipped out of the lunch line, Mina followed her.

She found her friend crying in the back of the classroom, clutching her backpack. When Mina sat beside her, she saw a beat-up felt snake sticking out of the top. Mina had known the moment she saw the stuffed animal that this was serious business. Fifth grade was too old to bring a toy like this to school, but today, Evelyn cared more about the comfort than the potential for teasing.

"They think my dad killed those people," she'd whimpered. "He says it's going to be okay, but it *won't* be. I know it won't."

Mina could've stayed quiet. But a few weeks before, she had found the instructions for a spirit summoning in Stella's jewelry box. Mina had stuffed the page in her pocket and copied every word before returning it, wondering if she'd ever be brave enough to use it.

She had decided to be brave that day because Evelyn needed help. And that was what Stella had always said mediums were for—helping people.

"I can fix this," she'd said. "I promise."

Everything after that was a blur. The sound of her and Evelyn's sneakers squeaking against the wet stones. The way it had hurt more than anything when the mark had appeared on her wrist. The week after, when Stella had taken her to the hospital after her fever got too high.

"Ignoring proper protocol is what got us into this mess," she said now. "Think about it, Evelyn—if my mark and your haunting are happening together, they're connected. *We're* connected. So, no, I don't want to break the rules again. I want to fix things."

Mina watched Evelyn consider this. Emotions passed across

her face like a swarm of minnows darting in the shallows—fear, regret, determination.

"Do you think we should tell your family?" she asked finally. "If we're in real danger, shouldn't they know I had something to do with this?"

The sand dollar on Mina's wrist throbbed, as if in answer. "They know someone's responsible for messing with the ghost. And to be honest, if they found out it was you, I don't know how they'd react."

Evelyn's eyes went wide. "They wouldn't think I did this on purpose, would they? What if I explained myself?"

Something twisted in Mina's stomach that she didn't quite understand, something that went beyond fear of what might happen if Stella discovered the sand dollar had reappeared on her wrist. But her prolonged silence seemed to be answer enough.

"I get it," Evelyn said finally. "I...I guess if I want to protect myself, I don't really have a choice."

She stuck out her hand, adorned with chipped black nail polish and a cluster of silver rings bearing various ominous symbols—a skull, a claw, a snake eating its own tail. "If you help me stop being haunted, I'll help you figure out a way to get rid of this ghost-demon thing."

Mina nodded, then took Evelyn's hand. She could've sworn she heard voices whispering in the back of her head as their palms clasped together, and when she pulled away, her warding necklace was hot against her collarbone.

Chapter Eight

If Evelyn's house felt like a graveyard, Nick Slater's felt like a mausoleum: fancy but grim, a place where voices were automatically hushed and memories of the dead lurked around every corner. Nick's parents both came from generational wealth, and they worked at Slater Enterprises, the family business, which as Evelyn understood it was just a company that bought and sold other companies to make more money. Yet nobody seemed to use any of the fancy shit they purchased with said money, from the massive sailboat down at the docks to the gleaming marble kitchen.

"So, you finally want to talk." Nick answered the door in house slippers and a button-down with crisp khaki shorts. Evelyn had always teasingly told him that he looked like a poster boy for the Hamptons, but secretly she'd liked how put-together he was—until it had started to feel stifling, like she had to box herself in, too.

"Yeah." Evelyn had lied to Mina. She didn't feel great about that, especially since Mina had promised to help her protect herself from some kind of wannabe demon. But she still didn't think it was fair to keep the fate of the Cliffside Trio a secret, and Nick was an easy place to start. "I know I could've called you, but it felt like telling you this in person might be better."

"I appreciate that." Nick gestured for her to follow him into the living room.

Pictures of Jesse were everywhere, crowded on the mantelpiece and hanging in artfully arranged clusters on the walls. Evelyn watched her ex's brother grow up with every step she took, from an adorable baby in a fluffy nightgown to a gap-toothed kid to a grinning teen. Some of the pictures had Meredith in them. It felt like a physical blow to realize that there would be no more updates coming. Jesse's story had ended before there could be photos of him at prom, or graduation, or college.

Colin Maxwell's and Tamara Winger's families had left town after the murders, but the Slaters had chosen to stay in Cliffside Bay. Evelyn knew firsthand how much those decisions had affected Nick. It was why she was here: to talk about Jesse's ghost. But as she sat on a white leather couch, squinting into the sunlight that streamed through the floor-to-ceiling bay windows overlooking the ocean, she couldn't get Mina's words out of her head.

That Nick believed his brother was at peace, and maybe it was better to keep it that way.

"I don't really know where to start," she said, swiveling to face him. He'd chosen a chair across from the couch, each plushy arm studded with brass anchors. "Uh. Maybe by making sure you know that I'm not trying to get back together with you."

Nick winced. "Blunt as always, huh, Evie?"

"You said you liked that I was blunt."

"I do," he admitted. "Most people don't know how to treat me. But you..." He shrugged. "You just acted like I was a normal person. You didn't make any special exceptions."

"But I did," Evelyn said. "That's why I said yes when you asked me to cheat for you."

Nick fiddled nervously with one of the anchors. "I didn't mean to guilt you into it, you know."

"I know. And I'm the one who agreed. That's on me."

"Then why are you here?"

You should tell him.

Evelyn tried to put the words together. But sitting in this memorial to Jesse Slater, staring at Nick's worried face, she didn't know what to say. What would really happen if she told him about Jesse's ghost? He'd have questions. He'd be hurt. He probably wouldn't even believe her.

Mina was right: It would make things a thousand times more complicated. All of Evelyn's convictions felt foolish now, half-baked and unprepared to be tested. Organisms in the intertidal zone had evolved with defense mechanisms to cope with its changes—a barnacle closing its shell during low tide to trap the water it needed to breathe, or a snail clinging to a rock with its foot to outlast a crashing wave. But Evelyn had always felt like those defenses were something she lacked. She had just enough energy to get herself into trouble, but not enough to pull herself out.

"No," she murmured, rising from her seat. "I—I can't do this."

"Evie." Nick rose from his armchair, too. He took one of her hands in both of his, uncurled her fingers from the fist she hadn't even realized she was making. "What's really going on? I thought you wanted me to leave you alone, but you're... you're here."

Evelyn stared miserably at his hands overlapping her own, like they were suffocating her palms. All she was doing was hurting him more. And all telling him about Jesse's ghost would do was make that hurt even worse.

"I'm sorry for coming here and confusing you. I did mean what I said. I think we should leave each other alone."

"You always do this." Nick's voice was lower, sadder. "When you're upset, you shut me out. No matter how hard I try to be there for you."

"That's not fair." Evelyn pulled her hand away from his. "We're not together anymore."

"But you did it the whole time we were dating. I took you to dinner with my parents, but you never let me meet your family. You never even let me come over to your house. You were ashamed of me."

"You know that's not why I didn't let you meet my family." Evelyn tried to hold back her tears. She wasn't even sure if it was this she wanted to cry about, or what had happened with Mina, or the creepy potentially demonic stuff at the Basic Bean. Maybe it didn't matter. "My life isn't like yours. And I knew that if I introduced you to my dad, your parents would freak. You were at that dinner, too—they hated me! They probably threw a giant party to celebrate our breakup!"

"I don't—I didn't—care about that stuff, all those conspiracy theories about your dad, all those rumors people spread about you after that party," Nick said hoarsely. "All I wanted was to take care of you, and you wouldn't let me."

"I don't need to be taken care of."

"Really? Because you sure seemed like you did when I met you."

Finally, Evelyn understood.

"You wanted to save me," she said. "At that party. On all those fancy dates. You...you liked that I wasn't comfortable, because then I'd feel like I needed you."

"I never meant to make you feel that way," Nick protested. "You get weird when people are nice to you, Evie. It's not the worst thing in the world to admit you need someone else. All I wanted to do was make you feel safe."

"Well, you asked me to cheat on a final exam for you," Evelyn said. "So I'm calling bullshit on that whole *safe* thing. I'm calling bullshit on you, actually. You don't mean a single thing you say."

"Then I guess we're done here, if that's really what you think of me."

Evelyn glared at him. "I guess we are."

She was so angry on the ride home, she almost crashed her longboard into a telephone pole. When she finally reached her driveway, still replaying her conversation with Nick, there was a car parked crookedly on the gravel. Not her father's beat-up minivan—a sleek little MINI Cooper, peppered with bumper stickers similar to the ones adorning Evelyn's helmet.

Evelyn dropped her board on the porch and bolted through the door. Someone waited for her in the living room, sitting on the couch beside her father in his recliner. A young white woman with a dark brown pixie cut and a pink, freckled face, her eyes—the same color as Evelyn's—magnified through a pair of black-rimmed glasses.

Evelyn was already crying a little bit, but the tears came faster now, clogging her throat and nose until the only sound she could make was a tiny, choking rasp.

"Meredith," she whimpered. "You came home."

Chapter Nine

It had been seven months since Evelyn had last seen her older sister in person, and far longer than that since Meredith had set foot in their childhood home. She'd fled the moment she graduated and found a whole new ecosystem at college—a boyfriend, a social circle, a future career as an accountant. So her return to Cliffside Bay wasn't just a shock, it was a monumental occasion. A seismic shift.

"What's going on?" Evelyn sat on the couch, sniffling. Meredith patted her shoulder gently. "Why are you back? Did someone die?"

"Shit, Evelyn, no." Meredith looked perturbed. "Nothing like that."

"Merry's staying here for the summer," her father said from the recliner, where he was scratching at his gray-streaked stubble—a nervous tic. The dusty TV screen, usually playing the soundtrack to his midlife crisis, had been muted.

Meredith scowled. "Please, Greg, don't call me that."

Their father had been *Greg* ever since the drowning summer. Evelyn was pretty sure it was because of how often their mother, Siobhan, had deployed their father's name like it was a swear word during one of their vicious fights. It didn't take long for Meredith to pick it up as a weapon of her own.

Evelyn knew her dad was innocent in a way that both Meredith and her mother refused to believe. He'd been the Cliffside Trio's sailing instructor, sure, but he'd also been with Evelyn all evening on one of their twilight nature walks. But because she'd been the only one with him, the detectives had refused to believe her statement by itself. They'd said Greg could have coerced her to lie for him, that she was just a kid.

But she wasn't a kid anymore, and she still remembered it. Evelyn's father was the one who'd sparked her love of nature, who'd taught her that life could flourish almost anywhere, from a scorching desert to the lightless depths of the sea. Their final walk along the shoreline before everything came apart would always be burned into her brain.

"I get it, Meredith," their father said. "You're all grown up now."

Meredith's hand froze on Evelyn's shoulder. "Yeah, which means I don't have to take your shit if I don't want to."

"You're the one who showed up uninvited and asked if you could stay for two months."

"And you said yes. So don't be a dick about it in front of Evelyn, okay?"

Greg sat up straighter in his armchair, his hand clenching a Red Bull can so hard, it collapsed with an awful screech. "You should be grateful I even let you back in here."

Meredith let out a mirthless chuckle. "And you should be grateful I was willing to come back at all."

After the divorce, their mother had refused to even petition for custody. She'd abandoned them all for a new life in New York City, and Meredith had made no secret of how angry she was about it. Since she couldn't take that anger out on Siobhan Mackenzie, she'd settled for the next best thing—their father.

Greg and Meredith's fights were unbearable. Things never got physical, but the horrible words they flung back and forth left Evelyn curled beneath the covers with her hands over her ears, unable to process how the two people she loved most could be so hateful to each other. She spent the next few years wandering Main Street, staring at the animal tanks in Scales & Tails, talking to Ruthie at the antiques store, or just sitting in the library, listening to Mrs. Morales's soothing voice as she read picture books to the preschoolers. Any stares Evelyn got were worth a few hours away from the screaming.

"Can you stop it?" she asked now, trying to sound the way both of them did when they got angry—sharp. Determined. Like there was nothing on earth that could possibly make them back down. "It's been five minutes since Meredith got back, and you're already fighting."

Meredith exhaled sharply, but her stance softened.

"You're right," she said, lowering her voice. "I can be civil if you can."

Their father still looked agitated, but his gaze turned toward Evelyn. And maybe he saw the fear on her face, because after a beat, he nodded. "Your old bedroom is still yours, if you want it."

"Great." Meredith rose to her feet. "Come on, Evelyn. I could use some help unpacking."

Meredith's bedroom had remained relatively undisturbed since her high school graduation three years ago. Evelyn poked her head in there every few months, but aside from raiding the leftovers in Meredith's closet, she hadn't touched anything. She watched Meredith survey the stripped mattress on a dusty bed frame. There was a suspicious stain in the center—most likely water damage from the leaky ceiling.

"Well, shit." Meredith dropped her duffel bag on the floor. "He's worse than I remember."

"Dad?" Evelyn asked, standing awkwardly beside a dresser encrusted with three years' worth of cobwebs and grime.

"Yeah. I don't know how you stand it."

"He's not usually like this," Evelyn said. "He hasn't yelled in . . . a while."

"Since I left, you mean." Meredith eyed the filthy blinds on the lone window. "You can say it."

"Can I?" Evelyn hated the quiver in her voice.

"Yes, you can." Meredith yanked the blinds up, coughing into a cloud of dust. Light flooded into the room, illuminating even more dirt. But it illuminated other things, too—the faded posters still taped up on the wall, the expired makeup scattered on the dresser. "I've been working with this therapist lately. Complex post-traumatic stress disorder. Anger management. You get the idea. You should probably talk to one, too."

Meredith's anger hadn't seemed particularly managed down-stairs, and there was no way Evelyn could afford to see a mental health professional on her dad's insurance. But she swallowed that truth as Meredith went to rummage through the hallway closet for cleaning supplies. Mackenzies were blunt and loud, with short, explosive fuses, and they didn't do well in a room together for all those reasons. If Evelyn was honest with Meredith...maybe she would disappear for good, just like their mother had.

Meredith was the first person Evelyn had come out to. She'd taught her how to use a tampon, how to put on eyeliner. She'd even helped her go vegetarian. Evelyn knew her sister wasn't perfect, but she loved her. And even though having her home was stressing out their dad, Evelyn had missed her.

"Why are you back?" she asked, when Meredith returned with every cleaning product in the house.

"Well. That's a fun question." Meredith grabbed a feather duster and brandished it threateningly at the windowsill. "Riku and I both got summer internships in the city, so we were going to share a sublet. But he got accepted by this amazing long shot at the last minute. So he went to Berkeley, and I couldn't afford to pay the rent alone...."

"So you came here." Evelyn picked up a broom.

"It's not like I had anywhere else to go within commuting distance." Meredith attacked the windowsill with the feather duster as if it had personally insulted her. "Greg's charging me rent, but that's fine."

Evelyn swiped the broom aggressively across the floor. She knew this place was a last resort for Meredith, but it still hurt to hear it.

"But you and Riku are good?" Evelyn asked. The floor was so dirty that sweeping it only seemed to make the problem worse.

A smile finally spread across Meredith's face, and she nodded. "I'm really proud of him. And we can definitely handle long distance for a couple of months."

Riku was Meredith's boyfriend of about a year and a half, a Japanese American guy who had taught Evelyn the basics of longboarding during her first visit to SUNY New Paltz. Evelyn had seen through her phone calls with her sister how good the relationship was for Meredith—it was part of how she'd known things with Nick weren't working.

"Hey, what about you and..." Meredith hesitated, her mouth twisting. Evelyn swore internally. It was as if she'd summoned the question with her thoughts.

"I dumped him." Evelyn shook her dustpan into a garbage bag and started to sweep all over again. When she looked over at Meredith, the relief on her sister's face was palpable. Evelyn's family sucked at hiding their feelings just as badly as she did.

"I told you dating him was a bad idea," she said.

"I know you did." Evelyn swept a cloud of dirt into the air; this time, she might have missed the dustpan on purpose. "That's why I didn't want to tell you it had ended. Because I knew you'd be all *I told you so.*"

"That's not what I'm saying." Meredith perched on the edge of the mattress, brushing grime off her jeans. "The idea of you dating him freaked me out so much because I...I didn't want you to be like me."

A knot of annoyance tightened in Evelyn's chest. "Being like you isn't the worst thing, you know. Your life's worked out pretty great."

Meredith's escape was basically Evelyn's blueprint. Survive another two years in the harsh, unpredictable extremes of Cliffside Bay before leaving to find a more hospitable environment.

"It's good now, sure. But I went through hell to get here." Meredith yanked off her glasses and began to polish them on her tank top, which only seemed to make them dirtier. "You know people still try to contact me about the drowning summer? Podcasters. Documentary producers. They've all got the same ridiculous questions about Greg, about Jesse."

"I bet you make them regret ever trying to talk to you."

Meredith gave her a slightly wicked grin. "Only when I'm in a bad mood. But the point is . . . I can't get them off my back. You can, and you deserve to be left alone. If you and Nick had stayed together long-term, it would've tied you to this forever."

Evelyn could have said a lot of things. How she was far more involved in the drowning summer than Meredith knew. How she was probably the only reason their dad wasn't in jail. How it was entirely possible that her sister's dead boyfriend (and her ex-boyfriend's dead brother) had been a victim of spirit cannibalism. But sharing any of that seemed like a really bad idea.

Mina was right, and Evelyn hated it.

"I'm sorry all those people keep asking you questions," she said finally. "But you don't have to worry about me and Nick anymore, okay? I promise."

"Good," Meredith said. "Because the questions they ask are

seriously ridiculous. Somebody emailed me just a couple of weeks ago asking whether or not Jesse was in some kind of paranormal trouble before he died, for fuck's sake."

Something stirred inside Evelyn's mind, and for the briefest moment, she smelled saltwater. "Wait, what?"

"It's some bullshit internet conspiracy theory," Meredith said disdainfully. "Look, I know how hard coming to terms with this is. There's so much out there about Dad, about Jesse, and the theories...they can get pretty wild. But Jesse, Colin, and Tamara are—were—real people, who really died, in a really terrible way. That's what matters."

"I just wish none of it had ever happened at all," Evelyn said. "And I don't know how to help you or Dad deal with it."

"None of that is your job," Meredith said gently. "All I want you to do is have a normal, fun summer, okay?"

Evelyn forced a smile. "Okay."

Cleaning Meredith's room took almost two hours. When they were finally done, Evelyn locked her bedroom door from the inside and flipped open her laptop.

She knew there was a lot of external information about the drowning summer. Over the past six years, many people had dedicated themselves to puzzling out the Cliffside Trio's murders, amateur detectives who thought that if they watched enough *Law & Order: Special Victims Unit* they were qualified to solve a real case.

It was a can of worms Evelyn had never felt the need to open.

All she would see were horrible things about her father. But Meredith's words had sparked a new curiosity.

She typed "the drowning summer paranormal danger" into her browser and hit *enter*.

There were thousands of results. Reddit threads and fringe forum posts. Podcast episodes about the "Sand Dollar Killer" and long, rambling articles discussing the exact positions of the moon and stars the night the murders had occurred. Some conspiracists claimed Jesse, Colin, and Tamara had been abducted by aliens then returned to Earth, or that they'd found some kind of government facility and their murders had been a cover-up. All of it seemed so obviously fake. Evelyn saw one post claiming her father was the Zodiac Killer despite being a literal infant during his first murders and almost chucked her laptop out the window.

But then she found something else.

The Cliffside Trio weren't just three random kids. Their parents had their YouTube channel shut down in the days after their bodies were found, but an archived copy of one video remains **here**.

Evelyn took a deep breath, then clicked through.

WE'RE ALMOST THERE, read the title of the video. The description was simple. *We're three friends—C, J, and T—who are* **this** **close** *to exposing the TRUTH about our town. We're going to prove something BIG. Link to our socials below!*

"This can't be real," she muttered, but she hit *play* anyway.

"Hey, everyone!" It was Jesse's voice, staticky but unmistakably his. A moment later, his shock of dark brown hair appeared on screen. Behind him were Colin and Tamara, both waving at the camera. They looked so alive, three white people her age with giant smiles and clothes that weren't quite cool anymore. The shaky camera quality made Evelyn pretty sure they'd propped a phone up on some cheap tripod. "We know we've been really cryptic about what's happening, and we know that anything to do with ghosts sounds impossible. But I promise, we'll be sharing everything soon."

"With proof," added Colin excitedly.

"Or so we think," said Tamara, elbowing him.

They went on, riffing back and forth for another thirty seconds and teasing their followers about "taking them along on the big discovery" before the video cut out.

Evelyn downloaded it immediately.

She paced back and forth as it loaded on her desktop. That was the Cliffside Trio, on video, talking about *ghosts*. How was it possible that Meredith didn't know this about her ex-boyfriend, and Nick didn't know it about his brother? Did this have anything to do with how they'd died, or why their spirits were now in such a terrible situation? She thought about Meredith's plea for her to have a normal life, and sighed.

Normal had gone away when the cops came to get their dad. When their mother left her own family behind. When Meredith heard the news about Jesse's death and howled for hours like a wild animal, sobbing so hard Evelyn could hear it all throughout the house.

She needed to know what had really happened during the drowning summer. Only then could her family heal. And she couldn't shake the thought that this had to be tied to Mina's own personal investigation.

"I'm going to figure out what happened to all three of you," she said aloud, gazing around at her empty room. "And I'm going to help you. I promise."

She heard absolutely nothing in response, of course. Evelyn looked ruefully over at Clara, feeling silly. At least when she talked to her snake, she could pretend Clara's flickering tongue or twitching tail meant she was listening.

Evelyn reached for the glass of water beside her bed—only to cough and sputter as soon as it touched her lips.

Something—some*one*—had turned it to saltwater.

Chapter Ten

Mina watched the video Evelyn sent her in bed, and even her cozy nest of fluffy blankets and some herbal tea wasn't enough to keep the bone-deep fear away when she was finished.

She'd wondered for years if the drowning summer victims had lingered in Cliffside Bay because of what she and Evelyn had done. But she'd never considered that their deaths might have had anything to do with a paranormal investigation.

It couldn't be a coincidence that three people who'd been actively pursuing a ghost had wound up being absorbed by one. But as for how, and why, and what it meant for her and Evelyn? Mina was less certain.

A few days went by without much progress. Despite Mina's best internet sleuthing, she couldn't find anything else tying the Cliffside Trio to ghosts, or anything about whatever supposed truths they were trying to expose. The ocean inside her stirred, restless.

Stella was working long hours at the Shorewell Community

Center, prepping for a wedding that Mina had already agreed to help out with, which didn't leave much time for the training she'd been promised. Evelyn was working, too. It seemed like every time Mina tried to text her about meeting up, she was in the middle of a shift at the Basic Bean or the newly reopened Scales & Tails.

Mina's patience was finally rewarded on a balmy evening at the beginning of July, when she got a text from Sergio telling her that he was two minutes away with some "medium stuff for you." She rose hurriedly to her feet, abandoning the wide-legged trousers she'd been fussing with. Her collection was starting to take shape, various pieces hanging neatly on the clothing rack by her door. Unfortunately, it was the only neat thing about her room. By the time she traversed the minefield of her bedroom floor and made it to the front door, Sergio's car was pulling into the driveway.

"Help me unload the trunk," he called from the front seat.

The last time Sergio had brought over something without prior warning, it had been a bunch of live lobsters in a cooler. Mina was pleasantly surprised to discover that this time, the trunk only contained a few cardboard boxes. They were heavy, but she'd take lifting them over handling anything with working pincers.

"You said this had something to do with my medium training?" she asked, as they lugged the boxes to the porch.

Sergio nodded. "Dad and Aunt Stella are both swamped right now, so they asked me to supervise this."

"Um, all right." Mina felt a familiar tug of disappointment. It wasn't that she didn't trust Sergio to help her, but when Stella had agreed to training, Mina had assumed she meant with her mom and her uncle.

"Yeah, yeah, I know, you didn't want the B-team." Although Sergio's voice was gentle, teasing, Mina didn't miss the resentment in it.

"That's not what I meant," Mina said. "I'm just…"

"Surprised you're being taught by me?" Sergio set his boxes down, then straightened up and stared out at the ocean. The sun had just finished setting, and the moon was the barest slice of waxing crescent beside a few winking stars. "I guess Dad figured that if I can't be a medium, I've tried to do the training enough times to teach someone else."

"You shouldn't have to do that," Mina said, turning toward him. "I'm sorry."

"It's fine." Sergio sighed. "Things are getting worse. They need you. I get it."

Mina knew he was right. A few days ago, during the new moon, Stella had gotten a killer migraine. She'd spent her night sheltering behind the wards on their house, icing her forehead and listening to podcasts. Mina couldn't remember exactly when the full weight of the spirits' voices had started to hurt her mother so badly, but after what Stella had told her about things changing, she couldn't stop seeing it everywhere. She tugged anxiously on her warding necklace.

"Why do you think the ghosts are changing?" she asked him.

"I don't know." Sergio turned away from the water. "Maybe it's because there's just less mediums in Cliffside Bay now. Things definitely got worse after everyone else left."

"So why did they go?" Mina asked. "If they knew it would put Cliffside Bay in danger?"

"I don't really know, but I do remember Dad fighting with our cousins a lot about all this medium crap." Sergio crouched down and sliced open one of the boxes with his car keys. "Eventually, they had one big final blowup, and then they were gone. I tried to contact one of our cousins on social after and he blocked me. They all did. Total scorched earth."

"What were they fighting about?" Mina had never really thought about her other family much, but she'd known some of them were mediums. More Zanettis out there somewhere, talking to the dead. Maybe if they'd stayed, she would have been trained by now. Maybe Sergio was right, and it would be safer.

Sergio shrugged. "Hell if I know."

He tipped the box over, and Mina's curiosity was overridden by awe as the contents spilled out across the porch. To an outsider, this would have looked like costume jewelry: clip-on earrings and gaudy bracelets, and pendants, so many pendants, glass in every color on strings that were hopelessly tangled together. To Mina, they were far more precious than gold.

"Oh," she gasped, kneeling beside them. "Are they really letting me try this?"

"Yep." Sergio picked up a plastic ruby that had fallen off one of the necklaces and chucked it back into the pile. "They want you to find a focus."

Mina had been waiting for this moment since her mother first explained to her why that lavender pendant always hung around her neck.

A scrying focus would allow her to sift through the spirits talking to her and listen to them one at a time. Since the only rule was that the scrying focus needed to be made of glass, the Zanettis kept a variety of trinkets in Dom's basement just in case they needed to replace theirs. Dom habitually lost his, but Stella had possessed that same pendant for as long as Mina could remember.

Mina was thrilled to finally be taking this step. She'd just... always thought this was something she'd be doing with Stella. Not with Sergio.

She sighed, pushed down the aforementioned disappointment, and turned to her cousin. "Where should I start?"

"I'll guide you through it. Dad tried to have me do this a bunch of times, so I'm basically an expert," Sergio said. "Hang on. You'll need this."

He reached into one of the other boxes and pulled out a scarf.

"I'm going to hand you the pieces one by one," he explained. "You'll be blindfolded, so that you can focus better and can't make any choices based on what Aunt Stella calls 'aesthetic appeal.'"

"Is that how Uncle Dom wound up with a novelty snow globe?"

Sergio grinned at the memory. "I think he lost that one on purpose."

He tossed her the scarf, which was plaid and scratchy.

"That's all?" Mina asked. It sounded pretty simple.

"Yeah, until you feel a connection to one of them. It should glow, too, so I'll be able to tell if you've found it."

"All right, then." Nerves fluttered in Mina's stomach as she lifted the scarf toward her face, but Sergio cut in quickly before she could tie it behind her head.

"Oh, I totally forgot. You need to take off your necklace. It blocks your intuition."

"What do you mean, 'intuition'?"

"I mean it keeps you from doing any medium stuff. Obviously."

Mina dropped the scarf into her lap and reached for the brass pendant. It was smooth and cool beneath her fingers. "I thought it just stopped ghosts from communicating with me when I don't want them to. Or attacking me."

"It also stops you from communicating with them even if you *do* want to," Sergio said. "Two-way street."

"But I saw the ghosts at the community center!"

"Because Dad and Aunt Stella summoned them, sure. There's no way you could do it solo with that thing on."

Mina felt as if something had been dropped into her ocean and she hadn't snatched it up in time. Ripples were spreading through the water now, growing larger and larger until she could no longer ignore them.

If Sergio knew the truth about her necklace, Stella had surely known, too.

"They didn't tell me." She pulled the necklace over her head, rubbed her thumb over the little red heart in the center, then squeezed the whole thing in her fist. "I don't have to wear this anymore after I find a scrying focus, right?"

"Right," Sergio said. "And, for what it's worth...you don't always have to do what they tell you."

"I know that," Mina grumbled, but the look Sergio shot

her told her that he wasn't so sure. She wondered how his face would change if she told him about her deal with Evelyn—or her rule-breaking during the drowning summer.

Still, she couldn't deny that something changed when she set the necklace down on the porch beside her. The world seemed a little more in focus, the colors slightly brighter. Although perhaps that was just the placebo effect.

Mina tied the blindfold across her eyes before Sergio could say anything else that might destabilize her worldview. The summer night air was cool against Mina's skin, like a shawl draped around her shoulders. She breathed in the familiar aroma of citronella candles mixed with salt blown in on the evening breeze.

"All right," she said, cupping her hands and stretching them outward. "Let's get started."

At first, it was almost relaxing. Every few seconds, a new glass object was placed in Mina's hands. She ran her fingers over it, finding chips and grooves, sometimes feeling the places where a metal piece or a semiprecious stone was embedded into the side. They waited a few seconds, occasionally a little longer, before Sergio asked her if she felt anything.

"I don't," she said, and they continued on.

After the tenth or eleventh object, it stopped being relaxing.

After Sergio dumped out the second box, it became downright frustrating—Mina touched pendants and pins, baubles and bracelets, an earring here, a tchotchke there, and none of them felt like anything other than ordinary glass. Sergio confirmed that none of them had glowed, either.

The scarf itched over Mina's eyes, which were now filled with unshed tears. But she kept trying. Hoping each time that this might be the one she felt that magnetic pull to, the glass object that would come alive for her. Until finally, instead of handing her an item, Sergio let out a defeated sigh.

"I'm sorry," he said. "That's all of them."

Mina tried not to sob, but her unconvincing cough was a pathetic alternative. She tugged off the scarf and immediately wished she hadn't—the massive pile of failed scrying focuses on the porch between them felt mocking.

She'd never failed a test before.

"Why didn't it work?" Mina tried to keep her voice calm, her tears unshed. This was just a problem to be solved. Clearly ghosts could talk to her, therefore she was a medium, therefore she would eventually find a scrying focus.

"I don't know." Sergio started placing handfuls of jewelry back in the boxes. He wouldn't make eye contact with her, and Mina wondered if he was thinking that he'd been wrong about her abilities.

"Do you have any idea how long it usually takes a medium to find a scrying focus?"

Sergio coughed. "I mean...when I help Dad, it's like, ten, max. He sort of seems to know which ones to grab—like they're calling to him. The blindfold and stuff is to help train you to feel that."

"And you're certain that when I touched all that jewelry... none of them glowed?"

"Pretty certain." Sergio looked at her gently. "It's kind of hard to miss that happening."

Mina could barely hear the waves anymore, barely smell the salt. Her world felt very small, and very numb.

"Hey." Sergio clambered closer and wrapped his arm around Mina's shoulder, pulling her into a brotherly hug. "It will. You've just got better taste than Dad and Aunt Stella's weird cast-offs. Next time we'll try something cooler, okay? Maybe more modern."

"All right," Mina mumbled. Her cousin was taking pity on her, which would have been sweet if it wasn't so embarrassing. Plus, he smelled like stale beer. Mina wrinkled her nose and pulled away. "Here. I'll help you clean up."

After the jewelry had been put back in the car, Sergio offered to stick around for dinner. But Mina declined. She heated up a plate of lamb chops in fennel-garlic sauce and ate it curled up on the orange velvet couch, sniffling. She'd thought the meal would make her feel better, but instead it felt like a reminder of Stella, of everything she could never live up to.

Eventually, she pulled her warding necklace out of her pocket and gazed at that tiny glass heart. She started to put it on, then hesitated and tucked it back into her pocket.

That night, Mina's imaginary net was very full. She scooped up her guilt, her shame, her fear, then pulled them into her tiny boat. Her catches wriggled there, sharp, spiky things, some oozing, some rotting, some snarling at her with too many mouths. She picked up the net to stare at them—and then she shoved them into an iron chest coiled with silver chains. Mina took a deep breath and pitched it over the side.

It sank very, very slowly.

Chapter Eleven

Lately, it felt like the Basic Bean had been eating away at Evelyn's life force. She'd worked a double on the Fourth of July that had made her contemplate withdrawing from society and spending the rest of her life wandering in the wilderness. The very next day, she'd shown up at the break of dawn for an opening shift at Scales & Tails to feed all the animals, clean their cages, and sweep the shop floor. She barely had time to take a nap before heading back to the Basic Bean, where it seemed like every customer was in just as much of a bad mood as she was.

"What's going on?" Kenny murmured, as Evelyn turned from the register to fill up a quick iced coffee. "You seem angry. Okay, angrier than usual."

Evelyn scowled at him as she held a shot glass beneath the espresso machine. "Asking me if I'm angry won't make me less angry."

"Do you have that caramel latte, extra foam?" called out Amy Cheng. Most of the time, the Basic Bean only staffed two baristas at once, but lately things had been so busy that they'd added a third on midday shifts. Amy, a Chinese American girl in Evelyn's grade who always came to work wearing a guitar-pick necklace and an unexpected shade of lipstick, was currently manning the cold bar.

"Yeah," Kenny said hastily, handing it to her.

"And have you texted her back?" Amy added, taking the drink from Kenny. Her hair was up in a messy bun, displaying her undercut, and her dark blue lips were curled into a knowing smile.

Kenny flushed. "I— No— I—"

"We can discuss this later," she said before heading over to hand the drink to a waiting customer. Kenny and Amy were friends—an odd pairing, since Amy had fronted a grunge band at one point and took no shit from anyone, while Kenny spent most of his time working on audio-engineering projects and twisting himself into a pretzel at the slightest provocation.

"You're texting some girl?" Evelyn asked Kenny, who looked as if he wanted to sink through the floor. She gave the iced coffee to her customer with a smile and forced out a *Have a nice day*. When she turned away from the register again, Kenny was waiting for her.

"Hey, do you want to work the hot bar?" he asked hastily. "It would give you a break from talking to customers, at least for a little while."

Evelyn knew he was changing the subject, and she didn't appreciate the insinuation that she was in no condition to be talking to people. But then she turned to the line of customers, almost out the door, and realized that making the drinks was by far the lesser evil here.

"Okay," she said, surprised by how grateful she was.

The next few hours passed in a blur. Evelyn didn't mind this part of working. She could turn off her brain, and as long as she kept moving, she didn't have to think about how tired she was. She heated up pastries and made drink after drink, fighting with the espresso machine and trying her best to turn the latte foam into a convincingly photogenic design Luisa would've happily taken pictures of.

Things finally slowed down around midafternoon. Evelyn scarfed down a stale pastry—there'd been no time for lunch—before returning to the register. She was much more willing to be there without a hundred people demanding increasingly ridiculous drink combinations. Amy and Kenny grabbed pastries of their own and picked up their argument beside the display case.

"Stop freaking out and just do it," Amy said as she touched up her lipstick in the espresso machine's reflection. "She'll text you back."

"You don't know that." Kenny fidgeted nervously with his glasses, pulling them off and cleaning them on his apron. "What if she hates me for trying again? What if I suck? What if—"

"Kenny." Amy stuck her lipstick back in her apron pocket and placed a hand on his arm. "It's a text, not a marriage proposal."

"Mystery girl again?" Evelyn asked.

"Yep." Amy rolled her eyes. "They keep flirting, but neither of them will do anything about it."

"Because it isn't flirting!" Kenny protested. "She's just being nice."

"She listened to that podcast after he recommended it," Amy murmured to Evelyn.

Evelyn couldn't quite choke down a laugh. "Shit, Kenny, that's true love. You should text her."

She turned back to the register to find a very familiar face waiting for her.

Unlike Scales & Tails, Mina came to the Basic Bean every once in a while. Evelyn had always made Kenny talk to her, but today she stayed behind the counter, relieved that there was at least one customer she wouldn't have to put on a fake smile for.

"Hey," she said. "Caffeine?"

Mina leaned over the counter a little. "Hello. Um. I really need to talk to you. I've been texting you—"

"I know," Evelyn said. The texts had been cryptic and carefully phrased—We need to meet soon and Any updates on your condition?—as if being haunted was a medical problem. "I've been working."

"Yes. I'm well aware." Mina fiddled with the wicker strap of her purse. Today she wore a floral-patterned midi skirt, chunky platform heels, and a cream-colored crop top that showed off a pale stripe of her stomach. But although her outfit made her look like she'd come straight from taking a bunch of perfect photos in a wildflower field, there was a slight vacancy in her eyes that even her perfectly made-up face couldn't hide. "It's important."

"My shift ends in fifteen," Evelyn said. "Can it wait that long?"

Mina nodded, visibly relieved, and hurried away from the register.

Evelyn turned to find both Amy and Kenny looking very curiously at her.

"What...," Kenny started. Evelyn gave him a look that he must have found truly ferocious, because he gulped nervously and looked to Amy for help.

"She obviously doesn't want to talk about it," Amy said, shrugging.

"But I don't want to talk about *my* personal life."

"You're the one who asked me for girl advice," Amy said.

Kenny flushed. "Because you flirt with girls all the time, so I thought you'd be good at it!"

"Yeah, I'm an expert. Therefore you should listen to me."

And then they were off again, arguing in the corner. Evelyn stayed at the register until her shift ended, then clocked out and headed over to Mina's corner table, armed with two iced coffees in biodegradable cups. She did appreciate that the Basic Bean's corporate offices at least pretended to care about the environment.

"Here," she said, sliding over Mina's. "Iced coffee with four sugars, a shot of chocolate syrup, and some whipped cream on top."

Mina was visibly surprised. "You know my coffee order?"

"It's impossible not to remember the person who basically asks for a sundae. You know Gino's Gelato is just down the street, right?"

Mina looked at her haughtily. "With much more charming staff, no doubt."

"Watch it, Zanetti," Evelyn said. "Your caffeine-adjacent monstrosity is free. I have the power to change that."

Mina chuckled, and for a moment she looked a lot less wrung out. Evelyn softened—it felt good to make her happier.

"Thank you," the other girl said, taking a sip. "And also, sorry. I didn't mean to bother you at work again. You're just rather difficult to contact."

"I get that." Evelyn took a long sip of her iced Americano. The caffeine rush would stave off her exhaustion for at least a little longer. "So what's going on?"

"Nothing really," Mina mumbled. "I— Why is your coworker staring at us?"

Evelyn turned to see Kenny watching them as he hung his apron up. So predictably nosy.

"He's probably just started to associate me with drama," she said. "Last time someone came to visit me here, it was Nick."

"Your ex? What did he want?"

"All his stuff back," Evelyn said. "But I think mostly he just wanted to talk."

"That sounds exhausting." Mina took another dainty sip.

"It was. What about you? Any lingering exes?"

"I...no." Mina sounded kind of wistful. "I've never dated anybody. Although I did have several nice conversations with people after I came out, but...none of them went anywhere."

When Evelyn had come out, she'd written a long, intense caption on social media about knowing who she was and wanting the world to know, too. Mina had just posted a makeup look with bi flag eyeshadow colors. Stylish, minimalistic, and elegant. Typical.

"Did you tell any of them how you felt?" Evelyn asked.

Mina's face twitched. "Absolutely not."

"Then of course it didn't work! They slid into your DMs. They were totally into it. You can't say they weren't interested just because you didn't ask them out."

Mina gave her a frosty look. "I'm not here to get your insights on my dating capabilities. Or the quality of my direct messages."

Evelyn felt a twinge of hurt—she would have liked to talk to somebody else about how it felt to be bi and out and sixteen in Cliffside Bay—but she pushed it down. Apparently Mina was not exactly the touchy-feely bonding type.

"Then what *did* you come for?" she asked.

"Ah. Right." Mina sighed. "Well, I've been doing a lot of thinking about the ghost, and their potential ties to the drowning summer."

"Me too." The ice cubes in Evelyn's coffee clinked together as she stirred her straw around. "I've been looking into things a little bit."

This was a massive understatement. After finding that footage, Evelyn had fallen deep into the drowning summer rabbit hole she'd spent six years hiding from. During her few moments of precious free time, she'd read a bunch of articles about the Cliffside Trio, listened to podcast episodes, and watched clips of a documentary online. Even the parts about her dad. The evidence against him had been purely circumstantial, but it still hurt like a bitch to listen to it all laid out.

Too much exposure to harsh and unforgiving conditions could kill any organism, no matter how strongly they'd adapted to their environment.

"I've done the same," Mina said. "But quite frankly, I think we should be viewing this as banishing a dangerous spirit, not a murder investigation. We have no proof that the deaths of Tamara, Colin, and Jesse, however tragic, are related to any of this."

"They were messing with a ghost, and then they wind up as victims of spirit cannibalism? No way that's a coincidence."

"I understand why finding the truth is important to you," Mina said. "But you shouldn't be distracted by that. You're in danger here—that's what matters most right now."

Evelyn's temper flared. "Oh, yeah, how dare I be *distracted* by that time my dad was falsely accused of murder. And besides, nothing's happened to me the last few days."

"Because the moon is in its first quarter, yes. That will change."

"I don't give a crap about the moon, Zanetti. You promised to help me deal with the ghost—maybe looking at how they're connected to the drowning summer is part of that deal."

"I know what I promised you. I..." Her voice wobbled, and Evelyn saw that careful facade crack again. "I came here to tell you that perhaps that promise wasn't...viable."

Evelyn had been ready for an argument, Amy and Kenny's judgment be damned. But Mina's tone made her hesitate, as did the way she rubbed hastily at one of her eyes.

Mina was upset. And Evelyn could tell she wasn't upset with *her*.

"Why?" she asked.

Mina relayed the story in short, stiff bursts of information— her cousin, her training, the failed search for a scrying focus.

"It's just...rather annoying," she finished. "I've tried again every day since, but it isn't working. And, well, I can't protect you *or* figure out how to banish a ghost without a scrying focus. It's the first step to becoming a real medium. And I can't seem to achieve it! Which is obviously so much fun."

Evelyn understood now. This was the first time in Mina Zanetti's life something hadn't come easily to her. No wonder she was freaking out.

"You're totally a medium," Evelyn countered. "Like...it's not as if you can't talk to ghosts. So there must be the right focus out there."

Mina gazed forlornly at her drink. "I suppose."

An idea budded in Evelyn's mind. She'd been looking forward to going home and resting, but...it was only 4:00 PM. She had time for this. And she didn't like the idea of leaving Mina alone and upset.

"I know you've already gone through a bunch of potential scrying focuses, but I know where to find more," Evelyn said. "Way more. If you're down to try again."

Mina looked up. "Really?"

"Really."

Chapter Twelve

Ruthie's was a few blocks down from the Basic Bean, right off the main square of Cliffside Bay. Mina walked while Evelyn coasted on her longboard. It gave her enough extra inches to be at Mina's eye level.

"The moon cycle matters to mediums because it's connected to when the high tides are higher and the low tides are lower," Mina explained. "How close the moon and sun are to the ocean alters that range."

"I know that." Evelyn thought about the tides a lot, actually, but not because of ghosts. Abnormally fluctuating sea levels were contributing to coastal erosion and messing with the creatures whose lives were tied to the Sound. The changing waterlines had outpaced evolution, and Evelyn was painfully aware of the consequences that would have for local biodiversity.

"Great! So can you tell me what times of month we can expect a larger range of tides?"

Evelyn hesitated. That, she was less sure about. "Um. No."

"At the new moon and the full moon, the tidal range is greater because the moon and sun are in alignment. That's called a spring tide. And when the moon and sun are at odds—canceling out their gravitational pull to each other—their range is lessened. This is further exacerbated by the moon's and sun's distance to the earth. That's what we call a neap tide—what we're in right now, actually."

"I've always thought that term was kind of silly," Evelyn said, barely able to hold back a laugh. She could remember the first time her Dad had said the words *neap tide* to her, how she'd cracked up and he'd joined her a moment later.

"You shouldn't take it so lightly, since it's what's currently protecting you," Mina said haughtily. "The tidal range is as low as possible right now, therefore the ghost is weak. But the night when my sand dollar came back? That was a full moon."

"The highest possible tidal range." Evelyn contemplated all this information paired with what she already knew about the shoreline and realized that contrary to what she'd said back at the Basic Bean, she *did* give a crap about the moon. "Do you think climate change will affect the way ghosts behave? Changing sea levels around the world mean more extreme tides."

Mina looked at her curiously. "Mom *has* been talking about how the spirits are more unstable lately. How they've been warping for decades, and it's getting worse. They need that cycle, too—highs and lows. It's the same way screaming all the time would tire any of us out."

A moment later, Evelyn coasted to a stop in front of Ruthie's and slotted her longboard into the rack at the front of the store. She breathed in deep as they walked in the door, soothed by the familiar smell of silver polish and mothballs.

Ruthie's was an antiques store, decorated with peeling curli-cue letters on the storefront and faded gold trim on the awning. The ground floor was for tourists making pit stops on their way to the North Fork or visiting rich friends, crowded with charming antiques with far less charming price tags.

"Evelyn, darling!" Ruthie, a white woman in her sixties, hurried out from behind the counter. She wore a loose cotton dress that fell to her ankles, a massive pair of glasses, and her signature pink lipstick. Her white wispy hair was tied in a neat bun behind her neck. "It's been far too long since you came to visit."

"I know," Evelyn said as Ruthie wrapped her in a hug. "I've been working a lot." When she drew back, the woman was appraising her as if she were a new find from an estate sale.

"You seem tired," she said. "Tell Mr. Clark and your managers at that coffee shop to give you some time off."

"I've been asking for the hours," Evelyn protested. "I need the work."

"You need your rest more."

Evelyn sighed. She'd learned the hard way that Ruthie wasn't worth arguing with.

"Fine," she lied. "I'll take more time off."

"Good. Then you can visit me." Ruthie smiled triumphantly, then turned her gaze to Mina. "Hello, young lady. I've never seen you in here before, but you look very familiar. . . ."

"You might know my mom," Mina volunteered. "Stella Zanetti?"

"Ah." Ruthie pushed her glasses up on her nose. "Of course. You know, your family used to be quite the subject of the Cliffside Bay rumor mill."

Evelyn was ready to cut her off, but Mina spoke up instead. "Why?"

"Well, it's quite fanciful." Ruthie spoke with mild amusement. "All that nonsense about seeing ghosts."

Evelyn was taken aback, unsure of what to say next. But again, Mina looked unfazed. She tipped her chin down—she had almost a foot on Ruthie—and smiled. "What a strange rumor."

"Listen, Ruthie," Evelyn said, before the old woman could ask any more questions. "We were wondering if you had any extra costume jewelry in the basement? My, uh, friend here is looking for some."

"Certainly." Ruthie waved a hand in the air. "Check the tables in the back of the basement. You should be able to find everything you want there, but if you can't, the boxes underneath have extras in them."

"Thanks," Evelyn said. "You're the best."

"Oh, darling, I'll only believe that if you agree to come to dinner sometime soon," Ruthie said.

"I will," Evelyn promised.

"And you could always work here if you wanted. A nice cushy job sorting clothes, polishing up estate-sale rejects—"

"It wouldn't be fair," Evelyn said. "I'd always be your favorite employee."

Ruthie's fond smile was answer enough.

They were on the stairs to the basement when Mina spoke again.

"You know Ruthie," she said. "I mean . . . you really know her. How?"

Evelyn hesitated. "I used to hang out around town when I

was younger. Ruthie's one of the people who took care of me a lot back then. I think she still feels like she has to."

"Why did you spend so much time on Main Street?"

"Home wasn't a good place to be."

Something changed in Mina's expression, a softening that felt dangerously close to pity.

"Let's get back to your problems," Evelyn said quickly. "Come on—Ruthie's has every possible kind of weird glass figurine and jewelry you could imagine. I bet you'll be able to find a scrying focus here."

The ground floor of Ruthie's was for tourists, but the basement was for the locals, and it was a treasure trove. Most of Evelyn's wardrobe came from the bins of $3 T-shirts and racks full of men's flannels—those plus Meredith's hand-me-downs had gotten her through high school so far. She'd made the mistake of bringing Nick here once and had realized that he saw it as a different kind of tourist attraction, a fun activity where they could buy some cheap shirts to cut into bonfire clothes.

"Oh, gross, they have bras," he'd said. "Who buys used underwear?"

Evelyn hadn't known how to tell him that the bralette under her band T-shirt had once been hanging on one of those racks. That she was lucky to fit into clothing sizes that were easy to find secondhand pieces for. That at least if it was thrifted, it was probably worn less than Meredith's old clothes. So she'd swallowed her pride and promised herself that she would never take him back there again.

She braced herself for any snide commentary from Mina, too, who she knew was really into fashion—an industry that didn't exactly do much to help those changing shorelines they'd just been talking about. But the other girl said nothing as they wove through the maze of clothing racks and old furniture. She just took it all in, brown eyes big and round as an owl's.

A row of plastic tables sat at the back of the store beneath a single basement window. They held the shop's odds and ends all crammed together on a series of old mismatched trays.

"What do you think?" Evelyn asked.

Mina smiled, long and slow. "Thank you. This was a really good idea."

Evelyn grinned back. "I know."

She also knew the exact moment the clouds shifted, sending sunlight through that lone half window, because it caught Mina's cheek, her throat, her collarbones. For a moment she was almost translucent. Her fair skin glowed; her lips parted slightly with focus. Then she reached for a ring with a giant green stone in the center, and the moment was gone.

Evelyn looked away hastily, aware that she'd been staring, even more aware that she hadn't wanted to stop. So Mina was pretty. So *what?*

"There's definitely a lot of possibilities here," Mina said, fiddling with the ring. "But I'm only supposed to use Mom's credit card for emergencies, and buying a bunch of costume jewelry doesn't really qualify, even if they are pretty cheap." She gestured to the handwritten sign tacked above them: CLEARANCE, $5 AND UNDER.

Evelyn nodded, like she understood. She was too familiar with the contents of her savings account to indulge in irresponsible spending. After watching her family go from comfortable to decidedly less comfortable financially, she felt guilty buying anything that wasn't a necessity.

"So we should test them in the store," Evelyn said. "It doesn't seem like it's that hard to do."

Mina cast a nervous look around, where several other customers thumbed through clothing racks. "I suppose we could. But I don't think it would be a good idea to do it in public."

"Hang on," Evelyn said. "I'll talk to Ruthie."

They wound up in a fitting room, crouching on the floor in front of a gigantic, dusty mirror with a gold frame—Ruthie liked using her favorite antiques as store decor instead of selling them. Curtains shut the girls away from prying eyes, and the box between them was full of possibility. Mina sat in front of Evelyn, a pink silky scarf tied over half her face. Her hands were cupped, and her teeth worried at her bottom lip in anticipation.

Evelyn was surprised to find she was nervous, too. This was her big idea, after all. She wanted it to work.

"So I just hand them to you and wait for them to glow?" she asked.

"Sergio said it would be quite obvious if it happened. And I should feel a pull to the object, as well—like it's a magnet."

Evelyn began, checking each trinket for glass and handing the relevant ones to Mina. The rhythm of it soothed her after a while—it was like riding her longboard or making drinks at the Basic Bean, a pattern, a sameness. This fitting room felt like its own little world, oldies playing faintly in the background, the gentle sounds of glass clinking, the occasional squeaking of Evelyn's sneakers against the floor. The familiar smell of Ruthie's had mixed with a soft citrus scent that might have been Mina's shampoo.

They finished the first box, but there was another one waiting. Evelyn lifted the cardboard lid...and felt something. As if someone had gripped her intestines like a rope and given them a painful, insistent tug.

She hissed and clapped a hand across her abdomen. "What the hell?"

Across from her, Mina stirred. "What's going on? Are you all right?"

Evelyn gritted her teeth. "It feels like I'm having a really bad period cramp. Except I'm not on my period."

"Do you think it's the ghost?" Mina tugged off her makeshift blindfold and looked around, worry creasing her face. Her reflection in the mirror was murky, blond hair blurred in the dim light.

"That feels different. There's no saltwater or anything, just...it feels like something's got, like, a hook in me. And it's reeling me in."

Mina's mouth tightened at the corners. "Would you say it's...calling to you?"

Evelyn understood then. Dread unspooled inside her, a box that couldn't be closed, a truth that couldn't be denied.

She denied it anyway.

"But I'm not—" she protested.

"Not a medium?" Mina's tone was devoid of all emotion. "Put your hand in the box."

"But—"

"If you're so certain, what do you have to be afraid of?"

Another cramp wracked Evelyn's abdomen. She shuddered. Then she reached into the cardboard box.

Glass touched her outstretched fingertips, figurines and paperweights, some wrapped in cellophane, others loose and rattling around. She plunged her hand deeper, until her nails scraped the cardboard at the bottom.

Something smooth touched her palm. The cramp in her side disappeared, replaced by immediate relief.

Evelyn lifted her hand out of the box, clutching the trinket, and held it up to the fluorescent light.

It was a shell, blue and tan whorls spiraling outward into a shape about the size of two quarters. Evelyn had walked past hundreds just like this one before, scattering the beach. She'd seen the snails that lived inside them, too, cruising the seafloor.

But she had never seen a shell glow. Blue-green light pulsed inside of it, spilling from the mouth of the whorls and bouncing off the mirror. Suddenly everything was awash in strange new colors.

"This isn't even glass," Evelyn whispered. The pull inside her had transformed into a satisfied, gentle humming. She could feel an answering hum emitting from the shell in her palm, as if the creature inside it was still there. She wondered if snails could become ghosts, too, and then decided she'd broken her brain enough for one day. "You said they had to be... I don't understand."

"Medium practices are different for everyone." Mina's voice was flat and careful. "Clearly this is part of yours. Congratulations."

"It was just supposed to be one time. One summoning, and I'd never do it again." Evelyn lowered her hand. The shell was still clasped in her fist, the glow slowly fading. She wasn't sure she could let go of it even if she tried. "I don't want this."

"The dead want *you*. That's all that really matters." Mina rose to her feet, stiff and precise as a windup doll.

"Wait," Evelyn said. "Don't you want to check the rest of them?"

"There's no point. I already know they won't work."

Evelyn tore her gaze from the costume jewelry to find that Mina's perfectly practiced control had fallen away. She stared at Evelyn with a fury that made her wonder what parts of herself exactly Mina was so determined to hide—but as soon as Evelyn noticed it, it was gone, and Mina's expression was neutral once more.

"So what happens now?" Evelyn asked, clutching the shell. A tendril of fear snaked through her, coiling in her stomach like that blue-green light.

"Well, you'll have to accept something my mother told me," Mina said, as casually as if they really were just two girls shopping for costume jewelry. "This isn't something you can turn on and off whenever you feel like it. It's forever."

Chapter Thirteen

Mina spent the next few days in an utterly wretched mood. It wasn't fair.

That Evelyn had opened a door she couldn't close, the same door Mina had spent her whole life getting ready to step through only to be forced to linger indefinitely at the threshold.

That her mother still wouldn't tell Mina anything about her and Uncle Dom's efforts to investigate the ghost.

And that even after more efforts to find a scrying focus, she'd come up with absolutely nothing.

The ripples in Mina's ocean were growing. Soon they'd be large enough to disturb those dozens of chests she'd sunk to the bottom, or maybe even wake up whatever lurked below that, some prehistoric sea creature she had tried very hard to forget.

She attempted to work on the Zanetti Collection, but it was all wrong. The fabrics Stella had helped her order suddenly seemed gaudy and impractical. It was all so fluffy, so basic—insubstantial as sea-foam. She didn't know how to fix it, or anything else.

Mina came to breakfast the next morning to find Stella waiting with a cup of coffee filled with whipped cream and a plate of biscotti. Mina's favorite. Which meant her mother knew something was wrong.

"Are you all right?" Stella asked her.

"Yes. Why wouldn't I be?"

Mina dunked a cookie half-heartedly into the coffee. It made her think of the drink Evelyn had made for her at the Basic Bean, which made her think about how she was genuinely considering telling Stella the truth about Evelyn. But she couldn't work up the courage to say something. It would mean admitting she'd gone behind her mother's back and that her own medium abilities seemed potentially nonexistent. Her warding pendant hung around her neck. She'd started taking it off for a few minutes here and there to see if it changed anything, but her guilt always kicked in before too long.

"You seem distracted," Stella said. "Is this about your scrying focus?"

"Oh. Um. Yes." Mina swirled the whipped cream into the steaming liquid below, watching it dissolve in the heat.

"I understand why you're disappointed. But you will find one, I'm certain of that."

"I can't continue my training until I do, though."

"It's an unfortunate roadblock. But we'll try again next week."

"I've tried hundreds of glass items. What if my scrying focus is something else?" Mina snapped her biscotti in half with a sharp, satisfying crack.

"Something else?" Stella looked perturbed.

"Well, do all the Zanettis use glass? What do their medium practices look like?"

Stella's coffee mug sloshed in her hand. She gasped and set it down hastily as steaming hot liquid poured across her fingers.

"Mina," she said quickly, but Mina was already on her feet, hurrying to the bathroom for a cold washcloth and a first aid kit. When Mina was done fussing over the burn, Stella seemed none the worse for wear aside from a small bandage on her finger. Which, her mother reminded her, was a frequent casualty of a day spent catering anyway. Together, they rose from the table and started toward the car.

"You've been so patient," Stella said as she locked the front door behind them. She'd looked older in the dim kitchen; now, in full daylight, she looked like she could be Mina's big sister instead of her mother. "You know what we should do? After this wedding tonight, I'll be free for a few days. We can go beachcombing, then have one of our classic movie marathons. All your favorites, snacks included."

Not so long ago, that would have been Mina's ideal evening: finding shells on the beach together and making new decorations for the living room, then pairing strawberry panna cotta and garlic-Parmesan popcorn with whatever movie she wanted. But she kept replaying the way Stella's expression had changed right before the coffee spilled all over her wrist. She hadn't looked surprised at all—she'd looked focused.

Mina had spent a lifetime studying her mother. And although she still had a great deal to learn, she could tell when Stella was desperate to hide something. Desperate enough to burn herself rather than answer a few questions.

"All right," she said weakly. "That sounds great."

The wedding was medium-sized, which meant the catering wasn't nearly as demanding as Mina had feared. Stella was still busy in the kitchen, helping her sous chefs finalize dishes and ushering the servers in and out of the door with trays of canapés and hors d'oeuvres. Mina and Sergio were both helping out that day, along with two other servers who'd been working with Stella since Mina was a kid.

Mina's job was to fill in the cracks. If Stella needed something chopped, held, or stirred, she'd be there. She also liked watching bits of the reception through the one-way glass, admiring people's outfits and choice of decor. Today, both the grooms had decided to wear white, although their bow ties were pale yellow and a soft, muted green. They sat at a table in the front, applauding seemingly endless toasts from their loved ones beneath a wicker arch decorated with vines and lilies.

Mina wanted a romance like that one day, a partner who looked at her as if she were made of magic. Unfortunately, her dating life thus far boiled down to a longtime crush on Graham Lee that had ended in one awkward slow dance and that time she'd been stood up by Kaitlyn Mallow. But perhaps Mina's bad luck was unsurprising, considering her family. Being a medium had messed up Stella's and her uncle's romantic relationships to the point where they'd both given up on dating altogether.

But maybe you aren't a medium after all, hissed a nasty little voice in her head. *And you're still too messed up for anyone to fall for you.*

"Mina?" Her mother placed a gentle hand on her shoulder. "Did you hear me?"

"I— No. Sorry." Mina turned to see sweat beading on her mother's forehead. A few loose strands of chestnut brown had escaped her hairnet, and there was a fresh oil stain splattered on her black catering clogs.

"One of the servers heard something strange coming from the basement," Stella said. "It's probably just an animal, but can you and Sergio go check it out? We don't want it disturbing the reception, and you know none of them want to go down there after the bat incident."

"Of course," Mina said. She found Sergio sneaking a glass of champagne in the hallway outside the kitchen and tugged him with her to the back staircase.

"Ooooh," he said, wiggling his fingers as he followed her to the basement. He was tipsy, but Mina didn't mind—she had more questions for him, and it would be easier to get an answer like this. "A secret Stella mission."

"Speaking of Stella," she said. "I was wondering if you could remember anything else. About the rest of our family, I mean. That fight you talked about."

"Hmm. Not much more than what I told you." He hiccupped. "I heard the word *dangerous* thrown around a lot, but Dad caught me eavesdropping before I figured out why."

Mina's disappointment struggled as she pushed it beneath her waves. "Well, let me know if you remember anything else."

It was strange to be back in the basement after what had happened with the Giacomos. It looked the same as always, dark and dusty, shelves crowded with long-forgotten items. Mina poked around, already annoyed by what all this grime would do to her sneakers. There were various kinds of animal droppings in the basement mixed in with the dirt. But she saw no evidence of any unwelcome wildlife, just cobwebs.

And then she heard it. An odd, high sound, somewhere between a whistle and a moan. She nervously followed the noise until she realized it was coming from behind the padlocked door.

"Sergio," she hissed. "Do you hear that?"

He nodded, face flushed but solemn. Mina's palms began to sweat. She could go get Stella. She *should* go get Stella. But all her mother would do was keep her out of this, like she was one of those hundreds of potential glass scrying focuses. Fragile. Impractical.

"I'm going in," she told him, then shoved the dusty curtains aside. The lock had been pulled shut again, but she knew the combination. She twirled it easily back and forth before it clicked open, then laid it on a nearby shelf.

"I didn't know you could get in here on your own," Sergio said.

Mina pushed the door open. "I follow far less rules than you seem to think I do."

The scene before her looked ordinary at first. The pool was calm, saltwater moving in slow, lazy rivulets as the filters did their work. Burned-out candles were scattered everywhere, and there was still a circle of salt around the water. The room smelled strange, though—brine and sulfur lingered in the air.

Her sneakers crunched against something on the concrete. Glass.

One of the floor-to-ceiling windows behind the pool had shattered, leaving broken pieces strewn across the floor. The wind whistled through the shards that still clung stubbornly to the wooden frame, and another moan rang out across the room.

She blew out a breath of relief as she stepped closer to the windows. Sometimes a noise was just a noise.

"Hey, Mina," Sergio called out. "Watch your step."

Mina yanked her gaze down and realized her white sneakers were both pressed firmly against a fault line in the concrete. That awful old superstition crept into her mind—*step on a crack, break your mother's back*. She hurriedly moved aside and surveyed the damage. The fissure went from the edge of the pool all the way to the broken window, rising until it hit the wooden frame.

"What do you think caused this?" Mina asked, unable to hide the tremor in her voice. When she turned toward Sergio, he looked shaken, too. He opened his hand to reveal a glimmering bit of glass shaped like a bird's wing.

"I found this," he said. "Part of Dad's scrying focus."

The disappointment Mina had shoved into her ocean tried to bob to the surface. She took a deep breath and held it down. "They must have tried something here." *Without me.*

He nodded. "Something big."

Mina bent to inspect the salt circle again, wrinkling her nose as the smell intensified. Something was off about it—the line of salt had been shoved outward, then broken, as if fingers had successfully pushed at the edges. She stared at it nervously. Rule number one of a summoning was *don't let the ghosts out of the circle.*

She touched a bit of the salt with the tip of her finger. It came away wet. And just like that, the warding pendant around her neck began to grow warm against her skin. Mina felt a brief burst of concern. But something else crystallized beneath it. Hope.

If this was happening, it meant a ghost was trying to talk to her. Which meant she *was* a medium. It was the waxing gibbous moon tonight—four days before it was full, not ideal—but maybe...maybe...

She pulled the necklace over her head.

"Sergio?" Mina turned toward her cousin. "Can I trust you?"

Sergio's eyebrows shot up as he took in Mina at the edge of the salt circle. "You took the pendant off."

"Yes. And I want you to hold it for me while I try something. But only if you promise to get me out of here if things get dangerous, and if you can also promise not to breathe a word about this to our parents."

A strange expression drifted across Sergio's face like a cloud obscuring the moon, and Mina wondered if he was jealous of her. But after a moment, he knelt beside her and held out a hand. "This is what you want." It wasn't a question. "You deserve a fair shot."

"Thank you." Mina gave him the necklace. Then she dipped her left hand in the pool until the water touched her wrist.

The change was instantaneous. Her sand dollar throbbed, and her mind widened—as if it had been inside one of those chests she'd shoved into the ocean, but now the planks had splintered, leaving her adrift in an endless expanse of water.

Mina had expected the dissonant chorus of voices she'd heard at the beach. But instead there was only one, whispering in a cadence too soft and muffled for her to make out the words, as if it was very far away and very much alone. Then it paused, and Mina felt a familiar presence brush at the edge of her mind, the same one she'd felt at the beach. It wasn't overwhelming or terrifying this time, it was...curious. A yearning unspooled inside of her, sharp and insistent, and she understood that it wasn't just coming from the ghost. It was coming from her, too.

The spirit pulled her in the same way the moon pulled at the tides, the same way she imagined two people were pulled toward each other when they fell in love. It was terrifying and undeniable and impossible to resist.

So she didn't.

When the sand dollar on Mina's wrist tugged her mind forward, she followed it willingly. And when she blinked again, the world around her had disappeared.

She was on the beach in Sand Dollar Cove. A full moon hung in the starry sky. Blue-green light unspooled through the water before her as that voice whispered in her mind, fading in and out. But tonight, she was finally strong enough to understand it. All she had to do was wade in.

Mina walked toward the ocean, waiting for the surf to touch her bare toes. But then something flashed in her peripheral vision—a burst of orange beneath the waves. The smell of rot wafted around her as the scene began to flicker. Her wrist throbbed with unbearable pain, and when she looked down at her palms, they were the translucent blue of a spirit—

And then a hand closed around her shoulder, and she was pulled forcibly back to reality.

"What," she gasped, whirling around. Sergio gazed back at her, his expression panicked. He tugged the necklace over her head, ignoring Mina's noises of protest. The moment it touched her skin, the pull began to fade.

"You were trying to dive into the pool," he said hoarsely, still gripping her shoulder. "You promise you won't try again if I let go of you?"

"I promise."

He released her, still looking wary, but the pull was gone.

"What happened to you?" Sergio asked.

Mina hesitated. "I...I'm pretty sure the potential demon wants to talk to me."

Sergio let out a low, uneasy whistle. "Well, shit."

"I know."

Mina had been given an invitation. She had four days until the full moon to figure out if she was brave enough to accept it.

Chapter Fourteen

Evelyn liked Scales & Tails best after closing. There was something soothing about the soft sounds of life all around her—the fish tank filters bubbling, the reptiles rustling in their cages, even the soft chirping of the crickets from their boxes in the storeroom. She liked it better when Luisa was there to help her, but unfortunately she'd been stuck with her least favorite coworker that day, a college student who always found a reason to leave early.

She still had company, though, not just the animals, but Mina, who'd texted the night before to demand they meet up. Evelyn hadn't been free until right now—it had been another long workday.

"I'm aware it sounds a bit ill advised," Mina said as they chucked the final garbage bags into the dumpster. Evelyn had been pleasantly surprised by Mina's willingness to help her close up, especially since she'd arrived in a white sundress and chunky sandals that were now looking the worse for wear. "But I think we'd be foolish not to consider it."

"It's a trap," Evelyn said as they washed their hands in the employee sink. It had been a few weeks since the bathroom incident at the Basic Bean, but she still felt a twinge of nerves each time she looked in a mirror, wondering if she'd see a figure hovering behind her. Instead, she saw Mina's tall, slim form beside her own, her blond hair almost white in the fluorescents overhead. "Do you *want* your soul eaten?"

"We have no proof the ghost can do that to the living yet," Mina protested. "Or that this even *is* that ghost."

"Who else would they be?"

"One of the drowning summer victims?" Mina's voice had remained calm throughout the entire story of what she'd seen at the community center, but there was an edge to it now that Evelyn didn't like. "I know you're interested in talking to them. This could be your chance."

Evelyn *did* want to talk to the Cliffside Trio. But the last time she'd messed with the dead, she'd wound up with abilities she didn't want and a scrying focus she didn't know how to use, not to mention a ghost haunting her. She wouldn't be reckless like that again.

"You said there was property damage from whatever your mother tried," she countered as they walked back into the main area of Scales & Tails, pausing beside the cash register. "That's got to be the potential demon. And if they can crack concrete, they can totally crack your skull."

Mina huffed and curled her hand around her gold bracelet,

fiddling with the thin row of metal that shielded her sand dollar mark. "Well, we can't hide forever. Confronting this ghost directly is the only way to stop them."

There was that tone again, and Evelyn understood now why it made her uneasy. Mina sounded *eager*.

"I agree we can't keep hiding." Evelyn stepped toward her. "But this is literally life and death. You're the one who told me that we're both in danger, that the full and new moons are overwhelming even for fully trained mediums. Neither of us stands a chance."

Mina's hand floated away from her wrist, and she stepped closer, too. "Maybe you're right," she said softly. "But if we ignore the meeting, aren't we passing up a valuable opportunity?"

"You could tell your mother," Evelyn suggested. "She could handle it." She knew as soon as the words came out that they'd been a mistake. Mina jolted backward, as if she'd been slapped, then turned her gaze away.

"Stella can't know yet," she whispered, staring behind Evelyn's head. "Not until I prove that I...that I..." The glow of the tank lights silhouetted her shoulders, brushed across the smooth, elegant skin of her neck. Evelyn hastily pulled her gaze away.

"That you...what?" she asked.

"That I belong in this world." Mina still wouldn't look at her. "That I can rectify the mistakes we made. That I can be the daughter she deserves instead of—of—" She broke off and strode to the door. The snake-shaped doorbell let out a discordant jangle as she fled into the night.

Evelyn swore into the absence she'd left behind. Then she grabbed her longboard and the store key and headed after her.

She found Mina sitting on the curb beside the parking lot, her head buried in her hands. The lot was deserted—it was a Sunday night, late enough that any weekend visitors had long since begun their drives back to New York City.

Evelyn sighed and sat beside Mina, laying her longboard on the tarmac at her feet. "You're not very good at running away."

"I thought you'd just go home." Mina's voice was muffled through her fingers.

"Do you want me to?" The thought made Evelyn hesitate. Part of why the drowning summer had made so many headlines was because Cliffside Bay was one of those towns considered sleepy and safe, plus the victims were all rich and white. But safe as it might be, Evelyn still wasn't going to leave a crying girl alone in a dark parking lot.

"Not really." Mina pulled her hands away, hiccupping slightly.

Evelyn hadn't turned off the lights in the store window—company policy—and they cast Mina in a soft yellow glow, enough that she could tell the other girl had been crying.

"I'm sorry. I'll have this under control in just a moment."

Mina took a deep breath, dabbed at her eyes with a tissue she'd fished out of her purse, and fanned her face with her hands. Then she turned to Evelyn, a false smile plastered on her face. "See? Back to normal."

Aside from a tiny mascara smudge and faint red splotches on Mina's cheeks, it was already hard to tell she had been crying at all. Evelyn wondered when Mina had learned to do that, and how often it came in handy. All Mina's perfect outfits and perfect grades were starting to feel more and more like a well-crafted adaptation, a shell that would help her survive the pressures of the world.

"You think you're not good enough for your mom?" It was a risky question, meant to crack right through that shell.

Mina flinched. "You don't understand. She gave up so much for me, and I don't want to let her down. But I've lied to her all summer. I know trying to talk to the ghost on my own is a bad idea, but I thought maybe if I could make things right before I confessed, she wouldn't be as disappointed. She wouldn't give up on me."

Give up. Evelyn knew she'd come out here to help, but those words clawed their way straight between her ribs, where they thumped like a cruel heartbeat.

"Trust me." Evelyn spoke a little louder than she meant to. "You can't make your parents do anything. If they want to give up on you, they will. If they love you enough, they won't."

"How could you possibly know that?"

"Because my mother gave up on *me*." Evelyn kicked viciously at the tarmac. "After the drowning summer, she decided she didn't want to be part of our family anymore. She signed her parental rights away. And at first I wondered if there was something I could've done to make her stay. I thought her leaving was my fault. But I know better now. She's just the kind of person who thought she could trade in her family the same way other people trade in a fucking *car*."

There was a long, long moment of silence. Evelyn was so overcome, she thought she might faint. She hadn't been this upset since the night she dumped Nick. The few lights in the parking lot had gone blurry, and she realized a beat too late that it was because of her tears. She didn't have Mina's protective shell. She didn't have anything at all.

Evelyn felt the soft, gentle press of palm on palm, fingers folding together, the cool metal of a cuff bracelet pressing against her wrist. She looked down and saw Mina's thumb moving in slow, gentle circles across her knuckles.

"I'm sorry." Mina's voice wobbled, but she made no attempt to hide it. Evelyn tipped her head up and saw a face filled with unmasked regret. "I knew they'd gotten divorced, but I had no idea she'd abandoned you like that."

"Yeah, well, she did." Evelyn was still upset, but Mina's touch felt grounding. For this one small moment, she wasn't facing down the world alone. "It's not okay, but...I've had time to get used to it."

"But you shouldn't have had to." Mina looked at her indignantly. "When Stella told my father she was pregnant with me, he said he wanted nothing to do with it. So I don't think about him, because he isn't worth it. But if he'd tried to be a dad and then decided he didn't want to anymore...that's *so* much worse. Your mother is...is..." Her face reddened. "A *heinous* human being."

"Asshole," Evelyn said. "*Asshole* is a better word."

Mina let out a startled chuckle. "I suppose so." Her grip on Evelyn's hand loosened, but she didn't pull away. "Look, Evelyn, the truth about why I ran out here is that I'm...jealous."

"Of me?" Evelyn fought the urge to laugh. "Because my life is so fun and perfect?"

"Because you're a medium." Mina's voice trembled again. "I know this is demanding and frightening, but it's what my family told me I was meant to do. Watching you fall into it, knowing that my mother and uncle would be thrilled to have your help..." She trailed off, but Evelyn understood. Mina had felt replaced.

"What about what you said? That they'd punish me?"

Mina sighed. "I was lying. I didn't want them to know what had happened during the drowning summer. I—I'm sorry about that, too. I see now that I've been selfish."

There was no denying that. But it wasn't like Evelyn had trusted Mina, either. And Evelyn knew in her gut that if she left Mina now, told her she was done here, that would be it. Whatever fragile thing was growing between them would be crushed.

"Yeah, you have been," Evelyn said. "But I was selfish, too. I summoned that spirit because Nick convinced me to cheat on a test, I got caught, and I knew it would wreck my college applications. There was this internship I wanted, and I didn't even get it....It seems so silly now. I can't believe I put us both in all this danger for *that*."

She'd been expecting judgment, but instead Mina's expression softened sadly. "You never could've known all this would happen," she said. "And honestly...I'm beginning to wonder if it was only a matter of time until what we did that summer came back to haunt us. Quite literally, I suppose."

Evelyn squeezed her hand. "You're really not mad at me?"

"Not unless you've got something worse to confess."

"Uh. Well. I...kind of tried to tell Nick Slater the truth about his brother."

Mina's head jerked up. "You what?"

"I chickened out," Evelyn said hastily. "All that stuff you said about making everything too complicated? You were right."

Mina relaxed, looking relieved. "It was a hard thing for me to understand at first, too. It still is, honestly. But everything you just told me makes it painfully clear that you need proper training, and my mom and uncle deserve to know what's going on with the ghost. I'll tell them the truth first thing tomorrow."

Maybe it was because both of them had forgone their survival mechanisms to connect with each other. Maybe it was because, evolutionarily speaking, a symbiotic relationship gave them both a better chance of handling this spirit. Or maybe it was because Mina was still holding her hand. But Evelyn shook her head.

"Tell them about the ghost, but don't tell her about me," she said. "I don't want to sell you out."

"But you need training," Mina protested.

"I know," Evelyn said. "But I don't want that training to come from your mom. I want to learn from *you*."

Chapter Fifteen

Later that night, Evelyn woke to whispers. A low muttering, snaking through the edge of her consciousness just softly enough for her to wonder if she was dreaming it.

She rolled over and clutched at her bedspread. The sky was still dark outside; her phone said it was 3:21 AM. Something flickered in her peripheral vision—Clara's forked tongue. Her snake's red and orange patterns writhed as she pressed against the glass.

"So you sense it, too, huh?" Evelyn murmured as her snake swiveled her head from side to side. The way Clara was acting right now meant she felt some kind of vibration she considered a threat.

Evelyn pulled down the covers and fumbled for the scrying focus on her night table. The shell. A quick internet search after she'd gotten home from Ruthie's had told her the creature who'd lived inside it was called a *moon* snail, which was so on-the-nose it made her want to scream. Now she sighed and touched the shell, which promptly began to glow that familiar blue-green. The light danced across her bedroom as the whispers became louder and clearer—like a radio switching from station to station, each of them full of a different kind of chatter. She still couldn't make out any words, but the voices were distinctly human.

"Whoa," Evelyn murmured, lifting the scrying focus close to her face. The blue light looked electric, almost neon; tiny strands of it twirled and coiled together inside the shell's mouth in hypnotic patterns that reminded her of Clara. She understood now what Mina had meant by it protecting her. This didn't feel like an attack the way the other hauntings had.

She squinted at the lunar calendar she'd copied off the internet and hung on her wall, trying to gauge how much she should be able to hear. They were in the waxing gibbous, a few nights from the full moon. A slightly above average tidal range, so Evelyn should be able to do...a slightly above average amount of ghost communication.

If she wanted to, anyway. Evelyn hesitated, remembering what she'd told Mina just a few hours ago. That she didn't want to talk to the dead without more training. But the voices were here, and she was still a little nervous that they'd pull a Basic Bean bathroom on her if she tried to pretend otherwise.

"Do you want something?" she asked aloud. Talking had worked last time—it was worth trying again.

A long moment passed before she heard a sloshing sound in response. When she turned, the bowl in Clara's cage was trembling.

"Oh!" Evelyn understood. "You need water to talk back, don't you?"

She fished the bowl out of the cave, working gently so as not to disturb Clara further. She could tell from the scent of salt that it was no longer freshwater.

Evelyn set the bowl down on her bedroom floor, wincing as water splashed over the sides. She still had the ingredients she'd taken for her ill-advised cave adventure. She grabbed the salt-shaker and sprinkled its contents in a messy circle around her rug, then lit the tea light candles and placed them around the ring. This was definitely a fire hazard, but that seemed like the least of her problems right now.

Mina had told her that Stella didn't use blood or personal items in her normal summonings, so Evelyn stared into the water bowl and hoped she'd done enough. Cool night air seeped beneath her cracked-open window, and she caught the smell of brine on the breeze. It didn't matter that she was inside: She was part of this now, and that meant she would always carry the ocean with her. For better or for worse, just as Mina had said.

"Go ahead," she said, feeling a little foolish even now. "What are you trying to tell me?"

The voices rose in an incomprehensible cacophony. The world around her swam, colors and shapes blurred together, and Evelyn gripped her shell so tightly it hurt. She felt a wave crash over her head, an assault of seawater. It was in her nose, her mouth, she coughed and choked and closed her eyes tight.

When she opened them again, she wasn't in her room any-more. She stood in an unfamiliar and overgrown parking lot beside a strange set of buildings. It was an odd scene, industrial yet strangely desolate, with several large cylindrical structures flanking a central hub that looked like an abandoned office tower. The ocean stretched beyond it, waves rolling in an endless line toward the horizon. The only sound was the constant rhythm of the water's ebb and flow.

Something ate at the edge of her vision—rusted orange. The ocean grew louder, and Evelyn smelled rot and brine, so strong it made her eyes water. Three forms materialized before her, indistinct and wispy. The sand dollars over their eyes glowed that same orange, a sharp contrast to their bluish-green bodies. They were the last thing Evelyn saw before the vision faded.

She knelt on her bedroom floor, gasping for air. A bluish-green tendril swirled through the water, pulsing in time with the glow emitting from her scrying focus. The bowl shook so violently that ripples splashed over the sides, but the salt circle held.

"What was that?" Evelyn demanded, trying to tamp down her panic. But the voices in her mind were silent. The bowl shuddered once more, then steadied.

Evelyn clutched her shell and watched its glow fade. She didn't feel safe enough to go clean up until the last bluish-green bits of light had winked out.

Mina had told her that her mom and her uncle hadn't been able to communicate with the Cliffside Trio. But there was no denying those three figures, or the sand dollars over their eyes.

She fumbled for her phone and texted Mina: holy shit, we have an actual clue about the drowning summer

She wasn't expecting a response so quickly, but her phone pinged before she could even get back into bed.

And how exactly did you obtain this
clue?

Evelyn typed back: ok 1. you text like a 10000 year old & 2.
spooky ghost shit. obviously.

Mina's response was even faster this time. I thought you
weren't going to talk to the ghosts.

they talked to ME ok. now ur not the
only one with a weird vision to decode

Fine. Now go to bed. We can discuss
further tomorrow.

YOU go to bed why are u even awake

Nightmares

oh. do u want me to call?

Mina typed for a long time, so long that Evelyn was half
asleep when the text finally came through.

No. It's under control.

Evelyn frowned, sent a response. that gets less convincing
every time u say it, zanetti

This time, Mina didn't reply. And when Evelyn finally fell
asleep, she dreamed of crashing waves and endless whispers and

a girl who waded to the bottom of the sea, snakes coiled around her arms and legs like anchors.

Evelyn woke up early and cranky. She spent a while googling different types of industrial complexes on Long Island, staring at various ugly cylindrical structures until she thought her eyes would fall out. But none of them were the one she'd seen in her vision. When she finally gave up and headed down to breakfast, she found Meredith in the kitchen, smearing jelly on burnt toast.

It was an unusual sight—Meredith's commute into New York City was brutal, almost two hours one way, which meant she left around dawn and returned home after sunset. They crossed paths only when Evelyn woke up early to work an opening shift, or in small, fleeting evening moments before Meredith vanished into her bedroom to video-chat with Riku.

"You want some?" her sister asked through a mouthful of crumbs. "I made coffee, too. It's...not great."

"Is it caffeinated?"

Meredith nodded.

"That's all I care about." Evelyn grabbed a travel mug out of the dish rack and proceeded to pour in half the pot. Working at the Basic Bean had given her a dangerously high caffeine tolerance. As she set the thermos down, their father walked in sporting yesterday's five o'clock shadow and a gray T-shirt that was possibly older than Evelyn herself.

"Morning, girls," he said. "Is that coffee?"

"Bad coffee, apparently." Evelyn passed the pot to him.

"Because your pre-ground beans are shit," Meredith said defensively. She was watching their father a little too carefully. Meredith and Greg hadn't fought the way they used to, or at least, they hadn't while Evelyn was in the house. But she could still feel their palpable dislike whenever they were in the same room.

Being around them both reminded her of the conversation she'd had with Mina last night. When her mother had left, the three remaining Mackenzies were vulnerable and unprepared. They had all evolved in order to survive, but they hadn't done it together. And now they belonged in completely different environments—her father buried beneath the sand, Meredith off the beach entirely, and Evelyn toughing it out in the surf. Alone. Always alone.

Could that change?

Evelyn grabbed a slice of toast and headed for the door.

"Hey, wait," Meredith said. "Where are you going?"

"Library." Evelyn took a bite, then winced. "This is basically charcoal."

"Why the library?" asked her dad. "I thought nobody your age cared about books anymore."

"I read sometimes," Evelyn protested, which was true, although the number of books she'd returned unread from her library app had gone way up since she got a second job. "Also, I'm meeting a friend."

None of this was a lie, but the detail that she'd texted Mina that morning to arrange a research session about a ghost-induced hallucination was probably a bad thing to bring up in casual conversation.

Meredith held up her car keys. "I'm heading into town, too. Want a ride?"

Evelyn felt a pleasant twinge of surprise. This was the first time her sister had actually tried to hang out with her since she'd been back. She followed Meredith out the door, trying to pretend she couldn't see the sadness on her dad's face. Trying to pretend it didn't make her feel like she was picking a side in a six-year-old argument.

"I thought you worked on Mondays," Evelyn said as they pulled out of the driveway. Meredith's car was exactly how Evelyn remembered it, down to the familiar smell of pine-scented air freshener mixed with burnt rubber. The jumble of clothes and textbooks in the back seat was basically fossilized, as much a part of the vehicle as the engine or the steering wheel.

"I worked the holiday weekend, so I get today off." Meredith slid on a pair of sunglasses as the car revved down the hill. She'd always been a bad driver, lots of stopping and starting, but Evelyn didn't mind. She wasn't the type to get motion-sick easily. "What about you? I think you work more than I do."

"I have a snake to support." Evelyn tried to keep her voice light. "It's important to maintain Clara's glamorous lifestyle."

"Is that why there's a freezer full of dead mice in the basement?"

"Snakes have to eat," Evelyn said.

"Of course they do," Meredith said. "But doesn't it gross you out?"

On Evelyn's first day at Scales & Tails, she'd been introduced to the breeding boxes for crickets, dubia roaches, and mealworms, along with a gigantic freezer filled with various kinds of mice and rats. Her father had explained the food chain to her well before biology class did, but she'd still been queasy the first few times she watched Mr. Clark feed the snakes.

"Nature isn't gross. It just is," Evelyn said as the car jolted down Main Street.

"Very philosophical," Meredith mused. "You get that from Dad?"

Evelyn had, actually. But she'd already experienced enough family weirdness for one day. "Hey, where are you going in town?" she asked, dodging the question. Meredith had shown no interest whatsoever in the rest of Cliffside Bay, and Evelyn didn't really blame her. Surely she had more bad memories here than good ones.

"Oh, meeting up with an old friend," she said, with a casualness that felt forced. "Here's your stop. You're welcome for the ride."

"I was going to say thank you." Evelyn cracked open the door. Mina was already waiting for her, sitting on a bench outside the building. She wore heart-shaped sunglasses, ruffled linen shorts, and a tightly fitted top with sheer cap sleeves. As always, Evelyn felt hopelessly underdressed for the occasion, even though there *was* no occasion. She grabbed her longboard out of the back seat and headed toward the library doors.

"Who's that?" Mina asked as Evelyn walked up, gesturing toward the MINI Cooper as it roared out of the parking lot.

"My sister."

"Meredith? I didn't realize she was still in town."

"She's back for the summer," Evelyn said, slotting her

longboard into the bike rack. "But like…barely. She's basically using our house as a B&B."

"That must be lovely," Mina said, looking a little wistful. "I remember her being really nice when we were kids."

Evelyn pushed open the library doors, welcoming the rush of AC. "It's a little more complicated than that."

Thankfully, Mina didn't push it. Evelyn could tell they were both still feeling out how things had shifted after their late-night conversation. Because there *was* a shift. Evelyn was used to backing off if things got too personal, but instead she'd chosen to get closer to someone else. Apparently talking to the dead was a shortcut to vulnerability.

The library had undergone a remodel shortly after the drowning summer. Evelyn still remembered how it had been before then—sagging old bookshelves and a row of computers that worked way too slowly. She also remembered how much the librarians had chuckled when she'd said as much to them, talked about how young she was and how much things had changed.

Nowadays the books were still there, slotted neatly into new shelves, but the whole place was sleek and gleaming like a corporate office. A few people were clustered around the bank of shiny laptops to the left of the front desk, and the sound of kids playing drifted from the children's corner across the hall. The library might have looked different, but it still felt safe to her. And during those years where she'd had nowhere else to go, *safe* had felt really, really important.

"Hey, Mrs. Morales," she said to the woman behind the front desk. Luisa's mother was a Mexican American woman with graying brown hair, a warm face, and a large pair of reading glasses perched on her nose. For as long as Evelyn had known her, she'd decorated the front desk elaborately, changing it every season. Right now it was beach-themed, with cardboard cutout waves, a big yellow sun, and plastic starfish and sand glued at the bottom. "Can I renew those books I borrowed?"

"Of course." Mrs. Morales took Evelyn's library card and tapped at the keyboard. "I hope you're enjoying them—they're my daughter's favorite series."

"The first one was really good," Evelyn said. "I had no idea Luisa liked them, too."

"She's the one who told me I should recommend them. Do you ever run into her at work?"

"Sometimes. She told me she's doing freelance photography this summer?"

"Yes, yes. She's very good. I keep telling her we should hang up her pictures here, but she won't let me, says it's too embarrassing." Mrs. Morales handed Evelyn's card back. "You know, I always thought it was a shame you two never became close."

Evelyn had seen Luisa at the library a lot during the year or two she'd spent avoiding home. Sometimes they'd even done homework together, or played some of the old-school board games in the children's corner. But she'd always been hesitant to hang out with anybody for too long, scared of the questions they might ask about her family. Now, she wondered how many connections she'd missed out on because of that fear.

"Well," she said, "maybe we will."

"Is there anything else I can help you with?" Mrs. Morales asked. "More book recommendations?"

"There *is* something I'm trying to research. But it's kind of a mystery."

Mrs. Morales's dark eyes sparked with interest. Evelyn knew from watching her match book after book with reluctant readers that she loved a challenge.

"What is it?" she asked.

"Um...an old building?" Evelyn offered weakly.

"And do you know where that building is?"

"Not exactly. On Long Island, though. I'm pretty sure of that."

"Or what it looks like?"

"Yes, but...I don't have a picture. All these big, ugly greenish cylinder buildings? Kind of looked like a factory, but it's abandoned." Evelyn glanced around for Mina, hoping for some backup, but the other girl had vanished during her catch-up with the librarian.

Mrs. Morales's forehead creased in thought. "There are some abandoned factories on Long Island, but what you're describing..." She typed into the search bar on her computer and swiveled the monitor around. "Is this what you're looking for?"

At first, it looked all wrong, a series of circles beside a neat central location. But as Mrs. Morales clicked through to another photo, Evelyn realized the first one had been an aerial shot. The second—a parking lot, tall ugly buildings—was unmistakably the complex she'd seen the night before, although here it didn't look abandoned at all.

"Yes!" Evelyn could've hugged her. "You should seriously be a detective or something. How did you figure it out so fast?"

"Well, it was in the news quite a bit when you were a kid,"

Mrs. Morales said. "Although I suppose it's not that strange you wouldn't know about it. If you want to read some newspaper articles, we've almost certainly got a few on file."

She tapped another key, and a nearby printer whirred to life. A moment later, it spit out the image in black and white.

"Thank you so much," Evelyn said, grinning as she picked it up. Printed beneath the image, in words she hadn't even noticed when they were on the screen, was BLUE TIDE WASTE MANAGEMENT PLANT: 1978.

Chapter Sixteen

Despite a promising start, Mina's research session with Evelyn hadn't gone according to plan. Oh, sure, Mina had learned plenty about the Blue Tide Waste Management Plant. It had been constructed in the seventies to manage sewage on Long Island, but complications arose after an anonymous employee leaked that its pollutant discharge system was being improperly managed. There had been protests and news coverage, but in the end what actually stopped the plant was time. The machinery started breaking in the early 2000s, and they'd shut it down shortly after.

It was only after the Blue Tide closure that it became clear just how right the protestors had been. The plant had leaked waste into Long Island Sound for decades. Evelyn was so upset by this news that she had to take a research break.

It had upset Mina, too, but she'd kept going. She scoured the articles and the internet for some kind of connection to the drowning summer, but she couldn't find one. There was no family involvement, no mention of the plant in the video Evelyn had found. No reason the victims would have had to care about it.

"If they could show me one thing, why would they show me this?" Evelyn complained as they left the library behind. "Do you think it has something to do with this potential demon? Or how the Cliffside Trio died?"

"I don't know," Mina said. "There were no casualties at the plant itself. We checked that, too. And you said they showed it to you as it is now, right? Abandoned?"

"Yeah." Evelyn groaned. They both stood beneath the library awning in a feeble attempt to avoid the sweltering heat—Mina had walked here, but Stella had volunteered to pick her up. "Maybe they just showed us a waste management plant because they wanted us to know we're in deep shit."

Mina let out a surprised laugh. "I think we already knew that." Something knitted together in her mind as she thought about the plant again, the pictures they'd seen of the sludge pouring into the water. It was a hideous diluted orange that reminded her of regurgitated bile.

Orange. Like the light she'd seen snaking through Mr. Giacomo's ghost.

"The spirits, Evelyn. You said you thought more extreme tide ranges in the Sound could be changing their behavior, right?"

"Yeah, I did," Evelyn said.

"What about pollution?"

Something about Evelyn snapped into focus when she talked about nature. Mina had noticed it before, but never so clearly. "Of course. All that waste leaking into the Sound...

it didn't just hurt the living. It's been hurting the dead. That's got to be why they showed me the plant."

"But the plant's closed now," Mina said. "It can't hurt them anymore. Why would the Cliffside Trio show you that when they could've shown you something about the ghost that's absorbing them?"

"I don't know." Evelyn's expression turned thoughtful. She'd barely had any freckles a few weeks ago, but now that summer was in full swing they'd started to grow into something you could only see up close. Mina couldn't help but notice how they clustered across her cheeks and nose like a spray of sea-foam. "But we're close to something—I can feel it."

Evelyn's phone buzzed. When she grabbed it, her face scrunched with surprise. "Huh. I thought she was kidding about that."

"Who's kidding about what?"

"Luisa Morales wants to set me up," Evelyn said. "Apparently her friend Talia is sort of into me, so she's invited us both to a party later this week."

It was a subject change that made Mina feel—not frustrated, exactly, but something close to it. Something a little uglier. "Well. Talia's nice. She was in honors chem with me."

"I already told her no." Evelyn finished tapping out a message, then slid the phone back into her pocket. "Talia's nice, yeah, but Luisa said that the two of us remind her of each other, personality-wise. Which means it would never work."

Mina's as-yet-undetermined feeling dissipated immediately.

"So you're uninterested in dating your clone," she said. "But you liked Nick?"

Evelyn shot her a look. "I thought you didn't want to talk about this. Shouldn't we be staying on topic? I'm sure we can dig up more horrifying supernatural realizations if we try hard enough."

It was true, Mina had been closed-off when Evelyn had brought up dating at the Basic Bean. But she was a private person, and a week ago, Evelyn had seemed like so much more of a stranger than she did now. She'd never talked to *anyone* the way she'd talked to Evelyn last night. "We're past that."

Evelyn gave her a hesitant smile. "I know. I was just teasing."

"It might sound strange to you, but I was scared," Mina said. "The last girl I talked to about being bi...well, I asked her out and then she stood me up."

"That sucks," Evelyn said. "I'm sorry."

"It's all right," Mina said. "It just made it a little frightening. I came out because I didn't want to feel like it was something I had to hide. But after my post, it seemed as if people wanted me to prove I was bi, somehow. As if me never having dated anyone meant I couldn't possibly know who or what I wanted, even though I'd had crushes on people. So I felt pressure, I suppose. To prove it. And when it didn't work out, I wondered if she'd talked to me and decided I didn't count."

"You know there are a hundred other reasons why she might not have wanted to go on that date, right?"

"I'm aware," Mina mumbled. "But it was hard not to fixate on that one."

"I understand." Evelyn shifted her sneaker on her longboard, sending it rolling back and forth across the pavement. "Not feeling like you're doing this right, I mean. I got this anonymous comment when I was dating Nick. Whoever posted it called me fake because I was with a boy. They said I had only come out to get attention."

"That's absolutely horrible." Mina's voice shook. "Why would anyone say something like that?"

"I don't know," Evelyn said. "And I'm not going to pretend it didn't hurt. Or that it didn't make me feel like I wasn't bi enough, either. But I know who I am, and I wasn't going to let some random asshole take that away from me. Especially when I'm lucky enough to live in a time and place where I *can* be out."

"I like that," Mina said softly. "I'm going to remember that."

"Thanks." Evelyn had a way of smiling that made Mina feel like she was in on some kind of secret. Like it was hidden somewhere between her cheek dimple and the curve of her lips. "You know, your post actually helped me come out?"

"Really?" Mina struggled to believe that she had influenced Evelyn Mackenzie to do anything aside from communicate with ghosts.

"Yeah. I mean, I knew I wasn't the only queer kid in our grade. People had been coming out for a while. But seeing you do it kind of gave me that push I needed." Evelyn shrugged. "Maybe it was the eye makeup. Very inspirational."

Mina knew she was blushing. She hadn't thought about how her post might have helped people, or made them feel more valid in who they were.

"Oh," she said weakly. "Well, I can teach you how to do the makeup look if you want."

"Sure," Evelyn said. "If we have time between our regularly scheduled ghost crises."

A truck pulled up in the driveway that Mina recognized as Uncle Dom's.

"Speaking of which," she said, frowning. That car should've been Stella's. "See you soon, all right?"

Evelyn nodded and headed off. It occurred to Mina as she climbed into the truck that Evelyn had stuck around just to talk to her, even though she'd told her in the library that she barely had enough time to go home and grab lunch before her next shift.

Mina wrinkled her nose as Uncle Dom pulled the truck onto Main Street. The inside smelled like it had been dipped in fish guts.

"Where's Mom?" she asked as he drove slowly through town. Uncle Dom was never really in a hurry—at seven years older than his sister, he was the quiet, steady anchor of the Zanetti medium duo. He and Stella had the kind of sibling relationship Mina had always craved. Sergio had felt a lot like an older brother when they were kids, but she wasn't sure if he wanted to be part of this family at all anymore.

"Stella's not feeling well," her uncle said as he pulled the steering wheel to the left. His ever-present baseball cap was strategically arranged across his bald spot.

"One of her migraines?"

"Yep."

"I'll take care of her. Don't worry."

She knew exactly what Stella needed at a time like this: calming music, ice packs, lavender essential oils.

"Actually, she asked if she could be left alone for a few hours,"

Uncle Dom said. "Do you want to come over for the afternoon? Sergio's off somewhere, but it's been a long time since we hung out. We could check out some more scrying focuses and order pizza."

They turned onto the side road that led to his house, not Mina's, like this was a foregone conclusion. Mina looked askance at her uncle—she'd lived with him for enough time to know something was off about this. There was a version of her that would have simply shoved that unease down and let him distract her for an afternoon. But the more time she spent around Evelyn, the less she seemed to be able to do that.

"You and Mom get spirit-induced migraines at the same time," she said. "And they generally correspond with the full or new moon, but that's still two days away."

Dom stared intensely at the road ahead. "Pushing this is not a good idea."

"Pushing what, exactly?" Mina's voice came out calm, unbothered. She was proud of that, because her ocean had begun to stir the moment his truck pulled up in the parking lot. Waves whipped into sharp white peaks as a storm brewed overhead. "She's having a migraine, you said?"

"I did," said her uncle. "Which is why you should come over, because she wants to be—"

"Left alone. Yes. But the thing is, I know how to do that when we're in the same house. I've had years of practice. So while I appreciate you inviting me over, I think I'd prefer to just go home."

When Mina looked over at her uncle again, his hands were white-knuckling the steering wheel.

"Unless there's something wrong," she said. "Something you don't want me to see."

"You promised her you'd stay out of this."

"She's my mother." Mina's voice was still soft, but it felt venomous. Inside her, thunder crashed above the roiling waves. She wondered what would happen if they broke over her boat, if she would break along with them. "Tell me what's going on, or I'll find out myself."

She had never said anything like that before to her mother or her uncle. It wasn't a question, or a plea. It was a demand. And to her immense surprise, it worked.

Uncle Dom pulled his truck over to the side of the road, then turned to look at her.

"The ghost attacked her," he said solemnly.

The waves in Mina's stomach lurched dangerously close to the sides of her boat. Perhaps it was her imagination, but the smell of saltwater inside the car had grown stronger. "Is she all right?"

"She will be." Her uncle adjusted his cap again, looking grim. "But she didn't want you to see her like that."

When Mina got sick after summoning that spirit with Evelyn, her mother had nursed her back to health. They'd gone to the hospital at first, then spent a week in the bedroom they'd shared at Uncle Dom's house as Stella monitored her temperature and fed her homemade soup. When Mina was lucid enough to be bored, Stella read her favorite books aloud and let Mina borrow her tablet to watch all her favorite movies. Now it was Mina's turn to repay her.

"Either you drive me there, or I walk."

Dom gunned the engine, maneuvering the truck so that it was going the right way. Toward home.

"She raised you to be just like her," he said ruefully. It felt a little like a compliment and a little like condemnation.

The lights were off inside the cottage, but the curtains were open. The afternoon sunlight illuminated chaos—a first aid kit still out on the living room table, a glass ward shattered on the floor. Mina barely stopped to take her shoes off before hurrying down the hallway to her mother's bedroom door. It was slightly ajar, but Mina knocked on it anyway.

"Dom?" murmured a faint voice. "Is that you?"

"It's me."

Stella immediately went silent.

"If you want me to stay outside, I will," Mina said. "But... please. I can help."

For another long moment, there was nothing at all. And then Stella's voice again, so faint Mina could barely hear it.

"All right."

The only light in Stella's room came from a few candles on the dresser and the night table, but Mina knew the topography well enough to side step the pile of recipe books on the floor and to swerve before hitting the antique coatrack Stella used as a jewelry holder. Her mother was curled up in bed, purple sheets bunched around her waist. Looming above her small frame was a massive wooden headboard, carved with moons and stars that seemed to flicker along with the candlelight.

"Mom." Mina pushed a few pillows away and sat on the edge

of the bed. Stella had at least a half dozen. Their first night in this house, they'd built a fort with them and camped out. Mina ate so much garlic-Parmesan popcorn and cookie dough ice cream that she felt sick the whole next day. "Tell me what you need."

"I didn't want you to see me like this, my seashell," she murmured. "Your uncle should have prevented you from coming here."

"He tried."

Her mother chuckled. "Sometimes I forget how stubborn you really are."

"I'm not— I—I just care about you. What happened?"

Stella hauled herself up and braced her back against the headboard. "Everything will be all right, Mina." Her voice was ragged. "I simply had a bad morning."

The candlelight illuminated the gigantic bandage on her mother's arm, stretching from her shoulder to her elbow. Smaller bandages dotted her face and neck. One right above her eyebrow, one on her cheek, one in the hollow of her throat.

"A bad morning? Mom, you need to go to the hospital. Uncle Dom can pick us up—"

"No. It's not safe." Stella wasn't as harsh as the last time she'd shut Mina down, but her tone was still firm enough to make Mina stop talking. "This house is protected. I checked the wards. As long as none are damaged, nothing can touch us here."

"There's a broken one on the floor."

"Yes, from outside." Stella coughed. "Hence why I rushed here as quickly as I could."

"So the ghost really attacked you?" Mina asked.

Stella nodded. "Your uncle and I have been trying to triangulate where the potential demon is most powerful, which would be far easier to do if we knew who this spirit *was*. For now, it seems best to avoid Sand Dollar Cove. Something most of this town does regardless."

Mina thought of her vision, the beach, the moon. "You think the spirit is strongest there?"

"Well, it was powerful enough to do this." Stella gestured ruefully toward herself, then to her night table. Mina turned and saw another casualty: the lavender glass pendant that had been her mother's scrying focus for as long as she could remember. All that remained of the necklace were a few purple fragments clinging to the setting.

It couldn't be a coincidence that this had happened right after Mina had heard a voice in her mind beckoning her to that beach, or that Evelyn had been contacted by the drowning summer victims.

"Are you absolutely certain this isn't the Cliffside Trio?" she asked. "The ghost that's threatening us, I mean."

Stella's lips thinned. "Yes, Mina," she said. "I told you, this is the ghost that absorbed the others."

"How can you be so sure?"

"Because this ghost was a problem before they died."

Mina gaped at her. "But you said you didn't know about this spirit until after the murders."

Stella met her gaze with steady, unwavering brown eyes.

You lied to me, Mina wanted to whisper—no, shout. *What else are you lying about?* Her ocean churned furiously. She'd tried to quell the storm she'd felt earlier, but instead it had only grown stronger.

"It was safer that way," Stella said. "You're highly vulnerable without a scrying focus—after today, I'm concerned that even your warding necklace may not be enough to protect you from this threat. But you don't need to worry about this. Once I've recovered, your uncle and I will find out who this spirit used to be. And we will stop them before they hurt anyone else."

"The ghost wants to talk to me." Mina blurted it out before her mind caught up with her mouth. "Isn't that an opening? A way you two could find out more about them?"

"The ghost...spoke to you?" Stella's voice turned harsh. "That shouldn't be possible. What about your necklace?"

Oh *no*. Mina gulped and clutched the pendant around her neck. "It was, um...I'd forgotten to put it on."

Stella obviously didn't believe her. "That's incredibly dangerous, Marina Elena. Of course the ghost wants to lure you in. You mustn't listen to a single thing they told you."

"I'm not planning on it," Mina said.

"Frankly, I'm unsure I can believe that. If you can't even listen to my instructions about keeping your necklace on, I don't understand how you *ever* expect to help us—"

"I *am* helping you," Mina protested. "I've found information that could change the way you're handling this. The Cliffside Trio were investigating ghosts! That can't be a coincidence."

Stella sighed. "Those kids came to me, Mina. They said they needed to know how to talk to a spirit. Our family's reputation has been around for quite some time. So they wanted to ask the local ghost hunters—their words, not mine—for help."

"And what did you tell them?" Mina asked.

"That it would be deeply unwise to do so, and that I couldn't in good conscience assist them. We don't summon random spirits here. We talk to the dead that need us."

"And you don't think what they were asking about had something to do with their deaths?"

Stella's expression was utterly neutral, her tone firm. "No. I believe they were murdered by human hands."

"What about the Blue Tide Waste Management Plant? Do you know anything about that?"

"Mina, please." Stella slumped against the headboard. "I don't know what conspiracy theories you've been reading, but I promise you, this path will bring you nothing but strife."

"But the spirits are changing, Mom. I think it's connected to the plant. The changing tide ranges, the pollution..."

"I need to rest," Stella said, her voice fading. "Please, Mina, enough of this."

Mina looked at her helplessly. She'd antagonized her mother while she was indisposed. It was impossible not to feel guilty about that.

"All right," she said. "I'm sorry. Can I bring you some water? Maybe some soup?"

Stella's eyes had fluttered shut, but she smiled, curling up in her nest of pillows once more.

"Thank you, my seashell," she murmured. "That would be wonderful."

Mina's mind whirred as she walked to the kitchen. She felt... foolish. Small. The Cliffside Trio had talked to her mother. But what did that even mean? What was Mina doing, pretending she and Evelyn were more qualified to handle this than two adults with a lifetime of experience?

Yet as she set about defrosting soup and stuck a glass of water beneath the tap, she realized there *was* something Stella didn't know about. The sand dollar on her wrist. Evelyn Mackenzie.

She could tell her if she wanted, but... Stella wouldn't listen. Stella *never* listened to her when she talked about the dead.

Mina put down the glass. Slowly, carefully, she lifted the warding necklace over her head. Then she stuck her hand beneath the tap, letting the water pool in her cupped palm.

The change wasn't immediate this time. It was slow, muted. The smell of salt crept through the room, and a faint bluish-green tendril appeared in the water running across her hand, flickering like a candle flame. Voices began to rumble in the back of her mind, and Mina felt that pull again. She knew it was wrong to seek this out. But she'd been craving this feeling ever since she'd been cut off at the pool—yearning met with yearning. A connection that hummed and fizzed beneath her skin.

But just as soon as Mina felt it, it stopped abruptly, as if she'd cracked open a chest and someone had just slammed the lid.

A frenetic clattering rang out from behind her. Mina whirled around. The three glass deer on top of the spice rack were vibrating, clicking against one another like broken toys.

She'd activated the wards.

Mina gasped and yanked her hand away from the tap, fumbling for her necklace. The figurines stopped trembling as soon as it touched her bare skin.

She *was* a medium, scrying focus or no scrying focus. Maybe this wasn't working for her because, like Evelyn, her practice was slightly different from the rest of her family's. Or maybe it was because Stella was holding out on her—she'd clearly withheld details about the drowning summer, after all.

Mina was tired of being sidelined. Cliffside Bay was in danger, and Stella was still treating her like a child.

This was her problem, too. And she was going to help fix it.

Chapter Seventeen

Evelyn's first official medium-training session began the day after Mina's mother was attacked by the ghost. No pressure. Evelyn asked Mina again if she wanted to tell Stella about her, but Mina refused. And after a quick rundown of Stella's lies, Evelyn understood why.

"I can't believe she talked to Colin, Tamara, and Jesse and didn't ever mention it to you," she said to Mina.

The other girl clutched a pillow close to her chest. Candles were clustered together on the windowsill behind her like gossiping friends. "I always knew she had secrets, but I didn't think they were...like this."

Despite her injuries, Stella was out visiting some produce supplier, a reckless attitude Mina was definitely upset about because, in Mina's words, "Does that mean she's lying about being in danger, too?" So they were in Mina's bedroom, which was the messiest living space Evelyn had ever seen. She'd wound up perched at the edge of the bed beside the vanity overflow-ing with makeup and a sewing machine. The mannequin in the corner would have given Evelyn nightmares, but Mina seemed comforted by it.

"So I guess we can't trust her," Evelyn said wearily.

"No, we can't," Mina said from the other edge of the bed. "We need to keep looking into this alone."

Just a few weeks ago, Mina had seemed so confident to her. Now, Evelyn could see the dark brown roots in her bleached hair, the zit on her cheek, the piles of laundry littering her floor. The girl before her was still accomplished, still smart, still annoyingly pretty—but she had a lot to lose and a lot to fear. Just like Evelyn.

"I know today is about training, but…I think you deserve a distraction from all this," Evelyn said. "Luisa's beach bonfire is tomorrow night. Do you want to go with me?"

"I can't," Mina said immediately, with such visceral panic that Evelyn jerked back, stung.

"I didn't realize hanging out with me was such a horrifying idea."

"That's not it. I— It's the full moon!" Mina whispered the last two words like they were an admission of some awful crime. "On the beach! Neither of us should be anywhere *near* the ocean."

Evelyn felt relief, followed swiftly by embarrassment. "Oh. Right. I just thought it might be nice to hang out with someone living for a change."

"What do you mean? You're always with people."

"What?" Evelyn was totally lost. "I don't hang out with

anybody, Mina. Except you. And Nick before that, I guess, but...that's it."

"But you know everyone," Mina protested. "Everywhere we go in this town, people line up to tell you how much they care about you. Ruthie, Mrs. Morales..."

"Are people who took pity on me when I was a kid."

"And your coworkers?"

"They're literally being paid to work with me."

"You truly don't see it." Mina lowered the pillow. "I...I don't even know what to say."

"How about starting that medium lesson I'm supposed to be here for?" Evelyn swung her feet off the bed and stood. She had no interest in explaining how alone she'd felt for the last six years. "We probably need space though, right? What's behind there?"

She pointed at a screen beside the closet, next to the mannequin.

"Uh, nothing," Mina said quickly, flushing from her neck up to her ears.

Curiosity prickled down Evelyn's spine. "I guess your mom isn't the only one with secrets."

"It's not a secret," Mina said indignantly. "It's unfinished. I'll show you when it's done, all right?"

A small part of Evelyn was tempted to unfold the screen and take a look for herself, but Mina was clearly uncomfortable.

"Okay," she said.

"Medium lesson?" Mina asked weakly.

"Medium lesson."

It wasn't as if all that much changed. Evelyn sat back on the bed and Mina straightened up, smoothing her hair and tossing the pillow aside. But Evelyn still felt that strangely formal sense of being in class and waiting for a lecture to start.

"I thought it might help to begin with the basics," Mina said. "Your relationship to the dead doesn't work exactly the way I was taught, but...I suppose mine doesn't, either. So we may have to improvise. But I *do* think you work with saltwater, and with Long Island Sound. Mom says it's special, that ghosts tend to collect here in a way they don't on the South Shore."

"Why *do* they get stuck here?" Evelyn asked.

The shadows on Mina's face flickered along with the candle-light, making the mole beneath her left eye look as if it were dancing. "For a while, I honestly just thought it was a mysterious thing she said. That she didn't really know why. But, well, if pollution can have an effect on ghosts...if the moon and the tides do, too...the whole Sound must do something to them as well, right? You know a lot about this area—is there anything special about this ocean versus another ocean?"

Something clicked in Evelyn's mind—another tiny puzzle piece in the vast mystery of the lingering dead.

"Well, first of all, the Sound isn't technically an ocean," she said. "It's an estuary. Fresh water mixed with saltwater. So it's got a way lower salt content than the Atlantic does."

"Mom calls salt a passageway," Mina mused. "Maybe the Sound is the perfect environment for ghosts to linger because it can't fully sweep them away."

"That's a really interesting idea," Evelyn said, her mind buzzing. "I wonder how that works? I wonder what ghosts are even made of. Maybe it's some kind of organic matter we just don't understand—what do you think?"

"I think you ask a lot of questions."

"Well, yeah! If I have to spend the rest of my life talking to ghosts, I'm going to try and figure out the details."

"I asked questions about the mechanics of being a medium all the time when I was younger." Mina looked at her hands, the sand dollar mark on her wrist peeking out from beneath her bracelet. "Stella didn't like it."

"Well, Stella isn't here," Evelyn said, with a sudden surge of protectiveness. "So what *do* you think about all my ghostly theorizing?"

"Huh." Mina hesitated. Evelyn had never seen someone try so hard to share an opinion before. "All right...well...I think that all my life, I've seen ghosts as these last echoes of a person, hovering at the edge of existence. But it's clear to me now that the world has an effect on them, just like it does on the living. The difference is, the dead have no power to change it."

"Until now," Evelyn said quietly.

Mina winced. "Yes. Until now."

She picked delicately through the clutter on her windowsill, then lifted out a glass figurine of a ballerina. "This is a ward— one of about a dozen in our house. After what happened to Mom, I think you should make some of your own. The problem is that you don't seem to use glass, but maybe if you substitute shells, or other organic matter, it will still work. You'll need to experiment."

"Why didn't you try and make one of these for me before?" Evelyn asked.

"I...would have had to ask my family for help," Mina

mumbled. "Since I wasn't sure it would work. And since I didn't want them to know about you..."

Evelyn grimaced. "Oh."

"You've been safe since you found your scrying focus, though!" Mina said hastily. "This is just extra protection."

Mina explained the basics to Evelyn—a bowl, saltwater, blood, dipping the object in until it glowed.

"But what makes the wards glow?" Evelyn asked. "Did Stella only pick ones she had a connection with? Or did the blood create a connection? And if the blood creates a connection, why don't all mediums just—"

"Slow down." Mina held out her hands. "One, wards don't work like a normal scrying focus—they're meant to dull a spirit's influence instead of amplifying their voice. Two, they glow because Mom's a medium. That's the only reason she's ever given me, and I don't think she really understands it. And three, the blood lets them know who to protect."

"What about Dad and Meredith?" Evelyn asked. "I can't exactly go up to them and be like, *Oh, hey, can I have some of your blood? It's for a thing.*"

"Since the ghost should target mediums before they bother with anyone else, your family will be fine for the time being. Stella has this saying, about how we stand on the bridge between life and death. Your family is firmly on the living side of that bridge."

Evelyn nodded, impressed. "Damn, Mina, you really do know your stuff."

Mina's face stayed mostly the same, but the corners of her

mouth twitched. Evelyn had learned this look—it meant she was happy but trying not to show it.

"Well, you know yours, too. The way you approach ghosts as natural phenomena instead of lingering souls that need to be shooed away...it's incredibly interesting."

Mina met Evelyn's eyes, and there it was again. That *thing* that had happened at Ruthie's and at Scales & Tails, a softening in Evelyn's chest that felt not like a weakening of her survival mechanisms, but an expansion of them.

Mina made her feel safe. And Mina made her feel *understood*.

Evelyn was so wrapped up in their conversation, she almost didn't hear the knock on the door. But Mina did. She jolted upward and shoved the glass figurine back onto the windowsill.

"Mom?" she called out.

"Open up, Mina. I've got something to show you."

There was a cheeriness to the voice that confused Evelyn— this did not sound like someone who was frightened of a potential demon. Mina shrugged, clearly bewildered.

"Don't tell her anything," Mina murmured before rising to her feet. She easily navigated the maze of junk on her floor before unlatching the door and pulling it open.

It had been a long time since Evelyn's last interaction with Mina's mother, but Stella had the kind of presence one didn't forget. Today she wore a sundress the color of a storm cloud with a gray shawl draped over it and a half dozen opal pins that kept her thick, waist-length brown hair out of her eyes. The green orb around her neck looked like cheap glass, but Evelyn knew it was far more than that. There were bandages on her neck and forehead; they only added to the impression that she was a force to be reckoned with. A *You should see the other ghost* situation.

"Evelyn Mackenzie," Stella mused. There was something sly and teasing in her voice, but no surprise. Evelyn remembered she'd left her sneakers in the front hallway. Of course Stella had known someone else was here. She felt hopelessly ordinary as Stella's brown eyes assessed her outfit: the flannel tied around her waist, her homemade cutoffs, and a graphic T-shirt that had once belonged to Meredith. It read WHATEVER FOREVER, and in that moment it felt deeply immature.

"How lovely to see you again. Now, Mina, you know the rules about having friends of any gender over: door open."

Mina flushed. "We were just—working on a school project—"

"In the summer?"

Evelyn had never seen Mina so outclassed before. Stella let the words hang in the air for a moment before she swung a tote bag over one shoulder and pulled out a giant tomato.

"You're staying for dinner," she declared, a statement, not a question. "We're refining my Bolognese."

"Mom," Mina choked out, now roughly the same color as the tomato. "Evelyn's a vegetarian. And I'm sure she has plans—"

"I don't," Evelyn said hastily, earning herself a glare from Mina. "Dinner sounds amazing, Ms. Zanetti. Thank you."

"It's Stella," said Mina's mother. "I'm so pleased to see you're friends again. Mina's really missed you, you know. And don't worry, I have excellent vegetarian options of all my best dishes."

She swept out of the room, that smile still fixed on her face. Mina sank to the floor, not even trying to hide her abject horror.

"You are not staying for dinner," she muttered.

Evelyn shrugged. "Pretty sure I was invited."

"It's far too risky! She could find out what's going on."

"Don't you think it looks weirder if I just run away?"

Mina sighed. "All right. Fine. But just a warning: Mom's kind of intense about food."

Kind of intense turned out to be a massive understatement. Evelyn had vague memories of Stella's cooking, but she'd only been friends with Mina while they were still living with her uncle. This was her first time watching the woman at full power.

Stella whirled around the kitchen like a tornado as she pulled out a collection of shiny utensils that looked like surgeon's tools, a food processor, and a ton of vegetables—celery, carrots, tomatoes, garlic. An oil-splattered speaker on the kitchen island blared out a bunch of old songs, and she sang along shamelessly even though her voice was awful. Mina flushed each time Stella tried to get her to sing, too.

"Can I help?" Evelyn asked, which turned out to be a mistake.

She was thrust into a dance filled with elaborate choreography that Mina and her mother already knew by heart. Evelyn struggled to position her knife correctly as she chopped unevenly at a celery stalk, while the Zanettis effortlessly diced tomatoes and garlic, bantering back and forth all the while. Mina handed her an apron at some point, and it hung awkwardly around her neck as she struggled to keep up. This was nothing like the Basic Bean.

The food processor whirred, carrots and celery were added to the sauce, and soon it was all lumped together in a massive pot on the stove, boiling like the contents of a cauldron. Evelyn hung back awkwardly as Mina stirred it with a wooden spoon that looked like it was older than all three of them combined.

"It needs more tomato paste," Stella mused as she tried a small spoonful. "What do you think, Mina?"

Mina tasted it. "More red pepper flakes."

"You always say that. We're not trying to burn the wedding guests' faces off, my seashell."

"It'll simmer out, Mom."

"Not the way you put it in."

Evelyn leaned against the far wall of the kitchen, a sharp pain building between her ribs.

She made it through dinner, nodding and smiling. The vegetarian pasta sauce was indeed delicious. But there was dessert, too—a strange white cylinder with fresh berries on top that she learned was called panna cotta. By the time she'd finished helping with the dishes, it was almost 10:00 PM.

"Thank you," she said for the umpteenth time as she headed for the door.

"Of course!" Stella cooed at her. "Come back soon!"

When Evelyn's world fell apart, when her mom left and her sister and her dad started fighting so badly that she didn't feel safe at home, she'd found a way to survive in hostile conditions because she'd had no other choice.

But after tonight, she understood more than ever that for all Mina's insecurities, she was surrounded by resources and support. Sure, Mina's family wasn't perfect. But they loved her, and they loved one another, and no matter how much her ecosystem changed, that wouldn't go away. It was a protective shell far stronger than anything Evelyn could hope to create on her own—and Mina had no idea how lucky she was to have it.

Evelyn pushed her sneaker against the pavement again and again, until she was going so fast that the evening air whipped painfully against her face, until the rows of houses blended together into one long, unbroken building in the darkness.

She rolled to a stop in her driveway, then pushed open the front door, her longboard tucked under her arm. Her father snored in his recliner. Upstairs, the light was on in Meredith's bedroom. Evelyn could hear the soft murmurs of her talking to Riku through the door.

All three of them were home, but that wasn't enough. They still didn't feel like a family to her. Maybe they never would.

Evelyn had intended to make wards once she'd come back, but she was far too drained to think about the ghost as much more than some abstract threat. Instead, she lay awake for a long, long time in her bedroom, clutching her scrying focus like a security blanket.

Just once, she wanted to fall asleep in a house that felt like people were living in it instead of dying in it.

Chapter Eighteen

The full moon hung outside Mina's bedroom window, taunting her. She'd spent her evening trying to turn away from it, tugging the curtains shut and hunkering down with the Zanetti Collection. It was more tempting than it should have been to think about what would happen if she took off her warding necklace and walked outside.

Stella had retired to her room earlier in the day with a migraine, a real one this time, so Mina had been left to her own devices. She stared at the contents of her clothing rack—a cream-colored blazer with a holographic star detail on one shoulder, some silky palazzo pants, a pale blue linen wrap dress with loose sleeves and a drawstring waist. The collection was filled with muted colors paired with statement details, meant to be a sort of elevated casual wear. There had been some earlier mistakes, but the surviving garments were well constructed.

Mina had known for weeks that it didn't work, but looking at it now, she finally understood why. The Zanetti Collection was boring. None of the garments took risks. They were bland, uninspired pieces with no heart at all.

But that wasn't the only problem with Mina's clothing designs that she didn't know how to fix.

Back at Ruthie's, when they'd been gathering up potential scrying focuses, Evelyn had made a bit of a backhanded comment about the fashion industry's impact on the climate. Mina had since googled it, and now she couldn't get the reality of it out of her head. Here she was, talking about pollution and ghosts, and the industry she wanted to be a part of was a massive environmental hazard.

Mina's phone buzzed. It was one of Evelyn's nearly incomprehensible texts, telling her she was going to Luisa's party after all.

Mina groaned and tossed her phone onto the floor. She'd gotten the sense last night that Evelyn was upset with her, although she wasn't quite sure why. This text felt like an invitation to a fight she didn't want to have. Mina had spent a lifetime pushing her frustrations down, so she decided it was best not to respond.

Besides, Evelyn wasn't foolish enough to go without her scrying focus. And she'd already shown such an aptitude for handling spirits—maybe she could handle this on her own. Maybe Mina was simply in her way.

Mina tugged at one of the pieces on the clothing rack. A pale pink romper. There was something to this one, though. She sat down with it, let her fingers linger on the fabric. It reminded her of the sun rising above the waves, the way the light bounced off the water. Mina didn't want to use any new fabric...but she'd already made this piece. Maybe there was another, better way to alter it.

She rummaged through her fabric bin, pulled out some

muslin, then went for her seam ripper. Her cuff bracelet made it difficult to draw a new pattern, so she tugged it off.

Mina was so engrossed in her work that she didn't hear the first knock, or the second. Or the door opening.

So engrossed that she didn't notice Stella until her mother was already looming over her, looking puzzled.

"Mina?" she asked. "I'm feeling a little better, if you want to watch a movie—"

Her mother stopped speaking abruptly. Mina looked up... and realized Stella's gaze had fallen to her wrist.

It was too late to hide the sand dollar again. Too late to do anything at all but watch the color drain from Stella's face, watch her sway back and forth, as if she was about to faint.

"How long." She pointed a shaking finger at Mina's arm. "How long have you been hiding this from me?"

"A month," Mina whispered.

"Living room," Stella said. "Now."

Mina dropped her sewing project and rose to her feet. She didn't say a word as Stella sat her down in the armchair and paced back and forth, preparing for an interrogation.

"So you did do something," Stella murmured. "That night, at the ocean. That spirit..."

"I didn't." The words came out soft and wavering. "It wasn't me."

Stella crouched in front of the chair and extended her hand. Mina obediently put her wrist out. It was a reflex: Stella asked, and Mina answered.

"Then who was it, Marina Elena?" Stella pressed down gently on the sand dollar mark, and Mina hissed in pain—it felt like a scab that hadn't quite healed. Her mother's brow furrowed with concern. "You did that summoning spell alone as a child to try and help with the drowning summer, and then you did it again. With no regard for the consequences. With no understanding of how much danger—"

"Evelyn," Mina whimpered. "Evelyn Mackenzie did it. I— She—she's a medium, too."

Stella's eyes went wide. "What?"

So Mina told her. There was no joy in spilling a six-year-old secret. Instead, it felt as if one of her many chests at the bottom of the ocean had cracked open, leaking poison into her carefully curated sea the same way that waste plant had leaked pollution into Long Island Sound.

Even now, it didn't feel as if it were her secret to tell. But she confessed anyway. She'd originally told Stella that she'd been trying to figure out who killed the Cliffside Trio six years ago in a misguided attempt to help, but now she explained that she and Evelyn had summoned a ghost to exonerate her friend's father... and that Evelyn had called a spirit again this summer. When she was finished, Stella released her grip and sat back, her gaze distant, almost vacant. She shook her head, massaging her temples, and Mina felt a stab of guilt. This couldn't be helping her migraine.

"This is my fault," her mother said. "I should have explained earlier, but I didn't realize it was all so complicated. And I'd hoped to resolve this without frightening you. But I see now that I have no choice. That sand dollar on your wrist—it means you're cursed."

Cursed. *Cursed*. The word ricocheted through Mina's skull like an assault. Like a massive gust of wind overhead, whipping up waves in her polluted sea.

She couldn't keep herself calm. Not when it was clear that even though Stella now knew all of Mina's secrets, Mina knew only a fraction of hers.

"I don't understand," Mina said. "I didn't— You've never told me— *How?*"

"When you were ten, you tried to talk to a spirit," her mother said. "But the more of yourself you give a spirit, the more they can take. You used your blood in that summoning—and it opened a channel to several of them. This allowed them to siphon some of your life force in exchange for completing your request. That energy let them linger in our reality for a bit longer."

"That's why I was so ill." Mina felt a little faint, as if a spirit was taking energy away from her right now.

"Precisely," Stella said. "I thought I knew who the spirits were that plagued you, and I thought I'd successfully broken your bond with them. Until today."

Mina already knew the answer, but she asked anyway. "Who did you think it was?"

Stella sighed, then reached out a hand. "Give me your warding necklace."

Mina obliged, curiosity and dread stirring in her as she fished out the pendant. Her mother wedged a fingernail beneath the red glass heart and pried it up, revealing a hollow interior. Mina realized with a jolt that there was something stuffed inside, something that had hung around her neck for six years.

Stella dumped the contents into her palm.

An earring. A scrap of dark blue jersey. And a class ring with SLATER etched into the side.

Mina's waves whipped higher.

"You thought it was the drowning summer victims," she choked out.

Stella nodded. "Personal objects like this have value. As you saw with Mr. Giacomo, they can allow you to summon a spirit—or banish one."

"That's how you do an exorcism?"

"Well…almost," Stella said. "Exorcisms require a sacrifice. A bit of you to make you stronger than the spirit you're trying to banish."

"That's why you can't get rid of the ghost," Mina breathed. "You don't know who they are. And you don't have anything that belonged to them."

Stella nodded grimly. "Yes."

"These items," Mina said, still staring at them. "How did you…?"

"Jesse, Colin, and Tamara gave them to me when they asked for help," Stella said quickly. "They had some rather misguided ideas about how contacting a ghost would work. But it did mean I had them on hand to try and break your bond with them later, after you summoned them."

"But it didn't work," Mina said.

"Not completely, no," Stella said. "The Cliffside Trio lingered, but they didn't seem to affect you or take any more of your life force. The necklace was a safety precaution—meant to be worn until your uncle and I found a way to usher them out of this world. We allowed you to take it off because we believed the bond had been broken. But whatever Evelyn did at the start of this summer renewed that connection between you, and the drowning summer victims, and the ghost that's consuming them."

Mina thought of that pull, that yearning. A channel she had opened by blood. She hadn't meant to keep the dead here—she'd only wanted to help Evelyn.

"There's one more thing," Stella said shakily. "Your connection with these ghosts means your communication abilities are...effectively stuck on one channel. It's keeping you from contacting any other ghosts."

Something broke in her then. It was as if her boat had capsized in the middle of the storm, and she was desperately treading water, searching for some scrap of debris to cling to.

"Is this why I can't find a scrying focus?" she whispered.

"Most likely."

"But—but what about Evelyn?" Mina protested. "She doesn't have a mark. She didn't get sick. And we both gave those spirits our blood."

"I don't know why they chose you," Stella said. "But they did."

Mina moaned and buried her face in her hands. Her words came out muffled and distorted. "Please tell me you can fix this."

Stella was silent for a long, long moment. Then Mina felt her hand on her shoulder, squeezing it gently.

"I will do everything in my power to keep you safe, my seashell," she said. "Just as I have always done. I know it's hard for you to hear all of this, but can you understand why I kept it from you?"

Mina knew her mother loved her more than anything in the world, and she had thought it was her duty to be grateful for that. To be the perfect daughter, worth all the sacrifices her mother had made. But right now her mother's love felt less like a bridge across her ocean and more like a hand holding her beneath the water; right now, *love* felt a lot like an excuse for fear.

That kind of love—stifling, smothering, terrifying—was the only kind Mina knew how to give. Stella had taught her that the same way she'd taught her how to steam a lobster and curl her hair.

"I understand," Mina whispered, moving her hands away.

Stella had been crying. Mina'd been crying, too. The room was blurred and fuzzy around the edges; she blinked and sniffled.

Mina understood, all right. But she didn't agree.

"Now," Stella said. "The matter of Evelyn Mackenzie."

In her mind, Mina clung to a bit of flotsam, bracing herself for another wave. But her mother's next words weren't what she was expecting.

"The summoning you two did to help Evelyn's father," Stella said. "It answers some questions I had from six years ago."

"About spirit activity, you mean?"

"No." Stella's lips thinned into a severe line. "It explained why he wasn't sent to prison."

"I don't understand."

"The evening those poor teenagers died, I was still waitressing at the Shorewell Community Center. I was waiting on a food shipment down by the pier when I saw Greg Mackenzie in his sailboat. With the Cliffside Trio. At sunset. At the time, I thought nothing of it."

"What are you saying?" The wind blew louder; her waves whipped higher. She struggled to stay afloat.

"I talked to several detectives. They think I was the last

person to see them alive." Stella locked eyes with her. "Evelyn Mackenzie seems like a lovely girl. I enjoyed our dinner together. But I want you to understand the full ramifications of what you two may have covered up."

"You—you think he killed them."

"I don't know for certain," Stella said. "Their spirits won't talk to us. The ghost absorbing them has made sure of that. But now that I know Evelyn was directly involved...well. It does beg the question, doesn't it? What would she do to protect her family? A young, brash medium with real power...she's dangerous, Mina. And she will need to be dealt with."

"Dealt with?" Mina gasped. "What are you going to do to her?"

"Oh, goodness, Mina, don't look at me like that. I simply mean that she needs to learn the rules of how this really works. She can't just run around misusing her powers, and whatever training she's received from you..." Stella trailed off. "Well. I'm sure you did your best."

Mina understood, then. Stella didn't just want to train Evelyn. She wanted to contain her. Mina couldn't bear the thought of Evelyn's natural curiosity dulled down, her questions left unanswered until she lapsed into silence.

Mina took a deep breath and stood up. It took a lifetime of self-control to keep her voice calm.

"I can't be here anymore," she said. "I need to process all of this."

"But after everything I just told you, surely you understand why you need to stay inside—"

"What I need is time to think." Mina dumped the objects back into the warding necklace. Pushed the heart back into place. Pulled it over her head. "I'll be safe with this on. Don't worry."

She walked into the hallway. In her mind, Mina grabbed at the wreckage floating in the waves. She bolted the debris together until she'd made a raft, and then she hauled herself up on it, shivering.

She grabbed her wicker purse and slipped her feet into her favorite sandals.

"Marina Elena." Stella chased her down the hallway, her voice shrill. "What has gotten into you? We aren't finished discussing the Evelyn situation."

"She isn't a situation," Mina said. "She's my—my—" Her throat caught on the word *friend*. She wasn't quite sure why.

"I see." Stella looked a bit shaky on her feet; Mina could tell the full moon was still hurting her. "Mina, as I've told you, I have nothing against Evelyn personally. I'm simply trying to make sure you're *both* safe."

Mina's hand trembled on the strap of her purse. The storm inside her didn't feel like something to be ashamed of anymore. It felt right. It felt true. "By lying to me? I told you, Mom. You need to give me time."

"Fine," Stella said. "But can you at least tell me where you're going?"

Mina turned around and smiled. "To a party. Like a normal teenager."

She made it all the way down the street before her panic caught up with her. She sank down on the sidewalk, dry-heaving, terrified and exhilarated and furious all at once.

She'd never stood up to Stella like that. And her mother had been right about at least one thing: It was all because of Evelyn.

Chapter Nineteen

Evelyn was nervous to show up for the bonfire alone. She hadn't been to a party by herself since the previous fall, the night that had ended with Nick taking her home. And she'd definitely never needed to be concerned about a full moon before. Whispers had started rustling in her mind that morning, fading in and out like crackling static. They weren't anywhere near as loud as the voices had been before she'd found her scrying focus, but they were still loud enough to worry her.

She wasn't completely sure why she was willing to risk potential danger to hang out with a coworker. But she knew it had to do with how Mina had made her feel the night before. Like Evelyn needed to cling to the few things she had going for her, because Mina had everything except this party invitation. It was petty, but she couldn't bring herself to care.

Evelyn fussed over her outfit and makeup way more than she usually would, frowning at a breakout on her chin and redoing her eyeliner until it was just right. She managed to bore a small hole in her scrying focus and string a cord through it, but it was kind of bulky, so she stuck the makeshift necklace in her tote bag alongside her wallet and phone. When she headed out the door, she wasn't sure what to expect at the party. But when she walked onto Cliffside Beach, her sneakers crunching across the belt of rocks and shells separating her from the sand, Luisa jumped up from her picnic blanket and gave her a big wave.

"You came!" she said, running over and wrapping Evelyn in a hug. "Do you know anyone else here? Or do you need intros?"

Evelyn was relieved to see that she'd correctly gauged the dress code—Luisa wore a casual yellow dress, gold eyeliner, and bits of metallic blush sprinkled across her cheekbones. Her fancy camera was slung across one shoulder. Cute, but still carefree, just like Evelyn's ripped straight-leg jeans and velvet crop top. She knew velvet was a bad choice for a sweaty summer night, but it was a Ruthie find that she'd never had cause to wear out before, so she couldn't really resist.

"I'm sure I know some of them." Evelyn glanced at the people clustered in small groups around the bonfire, maybe thirty total. Someone was playing guitar, and a few people sang along to the familiar melody of a pop song. One voice rose above the rest as if borne by the bonfire smoke, strong with a slight, gravelly rasp. "Who's the singer?"

"You definitely know *her*," Luisa said, tugging Evelyn toward the blaze.

Evelyn grinned, surprised, as the guitarist came into view. Amy Cheng looked at peace like this, her fingers dancing easily across the body of the instrument as she sang. She'd known the other girl was really into music, but it was another thing entirely to see her perform. She could totally see the grunge-band thing now.

"We work together," she said.

"Oh, I know." Luisa sounded amused. "You've both complained to me about the Basic Bean so much, I feel like I work there, too."

Luisa pulled off her lens cap and snapped a few candids of Amy playing as they watched the rest of the song together. Evelyn liked the way it felt to cluster among the others on the beach, to be part of the same moment, bound by the same appreciation for Amy's music. Sometimes living in Cliffside Bay felt like being trapped in a tidal pool, shoved too close to other organisms and roasting beneath the harsh gaze of the sun. But tonight, beneath the full moon, being close to others made her calm instead of frightened.

The full moon. Evelyn reached into her tote bag and grasped the shell, wondering if it was only her imagination, or if the murmurs in her mind were growing stronger. She could almost make out words, if she concentrated on them, which she didn't want to do right now. When she peeked inside, the shell was glowing, though barely visible through the canvas. She hoped anyone looking would mistake it for a phone screen.

Amy plucked out the last few chords of the song, then lay her guitar carefully on the blanket beside her. "Show's over," she said, although her blue-lipsticked grin told Evelyn she could've played all night. "Now someone put on something we can dance to. Gina didn't bring those speakers here for nothing, right?"

The small crowd scattered, and soon enough music was blasting from the aforementioned speakers, something upbeat and fast. Evelyn stayed by Luisa. She hoped the other girl didn't feel obligated to babysit her but wasn't sure how to convey that without making it weird.

"You're really good," Evelyn said as Amy placed her guitar back in its case.

"Thanks." Amy latched the case shut, then set it gently on a towel. It was covered in half-peeled stickers. "I'm practicing for my audition next week."

"There's this new band that's trying to recruit her," Luisa explained as the three of them meandered over to a cooler, half-buried in the sand. "They're sort of...Amy, how would you describe them?"

"Modern indie punk," Amy said immediately. "I'm playing my own stuff. They'd better like it, if they want me to be their frontwoman."

There was a story there, one that spilled out as Luisa opened the cooler and rummaged through the drinks. Apparently the grunge band Amy had been part of last year had talked over her ideas and ignored her suggestions until she felt like she was playing someone else's music entirely. Now, she was determined to find something better. Evelyn thought of her own journey—refusing to let Nick change her into someone she no longer recognized—and understood.

"We've got beer," Luisa offered. "Hard lemonade? Spiked seltzer? Somebody's got a fake, and somebody else has an older cousin."

Evelyn didn't want to know what happened if a medium got drunk during a full moon. "I'll just take a normal seltzer, actually."

To her surprise, Luisa and Amy did the same.

"I'm the DD, and her ex is here," Amy explained. "No bad decisions tonight."

"Well, no bad decisions we can blame on alcohol," Evelyn said, feeling a rush of satisfaction when they laughed. It was surprisingly easy to talk to these girls—she had no idea how she'd worked with them both for such a long time without noticing that they were close friends. They introduced her to most of the party, people she'd noticed while perched at the edge of a lunch table or talked to a bit in class. Luisa snapped pictures of everyone, careful to remind people to hide their alcohol first, then asked someone to take a few of her, Evelyn, and Amy.

No one brought up Evelyn's dad or looked at her like she was anything other than one of them. She was *normal*.

Except for the voices stirring in her mind, and a pull she'd begun to feel, a tether to the crashing waves.

"What did you think?" Luisa asked her after they talked to Talia, who'd been in Evelyn's history class. "Do you still want to be set up?"

"Don't even try," Amy said teasingly. She blotted at tonight's blue lipstick with a spare tissue, then continued, "Evelyn's got a thing for Mina."

"Zanetti?" Luisa's eyes lit up with curiosity. "Interesting."

"I do not." Evelyn's voice sounded unconvincing even to her own ears. *Have a thing*—was that even right? Was *that* what she kept feeling around Mina, or was it just frustration, or was it the rush of a rekindled friendship? It was hard to tell with other girls sometimes. Nick had felt like a pathway she knew how to tread, thanks to a million books and movies and TV shows, but with Mina there was so much less to use as a reference point.

"Hmm." Amy slid into a folding chair someone had abandoned for the dancing now taking place on the other side of the bonfire. Luisa sat in the sand beside her. "Not to play the lesbian card or anything, but I know two girls flirting when I see it."

"When have you ever seen us flirt?"

Amy raised an eyebrow, as if to say *Really?* "You called her drink order a crime against caffeine the first time she asked for it. Now you literally bring it to her, for free."

"I only did that once," Evelyn protested, sitting down on Amy's other side. But she could feel herself blushing, and could also feel that sense of connection—Amy was someone she could talk to about this. About girls. The rocky beach wasn't the most comfortable seat, but she didn't mind.

"There are rumors about Mina's family," Luisa murmured. "Strange ones."

"And we all know how Cliffside Bay loves to spread rumors," Amy said sharply.

Evelyn swallowed hard. Just when she was starting to believe no one here cared about her past.

"With Mina, I..." Evelyn sighed. "It's hard to explain. We were really close as kids, and I thought we were becoming friends again, but...I'm not so sure anymore."

"You don't have to talk about it if you don't want to," Luisa said hastily. "We know you're shy."

Evelyn had never once thought of herself that way. Guarded, maybe. Insecure. Intense. But never shy.

"Yeah, I'm surprised you came," Amy added. "I bet Luisa twenty bucks you wouldn't show up."

"Amy! Don't tell her that!"

"It's okay." Evelyn fought to regain the rhythm she'd found so comforting, like keeping her footing on her longboard, like the ocean ebbing and flowing across the intertidal zone. "I get it."

"I mean...I invited you to stuff after we started working together, and you never showed up," Luisa said. "Maybe I should've taken the hint when we were kids, but—I don't know. You've seemed different the last few weeks. So I decided it couldn't hurt to try again."

Maybe there *was* some truth to what Mina had said the night before, about Cliffside Bay. That the biggest thing holding Evelyn back from feeling like a part of something was...Evelyn.

"I'm glad you kept inviting me. It's just...hard for me to open up," she said, unable to keep the wobble from her voice.

Evelyn was scared to look at Amy and Luisa. Scared to see the inevitable pity on their faces. But instead, when Amy spoke, her voice was the gentlest Evelyn had ever heard it.

"I'm sorry. I didn't mean to make you uncomfortable."

"No, no, don't be." Evelyn turned to see that both of them looked concerned, but it was hard to be mad about that. They barely knew her. She thought of her decision to let Mina in and wondered if she were brave enough to make that choice again, now that she and Mina were in such a strange place. But she hadn't come to this party for no reason. She was here because she was tired of being alone. "I'm having fun. And I hope I didn't make your night weird."

Amy gave her the same confident smile she'd given her audience earlier.

"You're not making it weird," she said. "You know what's

weird? That one guy who comes to the Basic Bean and always orders an entire cup of foam."

"I'm sorry, he *what*?" Luisa asked.

"Oh, yeah," Evelyn said, latching on to the familiar rhythm of the conversation with relief. "He's totally got a bunch of bodies in his basement. There's no other explanation for that kind of behavior."

Amy was trying to convince Luisa to listen to her mom about hanging her work up in the library when Kenny walked over.

"Hi," he said nervously, adjusting his glasses. He was wearing a white pair of shorts—a bold move that Evelyn was willing to bet he'd regret—and a nervous smile. "Oh, um, good to see you, Evelyn. Didn't realize you were coming."

"Hey." Evelyn looked between the three of them, noting that Luisa had stiffened while Amy leaned back in her chair, watching them carefully. There was absolutely a weird vibe here, and this time, it wasn't coming from her.

"Um," he said, turning to Luisa. "Can we talk?"

She hesitated for a moment, but then she nodded, taking an offered hand and pulling herself up. Something clicked in Evelyn's mind as she watched them looking at each other. The moment they were out of earshot, she turned to Amy.

"Is *she* the mystery girl Kenny's been talking to?" she whispered. "The one who listened to that podcast he likes?"

Amy took a long, smug sip of her seltzer. "Yep. They had a thing last spring, and they clearly aren't over each other, but they're both too nervous to work it out."

"Oh my God," Evelyn said. "They've been talking to me about each other all summer, and I had no idea."

"Join the club," Amy said. "Dealing with it from both sides is super annoying. They should seriously just kiss already. Hey— I'm going to pee. You'll be okay by yourself?"

Evelyn nodded. She turned to watch the rest of the party while Amy was gone, her empty seltzer can hanging loosely in one hand.

She'd been lonely for so long, she'd forgotten how it felt when she wasn't. How a party could actually be welcoming instead of a place where she needed to hold Nick's hand to feel safe. Evelyn had worried about everything happening inside her house for a very long time. But maybe the defenses she'd constructed after the drowning summer no longer applied to her stretch of the shoreline. If these other people could treat her like she belonged...maybe she could start to treat herself that way, too.

Evelyn breathed in beach-bonfire air, salty and smoky, and when she exhaled, it was as if she'd also released some long-held breath deep inside her. She was about to go grab another seltzer when a figure clambered over one of the sand dunes. Evelyn knew that slim frame, that blond hair shimmering in the firelight.

Mina Zanetti had shown up to the party.

Something was wrong with Mina. There was the outfit—a simple tank top and shorts, a far cry from the elaborate looks

Mina seemed to thrive on putting together. There was the way she walked, slumped and strange. The way she clutched her wicker purse like it was the only thing keeping her afloat. And of course, there was the fact that she was here at all, when she'd acted like Evelyn was out of her mind for suggesting they go to this party.

Evelyn intercepted Mina before she could get too close to anyone else. "What's going on?"

"What do you mean?" Her voice was calm—too calm.

Evelyn tilted her head back, and at last she caught a glimpse of Mina's face. Red-rimmed eyes and blotchy cheeks that not even Mina's emotional guards could hide.

"Something happened to you." Evelyn pitched her voice as low as she could, drawing closer to the other girl. "Is it the ghost? Did they lure you here?"

Mina let out a high, shrill chuckle. "Oh, nothing like that! Just a small family disagreement."

"This whole *I'm totally not having a meltdown* thing doesn't work on me. You know that, right?"

"What thing?" Mina surveyed the party. "This looks fun, Evelyn. Let's go talk to people. Let's dance. Let's be normal."

"This *isn't* normal," Evelyn said. "Why don't we go talk somewhere else—"

"What?" Mina's voice had grown slightly less calm. "Are you going to stop me, too? Tell me what I can and can't do?"

Evelyn's temper flared. "No." She stepped aside, waved a hand at the bonfire. "If you're actually here to party, go ahead. But if you want to talk about what your mom said to you? I'm right here."

Mina's face contorted the same way it had back at Scales & Tails. Her smile slipped, but she didn't paste it back on this time.

"I..." she whispered, and then, "How did you realize— Mom—?"

"Because I know you. Or at least I'm starting to."

Evelyn met Mina's gaze, and there it was again. That feeling. Like the moment between jumping off the rocks and hitting the ocean—exhilaration and nerves and *no turning back now.* "Come on, Zanetti. Talk to me."

Mina sniffled, then extended her pale, slender hand. Evelyn noticed for the first time that her cuff bracelet was gone. The blue-green sand dollar on her wrist looked even more vivid than the last time she'd seen it.

"Stella found it," she whispered. "And I told her. I told her everything."

They wound up huddled against the place where the beach became a cliff, far enough away from the party for no one to see them but close enough to still hear the occasional snatches of pop music and laughter. It was hilly, sand and grass and rocks all mixed together, but Mina didn't seem to notice any discomfort as she explained what Stella had said. That she was cursed. That the sand dollar anchored her to the drowning summer ghosts, blocking her powers. That she couldn't break that bond without exorcising the spirit that had absorbed them—and they couldn't do *that* without learning who the ghost was.

"I have no idea how to process this." Mina's arm brushed against Evelyn's as she adjusted her seat on the sand. "I... she...she told me nothing. And it took me six years to even ask her why."

It was with no small amount of embarrassment that Evelyn realized Stella had charmed her at dinner the night before. It was an illusion just like the one Mina put up, but far more convincing due to those extra decades of practicing. Evelyn's family was a nightmare, sure, but at least she knew they weren't hiding anything from her.

"It's going to be okay." Evelyn had no idea how to break a curse, but that didn't seem important right now. Neither did her petty resentments about what Mina had and she didn't. All that mattered was that Mina needed help. "We'll figure this out."

"You're not mad that I blew your cover?"

Evelyn nudged her knee against Mina's. "Nope. I'm not scared of your mother."

Mina let out a sniffly laugh and nudged back, but didn't move away. Instead, she drew closer. She smelled like citrus and smoke, and when their fingers brushed, it took all Evelyn had not to take Mina's hand and—and—

"Can I tell you something?" Mina asked. Evelyn couldn't really see her face, but she sounded nervous. "I...I don't think you'll like it."

Evelyn's stomach contorted itself in a way that felt medically impossible. "You can tell me anything."

"All right." Mina hesitated, for a long, agonizing moment, and then— "Mom...said something. About your father."

Evelyn's whole body went cold. She yanked her shoulder away from Mina and turned to face her. "What?" she whispered. "What did she say?"

Mina knitted her fingers together in her lap. She didn't meet Evelyn's eyes.

"She saw him on the day of the murders. Going out on his sailboat with the Cliffside Trio."

"He was their sailing instructor. Of course he was with them that day."

"The detectives Mom talked to...they said...she was their last witness. To see them alive, I mean."

Suddenly their spot at the base of the cliff didn't feel cozy—it felt claustrophobic.

"I'm his alibi," Evelyn said. "I know what he was doing that night."

"But Mom saw him at about seven thirty." Mina gulped. "And their deaths were estimated to be between seven and nine o'clock. Didn't you tell me you were with your dad that whole time? You have to admit that the timing is suspicious."

Evelyn couldn't believe what she was hearing. "You...you helped me. I kept your secret for six years. Because I trusted you. Because even when we didn't talk at all, I remembered that you were the only one who believed me."

"I did!" Mina's voice rose. "I promise you, Evelyn, I wouldn't have helped you if I didn't believe you. But knowing this changes things. And it's got me wondering if maybe there's a reason you're seeing those same ghosts again and again, instead of the one that absorbed them. If maybe it's because we're the ones who made it impossible for them to get justice."

"He didn't do it." Evelyn was crying. She didn't even know when she'd started, only that she couldn't stop. "He didn't fuck-ing do it, okay?"

But what if he did?

It was a thought Evelyn had buried so deep, she'd forgotten

she'd ever had it at all. She hated that she was thinking it now. Mina was right: It didn't line up. And the police had *proof* of that. No wonder they hadn't bought her alibi.

"I know he's your dad. But I think we need to at least consider the possibility of his…involvement."

Evelyn had spent a long time honing her survival mechanisms as her ecosystem changed in ways she couldn't control or understand. She'd been miserable, sure, but she'd endured. And she'd chosen to try to change those mechanisms for Mina, despite the warning signs, because she'd thought the two of them understood each other.

Obviously, she'd been horribly wrong.

"We?" Evelyn swiped at a tear on her cheek. "There is no *we* anymore, seeing as you've decided exactly what you think about my family. I guess I'm your biggest mistake yet."

"That's not true," Mina protested. "I stood up to Mom. She said you were dangerous, and I defended you—"

"I don't need you to defend me." Evelyn's oldest survival mechanism of all was kicking in—her Mackenzie temper. "What I need are people who believe me. And you've made it very clear you aren't one of them."

"But I—I—"

"Look me in the eyes right now and say you're a hundred percent sure he's innocent."

"A hundred is—is a lot—"

"That's what I thought." Evelyn got to her feet, brushed the sand from her jeans. Her scrying focus glowed through her tote bag. For a moment she heard whispers again, but she pushed them away. She was far too mad at the living right now to worry about the dead. "You know your mother lies, right?"

"That's why I'm here." Mina rose to her feet, too. She looked utterly undone. "Because she lied. Because I needed some space."

"So, let me get this straight," Evelyn said. "She told you that she'd been deceiving you about curses and demons for most of your life. She told you I was dangerous, when I wouldn't be a medium at all if not for *her* summoning instructions. And then she told you that she thinks my dad is a killer. But out of everything she said... *that's* what you chose to fixate on?"

"No— I— It isn't like that."

"I think it is." Evelyn glared at her. "You're accusing my father of a triple murder because you can't handle the thought that your mother is the one with all the secrets. You think you're standing up to her, but all you've done is play right into her hands. Like you always do. You're too smart to fall for her bullshit. Or at least I thought you were."

Mina's face shut down then. Walls up. Expression completely neutral. When she spoke, it was cold and careful, as if the last month had never happened at all.

"I'm sorry you're upset about your father, but you don't know anything about my relationship with my mother. Don't project your denial onto me."

"My denial?" Evelyn was furious. "You're too far gone, Zanetti. And I'm done trying to help you see how messed up your life is."

She didn't look back at Mina as she walked toward the

parking lot and scooped up her longboard. Back by the party, her new friends laughed and danced as the bonfire cast wild, beautiful shadows across the sand.

Evelyn turned away from all of it and strode off into the darkness.

Chapter Twenty

The full moon hung above Evelyn like a watchful, wide-open eye as she skated home, her longboard swerving erratically across the pavement. She was angry in a way that felt dangerous. Most of the time, she was quick to explode and quick to apologize, but this fuse felt different—a long-buried slow burn that was finally ready to explode in a conflagration of fury.

She was angry with Mina, for being so easy to manipulate. Angry with Stella, for planting those ideas in Mina's head.

But most of all, she was angry with herself.

Because if what Stella had said was true, about that timing...it didn't line up with her alibi. Which meant she couldn't be sure her father was innocent. Not completely. And she didn't know how to live with the possibility that she might have single-handedly destroyed three families' ability to get justice for their children.

She'd pulled out her phone before she left the Cliffside Beach parking lot and texted Nick that she'd been at a party and it had gone badly, then called him. Because he still believed her. Because she needed to hear someone else say it. But she'd regretted the text immediately and canceled the call before he picked up. She couldn't do that to him, to both of them. Evelyn felt so pathetic for pretending she was stronger by herself when it so obviously wasn't true. When even after Mina had betrayed her trust, she was still seeking out the help of someone else who'd hurt her.

Evelyn was blinking back tears when she took a turn too hard. Her board grinded against the curb, then careened out from under her. The next thing she knew, the right side of her body was screaming with pain. She braced her palms against the pavement and pushed into a crouch. Her leg was a wreck, covered in skid marks that bled through the holes in her jeans. Gravel and bits of fabric were stuck in the wounds. Evelyn clumsily attempted to gouge them out, gasping in agony. Her shoulder throbbed, and blood trickled down her arm beneath her velvet crop top.

At least she'd worn a helmet. She was scratched and bruised, but she'd survive. Evelyn reached into her tote bag for her scrying focus and was surprised to find it intact. Then she scrabbled for her phone, frowned at the cracked screen, and stood up. Her longboard lay on its side a few feet away like a wounded animal, the wheels spinning uselessly.

Evelyn took stock of the damage: destroyed grip tape. New scratches in the plywood. But she was pretty sure it still worked. She hauled the board under her arm and limped the rest of the way home.

Her house looked abandoned. No lights shone from inside

the windows, and the roof sagged dangerously low over the porch, as if it were about to collapse.

Evelyn wanted a shower; she needed first aid. But that would have to wait.

She braced herself and opened the door.

Inside, the only light came from the TV, which buzzed like a fly in the living room corner. Greg Mackenzie sat where he always did, staring blankly at the screen. He looked more like a ghost than that blue-tinged spirit had—a mere shade of the parent he'd once been, unshaven and unkempt with red-rimmed eyes. To Evelyn's surprise, Meredith sat on the couch. She tapped absently on her laptop, headphones slotted neatly over her pixie cut. It was almost normal.

They both looked up as she walked through the hallway. Meredith reacted first, pulling off her headphones and shoving the laptop to the side.

"Evelyn," she gasped. "What happened to you?"

"I fell off my board. I'll be fine."

"You're hurt." Her father rose from his chair. "There's a first aid kid under the sink. Meredith, can you—"

"On it."

"I said, I'll be fine," Evelyn protested, but her father had already helped her into the kitchen. She didn't realize how much pain she was in until there was a chair to fall into.

In a moment, Meredith was back with the first aid kit. A mixture of warmth and sadness rose in Evelyn as her father and her sister pulled out bandages and peroxide—this was the closest the Mackenzies had felt to a family in a very long time.

"You need to fix those up before they get infected," her dad said. "Do you two remember when you played in those tide pools?"

"And then didn't tell you we'd gotten all scratched up because we weren't supposed to play there?" Meredith asked.

"And the cuts got all swollen and gross?" The tide pools were one of Evelyn's first memories. Her father had sat beside her and pointed out the limpets and snails going about their business in their tiny pocket of water. She'd been fascinated. And then she'd persuaded Meredith to wade in with her and sliced up her feet on barnacles. "I was four. Meredith was nine. We know how this stuff works now— Ouch!"

The peroxide stung, but Evelyn did her best to bear it with minimal outbursts. She wasn't always successful.

"Where did you learn to swear like that?" Meredith asked.

"Both of you," Evelyn mumbled. "It's a family trait."

Her father winced at that, and Meredith looked a little downcast, too.

"Well, I'm glad you came home," he said, as Evelyn tucked the last scrape beneath a Band-Aid. "And I'm glad you wore your helmet. I know you think they look ridiculous, but—"

"They save lives, I know, I know."

Greg had told her as much dozens of times. He was vigilant about safety. She looked at him now, closing up the first aid kit, and tried not to think about how easily those large, square hands could wrap around someone's neck and push them underwater.

It felt disgusting. It felt impossible. But she still couldn't get Mina's words out of her head.

"Dad. I want to talk to you about something," she blurted.

Meredith leaned against the sink, looking intrigued. "Should I leave?"

Evelyn knew her sister had doubts of her own. But this concerned all three of them, and if the situation was flipped, she'd want to stay. "No."

"What's going on?" her father asked.

"Um." Evelyn's throat was dry. This wasn't like any of the other scary conversations she'd had with her father—from her grades slipping (ended badly) to coming out (ended fine) to her getting caught sneaking out to attend a soccer team party (ended in mild fatherly amusement).

"I know you kept things from me when I was younger," she began. "To protect me. Because I was a kid. But...I'm not. A kid, I mean, not really, not anymore. And I have questions."

"Kept things from you?" Her father's brow furrowed. "What kind of things?"

"Things about...that summer."

Greg Mackenzie's face changed in an instant. So did Meredith's. She pushed off the counter and went to stand beside Evelyn while Greg backed away from them both. The doorway behind him framed his hunched shoulders, his thin, weary face.

"I have nothing to say about that summer," he said flatly.

"Not even to tell me you had nothing to do with it?"

"What's the point?" His eyes were haunted and sunken, his thin gray hair almost white in the fluorescent lighting. There was something frail about him that Evelyn had never noticed before. "I've said my piece. They named me a person of interest, sure, but they never charged me with anything. I..." He shook his head. "I would never hurt anyone—I mean, hell, I liked Jesse. He was a good guy. And the other two were my best students."

"Don't say his name," Meredith snarled. "Don't you fucking dare."

"I've given you a lot of leeway here, Meredith." The threat in Greg's voice made Evelyn tense up. If they started screaming now, she would break. Maybe she already had, back at the beach. "You know as well as I do that the police would have taken me in if they'd been able to tie me to the crime. My name is clear. I let you back into my house because I thought you'd finally accepted that."

Meredith didn't look happy about it, but she nodded. And Evelyn understood that if she said what she'd come here to say, it would change their family forever. But she couldn't keep it in.

"But there *is* something tying you to the crime," she said. "A witness."

Greg's gaze sharpened. "How did you hear about that?"

But it was Meredith's tone, Meredith's posture, that frightened Evelyn the most. "What witness?"

Evelyn had wondered for a long time if learning the truth about her father would drown them all, but maybe it was drowning them anyway. A waterline that kept rising ever so slowly until they'd all sunk beneath it.

"You just told us they had nothing," Meredith continued. "You've told me that for years, you fucking—"

"They *do* have nothing. I gave the kids their sailing lesson that day, then went home to see Evelyn."

"But you came home a little after eight," Evelyn said. "The

witness saw you in the boat with them at seven thirty. Their estimated time of death is between seven and nine thirty— and when you got back around eight, you said you'd finished work 'around seven.' I told the police you were home with me, but there's a window there where I can't cover you. I...I lied for you. I buried it for years because it hurt too much to think about, but I *lied for you*."

Meredith let out a long, low chuckle. "Shit, Greg," she said. "I thought you had Evelyn wrapped around your little finger. Guess she isn't your alibi anymore."

"Dad didn't brainwash me," Evelyn snapped. "But I do want to know what really happened that night. From him, not from anyone else."

Greg winced. "It's true, I've never told you this," he said. "Because I know how it sounds. But the town can say what they want—I didn't do anything to those kids except give them a ride. They were all students in my summer sailing class who asked for a lift across the bay to Sand Dollar Cove after class. I said yes and dropped them off. That's the last I saw of them. Someone saw me in the boat, and after everything that happened..."

"It didn't look good."

"Exactly." Her father sighed. "There was unknown DNA found on the bodies, but there was also mine. From the life jackets I had them all wear."

"But—but that's just circumstantial," Evelyn protested. "Easily explained. And you have no motive."

"That's what I told them. But it doesn't matter," Greg said, his voice hollow. "The town decided I was guilty six years ago. And people in Cliffside Bay don't like to change their minds." He gestured at Meredith, who shook her head.

"I've seen the docking records," Meredith said. "How long you were out in that boat with them, and how long it was until you came back. It's very quick. But there's still that time unaccounted for between then and your alibi with Evelyn. And the fact that you lied to both of us, that you let her lie for you when she was a child…"

"I just told you the truth." Greg's voice broke on the last word. "But after everything this town has taken from me… after you and Siobhan…I didn't want it to take Evelyn, too. She's all I have left."

Evelyn stared helplessly between them.

Do you think he did it?

For years, she'd needed to believe the answer was unequivocally no. Now she could no longer pretend it was that simple. And although the idea of wading into that doubt was terrifying, turning back to denial felt worse. She had crumbled a dozen times before. And just like the organisms in the intertidal zone, she'd learned to adapt. To survive.

"I'm not leaving you, Dad," she whispered. "But if you want us to believe you, I need to know you've told us the whole truth. We can't just keep dancing around it. All it's doing is hurting us."

"That *is* the whole truth," Greg said. "I won't plead my case any further. I've spent too much time trying to convince people who have already made up their minds."

He left then, disappearing into the dark hallway. His footsteps rang out on the stairs a moment later.

Evelyn turned to her sister, ready for a fight. But Meredith seemed surprisingly calm.

"So," her sister said. "You doubt him."

"I've got questions," Evelyn said. "I'm not sure that counts as doubting. Like you said, the boat docking records wouldn't give him enough time. And why sand dollars? They aren't even from Long Island—" She paused, shuddering. "I don't want to think about him like this. But if it's what I have to do...I'll do it."

"Baby steps." Meredith reached out a hand to pull Evelyn up from the chair. Everything still stung.

"I just don't understand," Evelyn said. "If you're so sure he did it...why are you even here?"

"I'm not," Meredith said. "Sure he did it, I mean. But being unsure is enough to make me uneasy." Meredith sighed, shook her head. "I never thought I'd see you confront him like that. Where did that come from?"

Mina. The thought crested in her mind, crashing across everything else. It had come from Mina. Denial. Secrets. Lies. Maybe they weren't in such different situations after all.

Mina had provoked her—and she, in turn, had provoked Mina.

It came to her all at once. The full moon. The things Evelyn had said to Mina, about her falling for Stella's lies time and again. The concept of meeting with the ghost was so dangerous, Evelyn had never seriously considered it. But Mina had.

Oh no. Oh *no.*

"I have to go." She left the kitchen behind and walked into the hallway. Her tote bag was crumpled carelessly on the floor. She fished around inside until she found her scrying focus, then looped the cord around her neck. The shell was heavy and surprisingly warm against her skin.

"You're going out again?" Meredith asked. "You're all cut up."

"What are you going to do, give me a curfew?" Evelyn didn't stick around to see if Meredith had a response. She grabbed her helmet and her longboard, then headed out the door.

Chapter Twenty-One

Mina did not consider herself the type of person who got angry. As a general rule, anger exhausted her—it led to nothing but regrettable decisions and illogical nonsense. But Mina was angry tonight, which was exactly how she found herself standing on the rocks at the edge of Sand Dollar Cove.

She wasn't in denial. She wasn't being manipulated. Evelyn was wrong. And to prove it, Mina was going to do what no one else could: face down the ghost.

She'd visited Uncle Dom's house for supplies instead of heading back to her own. She'd been worried about encountering errant family members, but when she ran into Sergio in the kitchen, he seemed intrigued by the idea of her going rogue.

"I totally support you kicking some ghost butt, but be careful," he said, through mouthfuls of a PB&J. "Remember what happened at the community center?"

Mina glared at him. "It won't go that way this time."

Sergio waved his partially eaten sandwich in the air. "If you say so."

She half expected him to try and come with her, but he didn't offer and she didn't ask. Which was fine, because she definitely didn't need any help.

The beach was empty and strangely silent. The only sounds were Mina's feet crunching across the ground and the high tide lapping at the shoreline. The full moon glowed in the cloudless sky, and although Mina understood there were scientific reasons for why the tides rose so high and sank so low in its presence, she liked to imagine they were quaking in awe of something so magnificent.

Mina couldn't help but feel nervous as she knelt on the rocky shoreline and got to work. She drew a small, circular trench on the driest part of the beach she could find, then sprinkled an unbroken line of salt into it. When she dipped her bowl in the ocean, her warding necklace grew hot against her skin. Mina gritted her teeth and set her makeshift scrying receptacle down in the middle of the circle, then placed candles around it. Their flames shook and shivered in the night air as she lit them one by one.

The air smelled of salt and smoke; the sand was wet against her bare knees. The moon regarded her from above, a great glowing orb that looked eerily like Stella's new scrying focus. Her hands shook as she touched the warding necklace. She knew what it contained now—more of her mother's secrets. She tugged the pendant over her head and lowered it into the bowl, then yanked her hands away.

As soon as she'd taken off the necklace, the sand dollar on

her wrist began to glow. Voices murmured in her mind, indistinct but vaguely alarmed. They were louder and crisper than they'd been back at the pool. She could even make out a word or two—*lost; cold; where?* Their confusion made her heart ache.

"You wanted to meet with me," she said. "I'm here."

In answer, the water in the bowl began to ripple, a small-scale mimicry of the ocean before her. A tiny ball of blue light coiled around the warding necklace. The voices grew louder, and Mina felt that pull again. It started at the sand dollar and wound up her arm, through her shoulder, then her chest. Her vision grew fuzzy, and suddenly the waves crashing on the shore beside her makeshift summoning felt like reaching hands.

Her bowl was so tiny. She didn't understand how she could expect to hear the spirits properly with such a small vessel, when such a large one waited right there. All it would take was a few steps and...

"Stop!"

The voice cut through all the others. It was low and a little husky and unmistakably belonged to someone *living*. The pull lessened slightly, and Mina turned, momentarily distracted.

A familiar figure stood perhaps thirty feet away. Her dark, wavy hair was wild, blowing every which way; a seashell hung around her neck. She ate up the distance between them in great, furious strides.

Evelyn Mackenzie was the kind of girl who knew how to be angry. Emotions blew through her like winds at sea; they buffeted her sails, and sometimes, when they were too strong, they threatened to pull her under. Yet she never sank. Mina did not understand how Evelyn could wade so easily into such treacherous waters while Mina could only ever skim the surface in her mind's eye. Submerging herself would be too painful, too much—the shock alone might be enough to send her permanently off course. Tonight proved that, if nothing else.

"Zanetti," Evelyn snapped, kneeling beside her. An eyeliner wing was smeared across her cheek; Band-Aids crisscrossed the skin peeking through her ripped jeans. "What the hell are you doing?"

"Breaking my curse," Mina said coldly. "The spirits of the drowning summer victims will come when I call. And they will tell me who killed them before I break our bond forever. Even if I have to exorcise them to get the truth out."

"Ghosts. Curses. Exorcisms. Great." Evelyn eyed Mina's summoning setup with obvious concern. The threads of light around the necklace had grown, filling the bowl with glowing blue-green tendrils. "I know you're pissed at me, but have you considered that this might be a colossally terrible idea?"

The voices wailed in Mina's mind again, the sand dollar on her wrist pulsed painfully, and for a moment she thought she might faint. But then she breathed in the crisp night air, and the smell of salt brought her back to reality.

"I am completely in control."

"No one actually in control has ever said that."

"If you don't like what I'm doing, you can leave." Mina pulled a penknife out of her purse and held her hand over the bowl. She'd thought this through. Giving the spirits her blood would complete the conditions Stella had given her for an exorcism. Just because her mother hadn't been able to do this didn't mean she couldn't.

"No!" Evelyn grabbed her wrist. "You're going to call the drowning summer victims, and they'll bring that ghost with them—"

"That's exactly what I'm trying to do, yes. If you'd just let go—"

"I won't." Evelyn pulled Mina's hand away from the bowl and locked eyes with her. Mina was stunned by the sheer emotion in her gaze. It made her want to drop the knife and grip Evelyn's hand the same way Evelyn was clutching her wrist, and that pulled at her in a different but no less powerful way than the ocean before her.

The sand dollar on Mina's arm throbbed beneath Evelyn's fingers. She wondered how it had come to this—Evelyn trying to hold her back, while she attempted to charge forward.

"Fine." Mina dropped the knife onto the sand. Evelyn released her grip and hastily scooped it up.

"I'm sorry I had to restrain you," she said. "I was worried."

Mina bit the inside of her mouth as hard as she could. Pain coursed through her, followed by the taste of salt and copper.

"You should be," she said, and then she leaned over the bowl and spit her blood inside.

What happened next happened very quickly.

The surf rushed forward, clawing at the sand. It splashed through the salt circle and over the top of the bowl, tipping the contents into the ocean. Mina lunged forward, grasping for the warding pendant, but Evelyn got there first. She snatched it up and clutched it to her chest, then turned to Mina, eyes wide.

"What the hell did you do?" she whispered.

Dread unspooled in Mina's stomach alongside the blue light that spiraled into the ocean, spreading outward like a trail of bioluminescence. The pull returned, stronger this time, and Mina felt as if someone had grabbed her hands and yanked her upward. She didn't remember kicking off her shoes or striding forward, only the cool relief of the surf against her bare feet.

The voices in her mind grew louder still, and tendrils of bluish green wove around her ankles. Everywhere they touched felt the same way the sand dollar did—awake. *Alive.* She stared at her wrist and realized the light from the sand dollar was spreading through her arm, pulsing softly. It didn't hurt anymore. Instead, it emitted a sort of pleasant, numbing warmth.

"Come back." Evelyn's voice was faint, distorted. Mina supposed she was on the beach behind her. She didn't think her body would let her turn to check. "Please, I—"

"It's all right." Mina heard her voice as if from a great distance. The water tugged Mina forward, but it stayed shallow even as she ventured beyond the surf. Although the tide was high, the ocean was receding far faster than should have been possible. "This is where I belong."

As if in answer, three figures began to shimmer in the water before her, their bodies bluish green. The sand dollars on their eyes pulsed alongside the one on Mina's wrist, and their lips spread into three wide, identical smiles.

There you are, said one clear, calm voice inside Mina's skull. *Are you finally listening?*

"Evelyn?" called out a completely different voice. "What are you doing here?"

Another person appeared in Mina's peripheral vision. The

voice in her mind fell silent, as if startled. Evelyn sprinted to the side, swearing, as the figure stepped closer.

It was Nick Slater. Evelyn's ex-boyfriend.

"You need to get out of here." Evelyn reached for Nick's arm. "How did you even find me?"

"The beach is public property," Nick said defensively. "Also, you texted me saying a party had gone off the rails, and then you called me, so I used Find My Friends because you still haven't taken me off your friend list— *Jesse?*"

The grip on Mina loosened for just a moment. She whipped her head back to see that the three figures in the surf had solidified. They were still a bit fuzzy around the edges, but even with the sand dollars, they were unmistakably the Cliffside Trio. And Nick was staring at them in horror.

Someone who knew absolutely nothing about any of this had come face-to-face with the ghost of his dead brother. It was a nightmare scenario.

Mina heard Nick's panicked voice, heard Evelyn try to respond, but they were already fading out. All she knew was that she had to stop this. It took all her concentration, but she stepped backward once. Then again, the water splashing against her legs as if in protest. She could leave the ocean and cut this cord. She was so close.

The ghosts' smiles flickered, then changed into three identical snarls. A glint of orange seeped into the sand dollars over their eyes and spilled across their faces, like tears. The voices in her mind began to hiss with panic as the light slid down their shoulders, their torsos. A stab of pain shot through Mina's arm, and her sand dollar glowed orange.

When she looked up from her wrist, the water behind the spirits was rising into the sky. Mina understood a moment before it crested across the horizon that the ocean had pulled back to make a wave.

This time, when it bowled her over, there was no Stella to grab her hand and pull her out. There was only a deluge of pain and panic, blue and green and orange light swirling around her limbs. Everywhere it touched her burned like acid.

She screamed, then choked on a mouthful of rotting seaweed. And then, just like when she'd knelt beside the pool, the scene around her *changed*.

Mina was no longer underwater. No longer on the beach at all. Instead, a vision unfurled before her like a movie set, a large living room paneled entirely in wood, with giant shaggy rugs and green and blue couches. She didn't recognize the furnishings at all, but the shape of the space seemed oddly familiar: the A-frame roof, the sloping beams.

In front of her was a girl. She was about Mina's age, white, short, thin, wearing a pleated skirt with a large plastic belt over it and a cropped knit top. Her hair was long, light brown, and perfectly straight, pressed so flat against her head that it obscured half her face. She stared at Mina with solemn brown eyes, then held out her hand.

A sand dollar rested on her open palm.

"Take it."

The voice was the same one that had spoken in her mind back on the beach.

"It's you," she gasped. "You're the ghost. Why—who—"

"Take it," the girl repeated. Mina stepped forward uneasily.

The shell flickered, and for a moment it wasn't a shell at all—it was a white piece of plastic, smeared with blood. Then it flickered again, and it was a sand dollar once more.

"What happens if I say no?"

"You can't." Her voice was soft, feathery, but when Mina glanced up again, those brown eyes were gone. In their place were two more sand dollars. A thick fluid the color of bile seeped from one of them, then the other, clogging the holes and spilling down her cheeks.

"Take it," she snarled once more, and Mina screamed again as the world dissolved around her.

Chapter Twenty-Two

Evelyn hadn't known where her night was headed when she'd left to try to stop Mina, but she never would have predicted it ending in Nick Slater's living room. She perched unhappily on the sofa beside Mina and glared at the giant silver orb that still hung in the sky, spilling light across the ocean. Evelyn knew it was unfair to blame all her problems on the moon, but right now, it was tempting.

"I need to know what I saw on the beach." Nick had chosen to sit in the same anchor-studded armchair he'd used the last time she was here. "You owe me that much, Evie."

"I know." Evelyn glanced to her left, where Mina looked utterly miserable in one of Nick's spare soccer uniforms. She'd gotten off easy—Evelyn had been forced to replace *her* ruined clothes with a pair of CLIFFSIDE CRABS sweatpants and a corresponding V-neck. The mascot jokes truly did write themselves. "Mina, are you ready?"

Mina looked between them a bit unsteadily. She'd knotted

one of Nick's soccer headbands around her sand dollar mark as a sort of shield, but that wasn't enough to muffle the bluish-green glow emanating from her wrist. "Not really. But I don't think that matters anymore."

After the wave swept all three of them into the ocean, Evelyn clawed her way to shore. It hadn't been easy—the voices in her mind had been harsh and demanding, and the water had folded around her in a suffocating embrace. But the shell around her neck had kept it all from overwhelming her. She'd emerged with seaweed tangled in her hair, her scrapes and bruises stinging from the saltwater, to find a semiconscious Mina and a bewildered Nick sprawled on the sand.

Mina was *glowing*. Orange starbursts flared from the sand dollar on her wrist, and bluish-green light snaked across her torso, tiny explosions that moved from her neck and shoulders down to her palms. She was lit up from the inside, incandescent and otherworldly, and for a moment Evelyn had been unable to do anything but stare in awe. Then Mina began to cry out and thrash on the sand, like a fish pulled from the waves.

Evelyn had run to her, panicked—but within seconds, the light beneath Mina's skin began to fade, and the pain had faded along with it. Or at least that was what Mina told them once she could speak again, but Evelyn wasn't sure she believed it.

She'd wanted to press Mina for answers and theories, but there had been no time for that. They had more immediate problems to deal with.

The ghosts were gone, but Nick had already seen them. And since his parents were in Martha's Vineyard for the week (Evelyn had rolled her eyes) and not currently furious with their child, his house had been the obvious option for a regrouping. Plus, all three of them had even been able to clean up a little.

Normally Evelyn would have delighted in taking full advantage of what she'd always called the robot bathroom. But she'd been far too worried about Mina's summoning and Nick's questions to pay much attention to the heated floors or the voice-activated shower commands.

Back in the living room, she studied Nick's face, sharpened with pain, and felt a deep swell of regret.

"Those three . . . things. In the water. Those were my brother and his friends." Nick didn't say it like a question, but Mina answered it anyway.

"Yes," she said. "Well, yes and no. Your brother as you know him is gone, Nick, but . . . that was his spirit."

"So ghosts are real, and . . ." Nick stilled. "And my brother's one of them."

"Exactly."

"How?"

Mina's eyes darted toward Evelyn in a clear signal for help. Mina might have been the medium's daughter, but Evelyn was the only common ground between all three of them.

"We're mediums," Evelyn said. "Ghosts talk to us, and we try to listen. Lately, Jesse, Colin, and Tamara have been, uh . . . reaching out."

"I don't understand," Nick murmured. "If his spirit can talk, why wouldn't he talk to me?"

Mina cleared her throat uncomfortably. "He most likely would have tried under different circumstances. It's quite common for spirits to attempt contact with the loved ones they've left behind. It's just that in this particular case, Jesse's spirit may not have full control over his actions."

"What do you mean, he doesn't have full control?"

Evelyn gulped. "You know ghosts are real now. Well. Demons are real, too, at least potentially."

She and Mina explained that, to the best of their knowledge, the Cliffside Trio were being slowly absorbed by another spirit that was beginning to hurt the living in addition to the dead. That they were caught up in the curse this ghost had cast on Mina. That it was all a mystery they were both trying desperately to solve.

When they were finished, Nick looked fairly shell-shocked.

"Does it hurt?" he asked shakily. "Jesse, I mean, and the others—does it hurt them?"

"We don't know," Mina said.

"And your curse... is that why you're glowing?" he continued, gesturing toward Mina.

"Maybe." Mina's hand strayed nervously to the headband around her wrist.

"How did you even *get* cursed by this ghost?"

Evelyn winced. "Well. Uh. I might have... we might have... summoned this ghost at one point. Without knowing what we were dealing with."

"You can do that?" Nick frowned.

"By accident," Evelyn said. "Neither of us had any idea what we were really doing. We were kids, or... or at least, we were kids the first time."

"The first time?" Nick's voice was dangerous. "Don't lie to me, Evie. This is my brother. I need to know."

Oh, this was going to suck. But as soon as Nick had shown up on the beach, Evelyn had known on some level that the truth was going to come out.

So she told him everything. About both summers. Even the parts that didn't make her look so great.

"You used a ghost to make sure no one found out about our cheating?" Nick looked ill.

"It wasn't my finest moment, okay?"

"And what about six years ago?"

"I believed my dad was innocent," she said, guilt twisting in her as she thought about what she'd discovered earlier that night. "I thought it was the right thing to do."

"But what if..." Nick trailed off.

"What if he did it?" Evelyn sighed. "I wish I could tell you I knew for sure that he didn't. But...he's my father. And I was ten."

"I was ten, too," Nick said. "When my brother died. And I dated you for four months, and you never said a word about this? You never thought, *Wait, this is a really big secret to keep from my boyfriend?*"

Evelyn tried not to crumple beneath the force of his accusatory gaze. "I promised Mina I would never talk about it."

"So you prioritized someone you hadn't spoken to in six years over someone who—who—" He broke off, shaking his head. "I don't understand."

"Don't make this about our relationship. That's not fair."

"What isn't fair is the way you two think you have the right to mess with my brother's spirit any more than you already have."

"We're not messing with spirits, we're trying to save your

brother's soul," Mina said sharply. "Along with the other two
people who died with him. Who also have families, who also
don't deserve to suffer."

"Well, he's my brother," Nick countered. "So if you're going
to keep doing this, then...then I want in."

Mina blinked. "Excuse me?"

Evelyn couldn't hide the panic in her voice. "You were on
that beach tonight. You saw how dangerous this is."

"I don't care." Nick set his jaw. "I can't know he's still out
there in some form, suffering, and not do something about it.
So either you let me join your weird supernatural club, or I'll
try talking to his ghost on my own. And something tells me you
really don't want me to do that."

Evelyn wanted to scream. The moon still glowed behind
Nick's head, and the soft lights he'd flipped on illuminated the
pictures of Jesse above the giant staircase. She knew it was just
her imagination, but she felt as if all those tiny versions of him
were watching her. Asking her what the hell she thought she
was doing trying to help the dead, when all of her attempts to
fix things had only upset the living.

"Welcome to the team," she spat out.

Nick's smile did a poor job of masking his fury. "Perfect."

Evelyn and Mina both wound up in the guest bedroom. Neither
of them wanted to go home, and sleeping in Jesse's old room
or Nick's parents' bed was definitely not an option. So instead
they sat side by side on the white, plushy guest bed, staring at
Evelyn's cracked phone. Somehow, it had survived the saltwater,

and they'd both used it to text their respective family members in a feeble attempt to head off how much trouble they would be in when they got home.

"Stella's going to kill me," Mina mumbled. "But I'm unsure I care."

Evelyn was pretty sure her father and Meredith would be upset, too, although their anger only frightened her when it was directed toward each other.

"Are you okay?" she asked, thinking of those orange lights coiled beneath Mina's skin. "What—what *happened* to you tonight?"

"I'm not sure. I want to talk about it. But first, I owe you an apology."

"No, you don't." Evelyn turned to face her. "*I'm* the one who's sorry. Now Nick's wrapped up in all of this, and it's all my fault again...."

"It isn't." Mina's voice was firm, but not unkind. "I accused your father of unspeakable things, and you *still* came to try to help me. I'm grateful—and embarrassed."

"Thanks." Evelyn's gaze strayed to Mina's wrist, still covered with the headband, still glowing bluish green. "Did the ghost do...that?"

"Yes. Well, I think so." Mina explained what had happened to her, the vision, the voices, the way the water had pulled her forward. Evelyn realized once she was finished that Mina had made no attempt to hide her fear.

"So you think that was her?" Evelyn asked. "That girl. You think she's the ghost?"

"She must be." Mina sighed. "But that's not all I'm worried

about. Obviously, my sand dollar glows when I communicate with the dead. It pulls me toward them, it creates a channel between us. What does that sound like to you?"

Oh. "Like a scrying focus."

"Exactly." Mina leaned backward on the bed and stared at the blank wall. "I'm starting to wonder if perhaps I couldn't find an object to channel my focus through because I already have one inside me. And it's stuck on a single channel, like my mother said."

"But my scrying focus makes the dead easier to manage," Evelyn said. "Your sand dollar mark seems to do the exact opposite."

"I know. But you have to admit, something strange is going on here."

"You sound incredibly calm for someone who's got a possible channel to the dead embedded in her wrist."

"I'm too tired to panic," Mina said matter-of-factly.

Evelyn glanced nervously at the warding necklace sitting on the night table, which she'd grabbed back on the beach. She didn't want to tell Mina to put it on again, but she wondered if maybe that would help. When she looked back at Mina, the other girl was staring at her wrist again.

"Can I see the mark?" she asked.

Mina hesitated, then nodded. "If you want." She tugged her makeshift bracelet away, then extended her hand, palm up. Evelyn caught it and raised it slightly, inspecting the sand dollar etched into Mina's skin. It was still glowing slightly, bluish-green speckles elevating what could have been a tattoo from a distance into something far stranger.

"It's kind of beautiful," Evelyn said. "Does it hurt?"

"Not anymore." Mina's voice sounded a bit high. "It was incredibly painful on the beach, though."

"I'm sorry." She curled her thumb around the curve of Mina's wrist and touched the sand dollar. Mina let out a soft, startled exhale and tipped her head up. Their gazes locked, and for a moment there was nothing in the world but Mina's surprised stare and slightly parted lips.

Evelyn hurriedly pulled her hand away.

"It's late," she said, practically leaping off the bed. "I think Nick said there was a cot in the closet. I can sleep there, if you want—"

"Don't be ridiculous. After the night you've had, you deserve a bed." Mina patted the duvet. "There's plenty of room in here for both of us, if you're comfortable with it."

Evelyn's brain turned to static. She had no idea what to think, or say. All she knew was that the idea of sharing a bed with Mina right now made her feel like she was about to catch on fire.

"Um," Evelyn managed. "I . . . um."

Mina knew she was bi, she told herself. They'd talked about it. She wouldn't ask to share the bed if she was uncomfortable with that.

"I'm okay with it," Evelyn said finally.

The bed was big enough for both of them, but Evelyn was still overly conscious of the fact that any shift, any movement, could mean their legs brushing or their arms touching. Mina's exhaustion turned to slumber within minutes, but tired as she was, Evelyn couldn't fathom falling asleep.

Mina was right there. Right *there*. She had somehow managed to pass out while facing Evelyn, and her softened face felt like a truth she hadn't meant to tell—it was so vulnerable, so gentle. Evelyn replayed that moment she'd touched the sand dollar again and again. How Mina's gaze had coursed through her like an electric shock.

She rolled over as carefully as she could, until her body was facing away from Mina's. Until she was inches away from falling out of bed.

Evelyn couldn't delude herself any longer. She had a massive crush on Mina Zanetti.

Shit.

Chapter Twenty-Three

They met by the abandoned pool. Mina, Stella, Dom, Sergio—and Evelyn.

They settled uncomfortably on plastic chairs, scraping over salt. Mina watched the sun stream through the broken windows behind Stella's head. The floor looked even worse than the last time Mina had seen it, cracks spiderwebbing all the way to the edge of the pool. But now didn't seem like a good time to bring that up.

Mina had spent the four days since the full moon thoroughly grounded, stuck in her room without her phone or laptop. Evelyn took the warding necklace, so Mina couldn't be forced to put it back on, but her mother had put up extra defenses around the cottage. Mina hadn't been foolish enough to raise her questions about her glowing sand dollar or share what she'd seen of the ghost with Stella. Instead, she'd written down everything she could remember about the girl she'd seen, sketching her clothes and trying to recall as much as possible about the shape of the room. The A-frame roof, the couches, the carpets. A basic knowledge of fashion told her that the features lined up with the late seventies, but without her laptop, that was all she could manage.

The silver lining was the Zanetti Collection. Something about that night had unlocked a burst of inspiration that kept her free of boredom. She'd been thinking about the pollution in the Sound, about how fashion was a big part of climate change, and wondered how she could make something that wouldn't make things worse. Mina had worried Stella would take away her sewing machine and sketchbook, but her mother apparently didn't have it in her to be that cruel.

This morning, Stella had informed her that she and Dom had made a decision: Evelyn needed to be evaluated as a medium before they could proceed further. Now she sat in the chair beside Mina, her brown hair pulled back in a neat bun, dressed in a white collared blouse tucked into a skirt.

"You look...different," Mina murmured to her. "Are you all right?"

Evelyn stiffened in her chair. "I'm just trying to seem like someone your family won't hate."

"They don't hate you," Mina protested. "They just have some questions."

"Yeah, just like the detectives had some questions for my dad." Evelyn tried to smooth back a loose bit of hair. "Don't worry, Mina. You'll be fine."

"I'm not worried about me," Mina said, as across the circle, Uncle Dom cleared his throat.

"We've never needed to do anything like this before," Uncle Dom began uneasily. "We don't go looking for other mediums. It's something we've always kept in the family."

Beside him, Sergio let out a sardonic snort. Dom glared at him.

"I didn't go looking for this, either," Evelyn said. "Why would anyone want to?"

"Because of power." Stella had dressed in one of her grander outfits today, a pale green dress that fell to her ankles with billowing sleeves. Mina could feel her cold fury even from a distance. The two of them had barely spoken since Mina refused to tell her *anything* about the night of the full moon.

"Power?" Evelyn echoed. "I have no power here."

"On the contrary. We've made a list of your transgressions, Evelyn Mackenzie." Stella scrolled through her phone. "Item one: You utilized a spirit as a tool in order to advance your own self-interests approximately one month ago. Item two: You interfered in a murder investigation in much the same way six years ago, causing an obstruction of justice."

Mina remembered what Evelyn had said. That she wasn't scared of Stella. But the Evelyn sitting next to her didn't look brave and brash. She looked frightened.

"And item three," Stella continued. "You are directly responsible for my daughter's curse."

Evelyn winced at that, but said nothing.

"Do you deny any of this?" Dom asked.

Evelyn's face was utterly stricken. "No. I understand that I've messed up. But I promise you, the last thing I would ever want to do is hurt Mina. I would never have put her in danger on purpose. I—I wish they'd cursed me instead."

Stella's expression softened a little, and she lowered her phone to her lap. "I know you care about my daughter. But none of this would have ever happened without your interference.

All the sneaking around behind my back, those risky, ill-advised attempts to contact ghosts..." She flicked her gaze toward Mina. "They were incredibly dangerous."

"I understand," Evelyn said.

"Then are you willing to admit you're the cause of all this strife?"

Mina understood now. This wasn't an evaluation, it was a trial. And Stella and Dom had decided their verdict before they'd ever set foot in this room.

They were going to blame Evelyn for everything. And Evelyn was going to let them.

Mina couldn't let that happen. "Bullshit."

The word hit Stella and Dom like a slap, because Mina didn't swear. Not ever. But the Mina who didn't swear was the same Mina who sank her problems in a fake ocean. The same Mina who had to be perfect because she owed Stella everything.

She loved her mother. She always would. But there was a difference between gratitude and suffocating obligation.

"This isn't Evelyn's fault." Mina stood and pushed her chair back. It clattered to the floor behind her, weak yellowed plastic against the concrete. "It was my interference that pulled her into this world in the first place. My choice to investigate my sand dollar mark without telling you."

"She is still the catalyst for your curse, and the reason it's come back to torment you." Stella's foot tapped against one of the cracks in the concrete, and Mina wondered what would happen if they kept deepening, if the whole room would fall into the ocean. A whisper unfurled in the back of her mind, but as soon as she noticed the sound, it faded.

"We were ten when we summoned those spirits," Mina countered. "We made a mistake, and the only reason Evelyn made it again was because you chose to shield me from the truth instead of educating me. You can't just pin all this on her and expect things to go back to the way they were, because they never will. *I* never will."

For once, Stella didn't have a retort. She turned to her brother, who looked equally shocked.

"Well, damn." Sergio had been leaning back in his chair this whole time, assessing everyone with obvious interest. "I wish all our family gatherings were this interesting."

"Sergio," Dom growled. "Behave yourself."

"Why? So you can tell me it's only a matter of time before the dead start talking to me?" He rose from his seat, too, then kicked the chair over. It toppled pathetically into the pool. "They're never coming, Dad. Maybe you should be grateful you get a replacement medium instead of trying to piss her off, too."

He walked out of the room then, standing taller than Mina had ever seen him.

"Why did you invite him?" Stella demanded.

"I—I thought it would be a good lesson—"

"In what, exactly?" Stella shook her head, then turned back toward Mina and Evelyn. "It's true, Mina, that I should have told you the truth sooner. And Evelyn, I don't want you to feel as if you're being attacked here. I'm simply concerned about how all of us are going to handle this situation. Together."

A month ago, this would have sounded like a dream scenario. But Mina didn't trust her mother anymore. If she bent now, if she told Stella about her vision and her worries about being some kind of human scrying focus, Stella would find a way to suck her back in. And Mina needed to believe she was worth something when she wasn't tethered to her mother's side.

"I don't want to handle it together," she said. "You can ground me if you want, Mom. But this is my problem, and I'm going to solve it. Come on, Evelyn. I'm done having this conversation."

She reached out her hand, and after a moment of hesitation, Evelyn took it. They walked out of the basement together.

Mina knew she would collapse when she stopped moving, so she waited until they were all the way back up the stairs, in the main room of the Shorewell Community Center. There were a few other people milling around, mostly in athletic wear, since the community center was hosting a fitness class today. But none of them paid the two girls any mind.

"Oh," Mina murmured as she slumped down on a bench. Her heartbeat was going far too fast. "I don't know— I— What was that?"

Evelyn sat beside her and tugged her hair out of its bun. It tumbled around her shoulders, loose and wavy, accentuating the tiny cluster of freckles on her nose. Her lips parted in the kind of grin that made it impossible to look anywhere else.

"*That* was one of the most amazing things I've ever seen."

Mina choked out a laugh. "I don't understand why you didn't just tell them off yourself."

"Because they're your family," Evelyn said. "I want them to like me."

"Why would you care so much about them liking you? They're being terrible right now."

Evelyn gave her a look that Mina felt she should understand, but didn't. "Never mind," she said. "The point is, Zanetti, you're kind of a badass when you want to be."

"Hardly," Mina said. "I would never have been capable of that without you."

"What are you talking about? All I did in there was a bad job of not crying."

"Not what you did today. What you've done all summer."

Mina had spent a lifetime learning to be a calm sea, doing her best to block out anything that could make so much as a ripple. Because ripples became waves if left untended, and there was no place for that kind of disruption in her careful world.

Evelyn Mackenzie was no mere wave—she was the kind of storm that whipped an ocean into tall, impassable peaks. She'd spent the last month dredging up the flotsam of Mina's past until it floated on the surface, impossible to ignore.

The old Mina would have hated it. But the girl she was now understood for the first time how *alive* the sea was during a storm. How that wind and rain and lightning could change an ocean into something absolutely mesmerizing. Something beautiful.

After her burst of bravery, Mina was suddenly far too terrified to meet Evelyn's eyes. Instead, her gaze roamed the space behind her—the people setting up for their fitness class, the tall, A-frame roof that sloped above them with its thick support beams.

And then it finally clicked. Mina couldn't *believe* it had taken her so long to figure this out.

"Evelyn," she gasped. "That vision the ghost showed me . . . it was here. At the community center."

Chapter Twenty-Four

Evelyn hadn't had a friend over to her house in six years. But tonight, she didn't really have a choice. Nick's parents were back in town, and Mina's house was totally out of the question. Which meant all three of them had reconvened at her place after she and Mina left the community center.

"Come on," she said, hustling them through the front hallway. Neither Nick nor Mina had said a word about the condition of her home, but she could still imagine their judgment as they took in the peeling plaster, the splintered floorboards, the hallway light that had been busted for a month. Their landlord was pretty lax about repairs, so Evelyn had gotten used to it, but seeing it through someone else's eyes made her embarrassed all over again.

"Evelyn," said a familiar voice from the living room. "Aren't you going to introduce me to your friends?"

Evelyn swore under her breath. She'd hoped her father's devotion to his recliner and whatever was on TV would keep him from noticing the two extra people she'd brought into their home. But of course it hadn't.

"Mina, Nick, Dad," she said quickly. "Now you're introduced."

"Hold on." Her father raised a bushy eyebrow. "Mina Zanetti? I remember you. You two dressed up as dinosaur princesses for Halloween."

That was *not* what Evelyn had been expecting. Beside her, Nick let out a soft snort. "Dinosaur princesses?" There was a cautious note of amusement in his voice.

"I was the T. rex," Evelyn said. "Mina was a stegosaurus."

"We had crowns," Mina volunteered shyly.

"Those costumes always confused me," Greg said thoughtfully, and Evelyn knew exactly what he was about to say before the words came out his mouth. "The dinosaurs were supposedly best friends, but the stegosaurus only appeared in the Jurassic period, while T. rexes—"

"Were almost a hundred million years later, therefore they never could've existed simultaneously," Evelyn finished. "I know. So does Mina, probably. They were also princesses, so like . . . accuracy was definitely not the point."

Her father's mouth twitched with amusement. "Well, I know you," he said to Mina. "But you—you're Nick . . ."

"Slater." Nick's voice was barely above a whisper.

Greg went still in his recliner. The tension in the room had nearly evaporated, but now it thickened again. Evelyn had never told her father that she and Nick were dating, mostly because she'd wanted to avoid this exact moment. They were two environmental factors that, once combined, could destroy her ecosystem forever.

"We're going upstairs," she said hastily, gesturing down the hall. Nobody protested.

"I remember him being different when we were kids," Mina said after Evelyn had herded all three of them into her room and locked the door. "But...I don't know. He's not different in the way I expected him to be."

"What, because he didn't try to murder anyone in the living room?" The words burst out of her unbidden, as they so often did when she was tense. Evelyn winced and turned to Nick, who sat against the wall, his long legs extended across the ratty carpet. But instead of responding with an outburst of his own, he let out a short, surprised laugh.

"This is all so messed up," he said. "Mina's mom. Your dad. My brother."

"Hopefully it's a mess we can clean up," said Mina. "That girl's outfit and her home decor are both from the seventies. We need to look up who lived in the Shorewell Community Center back then."

Evelyn scrounged around her unmade bed for her laptop, then sat stiffly on the edge of the mattress, cursing the itchy blouse and skirt she'd worn to the community center. Nick stayed on the floor but pulled out his phone, while Mina, who still didn't have access to any electronics, paced around the room. Evelyn knew she was supposed to be searching for information, but she couldn't help watching as Mina knelt beside the snake cage in the corner. It was so weird to see her in Evelyn's physical space when she already took up so much room inside her head.

"I've never really thought about snakes as pets," Mina mused. "But...she's beautiful."

Evelyn flushed. "Thank you. I think she's showing off. She doesn't exactly get tons of visitors."

"I think it's weird," Nick volunteered, still tapping through his phone. "It's not a dog *and* you have to feed it dead mice."

Evelyn bit back a nasty *I know you don't like her*—he was coping too well with all this to mess it up.

"Dogs are carnivorous, too," she said instead, trying to sound casual.

Mina spoke again. "Can I hold her?"

Evelyn had never let anyone aside from Mr. Clark touch Clara, although it wasn't as if she'd had any takers. But Mina was looking at the snake with abject wonder, and Evelyn had learned by now that undisguised happiness was something Mina only showed on rare occasions.

"Yes," she said.

It was always a little nerve-racking to handle Clara, but this time, the snake behaved herself pretty well. She wasn't in shed and she hadn't recently eaten, so it wasn't long before she was slithering through Evelyn's fingers and up her arm.

"Doesn't it scare you when she does that?" Mina asked as Clara coiled around Evelyn's shoulder.

"She wants to hide somewhere warm," Evelyn explained. Clara rested her head in the crook of her collarbone. "You're a beginner, so just be still and let her explore. She hasn't nipped in ages, and her bite won't seriously harm you. But if you're worried she might hurt you, we can just put her back in the cage."

"No, it's all right. I trust you."

Those words nestled a little too deeply in Evelyn's chest. "I'll make sure she stays on your wrist and arm, okay? We don't want to freak either of you out."

It took a bit of careful maneuvering, but Evelyn managed to transfer Clara over to Mina successfully. Mina gripped Evelyn's hand as Clara slid onto her wrist, then let out a gasp as the snake coiled around her arm.

"Her scales feel strange," she said, pulling her hand away and letting Clara weave through her fingers. "But the way she moves…it's almost hypnotic."

There was a smile on her face, the kind of look that Evelyn couldn't face head-on without wanting to collapse. Her feelings for Mina were simultaneously too tender to touch and too ferocious to tame. And they were a massive, dangerous distraction.

Although she and Mina had gotten close over the past month or so, she couldn't bring herself to hope that Mina might feel the same way she did. Sure, she'd stood up for her in front of her whole family, but that didn't change the fact that all Evelyn had really done to Mina's life was rip it apart. And Mina hated nothing more than things falling to pieces.

"Are snakes smart?" Mina continued. "Do you think she's attached to you?"

Evelyn watched Clara's tail twitch. "Snakes have small brains. Clara tolerates me because I feed her, but that's it. We don't have the same kind of bond people can have with a cat or a dog."

"But you care about her," Mina said. "Why?"

Evelyn cast a glance toward Nick, who had put down his phone and was watching them both. She couldn't read the expression on his face.

"Yeah," he said. "Why *do* you care about her?"

"Because I understand exactly what we are to each other," Evelyn said. "And I know what she needs to thrive. So I'll never disappoint her."

The room went quiet, and there was that tension again—a little different from what had happened downstairs, but no less stifling.

"Um," Mina said quickly. "I suppose we've gotten a bit off task."

"Not me," Nick said. "I found the Shorewells. It's pretty easy, once you bother to google them."

It *was* easy. Typing in their last name plus Cliffside Bay plus seventies brought up obituaries first, all from the nineties.

"Laurence and Mellie Shorewell, both died in a car accident in 1992," Nick read off his phone.

"Oh, look," Mina said excitedly, pointing at Evelyn's laptop screen. She was perched on the bed beside her, reading over her shoulder. "Laurence Shorewell was a scientist who specialized in Long Island's ecology."

"That's cool." Evelyn eyed the couple's picture: two old white people. They both looked unbearably sad and oddly familiar. She turned back to the text feeling a little unsettled, reading something about how he'd worked at Brookhaven Labs, and then—

"Holy shit!" Evelyn nearly knocked the laptop off the bed. "He worked at the Blue Tide Waste Management Plant!"

"The what?" Nick asked from the corner.

"I saw it in a vision," Evelyn explained, which earned her an eyebrow raise. She tried to fill Nick in while Mina grabbed the laptop and continued to scan the small print.

"He worked there starting in 1970," Mina read, "but 'left

to pursue new endeavors' in 1978, shortly before the plant's completion...."

"Wait." Evelyn hurried over to the bookshelf. She pulled out the folder full of printed info they'd gotten from the library and leafed through it. "Wait, wait, wait. I get it now. I've totally seen them both before."

It took only a second to find the digitized newspaper clipping: a photo of the crowd at the first protest against the Blue Tide plant, in 1978. Most people's names weren't listed, but a couple on the far right were unmistakably Laurence and Mellie Shorewell.

"There they are," she said, spreading the printouts on the carpet and stabbing a triumphant finger in the center.

"So this plant really messed up the Sound?" Nick asked, as he and Mina crouched beside her.

"Yeah, I mean, it's a small enough body of water that a change like this can really impact the whole ecosystem. So the plant's pollution had a highly concentrated impact." Evelyn's stomach churned as she thought of the damage to the ocean she loved and the creatures that lived in it. To the people who tried to make a life beside it. "Someone who worked at the plant is the one who started the protests, actually, because they knew the waste would leak into the— *Oh.*"

Mina turned toward her. "The source," she gasped. "Do you think..."

"It has to be him." Evelyn's mind buzzed. "Maybe he told his boss, and the boss didn't listen. If one of the Shorewells is the ghost, this is definitely a motive for their spirits to remain unsettled. It must've been horrible to see that plant operating even after everything they did to stop it."

"But why try to hurt innocent people?" Mina countered. "The plant was shut down years before the drowning summer."

"I don't know," Evelyn said. "But your vision showed you the Shorewells' house, and Jesse, Colin, and Tamara showed me the plant. The Cliffside Trio have to be part of this."

"That house was just the background in my vision," Mina said. "The girl was the most important part, I think."

"Girl," Nick repeated slowly. "Did they have a daughter?"

"It didn't say anything in the obituary," Mina said. "But her clothes were period-appropriate."

"Do you think there's anyone we could talk to?" Nick suggested. "There must be *some* old person who remembers the Shorewells."

Evelyn grinned. "I think there is."

Chapter Twenty-Five

The apartment above Ruthie's store was filled to the brim with antiques she'd kept for herself. Mina was generally good at navigating crowded spaces thanks to her messy bedroom, but this was on another level. She perched on a scratchy wicker chair beside a cabinet crammed with porcelain figurines and tried not to breathe on them too hard, lest they crush her. Evelyn sat across the table, while Nick was wedged in beside Mina. Discomfort radiated off him like the rotten-egg stench of low tide.

"It's so wonderful that you kept your promise to see me, and brought friends, too," Ruthie said, plunking cutlery on the table. "It's a shame Marvin is out of town. He would have loved to see you."

"Her husband," Evelyn explained, as Ruthie hurried over to the stove to mess with a giant pot of soup. "Old white dude who looks like Santa Claus. He's probably off at an estate sale."

"An antique clock convention," Ruthie corrected from across

the room. "And he *does* look like Santa Claus. Please tell him that the next time you see him, perhaps then he'll shave the beard."

Evelyn laughed, and Mina had the distinct sense that when her friend was old, she'd bear more of a resemblance to Ruthie than either of them realized.

Mina had spent the day since they'd linked the Shorewells to the Blue Tide Waste Management Plant trying and failing to put pieces together in her mind. How the drowning summer and a forty-year-old environmental disaster could be knitted together was currently beyond her, and although Evelyn had assured her that Ruthie was a gossip who knew almost everything about Cliffside Bay, she was skeptical that this dinner would give them anything more to work with.

"What the hell is that?" Nick demanded, sounding alarmed. A moment later, Mina felt something large and woolly brush against her leg. She yelped and jerked her ankles back.

"That's Lonnie." Evelyn still looked amused. "He's pretty quiet for a big dog."

Nick relaxed and scooted his chair back. Mina watched what appeared to be a living mop emerge from under the table and rest his head in Nick's lap. She was more annoyed than she should've been that he'd joined their investigation. He was technically a client, after all, and now that he'd seen the truth of what his brother had become, she couldn't think of a reason to leave him out of this. But the way he looked at Evelyn made her feel as if one of those chests on her ocean floor had broken again, releasing something vicious into the open water.

"Now tell me, darlings," Ruthie said as she poured them a

thick green soup that looked like a far cry from Stella's cooking. "What brings the three of you here on such a lovely summer night?"

"Your company," Evelyn said quickly. "Just like you said, you asked for a visit."

Ruthie let out a loud guffaw. "Nonsense. You have an ulterior motive, Evie. I'd know that look anywhere."

Evelyn flushed. "Okay, you caught me. We have a few questions we were hoping you could answer."

"Well, questions are an after-dinner subject," Ruthie said. "At least, for you. As for me, I'd love to get to know this young lady and gentleman a bit better."

Nick and Evelyn both answered Ruthie's questions with quick, easy charm, but Mina stumbled over even the simplest queries. She didn't want to talk about her family, or her summer, or the Zanetti Collection, and soon enough she'd zoned out. She was scratching Lonnie's woolly head when she heard Evelyn say the word *Shorewell*.

"Did you know them?" Evelyn asked. "It's just so weird, right? Their name's on our community center, and they don't even live here."

"Ah, yes," Ruthie said. "I knew them. Well, I knew her."

"Her?" Mina jerked her head up.

"Annette." Ruthie lowered her spoon into her empty bowl. "Their daughter. We were the same year in school, but she was too busy on all her trips to the city and such to pay much attention to the rest of us. She was too big for this place, always said she was going to move out west. She wanted to be an actress."

"What happened to her, Ms. Calhoun?" Nick asked.

Ruthie's wrinkled face was solemn. Lonnie reappeared on her side of the table and rested his head against her arm, as if to comfort her.

"She never came back to school in the fall of 'seventy-eight. The story was she'd gone to stay with family on the West Coast, like she'd always wanted. Some thought she was...you know." She gestured to her stomach. "But I knew different. Her parents stopped going out. They left the house to the town soon after, and then we never saw them again."

"And Annette never came back, either?" Mina asked.

"No." Ruthie looked a little sad. "Should've asked a few more questions back then, maybe. Why do you three want to know about that family now?"

"We're working on something for the community center," Nick lied smoothly, with an ease that seemed to come from practice. "Mina's mother is the head caterer, and my family's one of the primary maintenance donators who keep the place running. They thought it would be nice to set up a tribute to the family who donated the property all those years ago."

"It's a nice notion," Ruthie said. "But why come to me?"

"Well, we couldn't dig up much aside from their obituaries," added Mina. "So Evelyn had the idea to ask you, since you know everything that happens around here."

It made her feel kind of ill, lying to such a nice old lady. But Evelyn was a horrible liar, and Nick had already said enough. She felt even worse when Ruthie brightened up immediately.

"Well, I do consider myself a bit of an authority on this

town," she said in her low, creaky voice. "And I believe I have something that might help with your memorial."

Ruthie stood up and headed for a bookshelf crammed beside one of the porcelain display cases. Lonnie loped alongside her, his tail wagging furiously. Ruthie pushed aside almanacs and ancient yellow pages directories until her wizened fingers pulled out a book with faded gold lettering on the side.

"There we are," she said. "Cliffside High, class of 'seventy-eight. Marv graduated that year."

"You have a picture of Annette?" Mina breathed.

"Sure do." Ruthie flipped through the yearbook carefully, pointing out her husband—"So handsome, don't you agree?"—before flipping to the sophomores.

"There I am," she said, touching her own picture wistfully. "And over here's Annette." She turned a page, and Mina froze.

This was unmistakably the girl she'd seen in her vision. Flat-ironed hair, a pointed nose, wide brown eyes that looked liquid even in an old, faded photo. A whisper rose in Mina's mind, and she recognized it now as the same voice that had wormed its way into her head during the full moon, the same voice that had roared at her when she'd followed Stella into the water.

Mina knew who was talking to her now. It wasn't the drowning summer victims. It was Annette—it had *always* been Annette. The sand dollar on her wrist pulsed painfully beneath her cuff bracelet.

Mina didn't realize she was touching the page, her finger quivering, until Evelyn tugged gently on her arm.

"What do you think?" Evelyn asked.

Mina took a deep breath and pulled herself back to the present. She was learning that there were times where a stormy sea was appropriate, and other times where calm was best. This was most certainly the latter.

"This would be incredible to have as part of our tribute," she said. "Evelyn, can you take a picture of it? We can come back to scan it later this week."

"Scan it?" Ruthie cackled. "You can drop the act now, Evie. You're not working on a memorial."

Mina froze. So did Nick.

"Ruthie...," Evelyn said cautiously.

"Don't apologize, darling. I'm not upset with you—but I *am* worried." Ruthie looked as grave and unnerving as the porcelain figurines in the cabinet behind her. "You're not the first to ask me about Annette. Although your brother was a bit more polite than you are, Mr. Slater."

Nick recoiled. "My brother was here?"

"Along with his friends, yes." Ruthie picked up the yearbook and snapped it shut. "Three children at my table, asking about the Shorewells. A few weeks later, they were dead. I don't know exactly what you're chasing, but I've given you the answers I have because I believe you're not foolish enough to follow them down the same path. Don't prove me wrong."

As soon as the three of them were out the front door, Nick whirled around. The sun had just finished setting, and his fair skin was tinged bluish purple in the fading twilight.

"She was murdered," he said, without preamble.

Evelyn blinked at him. "You're going to need to be more specific."

But Mina understood. "Annette," she said. "You're talking about Annette."

He gave Mina a hesitant nod. "There was a lot I couldn't figure out yesterday. But now that I know what we're working with...I have a theory. Annette's dad was a whistleblower, but the plant kept operating. They shut down his protests somehow. It can't be a coincidence that his daughter went missing right before he disappeared from the public eye, too."

"I agree," Mina said. Perhaps it wouldn't be that bad to have Nick around, if he aligned so strongly with her own thoughts. Annette whispered in her mind again. She coughed uncomfortably as the smell of salt and rot crept through her, seizing up in her throat.

"You two think the company that ran the plant had Annette killed to scare her parents into keeping their corruption quiet?" Evelyn looked at them skeptically. "How would that even intimidate them, if she were dead? They'd have no leverage."

"That's a good point," Mina said. "But even if we don't have the full story...I think the plant must have had something to do with her disappearance."

"Even if that *is* true," Evelyn said, "there were no reports about her death. Not even an article about her going missing...."

"There was no internet." Mina's throat burned painfully as the whispers rose; she coughed again, eyes watering. The smell of rot was growing unbearable. "It was far easier for people to disappear."

"And you of all people should know how easily the media can lie," Nick said.

Evelyn winced. "Fine then, Slater, go right for the jugular."

"It's true, isn't it?"

Evelyn had called Nick by his last name, the same way she said *Zanetti*. Mina hated that she'd noticed, and hated even more how much it bothered her.

"Well, we have no way to prove any of this," Evelyn said. "We're out of leads. Unless anybody's holding out on us?"

Nick shook his head. "I've got nothing."

"Me neither," Evelyn admitted. She put her hands on her hips. "So what do we do next?"

Mina realized she'd addressed the question to her. But when she tried to speak, she felt something in her throat that hadn't been there a moment before, a thick, slimy blockage. She gasped and slumped forward, retching. The *thing* flew from her mouth and bounced onto the sidewalk.

"Mina." Evelyn's voice sounded muffled. Mina realized dimly that she'd slung an arm around her waist despite their height difference, propping her up. "Mina, are you okay?"

The stench of a hot summer day wafted around them. Although they were nowhere near the shoreline, she felt as if she were there. She could almost hear flies buzzing above the dried-out scum of seaweed left out on the beach. Mina's mouth felt raw and scraped-out. But the voice in her mind was already fading, as if Annette had made her point.

"Well. No," she said weakly. "But I think I'm all right now."

"What *was* that?" Nick knelt to poke at the object Mina had vomited onto the concrete. It was clump of seaweed, green and ragged, the tiny pods on the ends swelled with salt.

"I'm being haunted." Mina coughed again. "Clearly."

Nick's expression told Mina he was just now understanding

the gravity of this situation. "I didn't realize being a medium was so dangerous."

"It shouldn't be," Mina said, a bit harshly. "I'm a special case."

"Hey, you'll get through this." Evelyn released her grip on Mina's waist, and Mina felt a rush of disappointment. Then she realized Evelyn was reaching for her palm instead. The other girl squeezed it gently before turning it over, displaying the glowing sand dollar on her wrist. "The Cliffside Trio haunted me, too, remember? And we figured that out."

Mina looked unhappily at the bits of orange mixed with blue green. A fresh jolt of pain rolled through her arm, and it took all her self-control not to flinch. "I suppose we did. But you weren't bonded to them."

"That bond won't matter if we can break it," Evelyn said. "Your mom told us how to do an exorcism, remember? If we can just confirm that Annette is the ghost and find an item that belonged to her, we'll be good to go. And once she's not controlling the Cliffside Trio's spirits anymore...they'll probably be happy to leave you alone."

Mina was too tired to argue. She nodded along as Evelyn told her that she should wear her old warding necklace again, just in case. But she knew that wouldn't fix anything.

Evelyn thought Mina was being haunted by the drowning summer victims. Yet Mina knew in her bones that her mother had been wrong again. She was not connected to the Cliffside Trio—she was connected to the ghost that was absorbing them. The ghost that wanted nothing more than to ascend into a demon. And whatever Mina had done at the full moon had strengthened that connection to the point where even during a weaker part of the moon cycle, she was still susceptible to the spirit's whims.

At the new moon in a week and a half, the ghost would come for her again. Mina didn't know if she had the willpower to stop Annette's spirit from consuming her whole. But saying any of that aloud would only lead to panic and distraction. And it wouldn't matter what the ghost could do to her if she was able to destroy her before the moon winnowed away to nothing.

So Mina did what she had trained for her whole life. She pushed her fear down and constructed a fake, relieved smile.

"We *do* have one lead left," she said. "Someone who might know what the Cliffside Trio were up to." She turned to look at Evelyn. "Your sister."

Chapter Twenty-Six

There was nothing Evelyn wanted to do less than talk to her older sister about her ex-boyfriend's murder. But she couldn't deny that she, Mina, and Nick were closing in on something here, something that had happened between Jesse and his friends and Annette Shorewell's ghost. And if all it took was one uncomfortable conversation to stop a demon from ascending...well, Evelyn would tough it out.

It took her a few days to catch Meredith alone, thanks to their competing work hours and her sister's brutal commute. She tried to distract herself with the non-ghost-related things in her life—Amy, Kenny, and Luisa had added her to a group chat, one of the leopard geckos escaped from its cage at work and caused a mild panic, a couple had a dramatic breakup in the middle of the Basic Bean. Life happened all around her in Cliffside Bay, and yet Evelyn could not pull her thoughts away from the dead.

Finally, the stars aligned. Evelyn's dad had a late night at his part-time factory gig, and Evelyn was home and waiting when Meredith's car pulled into the driveway after a long day of work. The moon had shrunk past its first quarter and into a waning crescent, winking at Evelyn from behind a cloud as she stood on the front porch and waved Meredith inside.

"I've got extra pastries from work," Evelyn offered, holding up a paper bag. "Do you want some?"

The cinnamon rolls and croissants were kind of stale, but Meredith didn't seem to notice. She scarfed two of them down in as many minutes, then sipped a glass of water at the kitchen table. Evelyn nodded along to a rant about the LIRR and commuting and how expensive it was to do anything in New York City.

"It's just so frustrating." Meredith shrugged off her blazer. "All my friends can afford to stay in the city, so they're at happy hours right now doing valuable networking. And I'm *here*."

She'd looked so grown-up when she stepped out of her car, with her pantsuit and her conservative makeup and the edges of her heels poking out of a tote bag (she wore sneakers on commutes because she "didn't want to die falling down the stairs in Penn Station"). But Evelyn could tell Meredith was uncomfortable, as if adulthood were a costume she didn't know how to wear yet.

"What about Riku?" Evelyn asked her. "Does talking to him help?"

"Yes, and no." Meredith sighed. "He knows what happened to our family, but I still don't think he fully understands what it's like for me to be back here. I'm not sure anyone could."

"I do." It came out like an accusation, but Meredith didn't seem to mind.

THE DROWNING SUMMER 267

"Maybe you do," she said softly. "You're trapped here, too."

A few months ago, Evelyn would've agreed with her. Cliffside Bay had felt like an ecosystem she couldn't thrive in. But there were people here who'd helped her when she had nowhere else to turn, and regardless of how she felt about leaving now, she knew she couldn't go until she put the drowning summer to rest.

"I need to ask you something." Evelyn pulled out her phone. "And I want you to answer honestly. No—I need you to."

Meredith hesitated. "What is it?"

"This photo," Evelyn tapped her cracked screen, then turned it toward her sister. "Do you recognize it?"

She knew the moment Meredith registered Annette's face that her sister had seen her before.

"Where the hell did you find this?" she whispered.

Evelyn kept her voice firm. "What matters more is that Jesse, Colin, and Tamara found it first."

A crease appeared between Meredith's eyebrows. "Wait a minute. You confronted Dad. You talked to me about that summer last month . . . you're investigating the murders?"

Evelyn gulped. "Maybe."

"Well, you need to stop playing detective. These are real peoples' lives you're messing with, Evelyn. This is—this is *my* life."

"It's my life, too," Evelyn said. "I'm part of this, Meredith. More than you know."

"You have no right to dredge up everything I've fought so hard to work through," Meredith continued, like she hadn't even registered Evelyn's words. "You know that all I've ever wanted is to move past this—"

"But you haven't." Evelyn didn't know when she'd started crying, only that her voice was wobbly and her cheeks were wet. "I'm sorry about Jesse. I'm sorry about Mom. But I lost her, too, and when you left I lost *you*. I need to understand why that summer destroyed our family. I need to know the truth."

Meredith shoved her chair back and rose from the table. Evelyn was painfully reminded of a dozen other nights when she'd crept past the kitchen to see her father and her sister facing off like this, the air between them crackling with fury.

"You sound just like Jesse did when he was looking into that plant," Meredith snapped. "He kept saying he was trying to figure out the truth. And when I couldn't understand his conspiracy theories about that girl and that plant, he found new friends, and they started talking about her *ghost*, and the next thing I knew, he was dead."

"And you don't think any of that is suspicious?" Evelyn scrambled to her feet. She could feel her sister slipping further away than ever before. "Meredith, we could figure this out together. You could finally put the drowning summer behind you. For real this time."

But she knew before she finished speaking that Meredith was done listening. Her sister's expression was shuttered, her cheeks blotchy.

"Leave this shit alone," Meredith said. "And if you can't do that, leave me out of it."

She was halfway up the stairs before Evelyn could say another word.

Evelyn hadn't wanted to hurt Meredith. But she knew she'd broken something between them, all the same.

Meredith would rather forget the past than find out the truth of it. But Evelyn wasn't built like that. And she couldn't back down now just to spare her sister's feelings.

It had been a long time since Evelyn had cried in her bedroom and heard the telltale sniffles of Meredith crying in hers, through those too-thin wooden walls. It brought back the familiar pain of the months after their mother had left, of a house filled with regret and rage.

Back then, Evelyn had been a helpless child. But that was six years ago.

She touched the shell around her neck, a constant reminder that both the living and the dead were counting on her. She wouldn't let them down.

She wiped away her tears, opened her phone, and texted Nick and Mina about the clues she'd lost so much to find.

Chapter Twenty-Seven

Jesse Slater's room was a time capsule. Mina walked past posters of bands and video games that had been popular half a decade ago and an open closet still crammed with clothes. The place was eerily clean and well-kept, as though the Slaters were still waiting for their son to push open the door and walk back in. Mina couldn't shake the feeling that they were trespassing.

"Are you certain we should be in here?" she asked, turning to Nick.

"Don't get weird about it," Nick said roughly, striding toward a laptop in the far corner. After Evelyn's conversation with Meredith, Mina had known several things for certain: that the Cliffside Trio really had been looking into Annette Shorewell, that they'd also tied her to the Blue Tide plant, and that they'd known about her ghost. It had also revealed a new piece of information: Jesse had been looking into the plant before he stumbled on a ghost instead of the other way around.

The best way the three of them could think to proceed

was to find out why, and the best way to do *that* lay in Jesse's long-dormant computer, which wouldn't turn on without its old, dusty charger. No one wanted to risk moving it. So they'd reconvened at Nick's house the next morning, while his parents were both out. Mina was starting to wonder if they ever actually cared to spend time in their giant house.

"It's freaky in here," Evelyn mumbled, striding across the room to join Nick as he sat in the desk chair. "Those pictures by his bed—"

"Jesse and Meredith. I know." Nick tapped furiously on the keyboard. "I asked them if we could clean this whole place out years ago, but they refused. Mom still sleeps in the bed sometimes."

Mina shuddered. She had no idea what to say. But Evelyn seemed less lost—she bent close to Nick and placed a hand on his shoulder.

"I'm so sorry," she said. "We're going to figure out what happened to him."

Nick sagged into her touch. "I wish we'd talked more about... you know. This."

"I know. I wasn't ready."

Mina backed away as they kept talking, feeling like a different kind of trespasser. Her windpipe burned, and for a moment she wondered if Annette had come for her again, if she was about to hold out that sand dollar and demand she take it. But no—Mina was just having a feeling she didn't like and hadn't immediately shoved it away. Apparently, emotions could hurt just as badly as a potential demon did.

"Do you know anything about hacking the mainframe, or

whatever?" Evelyn beckoned Mina forward. "Nick tried this last night, too, but he keeps getting locked out."

Mina leaned over Nick's shoulder. "Are you saying you don't know his password?"

Nick scowled at the screen. "I've tried to think of everything he would've cared about—favorite books, favorite games, pets' names..."

"What about his girlfriend?" The words came out of Mina's mouth a little too sharply.

"I tried Meredith," Nick said. "But her name didn't work."

"Hang on." Evelyn glanced at something behind Mina's head, then elbowed Nick aside and tapped furiously at the keyboard. There was a ping of approval the moment Evelyn hit *enter*, and a loading bar appeared a moment later.

"What was it?" Nick asked incredulously.

"It was Meredith's name and their anniversary date."

He winced. "How did you know it?"

Evelyn pointed at the wall behind Jesse's bed, where a cluster of dusty photos were plastered beside the band posters. A date was written in metallic sharpie across a printout of Jesse and Meredith kissing.

Jesse's desktop was completely bare. The background was an inoffensive stock photo, and the few neat folders held nothing but homework and video game apps.

"Something's wrong here," Nick said. "This isn't his computer. It's been wiped."

"But it's got personal stuff on it," Evelyn said.

"No...it's curated. I can tell." Nick frowned. "Maybe this is what the police gave back."

"Or maybe your parents cleaned it up before the police could take it," Mina said.

Nick nodded slowly. "Money gets you a lot—including extra time to tamper with evidence."

"Do you think your parents knew he had something to hide?" Evelyn sounded uneasy.

Nick hesitated. "I don't know. But this isn't *him*."

"So what now?" Evelyn asked. "We could search the rest of his things...."

Mina suppressed a shudder. She did *not* want to do that. This already felt borderline disrespectful to the dead.

"No, if there's anything here, my parents would've found it," Nick said miserably. "They know every— Hold on a second."

Nick got to his feet. His gaze darted across bookshelves and the dark maw of the closet, then stopped above the bed. He climbed onto the mattress and reached up the wall, where an air vent sat unobtrusively beside several posters. It took him mere seconds to unscrew the vent and pull out something dusty.

"I knew it!" he said triumphantly, clambering back to the floor. "Jesse taught me this was the best place to hide stuff in a bedroom. It's where I keep my fake."

"What *is* that?" Mina asked. In answer, Nick brushed off the dust. It was a small black brick with a neatly coiled charging cable.

"An external hard drive," he said.

It took a few minutes for the computer to load the backup. When it did, it revealed a desktop crowded with random images, documents, and screenshots. The files were clustered so tightly that Mina couldn't even tell what the background behind them was supposed to be.

"This is the real Jesse," Nick said.

"This is my worst nightmare," Mina mumbled, gazing in horror at the virtual clutter.

"Hey, I've seen your room," Evelyn said. "It's a disaster."

"Yes, but my files are neat. How are we ever going to find anything in this mess?"

"We'll just check all of it, I guess," Evelyn said, shrugging.

It took them almost thirty minutes to search through outdated memes, scanned-in homework assignments, pictures of Jesse and his friends, and information about college applications. It was all so normal. Mina was starting to worry that there was nothing useful here when Nick found a locked folder lurking behind a screenshot of Jesse's SAT scores. This one had a password, too, but Nick cracked it pretty easily after some quick googling.

"Favorite video game *and* its release day." He clicked on the folder. "Oh. This is it."

The three of them leaned forward as Nick pulled up the same photo of Annette Shorewell they'd seen the day before. There were more images, too, pictures of the Shorewells, the Blue Tide Waste Management Plant, protestors marching outside the chain-link fence. Some of them had annotations on them, digital arrows and typed bits of text. *Related? Proof? Follow up.*

It became clear quite quickly that not all of this information came from Jesse. There were three different colors of text marking up the pictures, three different opinions often arguing back and forth. Colin and Tamara had become hidden behind Jesse in Mina's mind, and she understood now that this was a tragedy of its own, of people getting lost within the story of their own deaths. They were part of this, too.

"This must be a backup of another folder," Nick said. "They all had access to the real one, I bet. To share information."

"And argue about it," Evelyn added.

Mina would never get used to the feeling of intruding on the dead, reading words typed or scrawled by fingers that now lay rotting, sifting through the clues they'd left behind to try and end the suffering that still plagued them.

She didn't know if ghosts could feel pain, or if it was only a memory of it. If ghosts were echoes, or simply the purest distillation of a person's soul, if souls were even real, if any of that actually mattered. Mina wondered why she'd ever believed that her family's rules would hold forever when being a medium meant accepting that the world did not adhere to strict instructions. When ghosts broke the biggest rule of all: death.

"So do the police just not know about this, then?" Nick said. "Even if my parents wiped Jesse's computer...they must've found *something* on Colin's or Tamara's. Why didn't they think it was relevant to the case?"

"The investigation's still technically open," Evelyn said. "Are you really surprised they never told reporters this stuff? I mean, there are already enough weird theories about the drowning summer online."

Mina refrained from pointing out that "weird theory" was a relative term when the truth most likely involved ghosts.

"The real question is, why did your parents want to hide this?" she asked.

Nick's fingers paused on the keys. "I don't know. My parents don't talk about what happened to Jesse. They always say they're protecting me, but I'm done with that. I want the truth."

Mina felt a connection with him again, like that moment in front of Ruthie's. It was still a surprise. "My family throws around the word *protect* a lot, too."

"Wait, everyone," Evelyn said excitedly. "This picture's new."

It was a scan of some sort of form, crammed with numbers and incomprehensible abbreviations. Mina recognized the template.

"It's an expense report. Mom does them all the time for work, when her clients compensate her for catering costs."

"An expense report from the Blue Tide Waste Management Plant." Nick zoomed in on the form, where the plant's name was visible at the top. "Where do you think they even got this?"

"Nowhere legal," Evelyn muttered.

Below the company name was written PROJECT S BONUS REPORT. There was a note on the side, in red—*I think this is what you're looking for, J.* An arrow pointed to a specific row on the form. Mina's eyes leaped to the initials *LS*, then traced them across the row to a blank box. She looked at the other columns—more initials, but they had numbers typed in as an expense where LS didn't.

"Laurence Shorewell," Nick said solemnly.

"The only one who didn't get a bonus," Evelyn said.

"Not a bonus." Nick's voice was harsh. "A bribe."

There was an annotation beside his name—*A's disappearance a hostage situation gone wrong? Follow up on anecdotal leads.*

"They think she was kidnapped," Mina said.

Evelyn made a small noise of assent. "If her death was a mistake, that *would* explain the leverage issue."

Nick scrolled to the bottom of the form. Mina stared at the words printed there, beneath the final sum of the payments. Her mind hummed, and Annette unfurled within it, bringing the scent of salt and brine with her.

PAYROLL COURTESY OF THE SAND DOLLAR CO.

Mina finally understood. "The company that owned the plant—*that's* why. The sand dollars on their eyes were her trying to tell us the whole time what the company had done to her. Her trying to tell everyone."

"But I still don't understand," Nick said. "My brother was trying to help her. Why would she hurt him, Colin, and Tamara?"

Evelyn made a sharp, awful noise, and Mina felt a jolt of panic. But she didn't seem hurt—instead she was staring intently at the screen.

Evelyn pointed at an annotation beside the company name. "Zoom in on that."

Nick did. The note was typed in blue—Jesse's color. *Check the subsidiary company—SDC merged in late 80s, sold off in 90s, but was privately owned by SE. We don't have full proof, but we're getting close.*

"Wait," Nick said softly. "SE. Does that mean Slater Enterprises?"

"Your family's company." Evelyn's voice trembled. "They owned the waste management plant, Nick. They—they *knew.*"

Mina watched the way both of their faces twitched as they recalibrated, and felt her own ocean stirring, roiling, warning her. A soft, low rumble emanated from the walls around them, but the others didn't seem to notice.

"My family's owned a lot of companies," Nick protested. "That doesn't mean they understood the details of this one."

"Jesse must have thought they did," Evelyn said. "This could be why your parents had his laptop wiped. Because he told them."

Nick stood shakily and backed up. His face was pale, his blue eyes wide and wild.

Mina could almost feel his panic bouncing off the walls, off this tomb of a life lost in the depths of this same investigation. It fit together now, all of it. Jesse must have been digging into his family's past when he found the Blue Tide plant. It had led him to this discovery—and then it had led him to his death.

The shell around Evelyn's neck flared to life, sending a blue glow emanating through the room. She gasped and clutched at it.

"How is this possible?" she asked. "It feels like a summoning, but we didn't do anything. . . ."

"I don't know. But we need to stop arguing." Mina's wrist burned. Annette's voice echoed through her mind in an incomprehensible snarl.

"This is ridiculous," Nick snapped. "I asked you to help me put my brother to rest, and now you're accusing my family of having someone murdered?"

The rumbling came again, louder this time, and Mina knew she couldn't stop whatever was coming. Knew it wasn't hers to stop, even if it was her fault it was here. She smelled salt again, thicker this time, tinged with the rotting scent of a hot summer day.

"Remember what you said about your parents?" Mina asked. "About them protecting you? You knew they had something to hide."

"No." Nick's voice was raw. "Jesse might have seen a connection, but that doesn't mean Slater Enterprises— *Shit!*"

A moment later, something splattered against Mina's arm—a drop of water, then another, as if the ceiling had begun to rain. She tipped her head back and saw two stains on the plaster in the shape of handprints. Her entire body began to tremble.

"Get your ghosts out of here," Nick said, voice shaking. "I don't want to do this anymore."

Before she could formulate any kind of response, Mina *felt* the two hands rear back and punch through the ceiling. She cried out as holes opened in the plaster. The water that had lived in the house's pipes mere moments ago poured down, drenching all three of them in a deluge of salt and slime.

When it was done, Mina was surprised to find herself still standing, shivering and soaking wet. Evelyn was beside her, seaweed tangled in her hair. This was not mere saltwater—it was orange muck straight out of the pictures Mina had seen of the waste leaking into the Sound. Nick slumped to the ground, shuddering. Dead minnows were strewn around him, gazing at them all with glassy, accusatory stares.

Mina winced at the sting of salt in her eyes and the corresponding sting of the sand dollar on her wrist. Annette's voice was already gone, but she would never forget the anguish in it.

"Nick," she said hoarsely. "I—I'm sorry."

He locked eyes with her, gaze burning with regret and fury.

"Get the fuck out of my house," he said. And Mina listened, because she knew exactly how it felt to be betrayed by your parents—the people who were supposed to love you most.

Chapter Twenty-Eight

Victory was bittersweet. Mina learned that as she sat with the ramifications of what they'd uncovered. She believed whole-heartedly that the Sand Dollar Corporation—a.k.a. Slater Enterprises—was responsible for Annette's death. And then the pollution they'd covered up had infected her ghost, warping her spirit over all these years just like it had warped Long Island Sound. No wonder Annette had lashed out at Jesse, Colin, and Tamara when they'd tried to talk to her.

The new moon was three days away, but Mina no longer dreaded it. She wanted to tell Annette she finally understood why she was so angry. Perhaps they wouldn't have to banish her after all. Perhaps they could persuade her to leave in peace if they promised to get her some well-deserved justice.

"I still have questions," Evelyn said as she paced Mina's bedroom, trying and failing to navigate the cluttered floor. Mina had invited her over here because Stella was out at a catering gig, and because she had a surprise for the other girl. One she was too nervous to show her just yet. "We know the Cliffside Trio were investigating Annette because Jesse was digging into his family's secrets. But how did they jump from a company cover-up to believing in ghosts? That's a big leap."

"I don't know," Mina said. "But they spoke to my mother. They found out somehow."

"It's just... people don't try talking to a spirit without a reason. If the three of them knew Annette was murdered, why would they need to summon her? And how did she have the strength to kill them when she hasn't killed us?"

"They didn't know anything," Mina said uneasily. "Without protection or guidance, they were defenseless."

"You're probably right." Evelyn leaned against the wall, looking utterly exhausted. Mina suspected it was because they'd both spent the last day trying and failing to contact Nick. He was ignoring them, and she couldn't really blame him. She knew firsthand how much safer it could feel to shove something down and pretend it had never happened. "Sorry—you said you had something to show me? Something non-ghost related?"

Mina had a sudden urge to lie and say it was all nothing. Instead, she gestured toward the screen in the corner before she could lose her nerve. "Do you remember when you asked what was behind there, and I told you it wasn't finished?"

Evelyn looked at the screen curiously. "I do."

"Well, it's done now." Mina walked over to the screen and folded it back. Behind it was a clothing rack filled with the pieces she'd constructed since the full moon, each fully visible on a swiveled-out hanger. Instead of tossing out her rejected garments, she'd devoted herself to reworking each of her failures.

Sometimes she'd spliced two or three pieces together; sometimes she'd simply played around with the original structure. The resulting garments weren't technically perfect anymore, but they meant no more waste, the tiniest drop in the bucket of the fashion industry. And they felt like *hers*.

Mina watched Evelyn's face as she took the collection in, trying not to betray how nervous she was. She'd never shown her work to anyone but Stella before, and she had no idea what to expect.

The first thing Evelyn did was smile the exact same way she had at the community center: a wide, surprised grin that left Mina weak with relief.

"Whoa," she gasped, stepping forward. "You made these?"

Mina nodded. "I've been working on a collection all summer. But it hasn't felt right until now."

She turned toward the pieces again, trying to see them through Evelyn's eyes.

A romper the rich pink of the sunset reflecting off the water. A pair of wide-legged trousers that Mina had dyed by hand, as silky and ephemeral as foaming waves. A halter top in a deep blue with a brass key slotted through the neckline—like a chest languishing on the seafloor. Each piece a tiny glimpse into the world as Mina understood it best: through the lens of her ocean.

"What do you think?" she asked, voice a bit too high.

Evelyn hovered beside Regina the mannequin, who was clad in the centerpiece of the collection: a dress meant to convey the feeling of the ocean after dark.

"They're incredible," she said. "I knew you were into fashion, but these are something special. Seriously. Especially this dress." She reached a tentative hand toward the sleeve, then yanked it back, as if she thought her touch might ruin it.

"Thank you." Mina could barely get the words out. "And about that dress...I'm glad you like it. Because that's the real surprise. I. Um. I sort of...made it for you."

"What?" Evelyn gasped. "That's way too nice. I can't ever pay you back for this."

"It's a gift," Mina said softly. "For everything you've done to help me this summer."

"I..." Evelyn still looked utterly stunned. Mina noticed the tears glimmering in her eyes—had she overwhelmed her? But then Evelyn let out a shaky sigh and smiled again, and Mina knew it would be all right. "What if I rip it?"

"Then I'll be able to fix it," Mina said, fighting down a laugh. "You can try it on right now, if you want. I guessed at your measurements, but I'm sure it'll need alterations."

Evelyn exhaled, still gazing at the dress in disbelief. "I— Okay. Yeah. I'll try it on."

Mina waited as Evelyn fumbled around behind the screen. She didn't know why she was so anxious. Maybe because she'd never made clothes for anyone besides herself and Stella. Maybe because she had never really made *anything* that had meant as much to her as all of this did. Maybe because there was a lot to be nervous about in general.

And then Evelyn pushed the screen aside, and Mina forgot how to breathe.

The dress's slip was simple enough, a black scoop-neck frame with an A-line waist and a short, slightly flared skirt. But the sheer tulle overlay was where things got interesting. Mina had ripped it out of an old ball gown experiment and dyed it the dark bluish green of the Sound at night, then embroidered it with golden moons and stars. The high neckline and short sleeves were bordered by tiny metallic beads, and Mina had painstakingly sewn dozens more into the skirt.

Evelyn was always beautiful, but right now she shone. She was sea-foam and starlight, she was the moon's reflection on a crashing wave, and she was staring right at Mina, a cautious, bashful look on her face.

"Well?" she asked. "What do you think?"

They were only a few feet apart, but it felt like a mile. Felt too far, always too far, and Mina understood that Evelyn wasn't just talking about the dress. That somehow the entire time Mina was making it she had never realized it was actually her way of asking a question she knew, on some level, Evelyn had already answered.

Mina met her eyes. "I think I really want to kiss you right now."

When Evelyn spoke, her voice was low and soft and deathly, deathly serious. "Then kiss me."

So Mina did.

The kiss was gentle at first, patient, careful, not at all how Mina had thought it would be. The height difference took a little getting used to, but then one of Evelyn's hands found its way around her neck and Mina pressed her palm to the small of Evelyn's back, pulling her closer. When they broke apart, Mina's breathing was ragged.

"That was my first kiss," she whispered, pressing her forehead against Evelyn's.

Evelyn let out a noise at that, something between a gasp and a cough. "I never would've known."

"Really?"

"Really." Evelyn tucked a hand behind Mina's ear, drawing strands of blond hair away from Mina's face. Her lips landed on Mina's neck a moment later, and Mina shivered, her eyes fluttering shut. Every part of her ached for more of this, lips and hands and the gentle tug of teeth on her earlobe, the caress of fingers on her cheek.

"You're teasing me," Mina murmured as Evelyn pressed her nose into Mina's collarbone and chuckled, the sound reverberating through her chest. Evelyn smelled like salt and fresh laundry. Her body, warm and soft, was curled like a seashell against Mina's.

"It's just," Evelyn said, "that I've been thinking about what it would feel like to kiss you here—" She brushed her lips against Mina's shoulder. "And here—" Mina's cheek. "And of course here," she whispered, her lips now an inch away from Mina's again. "All summer long, Zanetti."

"Well, then." Mina's voice came out high and breathy. She thought she might collapse if Evelyn's lips touched her neck one more time, and then she thought that perhaps collapsing would be worth it. "Sounds like we have some catching up to do."

Mina had spent so much of her life below the surface of her own mind, pushing down her dreams and desires. Now, at long last, she didn't want there to be anything shielding her from someone else. They kissed until Mina's lips were swollen. Until the ocean inside her was the calmest it had ever been. Until everything that Mina had feared and grieved and hoped for was washed away by the rhythm of Evelyn's steady heartbeat, like the tide erasing lines drawn deeply in the sand.

Chapter Twenty-Nine

Evelyn had thought *before* she kissed Mina that she couldn't get the other girl out of her head. But now that she knew firsthand how it felt, all she wanted was to kiss her again. Unfortunately, she had other things to worry about. Like the new moon, which was coming in two days. If they could contact Annette then, Mina seemed to think they could put her to rest and free the other spirits she'd imprisoned. Evelyn hoped she was right. And whenever they were safe, she was going to ask Mina on a real date, one where they didn't try to solve a murder or summon a ghost.

"How many times has Amy texted *I told you so?*" Luisa asked. They were at Scales & Tails, although they had gotten very little work done once Evelyn had admitted exactly why she was in such a good mood.

Evelyn's phone buzzed. She snorted as she gazed at the screen. "That's one more. I can't believe you convinced me to tell her about Mina."

"You said you wanted girl advice," Luisa said, grinning. "Well, you're definitely going to get it. Although I don't think anyone's ever made Amy a dress before."

"I still can't believe Mina did that." Evelyn couldn't quite keep the giddy wobble out of her voice.

"Neither can I," Luisa said. "Show me those pictures again."

Warmth spread through Evelyn as Luisa gushed over the dress. It was currently sitting in her closet, a reminder that as stressful and strange as this summer had been, it had brought her and Mina together.

She touched the seashell around her neck and wondered how it was possible that she could hold so much joy for Mina and so much pain for everything else. The way Meredith had bolted up the stairs after Evelyn asked about Jesse. The look on Nick's face as he told them to get out of his house. The secrets they'd uncovered about the Slater family, secrets they couldn't prove without evidence Nick had probably destroyed by now. Even if they put the ghost to rest, they couldn't fix the Blue Tide plant's impact on Long Island Sound.

Yet Evelyn was smiling. Mina didn't cancel out the terrifying, messy world. But she made it a lot less scary to live in.

"She said she wants to set up a store eventually," Evelyn said. "When she feels like the collection's finished."

"Does she need a photographer?" Luisa asked. "Or at least someone to give her tips on how to make clothes look good in pictures?"

"You can ask her yourself at Amy's show," Evelyn said. "She'll get a little overwhelmed if you're too nice to her, but I know it would mean a lot."

"Oh, right!" Luisa brightened. "I'm glad you're both coming."

Amy had aced her audition, and her new band was playing at a venue a town over next week. Evelyn hadn't expected much when she asked Mina to go with her, but the other girl had said yes before she could even finish asking the question.

"I am, too," Evelyn said. "She seems excited. I know she's spent a lot of time on her own, but I'm not sure that's what she actually wants anymore."

Luisa coughed.

Evelyn frowned at her. "What?"

"I mean, I could've said the same thing about you at the beginning of the summer," Luisa said. "I hope you don't take this the wrong way, but... you seemed so lonely. Even when you were dating Nick."

Evelyn flushed. "Please don't tell me you tried to be my friend out of pity."

"I think we're way past that," Luisa said. "That year when we were both in the library a lot, we'd just moved here from Staten Island, and I didn't have any friends. But Amy made me feel at home, and we're still close all these years later. So when you and I started working together, I thought... maybe I could be that person for you."

A few months ago, Evelyn would have insisted she'd been fine on her own. But that obviously wasn't true. So many people in Cliffside Bay had taken care of her when her own family couldn't. They'd been rooting for her all along. She'd just never been ready to notice it until now.

"You were," she said, surprised by how close to tears she was. "That person for me, I mean. Thank you. Seriously. I've spent a long time trying to convince myself that I'm better off alone. I'm really happy to be wrong."

"I'm happy you're wrong, too."

Evelyn rolled her eyes, but she was still grinning.

Luisa's phone buzzed. She reached for it and paused, staring at the screen. "It's him."

"Look, I know it's none of my business, but the two of you..."

Luisa groaned and shoved her phone away. It spun across the counter until it hit the cash register. "Not you, too."

"I just don't get it. You like each other, right? What's holding you back?"

Luisa gave her a rueful look. "I get scared when things mean too much to me. It's why I can't show people my photos. It's why I dumped Kenny the first time, because my feelings freaked me out. But they didn't go away. And now, the thought of telling him I want to get back together after being the one who tore things apart...it's embarrassing."

Evelyn remembered what Amy had said: *They're both too nervous to work it out.*

"I don't think he'd care," she said. "I think he'd just be happy. And for whatever it's worth...maybe you *should* take your mom up on her offer to hang your photos in the library."

Luisa hesitated. "I'll think about it."

The door opened, and Luisa went to take care of the customer. Evelyn was about to put her phone back in her pocket when it started vibrating furiously. Texts were coming in from everyone she knew—Amy, Kenny, Mina, random people from school. Then calls, some from numbers she didn't even have in her contacts.

Are u okay?

Call us if you need to talk

What's going on?

Did you know about this?

And over and over again, the same link, some news outlet she'd never heard of. Her stomach began to churn as she swiped one open at random.

"I THINK HE DID IT": THE DAUGHTER OF SUSPECTED "SAND DOLLAR KILLER" SPEAKS OUT

Evelyn didn't remember collapsing behind the counter, but she did, her back to Hal's glass enclosure, her breath coming in small, choked gasps like a trapped animal. It was all she could do to pick up her phone and swipe at it, then hold it to her ear.

"Meredith," she whispered as the phone rang and rang, as if her sister could hear her without picking up. "What did you do?"

Mr. Clark let her go home early. Luisa helped her pack up her stuff and leave through the back door, just in case the article had stirred up any unwanted media attention.

"Call me if you need anything, okay?" she asked, then gave Evelyn a hug.

Evelyn nodded numbly. She managed to longboard home through muscle memory only. Her mind was elsewhere. The whispers she'd heard as a kid. The vicious rumors about her dad all over the internet. Her hope that she'd finally moved past all this seemed pathetic and flimsy. Her new friends, Mina—would any of them even want to be around her now?

Meredith's car was in the driveway when Evelyn coasted to a stop. Her sister stood behind it, loading a garbage bag of clothes into the trunk.

Evelyn picked up her longboard and marched forward. She was so angry she could barely see, or maybe that was because of the tears.

"Why did you do it?" she demanded.

Meredith's aviators were perched atop her forehead, her gray-blue eyes rimmed with red. Everything about her looked worn-out and miserable.

"Shit," she said. "I thought I'd be out of here before you saw."

"You thought you could just sell out our family and run away?"

"I'm not running away," Meredith said, shutting the trunk. "I'm going to stay with Mom. If you had any sense, you'd join me."

"Mom doesn't want us. She hasn't talked to us in four years."

"She's talked to *me*," Meredith said.

Evelyn felt as if she'd been struck. "What?"

"Last year," Meredith said. "She visited me at school. Met Riku. Told me about her new life. She said she wants a relationship with me again—but only if I promised not to contact Dad anymore."

"That's so messed up," Evelyn said. "You know that, right?"

"More messed up than Dad killing three people?"

"He didn't. Fucking. Do it."

"You've been very adamant about that opinion," Meredith said. "So after my plans fell through for the summer, I figured

I'd come check it out and make up my mind for myself. Maybe poke around a little bit."

"You were spying on Dad?" Evelyn stared at her in disbelief. "On me?"

"I wasn't spying. I was trying to give him a fair shot. I talked to some people, asked some questions, and then..." Meredith hesitated. "A reporter reached out. I talked to her off the record and told her I wasn't interested in a story, but after you confronted Dad... after our little spat the other day... I felt differently."

The "friend" Meredith had been on her way to see when she'd driven Evelyn to the library. Of course. For one moment, Evelyn felt horribly guilty. If she hadn't pushed Meredith, none of this would be happening right now. But then she thought of how resistant Meredith had been to change all summer. Her sister had no interest in adapting to her environment at all. If reality didn't suit her, she would shut it out. Whatever consequences that led to were her fault, not anyone else's.

"Don't you dare blame this on me," Evelyn said. "You said you wanted to move past this. Well, all this has done is guarantee we never, ever will."

"Meredith." Their father's voice was hoarse and weary. He stood on the porch, silhouetted in the afternoon sunlight. "Didn't I tell you to be out before she came home?"

"I didn't know she'd find out so soon," Meredith snapped. "I'm leaving."

"So that's it?" Evelyn looked from him to Meredith. "You're just going to abandon us again?"

"I'm not abandoning you," Meredith said. "I'm just trying to tell the truth."

"You've never wanted the truth," their dad said sharply. "You just wanted Siobhan to come back. Don't you understand that she left you?"

"No, she left *you*," Meredith snarled. "She wanted to take us, but you fought her—"

"That's not true." Greg stared at them both from the porch. "Your mother could have easily gotten full custody of both of you. She signed her parental rights away, Meredith. You *know* that. Telling the world you hate me won't fix that. It only makes you a pawn in whatever game she's playing now."

All summer, Evelyn had hoped she could pull her family back together one tiny piece at a time. Now she understood that they'd always been too broken for that. That she'd been a fool to ever think otherwise. There were some conditions even the strongest creatures in the intertidal zone couldn't survive.

"You're lying," Meredith whispered, trembling. "You made her sign them away."

Greg shook his head. "Come on, Evelyn. Get inside. The Kowalskis are staring."

Evelyn turned to see the curtains next door hastily fluttering shut. Great—they were probably taking pictures. She had a distant, hazy memory of the media frenzy during the drowning summer, and shuddered.

Evelyn stared at Meredith's face for one final moment. It was slightly blurred through her tears, but she tried to commit her sister to memory anyway. She didn't know when she would see her again—*if* she would see her again.

"Don't ever come back," Evelyn said. Then she rushed past her father through the safety of the front door.

"Evelyn," her father called after her. "Don't answer your phone. I don't want you dragged into this."

Evelyn rounded on him, still crying.

"I've always been part of this," she snapped. "You can't protect me from it. You can't protect either of us."

She could only think in small steps: walking up the stairs. Shutting her bedroom door. Curling up beneath the covers, all tears and snot and deep, wracking sobs.

Evelyn had tried six years ago to protect her father. And she'd thought that she'd succeeded. But now every bit of joy she'd found this summer seemed like a joke.

What use was communicating with the dead when she couldn't even protect the living? When everything she'd ever done to help her family had failed?

Chapter Thirty

For the first time in recent memory, Mina had been happy.

Then Meredith's interview dropped, and the Evelyn Mackenzie who Mina had spent the last month and a half falling for was utterly broken. The last two days had been hellish. Evelyn was stuck inside, hiding from the reporters who'd descended on her driveway, while Mina watched helplessly from a distance. She'd texted her and called her, but it felt futile, a tiny boat tossing on the waves in an unending storm.

And then she got a phone call.

She'd been in her room as usual, working on SAT prep of all things, when Sergio's number popped up on her screen.

"Hello?" Mina said. He didn't usually call her unless he was in hot water with Uncle Dom, so she was uncertain what to expect.

"Hey." His voice was low, a little agitated. "Remember when you told me to tell you if I figured out why the rest of our family left town?"

Mina sat up straight on her bed and shut her laptop. Her online practice questions could wait. "What did you find?"

"I started reaching out to a few of them again, and one of our second cousins talked to me. Do you remember her? Giulia?"

Mina could call up a vague memory of dyed red hair and a gap-toothed smile. "A bit. She's around your age?"

"Yeah," Sergio said. "She told me the truth, or at least as much of it as she knew. She and the rest of her family left because Aunt Stella and Dad weren't just putting spirits to rest—they were bargaining with them."

A chest at the bottom of Mina's ocean began to tremble. She could feel whatever lived inside of it rattling against the rotting wood. "Bargaining? For what?"

"Asking them to do things in exchange for life force," Sergio said. "I guess that helps ghosts hang around a little longer. Giulia called it a sacrifice. Some of you for some of the spirit. Apparently it's a bad idea to use dead people as tools."

His tone was cavalier, but Mina knew he was trying to sound like he wasn't incredibly upset. She understood the impulse.

"But they taught us not to do that," she protested weakly.

"Where did you find that summoning spell that got you into all that trouble?" he pointed out. "That was Aunt Stella's, right?"

Mina's voice came out a whimper. "Right."

"Anyway, something awful happened. It was related to the drowning summer. That's all Giulia could tell me. But apparently there was some big sacrifice the family couldn't ignore anymore, and they disowned our parents because of it."

A big sacrifice. Mina's mind whirled, trying to knit the whole thing together. Her curse, her own life force siphoned. How she was bound to Annette, not the drowning summer victims. The way Stella had blamed Greg Mackenzie for everything. And a final memory of her mother lying in bed, exhausted, whispering: *I believe they were murdered by human hands.*

Evelyn had been right. There *was* a hole in the story they'd constructed. A hole that could only be filled by a medium.

"You don't think," she said. "That sacrifice they're talking about. Sergio—you don't think they had anything to do with…"

"I don't know. But I'm not ready to talk to Dad yet. I'm spending the night at a friend's. Maybe you should do the same."

"No." Mina swallowed. "I have to know the truth."

She was warded inside the house, and yet she still felt the barest whispers in the back of her mind, as if Annette had been awoken by her thoughts. Tonight was the new moon—with everything happening to Evelyn, she'd almost forgotten.

If Stella had pinned the murders on Greg on purpose, Evelyn's suffering had come directly at the hands of the Zanettis. Handling this would be the biggest challenge of Mina's whole life. But she needed to know what her mother had done. For both their sakes.

When Stella came home from work that evening, Mina was waiting for her. She'd even made her coffee and put together a little antipasti, as a peace offering. Stella eyed the cutting board stacked with cheese, prosciutto, roasted red peppers, and a small bowl of olives with visible delight.

"Goodness, it feels nice to be inside," she said as she sat down and sipped her coffee. "The wards are such a relief."

"I'm sure they are." Mina wrapped a hand around her own

coffee mug. "I'm assuming you heard what happened with Evelyn's dad."

"Yes." Stella sighed. "It's quite upsetting. The whole town is
stirred up."

"Do you really think he did it?"

"I..." Stella hesitated. "Nobody knows for certain, do they?"

"This mystery," Mina continued. "And this ghost. They both
seem so tied together. They've messed with both our family and
Evelyn's. But I finally think I can solve the problem. If you help
me, we can exorcise this ghost."

"If I knew who she was, Mina, I would have already—"

"She?" Mina had trained her whole life to be an impervious,
emotionless dam against the waves inside her. But it took everything she had to keep her voice calm.

"I misspoke," Stella said quickly. "You know as well as I do
that the potential demon's identity remains hidden."

"So the name Annette Shorewell means nothing to you?"

Stella flinched, her coffee trembling in her hand. Mina
swallowed her disappointment. Whenever she thought she'd
reached the bottom of Stella's lying, there was always more. All
she'd done this summer—no, her whole life—was sink into a
bottomless ocean of deceit.

"Careful, don't spill it on yourself again," she said. "That
worked well last time, didn't it? Distracting me before I could
ask more questions about our family?"

"Mina," her mother protested. "That's not what's going on
here—"

"Enough." Mina set down her coffee mug. She had never
been so frightened. She had never been so furious. "You've

known who she is this whole time, Mom. And you've hidden that from me."

"You don't understand." Stella sounded frantic. "I kept the truth about Annette from you to protect you."

"Stop pretending you were trying to protect anyone but yourself," Mina snapped. "I know I'm bound to her instead of the Cliffside Trio. You hid that from me, too, didn't you?"

The anguish on her mother's face told Mina she was right.

"Please, Mina. You don't understand the choice I had to make—"

"A choice? Or a bargain?" Mina heard whispers in her mind again. The sand dollar on her wrist throbbed, and she knew it was only a matter of time until even the wards couldn't hold Annette back. "What sacrifice did you and Uncle Dom give her that was so horrible, it made the rest of our family leave?"

Stella blanched. She stared at Mina with wide, beseeching eyes, as if begging her to say something else. So Mina did.

"Was it them?" she asked. "Did you feed Jesse, Tamara, and Colin to a ghost?"

"What?" For the first time, Stella seemed genuinely shocked. She set down her coffee, brown liquid sloshing over the rim. "Mina—how could you ever—I would never do something like that."

Mina searched her mother's face for another lie. She couldn't find one, but that didn't mean it wasn't there.

"Then tell me what happened during the drowning summer," Mina said. "What really happened. Please, Mom—this is your last chance before you lose my trust forever."

"All right." Stella was still pale and trembling, but she looked resolute. "I suppose this is what I deserve. I should have told you the truth a long time ago.

"There has been a budding demon in Cliffside Bay for as long as I can remember. But it takes many souls to convert a ghost to a demon. We believed that was why everything was warping— that the draw of that one spirit was changing all the dead in the area. Your uncle and I had been working on ways to contain Annette's spirit without knowing who she was. We were willing to use more... experimental methods than the rest of our family."

"Bargaining," Mina said.

Stella nodded. "We thought developing relationships with other ghosts would be necessary in order to prevent her ascension to demonhood. These ghosts made us more powerful, and we gave them a little longer to stick around. It felt like a fair trade—a necessary one, if we wanted to make an exorcism work. The rest of our family felt differently, but things didn't reach a tipping point until the Cliffside Trio got involved."

"So they really did come to you about Annette."

"Yes. They solved a mystery that had baffled us for a generation. They figured out who Annette was, and we thanked them and told them we'd take it from there. Yet they summoned her anyway. I still don't know where they found out how to do so— how they even figured out there was a ghost at all. But they were unprepared for how powerful she would be. When she killed them, we feared it meant she had ascended. But she was still a ghost."

"So she was powerful enough to kill three people, but she's

only targeting mediums now? What happened to *We stand on the bridge between life and death*—was that a lie, too?"

"It wasn't." Stella sighed. "The rest of the family blamed us for what had happened. They believed *we* had given the three of them access to our summoning techniques."

"Is that why they left?"

"No." Stella's voice was trembling so hard now, Mina could barely make out the words. "They left because of you."

Mina's sand dollar pulsed painfully. Annette's voice whimpered in the back of her mind, and Mina wanted to whimper back, because as much as she needed to know the truth, she feared she wasn't ready for whatever she was about to learn.

"Why?"

"We only needed to find an object that had belonged to her. We were so close to finishing all of this, even though she was more powerful than ever. But then...you found my experimental summoning instructions. And you called her. The reason she must have chosen you over Evelyn is because of all the work your uncle and I had done. We'd dabbled in something we shouldn't have, and so the ocean knew our blood. It knew us. And it knew you, too."

"And then?"

"She started sapping your life force," Stella said. "She couldn't kill you right away, like she'd killed the Cliffside Trio— you knew enough even then to shield yourself better than they would've. But it wasn't enough. I knew I had to do whatever I could to fix it."

"Fix it?" Mina whispered. "What did you do, Mom?"

"You have to understand, Mina, her spirit was absorbing you.

You were admitted to the hospital with a fever so high you were hallucinating, and no matter what the doctors did, you weren't getting better. I knew—" Stella's voice broke. She shuddered, then continued. "I knew you were going to die. As mediums, we're taught that death is natural. That we must learn to accept the inevitable as part of our calling. But you were so small, with so much life to live. And I loved you too much to let you go."

"So you made a bargain," Mina said.

Stella couldn't meet her eyes anymore. "Yes. I made it so that as long as you lived, Annette could feed off your life force but not take it entirely. You sustain her, and in exchange, she spared you. An imperfect solution, but I didn't know just how imperfect until you began to insist on training to become a medium."

One of the chests in Mina's ocean cracked open, then another. She couldn't stop every awful thing she'd stored inside them from swimming out into the open water. "This goes against everything you've ever taught me."

"I knew it would hurt you to find out. But I had to keep you safe."

But Mina was so far past believing her. Annette's voice snarled in her mind, and it no longer sounded like a threat. It sounded like a warning.

"And the warding necklace?" she asked.

"I didn't want the Cliffside Trio to tell you the truth," Stella said. "I couldn't block you from Annette directly, not without something that belonged to her. But cutting you off from her three strongest spirits—the lives she'd taken herself—seemed as if it would help."

"And what about Greg Mackenzie? You were a witness against him."

"I wasn't lying about seeing him that day. He was in the right place at the wrong time... and it was easier to keep the authorities suspecting him than digging into our family. If I'd known it would lead directly to your situation, I never would have done it."

"So you destroyed Evelyn's family," Mina said. "And you've let us run around trying to fix this all summer when you knew that there was nothing we could do. Hoping all the while that we'd fail and I would crawl right back to you."

"You assume the worst of me." Stella sounded utterly broken. "I have spent this summer trying to find a way to break your bond with Annette, before it's too late."

"Too late?"

"Annette is still trying to become a demon," Stella said. "And an ascension like that is impossible without help from someone living. A medium must help a ghost cross back into this world. And the bond you have with Annette... it is most likely strong enough to do that."

Mina thought of whatever had happened at the full moon. Of Annette holding out that sand dollar.

Had she been trying to bargain with Mina? To cross back over? To wreak havoc?

She'd thought of Annette as a victim in all this. But maybe it wasn't that simple. She'd murdered three people. She'd nearly murdered Mina, too.

And Mina was bound to her for the rest of her life.

"You've hidden too much from me," she told her mother.

All her life, she'd wanted nothing more than to be just like Stella. But now Mina understood that the person she'd wanted to be was a fantasy, an idealized version of someone who had preached control and consequences, yet flung all of that to the winds as soon as it suited her.

Mina couldn't even look at her.

"I don't want your help," she told Stella. "And I don't know who you are anymore. I'm not sure I ever did."

Mina left her sitting at the kitchen table. When she turned back in the doorway, her mother was watching her go, one arm slightly outstretched, as if to try and take her hand once more.

Mina didn't know when she'd fallen asleep, but she woke to the sand dollar on her wrist jolting with pain. She groaned and rolled over in bed. Light coiled beneath her skin, flashing between blue and orange. But for the first time in days, there was no presence in her mind to accompany that pain.

It was still the new moon, and Annette was quiet.

Something was *wrong*.

She swung out of bed and bolted to her door, careening into the hallway. Stella's door hung slightly open. Mina pushed it open frantically and scanned the space—empty. Stella wasn't in the kitchen, the living room, the bathroom. She wasn't anywhere.

Maybe she had gone to stay with Uncle Dom—but no. Mina knew that wasn't right.

She found Stella's opal headband on the porch. It was

cracked and broken, a trail of stones strewn down the first few stairs to the beach.

Oh no. Oh *no*. Stella had gone back to Sand Dollar Cove.

The stairs seemed even steeper and more precarious now, lit by nothing but her phone flashlight and the weak light of dawn slowly creeping across the sky. A sulfuric, rotten smell wafted through the air the closer she got to the water.

She saw why as soon as she reached the bottom of the stairs. It was low tide, and the descending waterline had left a trail of sludge in its wake, the same kind of waste that had rained down in Jesse's bedroom. Dead fish and horseshoe crabs were scattered across the rocks, the latter flipped on their backs with their legs hanging limply in the air. Flies buzzed around their corpses.

Standing in the middle of the carnage, knee-deep in the surf, was Stella Zanetti. She gazed out at the horizon as a bluish-orange light spread through the water around her, seeping from her body like a bloodstain.

"Mom!" Mina's bare feet squished through the sludge as she waded into the foam. The sea was pulling backward so fast she could see it moving, just like it had the night of the full moon. "What are you doing?"

Stella turned, her hair whipping in the wind. The expression on her face was frightening in its tranquility: She looked resolute and calm, as if this were any ordinary morning.

"Get out of the water, Mina. It's not safe."

"Mom, please, just come back to the beach—"

"It's too late," Stella said dreamily. "It's already done, my seashell."

"What's already done? What did you do?"

Mina spun around frantically. Discarded in the sludge were items she'd missed before: candles, an overturned bowl, a bloodstained silken scarf.

"You made another deal with her," Mina choked out as she waded deeper into the surf. She only had to make it another thirty feet to grab Stella and force her out of this. She could get her back up the stairs and into their warded house, far, far away from Annette Shorewell. She had to.

"A trade." Blue and orange light spread beneath Stella's skin, snaking up her arms. "Annette will siphon my life away in place of yours over the next few days. And when it's done, you won't belong to her anymore. I will."

"No! I won't let you bind yourself to her the way you bound me." Mina's sand dollar flared again. This time, the pain was everywhere, prickling beneath her skin like an electrical current. She screamed and fell to her knees. She was on fire at the edge of the sea; she clawed her wrist, as if she could scratch the sand dollar away with her fingernails.

And then a translucent hand reached up from the surf. Then another, then another, restraining her limbs and forcing her into a crouch.

"It's all right, my seashell," Stella said gently, leaning down and tipping up her chin. A burst of bluish green appeared on her cheek, right under the mole below her eye. "It's not the same bond. She's agreed to take all my life, to leave you alone. It's the trade I should've made six years ago. But it's not too late. You'll be safe, Mina. That's all I've ever cared about."

Mina cried out and thrashed against the hands, but they didn't budge.

"Don't leave me," she whimpered. But just like always, Stella didn't listen. Instead, her mother waded farther into the ocean. A wave built before her, just like the one at the full moon.

Mina heard no voices in her mind, but she spoke anyway.

"Please," Mina murmured, "please, please, just let her go, just let her live. . . ."

In front of her, there was a flicker, and then there was Annette, a ghostly blue green, sand dollars plastered over her eyes. Her spirit was a warped, grotesque thing. Seaweed twined through her hair; barnacles grew on her arms and legs. Orange light had corroded her lower jaw and half her shoulder, and Mina made out a few cigarette butts sticking out from her neck, broken glass studding her skin. Pieces of plastic hung off one of her wrists like jewelry.

Annette lifted up a hand, and three figures appeared behind her, their faces glowing and indistinct—Tamara, Jesse, and Colin. And then more figures behind them, and more behind them: twenty, maybe thirty spirits, all of them with sand dollars over their eyes, too. Mina caught a glimpse of Mr. Giacomo flickering in the waves, his mouth open in anguish.

In the center of it all was Stella, so full of light that she could have been a spirit, too. The wave rose above her, so tall it seemed to blot out the sun.

"I can't," Annette said.

Mina barely had time to scream before the wave crashed over Stella's head and pulled her mother into the ocean.

Chapter Thirty-one

In the days after Evelyn's world crumbled, strange, sludgy liquid began washing up all over Cliffside Bay. It left behind hundreds of dead sea creatures and a horrible, inescapable stench, which the breeze carried all over town. No one was allowed on the beach aside from the cleaning crews dispatched to handle the mess, but that didn't stop it from returning each morning. Evelyn didn't need to get close to the carnage to know what was happening—she could hear the panicked voices of the dead well enough through her shell necklace. She tried taking it off, but that only made it worse.

Mina's mother wasn't among the dead, at least not yet. She'd washed up on the shore like a piece of driftwood and been taken to the hospital, where she remained alive but unconscious.

"So she took your place in the bargain?" Evelyn asked Mina. They were sitting in Mina's uncle's house, in the bedroom that Mina had slept in when they were children. It had been two days since the incident, but Mina had spent most of that time in the hospital, then at the police station, until the officers were sufficiently satisfied it had all been a terrible accident. Evelyn was relieved to be back in the same room as her.

Mina nodded and held out her wrist. The blue-green sand dollar was visibly faded. "The bond was too strong for her to transfer it all at once," she said. "But every day, I feel it—*her*—a little less."

Evelyn listened as Mina told her the rest of it. Not just about the bargain that Stella had made to save her life, but the lies she'd told to protect the Zanetti family. And the bond that Mina had felt with the ghost herself, one that had gone beyond fear and into some sort of understanding. Evelyn could tell that was the part that frightened Mina most of all.

"Your dad is innocent," Mina said. "Annette Shorewell killed Jesse, Colin, and Tamara. And my family covered it up."

Evelyn struggled to find any sort of relief. Greg was innocent, but if the true murderer was a ghost, she had no idea how to prove that innocence. And it was hard for her to be furious with Stella Zanetti when she was currently in some kind of coma.

"I'm so sorry," Evelyn said. "If we hadn't done that summoning six years ago, you would never have been put in this position. And your mom probably would've figured out how to banish Annette by now."

"I'm not sure that's true." Mina stared mournfully at her faded sand dollar. "Mom doesn't think about the consequences of her actions. Even now, she's dying in there to break my bond with Annette. But if she gives all her life force to that ghost..."

Mina trailed off, but Evelyn had already put the pieces together.

"You think she won't be a ghost anymore," she finished.

"Mom said a medium has to help a ghost cross back into our world in order to finish a demon ascension. What she's doing feels like the biggest help a ghost could possibly get. And all that just to save me?" Her voice broke. "That's not what I want. That's not *right*."

Something gave in her then, as if the story of how she'd gotten here had been the only thing keeping her together. She let out a soft, choked whimper and crumpled into Evelyn's arms, sobbing. Evelyn held her as she cried, nestling her nose into the crown of Mina's head. She knew how it felt to be flooded with emotions too big for a body to hold.

"I don't know what to do," Mina said at last. She was the taller one, but she'd folded herself into Evelyn anyway, her face pressed deep into her shoulder. Evelyn could feel her tears through her T-shirt. "I'm so scared."

"Me too," Evelyn said. "But I know we can find some way to stop Annette. An exorcism would save your mother, right?"

Mina sniffled. "Maybe. We don't have anything that belonged to Annette, though. We can't do anything without that."

"Remember what you told me?" Evelyn asked, stroking her hair. "Practices evolve over time. So do mediums. Maybe it's time for us to try something new."

Mina pulled away, and for a moment Evelyn thought she'd gotten through to her. Her eyes were swollen, her nose red. But then her mouth hardened, and her expression flickered back to closed off.

"My mother thought she could evolve, too," she said. "It only made things worse."

"But, Mina—"

"Please," Mina whispered. "Stop."

Evelyn wanted to tell her that she wasn't her mother. That burrowing inside herself and refusing to fight would only make it worse. But she couldn't bear to be hard on Mina right now, not when she was so fragile.

"Okay," she said uneasily as she let Mina curl up against her once more.

But Evelyn couldn't ignore her worry that if Annette obtained Stella's full life force by the full moon next week, she would probably ascend. The ocean Evelyn loved so much would be at a demon's mercy. And she had no idea how to stop it.

Evelyn's family problems felt trivial compared to Mina's, but coming home to reporters in her driveway still hurt. The local news had been in and out for the last few days, taking footage of the Mackenzies' home as if it were going to give them an interview. Evelyn cut through the Kowalskis' backyard, hopped the fence, and landed a little clumsily in the dry brown grass behind her house. She pushed open the back door to find Greg staring at the blinds, a feather duster in his hand and an expression of pure determination on his face.

"Oh, good. You're back," he said. "Do you know where the broom is?"

Evelyn lowered her longboard. The lights were on, illuminating the dirty living room. The TV was off. A vacuum cleaner sat against the wall, which had visibly been put to use on the hardwood floor.

"Dad," she said. "What are you doing?"

"Cleaning the house, of course. I should've done this years ago."

"I mean...yeah," Evelyn said cautiously. "But why now?"

Greg didn't look like a man who currently had reporters sitting outside his house, gawking at the potential home of a triple murderer. He seemed almost content. "It felt like it was time. Now, about that broom?"

"It's upstairs," she said. "You want help?"

He nodded. "If it's not too much trouble."

Together, they mopped and dusted and swept, moving the furniture around so they could give the floors a true deep clean. The living room looked different with everything askew. Like it belonged in some other house, with some other family.

"Don't you have a shift today?" her father asked after a little while.

"Nah." Evelyn swirled the mop around in the water bucket. "I've kind of called out of both jobs for a little while. Until this, uh...blows over."

Greg nodded, looking resigned. "Did your bosses give you trouble?"

"No. I think they're happy they didn't have to cut my hours themselves. They don't want reporters hanging around."

It had been only a couple days, but she knew everything had changed again. She'd avoided looking at any texts that weren't Mina's. She couldn't bear to read the inevitable hatred, or any excuses from her supposed friends about needing space.

"Those reporters should be ashamed," Greg murmured. "You're a kid. None of this has anything to do with you."

"Aren't you scared of them?" Evelyn swabbed the patch of floor where the recliner used to sit. There was a massive stain on the wood, but the more she attacked it with the mop, the less awful it looked.

Her father's voice was incredibly weary. "I've been scared for six years. Hiding in here. Hiding from you."

"I think I was hiding from you, too," Evelyn said. "The drowning summer felt like an impossible thing to talk about."

"Some things are hard to reckon with, even from a distance," her father said gravely. "I used to be furious with your mother for what she'd done, and I still am, but I understand it. Meredith, too."

"You understand why Meredith gave that horrible interview?"

Her sister had texted and called her, just like everyone else in Cliffside Bay. She'd stopped only because Evelyn had blocked her number.

"Well, not that part," Greg said. "But I do understand why she left. This place has caused her nothing but pain for a very long time."

"Why did you stay, then?" she asked him. "Cliffside Bay has hurt you, too."

"I know. But I didn't want to let it win. I wanted there to be something those rumors couldn't take away from me. The truth is, though, that I don't get to choose whether people believe me or not. Whether they stay or go. No matter how much I try to hold on to things . . . they tend to float away."

Evelyn put the mop back in the bucket and shoved it into the hallway. The walls and windowsills were free of dirt and dust;

the hardwood floors gleamed. Sure, the furniture was still old and the house was still rickety. But it was a real improvement.

"I get to choose, too," she said. "And even if those reporters never leave us alone, I'm staying."

Greg coughed and turned his head away. Evelyn knew he was doing a bad job of trying not to cry.

"You want to know why?" he asked finally. "Why I'm cleaning?"

"Because our living room was disgusting?"

He chuckled. "Well, yeah. But even though I can't make those reporters go away, and I can't clear my name...I can make damn sure that our house looks like people actually live in it."

Evelyn didn't know what to say to that. She felt guilt, that her dad was still here and Mina's mother was in the hospital. Relief that he was doing all right. Anger that he hadn't been able to function like this sooner. And something else, too. A tug of hope. Maybe they could find some way to survive this together.

Before she could find a response, there was a knock on the back door.

"Shit," Greg said. "They jumped the fence?"

Evelyn retreated, hoping they could get away from the open blinds before the reporters got a picture. But before she'd taken more than a few steps, she recognized the figures on the other side of the window.

"Wait. Those aren't reporters."

Kenny looked like he was about to collapse, but then, he always looked like that. Luisa and Amy seemed far less fragile, although she could feel the nervous energy radiating from all three of them.

"Hey," Kenny squeaked out. "Um. Glad we got the right house. Would've come through the front door, but..."

"It's a nightmare out there," Evelyn said flatly. "Why are you here?"

She couldn't know if this was some kind of trick—maybe someone had planted a camera on one of them. But no, Kenny was way too neurotic for that to ever work.

"You haven't been answering our texts," Luisa said. "We just wanted to make sure you were okay."

"And let you know that we're thinking about you and Mina," Amy added. "It's super messed up that you're both dealing with so much right now."

"You're not..." Evelyn swallowed. "You don't have to pretend to be nice to me."

"Well, I'm sure as shit not pretending," Amy said. She looked from Luisa to Kenny. "Are you?"

"Don't be silly," Luisa said gently. "You're our friend."

"And work's way more boring without you," Amy added. "You've missed some real scandals. Kenny put his podcast on the speaker system and almost got fired."

"Amy!" Kenny looked like he wanted to sink through Evelyn's back steps. "But, um. Yeah. We miss you."

"And we thought you might want to get away from all this," Luisa added. "There's half-price movie tickets at this place about thirty minutes from here. Want to come?"

They weren't embarrassed to be her friends because of her father. They weren't giving up on her after all. Evelyn didn't even try to suppress her tears.

Evelyn had thought of herself as a lone organism in the intertidal zone, trapped but tough enough to weather anything. But that wasn't how an ecosystem worked. No creature survived without the rhythms of the larger world, the complex, fragile web of life that left everything and everyone inextricably connected.

And Evelyn was finally ready to accept that not only had she always been part of this particular ecosystem—she *wanted* to be.

Cliffside Bay was her home.

She swore in that moment that she would find some way to protect that home from Annette, no matter what. But right now...right now, she really wanted to sit in a dark, cool theater and watch a movie with the friends who'd chosen not to run away.

"Sure," she said, sniffling. "Let's go."

Chapter Thirty-Two

Mina had never known it was possible to miss someone so much. She found herself clinging to every good Stella memory she had: her mother's off-key singing, her food, the opals in her hair glimmering as she laughed at all their inside jokes. Mina had spent the past few weeks avoiding her mother, but she'd believed that eventually, they would curl up together on that orange velvet couch and talk it out. Now she wondered if that day would ever come.

The foundation of her ocean was not sand and sediment. It was her mother. And even after Stella's lies and betrayals, she couldn't live in a world where her mother had been taken away from her like this. There was nothing to cling to. Nowhere to run. All she could do was sink into the abyss.

She didn't notice time passing. Sometimes Evelyn was there, and sometimes she wasn't. Sergio and Dom drifted in and out of her childhood bedroom as she tunneled beneath the covers, clutching one of her mother's gauzy scarves like a stuffed animal. Her ocean was beyond storms, beyond waves—it lay flat and colorless, reflecting the sky back without a single ripple. It had surrendered, just like Mina.

Until a pair of Sperrys and salmon shorts appeared in her sightline.

Mina groaned and yanked the duvet over her head. Nick Slater was the last person she wanted to talk to right now.

"I know we don't know each other very well." Nick's voice wafted through her blanket cocoon. "But I think I can help you."

"You?" Mina couldn't hide her disdain. "No."

"I'll leave if you want." Nick sounded different than he usually did. Sad. Quiet. "But I know how it feels to lose someone who's kind of your whole world."

Jesse. Of course. Despite herself, Mina felt the slightest stir of interest. She pulled the blankets down to see Nick hovering beside her bed, an awkward, hopeful expression on his face.

"You don't even like me," she mumbled. "The last time you saw me..."

Annette Shorewell had attacked him through her. And then he'd yelled at her and Evelyn to go away.

"I know what I said. But I don't hate you. And even if I did, nobody deserves to go through what you're going through."

"Maybe I do." Mina had been thinking that from the moment the wave took her mother away. "I bound myself to Annette's spirit during the drowning summer. Stella broke all her rules to save me."

"I... I didn't know that."

"It doesn't matter anyway." She waved her wrist in the air. The sand dollar on it was half gone now, like a temporary tattoo slowly fading away. "When it disappears, she'll die. And there's nothing I can do about it."

"You sure?" Nick lowered himself onto the floor and sat cross-legged on the carpet. He was tall enough that this put him at Mina's eye level. "She's alive. That means it's not too late."

"I told Evelyn this already," Mina protested. "No more plans. All they've done is destroy my family."

Her voice wobbled on the last word. Nick's face softened.

"When Jesse died, I was so scared," he said. "I didn't understand why he'd left me, and my parents were too wrecked to really help. But now I know the world's unfair, and horrible things happen all the time that are way out of our control."

"What are you trying to say?" Mina hated that she was close to tears. She didn't want to cry in front of Nick Slater.

"That this *isn't* out of your control. Not yet." Nick met her eyes. "Mina... if I knew there was even the tiniest chance I could save Jesse's life, I would take it. No matter how dangerous."

Mina sat up slowly, blood rushing to her head. When she touched her hair, she could feel the grease in it. When was the last time she'd showered? Eaten?

"This is different," she said. "Every time I've tried to do something about this, I've made it worse. I bound myself to Annette. I strengthened that bond. Now I've given her everything she needs to become a demon. If I interfere again... with my luck, I'll find some way to make her even *more* powerful."

Nick's voice was firm. "Does Evelyn know you've given up like this?"

"I haven't given up," Mina snapped. "And ask her yourself. Isn't she the one who put you up to this?"

"Actually, when I finally managed to talk to her, she told me to leave you alone. But I'm not going to let you grieve someone who isn't gone yet."

"You can't make me do anything," Mina said. "Why are you even worried? Are you scared Annette's going to come for your family once she ascends?"

To her surprise, Nick didn't even flinch. "If it were only my family she would hurt, I'd care a whole lot less. But Annette is out of control. I've been going through Jesse's files. He wanted to expose our family for what we'd done and who we'd hurt, even though he knew it would ruin us. Annette killed him, Tamara, and Colin anyway. If she ascends, she'll do worse."

"So you believe it?" Mina asked. "That your family's company really did have someone killed?"

"I think Jesse was right that the murder was a kidnapping gone wrong, but...yes, I believe it," Nick said. "Even though I can't prove it. That's what Jesse was looking for when he went to contact Annette, I think. Some final link that would put all the pieces together and make it impossible to deny."

"How can you stand it?" she whispered. "Knowing they did something so horrible?"

"I don't know." Nick sighed. "I wanted to pretend it wasn't happening at first. I was so worried I couldn't be the son my parents wanted that I made Evelyn cheat on that test, and now here I am, trying to figure out if they know part of our money comes from a murder cover-up and an environmental disaster."

"Maybe they don't know," Mina suggested.

"Maybe," Nick said, but she could tell he didn't believe it. "Look, I didn't ask for these problems. Neither did you. Neither did Evelyn. But if we just give up, you lose your mom forever. And Annette becomes a demon…which is really, really bad, right?"

She remembered what her mother had said—that a demon would be on par with a natural disaster. "Right."

"Then help me figure out how to stop it," Nick said. "Because we can't change the mistakes our parents made, but if we don't try to do something about the consequences of those mistakes now…"

"Then they'll become even worse. I know."

Mina had always thought of the bottom of her ocean as uninhabitable. The thoughts that belonged there were as unfathomable and cruel as the uncharted territory of the deep sea. But now she pictured herself in the water, no boat to ride in, no raft to cling to. She sank through her own mind until she reached the chests scattered on her ocean floor. Then she planted her feet in the sand and spread her arms wide, beckoning in all those memories she'd sunk. One by one, the chests cracked open, and Mina let their contents spill through her sea.

She thought of Stella sending the Mackenzie family into chaos. Of Slater Enterprises covering up the Blue Tide leak. Of orange light corroding the blue-green aura of a spirit, of waste washing up on the rocky shores of Cliffside Bay. Of Jesse, Colin, and Tamara sitting in that cave in Sand Dollar Cove, trying to find peace for a spirit that was too far gone.

She'd believed her part in this was finished, that she'd hurt too many people to go on. But the truth was, she'd just been too scared to fail again. So scared she'd been ready to let Stella go. So scared, she'd been ready to step aside as Annette ascended into a demon that could destroy Cliffside Bay.

Mina would never let fear control her like that again.

She turned to Nick and gave him a sharp, steady nod.

"All right," she said. "I'll try."

The first order of business in Mina's extremely impractical plan was talking to her uncle. Evelyn was working on a theory about adapting the summoning ceremony for their individual medium practices, and Nick was digging up as much as he could find about Jesse, Colin, and Tamara's plans. So while they were off putting together puzzle pieces, she went looking for her own.

She found Uncle Dom out on the pier behind his house, docking his motorboat.

"Mina," he said, looking relieved. "You're out of bed."

Mina had taken a shower, forced down a meal, even put on some concealer. It had been incredibly difficult, but she had to try, for Stella's sake.

"Do you have a minute?" she asked. "I want to talk to you about something."

"Anything for you." He gestured back toward the house. "Walk with me?"

The waste swirling through Long Island Sound had made going anywhere near the ocean unpleasant. Uncle Dom had been trawling in nets filled with dead, rotted wildlife every day, until the local government formally banned fishing of any kind. Mina was more than happy to leave the smell and the sight behind.

"It's about Mom," she said quietly. "I know we fought before all of this, but..."

"That's done now." Uncle Dom wrapped an arm around her

shoulders. "We're your family, Mina. We'll get through this together."

Mina felt a swell of warmth at that. She knew her uncle had been part of her mother's scheming, but she also knew he loved her.

"I know," she said. "But we need to talk about what to do next."

"I couldn't agree more." Uncle Dom pushed open the back door. Mina followed him into the kitchen. It was nothing like the one at the cottage—Stella had taken all her supplies when they moved out, and Uncle Dom hadn't really bothered to replace them. "I know this is difficult, but...I think it's time we talked about what to do with the house. We can bring over your things from your bedroom, but I'm afraid there won't be enough room for all the furniture in storage. Perhaps we could sell it—"

"What?" Mina shrugged out of his grasp, uncomprehending. "I—I'm just staying here for a little while. Until she wakes up."

The look on her uncle's face threatened to break her. "I've been talking to the doctors. She isn't going to wake up."

It was a line right out of Mina's worst nightmares. And for a moment it sank through her, pushing down her newfound determination. Maybe he was right.

But this summer had taught her that maybe he was wrong, too.

"That's because they don't know why she's sick," Mina protested. "We do. We can make a plan. We can break her bond with Annette, find some way to save her—"

"Enough. We need to accept the way things are."

"You're accepting that Mom's currently helping create a demon?"

"We don't know that for certain," Uncle Dom said. "But even

if she is, we've already spent this summer trying to exorcise Annette's spirit. Her bargain has made that far more complicated than it already was."

"That doesn't mean we can't fix it," Mina protested.

But her uncle hesitated, and Mina understood that he would be no help.

"Fine." She kept her voice flat. "Just don't try to stop me."

Mina couldn't be in this house anymore. She wasn't sure where she could go—Evelyn's home had been a minefield of reporters since the news about her father broke—but she wouldn't stay here.

Before she could reach the doorway, though, her path was blocked by Sergio.

"Hey." He looked troubled, although Mina supposed they all did. "I heard your argument."

"Fantastic." Mina moved to shoulder past him, but he held up his hands.

"Wait. I think I can help you."

"Really? I thought you didn't care about any of this."

"I can't be the medium Dad wants, no," Sergio said, his voice hushed. Mina understood—at any moment, Uncle Dom could walk out of the kitchen. "But if you're going to try to save Aunt Stella, I want in."

Mina hadn't been in Sergio's room in ages. It was dimly lit and messy, with an overflowing laundry hamper and a few poorly hung posters on the dark blue walls. She sat on a beanbag chair, trying her best to avoid any suspicious stains.

"Dad's too scared to confront Annette," Sergio said, sitting on the side of the bed. "But it's the only way to make this right."

"I know," Mina said. "But I can't think of a way to call her that doesn't put us in even more danger. Even if we try when we're most powerful...she'll just overwhelm us."

"I think that's actually one of the biggest things Dad got wrong," Sergio said. "It's the spirits that are at their strongest during the new and full moons. Not the mediums. Sure, you can hear them more clearly, but they have way more power to mess everything up. If you want your best shot...I think you should go after her during the first-quarter moon, when the tidal range is lowest. She'll be weaker."

Mina hadn't thought of this before. It made a strange sort of sense. "But that's in two days," she said. "That's not a lot of time."

"Your mother doesn't have a lot of time."

It was blunt but true. Mina forced back more tears; there would be time for that later.

"I'll think about it," she said. "I still don't have an exact summoning in mind. And I don't think Annette will fall for it—she must know we're going to try this."

"So what *would* she fall for? What does she want?"

Mina frowned. What could she possibly want now that she had Stella in her clutches and an ascension on the horizon? Mina thought of the vision she'd seen, the way Annette had told her to take the sand dollar. And she had an idea.

"She wants to make a bargain," she said. "So I'm going to offer her one that she can't possibly refuse."

Chapter Thirty-Three

The Shorewell Community Center looked lonely at night, its glass arms extended in an empty embrace. The quarter moon hovered above its sharp widow's peak of a roof, barely visible through the clouds blanketing the sky. Humidity clung to Evelyn's skin, and she knew a storm was coming soon. One of her hands clutched the strap of her canvas tote. The other was clasped tightly in Mina's.

"This is it," she said as they walked through the deserted parking lot. She could barely see Mina beyond a silhouette, but she caught the other girl's nod.

If they could stop Annette from ascending, they'd save lives. Including Mina's mother's.

Or they'd fail, die horribly, and be absorbed into a demon.

No pressure.

The building was locked, but Mina used her mother's employee ID to buzz them in. Evelyn followed Mina and her battery-powered lantern down the mazelike hallways, periodically touching the shell around her neck for comfort.

When they reached the basement, Mina stopped and set down her lantern on a shelf. Everything was swathed in dim, golden light—discarded wedding decorations and pantry supplies, old paint cans and dusty glassware.

"What's going on?" Evelyn asked nervously. They stood beneath a wooden archway draped in moth-eaten lace, mere feet from the padlocked door to the pool. "Is something wrong?"

"No," Mina said. "But I don't know what's going to happen in there. And in case things go wrong...I wanted to. Um. Kiss you. One more time."

Evelyn was surprised to find herself on the verge of tears. She could just about look Mina in the eyes when she stood on her tiptoes and wrapped her arms around the other girl's neck. Mina clutched her fiercely, as if Evelyn would disappear if she let go.

But when their lips were a hair's breadth apart, Evelyn stopped. Mina's face was split between light and shadow, her eyes closed. She'd worn a full face of makeup to stop a demonic ascension. Evelyn knew her well enough now to understand that it was another defense mechanism, like a salt circle for Mina's self-control.

"This isn't a kiss goodbye," Evelyn whispered. "This is me promising you that we're going to do this again."

Mina's brown eyes fluttered open.

"I promise, too," she whispered back. And then her lips were on Evelyn's, and for a moment Evelyn forgot where they were and what they needed to do. There was only Mina, and that was enough.

The cracks in the floor spiderwebbed across the concrete, spreading from one wall to the foundation of the pool itself. As Evelyn finished sweeping away the salt circle Dom and Stella had left behind, her sneakers crunched across shards of broken glass. The smell of rot wafted through the broken windows as she studied the fissures that crisscrossed below the water. Thunder boomed in the distance, and Evelyn felt a smattering of rain on her face.

On the other side of the pool, Mina opened her daisy-printed backpack and pulled out a lifetime supply of candles, three different scrying bowls, and a bunch of bubble-wrapped glass. A giant container of salt already sat on the ground beside her.

"You know we're only summoning one ghost, right?" Evelyn said.

Mina looked up ruefully. "I was worried we wouldn't have enough supplies."

"You are totally that girl who overpacks for trips."

Mina flushed. "It's important to be prepared."

It didn't take that long to pour salt around the pool, or to place tea light candles around the circle they'd made. As Evelyn lit them one by one, each flickering flame reminded her just how fragile her and Mina's lives felt in the face of something so dangerous.

Once they were done, Evelyn dug out her own contribution to this makeshift summoning. She'd given a lot of thought to Annette Shorewell's spirit—more specifically, the ways Annette had been altered by the chemical composition of the Sound. If she and Mina wanted to have any chance of surviving this, they'd need to figure out how to defend themselves against that power.

She'd gone to the beach yesterday morning and taken samples of the sludge Annette had washed up on the shore, along with some vials of murky water. Then she'd poured it all into a bowl on her bedroom floor and dunked the Cliffside Trio's personal objects inside. Together, Evelyn and Mina spilled their blood into the water as Clara watched from her tank. Evelyn left the bowl in her room overnight, covered in Saran Wrap, and when she checked it the next morning, blue and orange light swirled inside. She could feel the charge it held even from a distance.

Now, she held two vials of that water in her hands. A new kind of ward, or at least she hoped so, the Zanetti glass and the Mackenzie natural world mixed together. If this all went according to plan, which Evelyn found unlikely, the wards would serve as a way to block out the influence of the drowning summer victims and force Annette to show herself to them directly. Ideally, it would also make it more difficult for her to hurt them.

"Here," Evelyn said, handing one of the vials to Mina. Blue light crackled inside for a moment before disappearing behind a swirl of sludge. "Can you feel the power in it?"

"Yes." Mina closed a hand around the vial. Evelyn could barely make out the faded sand dollar on her wrist.

Their plan wasn't that complicated. They would summon Annette and tell her that they'd learned who she was, just like Mina had originally intended, and that they wanted to lend their strength to her vengeance instead of trying to stop her. In order to do that, she would need to renew her bond with Mina...and *that* was when they would try to banish her.

"We don't have an object that belonged to her," Mina had explained. "But we have *me*. If I can pull her through to our world...shouldn't I be able to push her back, too?"

Evelyn hoped Mina was right as they dipped a wooden scrying bowl in the pool. Mina pulled out a pink Swiss Army Knife; Evelyn opted for her trusty box cutter. They slashed their palms, then clasped their hands together. Their combined blood dripped down their wrists and into the bowl.

Evelyn's hand throbbed as she pulled it away, but she didn't wipe the blood off. Something buzzed in the tote bag beside her—her phone. Evelyn frowned at the light glowing through the canvas. She didn't have time to deal with someone texting her right now.

"You ready?" she asked, turning back to Mina.

"No." But Mina grabbed the bowl in her hands, leaned over the salt circle, and dumped the contents into the pool. She jerked back hurriedly so as to get behind the barrier, and Evelyn followed her example.

As their blood swirled through the water, lit by the glow of three dozen candles, Evelyn began to recite the words they'd practiced.

"We call upon you, Annette Shorewell," she said, clutching the vial in one hand and the shell around her neck in the other.

"Show yourself, and we will bargain with you." Mina sounded eerily calm.

"We call upon you, Annette," they chanted together.

Evelyn's phone buzzed again. She felt a knot of déjà vu in

her stomach—what if something had happened to her father? Another news story? Some kind of arrest?

She stared at the pool, determined to focus. Rain fell steadily now, speckling the glass, washing out the smell of rot. A soft hissing came from the water. Her scrying focus glowed a moment later, sending blue light emanating from where it rested between her collarbones. The vial in her bloody palm began to heat up.

"Oh," Mina murmured from beside her. The sand dollar on her wrist was glowing blue as well.

The water in front of them came to life all at once, frothing and swirling into several tiny whirlpools. A glowing hand burst from one, then another, until there were three clawing desperately at the air. But instead of spirits rising from the ocean, orange light crackled at the edge of the whirlpools, and the hands slowly descended. The vial flared hot against Evelyn's skin.

Triumph coursed through her. They'd stopped the Cliffside Trio from materializing. This was actually working.

Another whirlpool began to form in the center of the water, bigger than the other three. Evelyn took a deep breath and braced herself as a spirit began to rise. First a bent head, then two shoulders, then hands, which Annette Shorewell braced against the thrashing water as if it were a solid object. She tilted her head up, her face flickering.

Mina had told Evelyn what the spirit looked like, but it was nothing compared to the sight of her in person. Sand dollars were pressed over Annette's eyes; seaweed, candy wrappers, and cigarette butts twined in her hair. Her fingernails were barnacles, her teeth shards of broken glass. She smelled so strongly of rot that Evelyn nearly gagged. And she looked like she was rotting, too, because that orange, corrosive light flared like a tiny sun inside her sternum. Tendrils snaked from a pulsing knot in her torso out through her limbs, eating away at her from the inside out.

"Annette Shorewell." Mina's voice was still calm. "How lovely of you to join us."

In response, Annette raised her too-long arms in the air. The pool churned furiously until water sloshed over the sides. Evelyn eyed the circle of salt nervously, but it remained unbroken.

"We would like to bargain with you," Mina continued, raising her voice as thunder boomed across the tossing sea beyond the windows.

Annette's voice was a low, creaky rasp. "Why would I bargain with you? I have all I could ever want."

"We don't want to stop you anymore," Evelyn said. "We know what you've been through."

"We know how you've suffered, and we want to help."

Annette swirled in and out of focus. "You... did not want this before."

"I changed my mind," Mina said. "If you break your bond with my mother, we can help you ascend right now. And you will have the strength of two young mediums on your side. A better deal, isn't it?"

"I...n—" Orange light flickered brighter inside of her, and she winced, body trembling. "Yes."

Evelyn felt a stab of unease. Had the ghost just tried and failed to say no?

"Excellent." Mina pulled out Stella's scrying focus from her pocket, the green glass orb she'd picked up after her pendant was destroyed by the ghost. "Here."

She tossed it into the pool. Immediately, water began to swirl around it. Annette bent down, her hands clutching at the pendant. She murmured at it softly, as if whispering sweet nothings—then crushed it in her palm. Light swirled up from her hand and dissipated into the air, and Evelyn felt something shift. Annette's form flickered at the edges, fuzzy and static.

"How do we know if she actually did it?" Evelyn asked.

Mina hesitated. "I...I felt something. And, well, look at her."

"I have weakened myself," Annette hissed. "Now you."

This was too simple. Too easy.

"Annette," Mina began. "We banish—"

The ceiling began to shake. Evelyn gasped as a chunk of wood fell to the ground, then another. Water streamed through each of the holes, intensifying the smell of salt and rot.

"Tell me this was supposed to happen."

"It—it wasn't." Mina rose to her feet and stared frantically at the water pouring from the ceiling. "Stop this, Annette—"

"I can't." Annette's voice was still raspy, but there was a note to it that felt almost...panicked. A gust of wind whipped through the room, bringing more rain with it, and the water pooled against the concrete, washing away the salt circle. Evelyn scrambled to her feet as well, slinging her tote bag over her shoulder. Her phone still buzzed furiously inside.

"Yes, you can," Evelyn snapped. "Didn't you just weaken yourself?"

Annette let out a soft, pained wail. She was so many

contradictions at once: human and inhuman, natural but unnatural, trapped between life and death in a maelstrom of orange and bluish green.

"She's going to get out," Mina gasped. "We need to run."

Evelyn shook her head. "Wait." The sand dollars over Annette's eyes, the frenzied fear in her voice—she wasn't sure the ghost was lying when she said she couldn't stop this. There was no control here. It felt way more like some kind of emotional meltdown than calculated fury. Like a wave that had built too high and was about to come crashing down.

"Annette." Evelyn couldn't meet her gaze, but she stared at the sand dollars anyway. "Is someone doing this to you?"

"She's almost a demon," Mina protested from behind her. "She only wants to hurt us—"

"Him," Annette wailed. "Help—"

And then she cut off, her head whipping to the side as if she'd been slapped. The ceiling shook again, and this time, the floor shook with it. Evelyn fell, skidding painfully onto her side. Her phone buzzed on the concrete behind her, and she swiped it away from a puddle on instinct.

She glanced at the cracked screen, and then she gasped.

An uncountable number of missed calls from Nick—and two texts.

FOUND MORE JESSE BACKUP
FOOTAGE. MINA'S COUSIN HELPED
HIM.

PLEASE CALL ASAP.

"Mina!" Evelyn threw her phone into her bag and braced her hands against the slippery floor, which had begun trembling again. Maybe it had been the storm, maybe it was the result of many years of waves eroding the cliff below it. But the foundation of this house was crumbling. "Sergio was friends with the Cliffside Trio. I think he—he—"

"That's enough."

Evelyn swore and rolled over. She tipped her head up to see Sergio Zanetti's dispassionate face. One of his hands was clenched in a fist.

The other held a gun.

Chapter Thirty-Four

Evelyn's words swirled through Mina's mind. Sergio had been close to the drowning summer victims. It was the missing piece they'd been looking for: *He* must have been the one to set them down the path of contacting a ghost. And if he'd known about that investigation, the only reason he wouldn't have told them about it...was because he had something to hide.

"You don't need a gun for a ghost," Mina said softly. Water poured onto the concrete around them as another chunk of the ceiling fell at Sergio's feet.

"Good thing that's not why I brought it," Sergio said. "You've both done what I needed. Now it's time to finish this."

"What are you doing to Annette?" Evelyn snapped. Behind her, the ghost swayed from side to side, moaning softly as she floated in the pool. Orange light crackled through the water around her. Mina had felt Annette's presence return to her mind the moment the ghost appeared to them, frizzing through her brain like static. She understood now that she'd been listening to pure, unadulterated panic.

Sergio only shrugged. "Nothing you two didn't do first."

Mina turned slowly, scared to provoke him while he held the gun. "You're bound to her, too, somehow. I . . . I thought you weren't a medium."

In answer, Sergio opened his clenched first.

Mina recognized the white plastic object inside as the same one she'd seen during her vision with Annette, flickering in and out with the sand dollar. It was some kind of hair clip, smeared with crimson, as was the rest of Sergio's palm. He must have used his blood on it.

"You have something that belonged to her," Mina whispered. "You've had it the whole time."

She'd thought Annette was trying to bargain with her. But when the ghost had said *take it*—she must have meant *take it away*. From Sergio.

Annette wailed in what might have been agreement. For once, Mina wished her bond with the ghost were stronger. Maybe then she could figure out how to stop this.

"I'm surprised it took you so long to figure it out," Sergio said.

"You murdered them." Evelyn glared at Sergio with undisguised fury. "Jesse, Colin, and Tamara—did you feed them to Annette so that she'd grow stronger? Did you *want* to make a demon?"

"No!" His voice cracked. "I— No. It was an accident."

"Yeah, some accident," Evelyn said. Sergio trained the gun on her in response, and Evelyn's face paled, her summer freckles standing out against her skin.

Mina pushed her panic down. She could feel it all later, but all that mattered right now was her and Evelyn's survival. The best way she could think to give them a fighting chance was to make Sergio believe she understood his side of the story.

"So it was an accident." She tried to sound soothing. "You didn't mean for anything to happen to your friends."

"No!" A horrible crack rang out from above, and the entire room trembled. "I had...plans. For a ghost. But they wouldn't show themselves to me like they did with Dad and Aunt Stella. So when I found out some kids in my grade were already looking into a dead girl...I figured they might want to know that if she had a good enough reason to be hanging around, there was a chance they could talk to her. They could find out everything they needed to know about her murder. And I could benefit from that summoning, because it would finally force a ghost to see me. I thought Aunt Stella might give them what they needed, but even without her I knew enough to help on my own. I told them we needed something that had belonged to the ghost...and Tamara actually found it. Apparently some of the Shorewells' stuff was left behind in the basement when they moved out."

Mina thought of the dusty old props she'd played with as a kid and shuddered. Had any of them belonged to Annette?

"When we went to the beach that day, I thought we were prepared. I had no idea she was already so strong. I didn't mean for them to die."

"But *you* didn't die," Mina said hollowly.

"No." Sergio's mouth twitched. "When the summoning went wrong, I grabbed this." He clutched the hair clip more tightly. "It kept me safe."

Because he was the only one who'd known how important it really was. Mina couldn't stand it. That he'd had the solution the entire time, that he'd seen how much Annette was hurting her...and he hadn't done anything to stop it.

"I was going to use it to make a bargain with Annette," he continued. "But Dad and Aunt Stella were on high alert right after the murders, and then the two of you summoned her, and you somehow wound up bound to her instead, and...well. I thought I'd never get another chance at power until this summer. All I've done since June is wait for you to loosen that bond on her so that I can replace it with my own. And now I have."

"Why would you bind yourself to her at all?" Mina asked, trying not to let her horror show.

Sergio smiled grimly. "I'll show you." He gripped the plastic tightly, and Annette shrieked again.

"It lets you control her," Evelyn cried out. "You want her to ascend so that she can be your...your *pet demon.*"

"Your girlfriend's got it," Sergio said, with false admiration. "That bond is a two-way street. Did you really think that if you pulled a demon through to this world, they wouldn't owe you something? Stella never told you. And you were too scared to find out for yourself."

It shouldn't have surprised Mina that a demon could be used as a tool the same way a spirit could, but the thought still horrified her.

"Dad and Aunt Stella had the right idea, experimenting with bargains," Sergio continued. "They just didn't think big enough. They should've taken advantage of the way the world is changing these ghosts, turning them into perfect weapons. Now I can show Dad that I'm a more powerful medium than he *ever* could have imagined."

Mina was still terrified, but she felt something new stirring inside that terror—understanding. He had only ever wanted to be like Dom, just like she had only ever wanted to be like Stella. But that want had warped him the same way Long Island Sound had warped Annette's spirit.

He had taken all the wrong lessons away from their parents' mistakes. Instead of trying to fix the damage they'd caused, he wanted to make it even worse to benefit himself. Mina had to stop him, no matter what.

"You have no idea how much damage an ascension will cause," Mina said. "Innocent people will die. Is that really what you want?"

"It'll be fine," Sergio said. "How big of a deal can this *really* be? Aunt Stella probably just lied to scare you, and you fell for it. Again."

The floor tilted, and Mina slid to the side, grasping frantically at the concrete. Water splashed everywhere; extinguished candles and debris pooled in the space between the wall and the window frame. Her warding vial smashed to bits. The lantern skidded toward the glass and fell through the shattered window, its glow fading into the storm as it tumbled toward the ocean. Mina's stomach lurched as she took in the view below them—the cliff's edge, the tossing waves, the rain pouring down from a bruise-colored sky. The building was collapsing. If they didn't get out soon, it would take all three of them with it. Maybe it was already too late.

Evelyn slid, too, but Sergio managed to keep his footing. Mina tried and failed to scramble toward him as he knelt at the edge of the pool, still holding the gun loosely in one hand.

"It's finally time," he breathed, stepping across the remnants of the salt circle and dunking his hand in the pool. "Come on, Shorewell. Show us what you've got."

The water in the pool crackled orange, then roared to life, a whirlpool spinning upward. Annette spun with it, orange and blue exploding across her fragmented form. Sludge spread through the water and sloshed over the edge of the pool as she clawed at the edge of the circle—then *broke through*.

Mina felt the ascension in her very bones. It was that same yearning she'd experienced all summer magnified by a thousand, crashing through her like a tidal wave. The sand dollar on Mina's wrist burned, and Mina burned with it, longing for the world she had left behind, longing to feel breath in her lungs and the sun on her face—no. *No*. Those were not her thoughts. She gasped and forced her mind back from Annette's spirit. Sergio had miscalculated: Mina was still bonded to the ghost. No—the *demon*.

Annette stood on the concrete floor, sludgy, tainted water dripping from her hands. She looked almost as solid as she had in Mina's vision. Light still spun beneath her arms and legs, but with every second that passed she was less translucent, her body returning to pale, wet flesh. Waste still seeped from beneath the sand dollars on her eyes, dripping down her cheeks like tears, and orange-gray muck pooled around her feet. She reached for one of the sand dollars and tugged, but it would not come off.

"Not so fast," Sergio said quickly. He dangled the hair clip in front of her. "I control you, remember? If you want to cross over, you need to do my bidding."

But Sergio was wrong.

Something lurched inside of Mina like a brand-new muscle

flexing for the first time. She could feel Annette's fury. Her pain. And for the first time, she didn't push it out, just like she'd let herself sink through her ocean. She reached for Annette the same way Annette had always reached for her. The sand dollar on her wrist glowed orange, but she no longer felt any pain.

"You don't control her." Mina didn't recognize her voice. "I do."

Now, she thought.

A spigot of sludge rose from the pool behind them, slamming straight into Sergio's torso and pushing him onto the floor. His gun flew across the concrete, a shot firing wildly as it slammed into the window. Evelyn screamed as crimson poured from her arm.

Mina cried out, struggling to crawl forward. But Annette was crouched between the two girls, her long, thin hands clasped around Sergio's throat. Her lips parted, chin gaping nearly to her chest as she revealed the full length of those glass-shard teeth. Orange light sparked across Sergio's slackened face as bluish-green tendrils emerged from his nostrils, then his mouth. Annette drank it in, her form growing more solid by the second.

No, Mina thought frantically. *Not like this*—

But whatever moment of control she'd had was already fading. Annette would not be stopped.

"We need to run," Evelyn called from across the room. Her arm was still bleeding, but she'd been scrabbling on the floor for something. Her hand closed into a fist—was that her warding vial? "Let's go, Mina, this whole thing's coming down—"

The floor tilted again. Water poured from the ceiling as it gaped open, and Mina was knocked backward. The wind screeched like a banshee. She slammed her head against the concrete before she punched through the broken window.

And then she was over the cliff, hurtling toward the water, and as Mina fell, she wondered if what she'd heard about drowning was true. If it only hurt when you struggled.

Mina hit the ocean so hard, it didn't feel like water at all—more like crashing against a flat surface and splintering into thousands of tiny, painful pieces. Her body was in agony, any movements useless against the pull of the current. She had no idea which way was up or down. There was only the cold, murky sea and a foggy sense of panic.

She opened her eyes and saw nothing at all. She wanted to scream but didn't—her breath was all she had.

Thirty to sixty seconds. That was how long the average person could hold their breath. How long Mina had before the water would rush into her lungs where air used to be.

She didn't want to go like this, so messy, so painful. She didn't want to go at all, but she wasn't sure she had a choice.

A light flickered in the ocean beside her, blue and faint, but there. She kicked, and it was closer. She kicked again, and it was all around her, twisting and writhing like one of her imaginary sea creatures.

And then she wasn't in the Sound anymore. She wasn't anywhere.

"You're dying."

Mina opened her eyes. The first thing she saw was the A-frame ceiling of the Shorewell Community Center. The second thing she saw was the girl kneeling beside her. Sand dollars were pressed over her eyes and sludge had congealed on her cheeks, but she looked otherwise human, and somehow that was far more disturbing than the demon Mina had seen at the pool.

Mina gasped and sat up. She could breathe, or at least she thought she could, although there was a strange tightness in her chest. When she looked down at her hands, they flickered from translucent and blue green to human flesh.

"What is this?" she whispered. "Why am I here?"

"I told you. You're dying." Annette stood, her shoes clicking on the hardwood floor as she stepped back. "Her, too."

Evelyn appeared on the hardwood floor a moment later, just a few feet away. She was curled up on her side, one arm flung out as if in protest. Blood still trickled from the wound on her shoulder. For a moment her body was blue green, just like Mina's had been, before it flickered back to normal. Her eyes opened, and she snarled out a truly impressive string of obscenities as she rose to her feet.

"Are we ghosts?" Evelyn demanded. "Because if we are, I'm going to make you wish you'd never—"

"Not yet," Annette said calmly. "But soon."

They'd both fallen into the Sound. They were drowning. And Annette's spirit was absorbing them, just like she'd absorbed Sergio.

Just like you told her to. Mina pushed that thought away. It would only make her sink faster.

"I'm tied to you," Mina said instead. "If I die, won't you?"

"You have let me cross over," Annette said. "That no longer matters to me."

But there was the slightest twinge of hesitation in her voice.

Mina remembered how closely she had felt that ascension. The bond between them wasn't broken yet.

If she could pull Annette into this world, surely her theory was right. She could push her back out.

She took a deep breath and tried to focus on that muscle again. Annette winced, flickering, and for a moment Mina saw a glimpse of seaweed twined in her hair, of the glass shards glinting in her mouth.

"Stop that," she hissed.

Encouraged, Mina reached for that pull in her mind once more, but she couldn't find it. She glanced at her wrist—her sand dollar was no longer glowing. The connection was fading fast. For a brief moment, Mina could feel the dark, cold water pressing against her skin; her lungs burned for air, her lips opened in a final breath—

And then she was back, shuddering. They didn't have much time left.

"I'm sorry for getting you into this mess," Mina said to Evelyn. She wanted her face to be the last thing she saw—that wavy, tousled hair, those wide storm-cloud eyes. "I'm sorry for everything."

And then Evelyn gave her that smile. The one Mina had seen a hundred times this summer. The one that meant *We've got this.*

"Don't be," she said, and took her hand.

Mina felt it immediately: the plastic shape of the hair clip clasped between both of their palms. Somehow, some way, Evelyn had kept hold of it. Hope surged in her as they turned back toward Annette, together.

Maybe they couldn't give this exorcism their blood. But Mina hoped they had both offered up enough of a sacrifice the moment they hit the water. That two mediums would be enough in a way even her bond with Annette couldn't be.

Mina's wrist began to glow bluish green, and for once, its pulse felt comforting.

"I banish you, Annette Shorewell," Mina said, the words ringing out through the illusory living room. "You have no power here."

A great groaning rang out through the room, and the floor began to shudder. Cracks appeared in the wooden floor, eerily similar to the ones in the concrete beside the pool.

"What are you doing?" the demon snarled, advancing toward them. Her body was turning translucent again, glass bristling in her mouth, seaweed winding through her hair. Her arms were too long, her extended nails jagged, broken bits of shell. "I hold your lives in my hands. I—"

Both of them squeezed the hair clip, and the demon let out an agonizing wail. Mina was overcome by a sudden surge of guilt. She was a girl who had been murdered, then warped, then controlled by Sergio.

But no—she was not a girl anymore. She was a *demon*. She had bent the rules of life and death so hard, they'd broken. And it was Mina's job—no, Mina's calling—to find some way to send her back where she belonged.

"I banish you," Evelyn said. "Leave the spirits you've taken and the people you've hurt."

Another crack, this time from the ceiling. The whole room was shuddering now, flickering in and out. The furniture had disappeared. The A-frame ceiling slid apart, and murky water poured through. It coiled around Annette like a whirlpool. She wailed, clawing at the air with her hands. Orange light spread through her again, so bright it hurt to look at, and Mina's sand dollar pulsed again.

"I banish you," they said together. Annette fell to her knees, snarling. Voices swirled through Mina's mind, shrieking and wailing; wind blew the world away. But she and Evelyn were still standing as the water rose. Still holding hands. Mina would die before she let go.

Annette's body convulsed, twisting into strange, incomprehensible shapes. She stretched out one blue-green hand—and for a moment, just a moment, she changed.

She was still translucent. Still a ghost. But a girl now, the sand dollars gone from her eyes. Mina met her wide, horrified gaze.

"It's time," Mina said, and Annette's face softened for a moment. Maybe it was resignation. Maybe it was relief.

"I know," the demon whispered. And then her body unspooled, blue and green and orange twisting away from one another into a thousand tiny tendrils. The water crashed over their heads, and Mina's hand was wrenched away from Evelyn's.

The last thing she felt before her consciousness faded away was the cold, numbing embrace of the sea.

Chapter Thirty-Five

Evelyn woke up in the hospital, where she spent the next few days being treated for the bullet wound in her arm and the water she'd aspirated into her lungs. Mina had been admitted, too, but she'd gotten some kind of poisoning from the waste in the water *and* suffered a cerebral injury that required more extensive care. The doctors wouldn't let anyone but family see her, despite Evelyn's best attempts to persuade them otherwise.

She did have distractions, though. First there were the police, who asked her a lot of questions about Sergio Zanetti. She told them he had lured her and Mina to the community center and shot her before the whole thing crumbled into the ocean, which was technically true. They told *her* that his body had washed up on the shore, drowned. And they asked if she knew anything about recent evidence that had come to light connecting him to Cliffside Trio.

Evelyn knew they were putting pieces together, telling themselves whatever story would suit this whole mess. She didn't trust them, but she knew they no longer suspected her father. She hoped that would be enough. And when she considered Sergio's death, she could only manage to view it as a tragedy when she thought of the pain Mina must be feeling.

As for his ghost… well. Evelyn hadn't felt any trace of Sergio's spirit yet, but she looked forward to exorcising him.

Once they were finished questioning her, more visitors came. Her dad, of course, who told her in a low voice that her mother had paid for the hospital bills. Evelyn tried to find the energy to be upset about that and decided it was the least Siobhan could do for them both. Ruthie and Marvin brought her soup and a GET WELL SOON card from Mr. Clark. Mrs. Morales gave her a tote bag full of library books. And Luisa, Amy, and Kenny showed up with leftover Basic Bean pastries plus reptile videos from Scales & Tails. Luisa and Kenny also admitted they were dating, which Amy was appropriately smug about.

"So she's gone?" Nick asked her. "Annette, I mean." He'd come to see her the day she was supposed to be discharged. Her dad had brought her favorite cutoffs and T-shirt to the hospital. Putting them on had felt so good, she'd nearly cried.

"Yeah," Evelyn said. "We exorcised her. Your brother and his friends are free."

"What about Jesse's spirit? Is he gone, too?"

Evelyn had lost her scrying focus during the exorcism, which had led to strange dreams and stranger visions, brief glimpses of other lives and whispering new voices. She could feel the drowning summer victims, but they didn't linger out of pain the way they had before. Although there *was* something expectant about their presence in her head.

I'll help you soon, she promised them, swirling the water glass on her nightstand.

"I don't think so," she said. "When Mina and I are out of here, we'll give you the goodbye you deserve."

"Tamara's and Colin's families are back in town," Nick said. "Because of... everything. The sixth anniversary of their deaths is this week, and they're holding a private memorial for their kids."

Evelyn didn't ask how he knew that. Obviously, he'd been invited.

"Maybe that's what their spirits are waiting for," she said. "One final goodbye."

"Maybe," Nick said. "But I don't think that's the whole story. I confronted my parents about Jesse, and they admitted that they knew about the Blue Tide plant. So I... I've been talking to a reporter. I've handed over copies of everything Jesse found. The world needs to know the truth, even if we can't prove it."

Evelyn felt surprised, then vindicated. What the Sand Dollar Corporation and Slater Enterprises had done was unequivocally wrong. But what had come after was far more complicated. A ghost left to the mercies of a changing world and an erratic ocean. And a family of mediums with just enough ego and desperation to give Annette's spirit the power she'd wanted.

Two months ago, Evelyn would have been determined to expose the Slaters and the plant's corruption to the world regardless of how Nick felt about it. But she knew how painful it was to be forced into the spotlight for something she hadn't personally done. It was not a decision she wanted to make for Nick. She was glad that it was one he'd made himself.

"I hope you're ready for the consequences," she said.

"I know I'm not. But it's what Jesse would have wanted. And I'm not going to stay quiet just because it makes my life easier."

"I think he'd be proud of you," she said. "Jesse, I mean. You're way less of an asshole than you could be."

Nick snorted. "Thanks, I guess." But Evelyn could tell he wasn't mad at her.

There was one more thing she wanted to say to him. She felt obligated, even though she knew it would hurt him, and this summer had already hurt him a *lot*.

"And I...I know this summer hasn't been easy on you, for a lot of reasons," Evelyn said. "But you should know that Mina and I are kind of dating? I think?"

Nick's mouth twitched, but his voice was calm. "You think I didn't notice you two were into each other?"

Evelyn flushed. "I just don't want you to hear it from someone else."

"I get it." He hesitated. "I'm not going to pretend I wasn't jealous. Or that this won't be weird for me, at least for a little while."

It was hard for Evelyn not to wonder if any part of that weirdness was because Mina was a girl. But then she studied Nick, who was looking at her so earnestly, and she decided that wasn't a fair judgment to make. Nick was still handsome, still careful with that artfully mussed dark brown hair, but there was a gentleness to his face now that Evelyn hadn't noticed before. Neither of them were the people they had been two months ago.

"I understand," she said. "But if you ever need someone to talk to about your family being in the news, and your life being harder because of it...I've got your back."

Evelyn's final visitor was Stella Zanetti.

She hadn't even known the woman was awake, let alone at the point where she could visit other patients. But there she was, still managing to look intimidating and cool in a hospital gown.

"Evelyn Mackenzie," she said, lowering herself into one of the plastic visitor chairs and gesturing for Evelyn to join her. "I believe we need to have a chat."

"Uh," Evelyn said, "have you talked to Mina?"

"A little bit." Stella folded her hands in her lap primly. The gesture reminded Evelyn so much of Mina that it physically hurt. "She's still in and out of consciousness. I'm afraid I've only been able to catch her awake for a few minutes."

It took everything Evelyn had not to run down the hallway and try kicking Mina's door open. "Is she going to be okay?"

"The doctors are almost certain she will make a full recovery."

Evelyn didn't like that *almost*, but she'd heard the same thing about herself a few days ago, and she was fine. Or at least mostly fine. Breathing still felt like throat knives sometimes, and her shoulder ached, but she could handle that.

"She better," Evelyn mumbled.

"Or what? You'll threaten the cosmos?"

"Isn't that basically what you did to save her life?"

Stella's expression remained neutral, but her voice sounded amused. "Touché. Listen—I'm here to apologize. I know what happened with Sergio. And I also know how difficult I made your life this summer. I wanted to blame anyone but my family for our own mistakes, but it was completely inappropriate of me to target my misplaced rage on you."

"Thanks," Evelyn said cautiously.

"We owe you a great debt. Without you, my daughter and I would almost definitely be dead."

"Hey, Mina's pretty smart. She probably could've figured this out alone."

"Perhaps, although you certainly made it easier," Stella said. "You aren't a Zanetti medium, Evelyn. But I never should have asked you to be. You are building your own practice. Making rules that work for you. It's all right if you want nothing to do with me, but...I am happy to offer any guidance you might need."

Part of Evelyn really wanted someone around to answer questions. The Zanettis were why she could speak to the dead—even if she wasn't going to be just like them, she couldn't deny that Stella's experience might come in handy. But that didn't feel like enough when stacked up against everything else Stella had done.

"You pushed the police toward my dad after the drowning summer," she said. "I don't think I can forget that. And you're right that I'm not a Zanetti medium. I pay attention to what's really going on here. The Sound *is* special, and it's also hurting. So I'm going to figure out how to protect it as best I can and make it as safe as possible for the living and the dead. Without you."

Stella's small, pointed face remained unchanged. But Evelyn had spent all summer watching Mina's emotional control, and she could tell from the small stiffening in her shoulders that this had hurt.

"I'll respect that decision," she said. "But Mina told me that you two are seeing each other. And so all I can do is hope that one day, you'll have forgiven me enough to come to dinner at our house again. Consider it an open invitation."

Evelyn understood in that moment that Stella wasn't doing this for her. She was doing it for Mina. Trying to be the best mother she could in the wake of this summer's disasters. She hoped for Mina's sake that the two of them would be able to heal.

"Mina's important to me," Evelyn said. "And I know it would mean a lot to her if I could forgive you. So I'll try. But if I *do* accept that invitation, it'll be for her sake. Not yours."

Stella nodded once, sharply. "I understand."

Chapter Thirty-Six

The first thing Stella Zanetti did the day Mina got home from the hospital was make stuffed artichokes. Mina hovered uncomfortably in the back of the kitchen as her mother mixed together bread crumbs and cheese, then cut the tips off the artichokes with kitchen scissors and cored them until the feathery choke at the vegetable's center was gone.

Mina had been in the hospital for a week. For the first few days she had been in and out of consciousness, a weak, feverish shell of herself. She'd hit her head as she fell, and the resulting damage of nearly drowning hadn't helped. But she felt mostly better, aside from a small shaved patch on the back of her head that was easily covered and a lingering sensation of saltwater in her mouth.

The sand dollar on her wrist was gone. Mina didn't know exactly when it had disappeared, but she was certain it would never come back.

"I'm thinking of making these part of my new catering

menu." The Shorewell Community Center had collapsed into the ocean along with a great chunk of the cliff, so Stella was in the market for a new job. She already had a few offers from local hotels. "Pull off the leaves and they'll be two dozen little herbed artichoke bits. They're a perfect appetizer."

Now that she was home, Mina could tell neither of them knew where to begin, so her mother had started the only way she knew how: food.

"Mom," Mina said quietly.

Stella turned to face her properly. The corners of her mouth were quivering. For the first time, Mina noticed streaks of gray in her long brown hair.

"Yes?"

And then Mina pulled her into a hug, and Stella's arms gently closed around her shoulders, still covered in artichoke and bread crumbs. She wasn't sure which of them started crying first, only that they were both unable to stop for a very long time.

They wound up on the kitchen floor, which felt right.

"I lied to you about so much," Stella said. "*I'm sorry* doesn't feel big enough. I struggle to believe any words could."

Mina had done a lot of thinking once the haziness in her mind faded. About what her mother had done and why. About how it had felt the first time she saw Stella's face hovering over her own in that hospital bed—like she could finally remember how to breathe again.

"I lied to you, too," Mina said.

"Well, yes, but you're sixteen, my seashell." Stella patted her hand. "You're supposed to lie to your mother."

"About partying, maybe. I don't think any of the normal adolescence stereotypes cover demonic ascension."

"Perhaps not," Stella admitted. "But my point still stands. I deceived you, and that's unacceptable."

"It's not—I—" Mina sighed. "The lying isn't what I'm upset about. At least, not anymore."

"Then what is it?" Stella asked. The oven glowed behind her—Stella had insisted on putting the artichokes in before she sat down. The smell of lemon-herb-Parmesan dip was starting to spread through the room, but when Mina tried to inhale it, she got a mouthful of salt instead.

She winced and braced her back against the cabinet. It came in waves, this pain, and it always brought a cascade of memories with it.

"You tried to sacrifice yourself for me. Why did you think that would make things better?" It came out like the accusation it was.

Stella's face trembled, but she squeezed Mina's hand.

"I've had some time to think about that," her mother said. "It's true that I felt I was to blame for what had happened to you, and that I wanted you to be safe. But I also know it's in my nature to self-destruct when I feel as if I've failed."

Mina remembered herself on the beach the night after her and Stella's first big fight and shuddered.

"Mine, too," she whispered. "But I've learned that doesn't actually help very much. Mostly it just makes the whole situation worse."

"I wish I'd understood that earlier," Stella said. "It would have saved us both a lot of trouble."

Mina sniffled. "Yes. It would have."

"There's something else," Stella said quietly. "Uncle Dom would like to come stay with us for a little while, if that's all right with you."

"I understand."

He'd visited her in the hospital once she'd improved, but it had been difficult. Mostly her uncle had cried in his gruff way—reddened eyes, blowing his nose a lot—as he had told her, over and over again, that he'd had no idea what Sergio was up to. Mina believed that neither of them had known. Her mother and her uncle were imperfect, but they weren't monsters.

"I don't know how I could have missed his involvement," Stella said. "I feel such guilt. We both do."

"He didn't kill them," Mina said. "The ghost did that."

"But he still bears the responsibility for their deaths."

The betrayal Mina felt at Sergio's deception would take a long time to parse through. She was shaken to her core by how terrifying he'd been in the community center, how he'd used her grief for Stella to his own vile ends. She couldn't understand how he had seen the way the ghosts were changing and wanted to take advantage of it instead of being horrified by it.

They'd stopped him, but only just. And now that he was dead, Mina faced the complex calculus of grieving...and waiting for his voice to appear in her head.

"It's curious that he hasn't arrived yet," Stella continued, touching her new scrying object—a small dove on a bracelet. "His spirit is most certainly unsettled, but I haven't felt it at all. Nor has Dom."

Mina had her own theory as to why his spirit hadn't shown

up yet. One that made her feel both hollow and relieved. She knew what she had commanded Annette to do to Sergio after her ascension. She didn't know what absorbing a living person's spirit did to them, but maybe it destroyed their soul for good. Maybe she had been responsible for the unimaginable.

Mina never wanted to use that kind of power again. She felt the beginnings of something she could stuff in a chest, bury in the endless depths of her ocean, but no. She wouldn't shove her fears away anymore. She'd already thought about talking to a therapist about some of it, but there were pieces she couldn't share with anyone but Evelyn. It would hurt, but it wouldn't fester, and maybe that would be enough.

She knew not sharing this with Stella would mean one more lie between them. One more secret. But she hoped it was a secret she'd be ready to tell one day, when the time was right. And after all her mother had done to both of them... Mina felt she was owed a little processing time.

"We'll be ready for him," she said.

The timer went off, and Stella retrieved the artichokes, her hair illuminated in the glow of the oven. They ate in the living room, sitting close together on the orange velvet couch. The leaves were delicious, stuffed with bread crumbs and cheese all melted into the meat of the artichoke.

"I figured we could have garlic-Parmesan popcorn for dessert," Stella said. "And then a movie marathon. Whichever ones you want."

"That sounds excellent," Mina said. "But I do want to talk about how it's going to be with us. From now on, I mean. With medium training... and with everything else."

"Evelyn has elected not to work with me," Stella said carefully.

Mina was unsurprised. "I'm more willing than she is. But I don't ever want to go back to the way things were before. I don't think I can."

"Well, what *do* you want?" Stella asked her.

"I'd love to talk to the rest of our family," Mina said. "I believe that even though my sand dollar mark is gone, my bond with Annette shaped the way I communicate with ghosts. I don't need a scrying focus. I'm already attuned to the dead. I'm hoping that if I can get access to more mediums, I can find some tips on how to handle this kind of connection."

Stella looked at her gravely. "I suspected as much," she said. "Dominic and I have already reached out to them about the Sergio situation. I'm unsure they'll listen to us, but if they respond, I will put you in contact with them."

Mina nodded. "That sounds good. And I—I want you to listen to me, Mom. Answer my questions. Where we go from there—I don't know."

"I will try my best," Stella said.

It wasn't perfect. But it was a start.

Mina had always known that Stella loved her more than anything in the world. Now, she wondered if her mother loved her enough to change.

She wanted to believe she could.

The Basic Bean was winding down. It had been a long day of oppressive August heat, and Mina had watched customer after customer ask for something iced and soothing to beat back the humidity. She stirred her drink—it had been on the house— as she watched Evelyn flit to and fro behind the counter in a whirl of energy, ringing up customers and calling back orders to Kenny and Amy.

"What do you think?" Luisa asked from her seat across the table. Mina swiped through the photos on her phone. The two of them had spent the afternoon at her house, staging a photo shoot with the Zanetti Collection before they went to meet up with the others. Luisa looked amazing in the romper, while Mina had sheepishly donned the wide-leg trousers. She eyed her face with surprise—she looked hesitant, but happy.

"I think they're perfect," she said. "I can't wait to do the rest."

"Amy's already called dibs on modeling that new jacket you're working on. She says it's going to make her look like a goth pirate."

"And that's a good thing?"

"Coming from her, that's a high compliment."

"Well, all right, then," Mina said. "I can take her measurements today, if she wants."

The two of them had teamed up—Luisa wanted to take photos to submit as her portfolio for a photography internship in the city, and Mina needed the photos so she could finally start promoting her work on social media. It was nowhere near ready to sell, but she wanted to get the word out there. She'd committed to creating everything out of secondhand materials as much as possible. It was better for the environment *and* it made for a cool challenge with every garment.

While they were working together, Luisa confessed to Mina

that she had a secret photography page with more than twenty thousand followers, but she'd been too shy to share it.

"Trust me," Mina had told her. "It's worth telling your friends what you care about."

The others' shift ended, and they crowded around the table. Mina wound up squished between Kenny and Evelyn, who grabbed her hand and squeezed it reassuringly.

"You're all in for my show tonight, right?" Amy asked, leaning across the table.

"Mina?" asked Evelyn.

"I'm not great with crowds, but I'll try."

"Us neither," Luisa said. "But the band's really good."

"They are," Kenny confirmed. "I've been helping them record an EP."

Evelyn had told Mina that Kenny was really into podcasts, but apparently he was also into audio engineering. Mina studied all of them and wondered how it was that they'd accepted her so readily when she was a total stranger. But they'd accepted Evelyn, too, and Mina's afternoon with Luisa had felt so . . . easy.

If she wanted to protect Cliffside Bay, she needed to be part of it just like Evelyn was. Which meant she'd need to build a community in her own way, with her own goals. Actually trying to make friends seemed like a good first step.

The others began to pack up, talking excitedly about the concert ahead. But Kenny lingered behind. He cleared his throat and adjusted his horn-rimmed glasses.

"Um, hey," he said. "There's something I've always wanted to ask you about. I hope it isn't too weird."

"If it's too weird, I'll tell you," Mina said.

"Okay. Well—your family. You know those rumors that you're all kind of...witchy? How true are they?"

Mina allowed herself a slow, self-indulgent smile. "Would you believe me if I said they were?"

Kenny gulped, looking rattled. Mina could tell he had absolutely no idea if she was kidding.

"Do you want a ride or not?" called Amy. "I borrowed Dad's car."

"Well?" Evelyn asked, but Mina knew she was mostly asking her. "Are you coming?"

"Yes," Mina said. And Evelyn's grin made it impossible for her not to smile back.

Chapter Thirty-Seven

The August humidity was an unwelcome blanket against Evelyn's skin. She squinted through her sunglasses at the beach before her, taking in the view—strips of timber, some as tall as her and others as small as splinters, a few plastic corsages from the wedding props, and, as always, the inevitable shower of glass. New debris from the Shorewell Community Center washed up on the coast each morning. And Evelyn was there to meet it three times a week, armed with gloves, a trash bag, and whichever volunteers had joined her.

"Do you think you can help me lift that?" she asked, pointing to the largest slab of wood.

"I know a challenge when I hear one," said her father. He'd been Evelyn's most constant beach cleanup companion, dutifully meeting her at the front door with his car keys, his bucket hat, and a tube of sunblock. "You think your old man's not strong enough?"

"Go prove me wrong, I guess."

The investigation into Sergio's death had lifted the six-year cloud of suspicion that had hovered over Greg Mackenzie. And while his exoneration hadn't fixed everything, it had helped in the ways that Evelyn cared about most. Her father left the house again for reasons other than a work shift. He went on nature walks. He kayaked. He'd even tried to make veggie burgers from scratch, although they'd come out terribly.

She had a father again. But for all she'd gained this summer, she'd lost someone, too. Evelyn thought about unblocking Meredith's number every day, but she wasn't ready yet. She was pretty sure she would be one day, but it would be a long, long road before she could trust her sister again. She'd even gone to the trouble of transferring the account info at the bank—her father was the one who could technically see her balance now.

"Am I late?" called a familiar voice as Evelyn and her father heaved the slab of lumber into the parking lot. A truck pulled into the nearest spot, maneuvering clumsily before revving to a halt. Mina stepped out a moment later, wearing her best approximation of beach cleanup gear. It cracked Evelyn up how hard it was for her to look truly dressed down.

"Nope," Evelyn said. They'd gone on that date, kind of. It had been intended as a picnic, but mostly they'd just talked and forgotten to eat their snacks, then laid close together on the blanket while arguing about cloud shapes. Inevitably, the conversation turned to strategizing about the way the Sound was still warping ghosts. And then to the Slater story, which was still in the works. Neither of them knew what to expect when it dropped. But there were peaceful moments, too, when Evelyn could just feel lucky that she got to hold hands with the girl she liked in public and feel at home.

"Here's your cool claw thing," she said, handing Mina a reaching aid. They'd gotten an anonymous donation to purchase supplies last week. Evelyn suspected it had come from Ruthie, although she wasn't saying anything. "And a garbage bag. Stick whatever trash you've got in the truck."

It hadn't been too hard to get people to sign up for her project. She'd made a social media group that had gotten shared pretty widely, leading to some helpful conversations with people organizing similar cleanup efforts in their own towns. Today it was just her, her dad, and Mina, although her friends and Nick had started coming, too, along with a few others. But she wasn't stopping there.

There was a binder in her room growing thicker by the day with ideas for what she'd started calling the Cliffside Bay Conservation Initiative. Forget waiting for someone to give her an internship: She was making her own.

And Evelyn was making her life as a medium her own, too. Part of that binder was dedicated to her new ecological focus: how she could combine mitigating the effects of pollution and climate change on Long Island Sound with her work communicating with ghosts.

She'd found a new scrying focus during one of these beach cleanups, a tiny piece of the debris, and she understood that her bond to this ocean was just as complex as the range of life that dwelled inside it.

It was overwhelming sometimes to consider the mess that she and Mina were still in. Banishing Annette had been a victory, but that felt incredibly small when stacked up against the dual pressures of the unsettled dead and the fragile, precious life that fought to survive in an increasingly hostile ecosystem.

Whenever Evelyn felt like she was drowning in the unfairness of it all—how little they had asked for this, how much it had already hurt them—she remembered that at least she had an excellent partner working on it with her. She didn't understand how she'd ever thought she could survive alone, but she was glad to know better now.

"What do you think?" her father asked when they were done. It had been a long, exhausting morning. But Evelyn felt good. The truck was full of garbage bags, and Mina had agreed to drive them all to the dump this afternoon. She hugged her goodbye, then snuck in a kiss on her cheek while her dad was busy clearing up more debris.

"Does the beach look a little better?" her dad asked, finally peeling off his gloves.

"It does." Evelyn took a long sip from her water bottle. "You know, Dad—I've been thinking about something. I still really want to study wildlife ecology, but I'd like to focus on the Sound. Stony Brook University is only thirty minutes away, *and* it has an amazing environmental science program."

"The world's a big place," her father said. "Don't feel like you need to stay here."

"I don't," Evelyn said. "I used to think I was trapped in Cliffside Bay. And I *do* want to travel, to understand more about the world. But I love the Sound so much. I want to spend the rest of my life helping it."

Her father's voice was gruff. "You have no idea how proud I am of you."

They stood like that for a while, watching the surf roll in and out. Evelyn loved the rhythm of it, like the Sound was breathing. She thought of the ghosts buried beneath the murky water, of the debris that hung around her neck. It was a place of so much joy and so much pain. And she was just as much a part of it as each of the waves that crashed upon the shore.

She wouldn't have it any other way.

Chapter Thirty-Eight

This time, the dead came calling at sunset. Mina felt them tugging at her from the living room, where she and Stella sat in the candlelight, trying an assortment of appetizers from her updated catering menu.

"Do you feel that?" she asked her mother, setting down a spoonful of homemade ravioli.

Stella nodded, her hand moving automatically to her new scrying focus. "They're here."

Mina looked at the place on her wrist where the sand dollar mark had been. Bluish-green light pulsed beneath her skin, and voices murmured through her mind. She clutched the new warding necklace Evelyn had made her from a glass vial filled with ocean water, then honed in on the spirits she was trying to listen to. It was something they were working on together as a way to keep Mina's abilities under control. They were still testing it out, but Mina knew these spirits meant her no harm.

"They're ready," she said.

"Good." Stella hesitated. "I assume you two will want to take this one on your own."

"Yes."

"You know I'm here if you need help, though."

"I know," Mina said. "But we won't."

She swung open the back door and stepped onto the porch as blue light teased gently around the veins at her wrist. Her phone began to buzz, and she lifted it to her ear, smiling at the familiar sound of Evelyn's voice.

"Meet me on the beach," Mina said.

The stairs didn't feel nearly as treacherous as they had at the beginning of the summer, although they were still crunchy with salt. She kicked off her sandals the moment she touched down in Sand Dollar Cove, her breathing a little labored. The damage done by her head injury and near-drowning was mostly healed, but her lungs still ached if she did too much physical activity.

It didn't take long for Evelyn to join her on the beach, wearing cutoffs, a cropped T-shirt, and a flannel tied around her waist. She hurried up to Mina and wrapped her in a hug, then planted a kiss on her collarbone. She'd started to make a habit of that. Mina had pointed out multiple times that her lips were available, and Evelyn had countered by making a big show of their height difference and how far she had to stretch to reach them.

"The sacrifices I make for pretty girls," she'd declared dramatically, while Mina tried and failed not to laugh.

"You ready?" Evelyn murmured now, her breath soft against Mina's shoulder.

Mina kissed the top of her head. "Now I am."

There wasn't much setup to do when they used the ocean as a scrying bowl. There were still candles—a barrier between the living and the dead, each placed in the sand. But the salt in the water seemed to work well enough by itself now. The Cliffside Trio's personal items had been lost along with the community center, but Mina knew it wouldn't matter. Blue lights had already appeared on the horizon, bobbing and shifting on the waves like bits of debris. These ghosts had waited until the new moon, but they were ready to go now.

Nick arrived just when they were lighting the last few candles.

"There was traffic," he said hastily.

"We wouldn't have started without you," Mina said.

"Thanks." His eyes strayed to the ocean. "Is that..."

"Yeah," Evelyn said. "Are you going to be okay?"

"I mean, no," he said hoarsely. "But also yes. Does that make sense?"

It did, at least to Mina.

They barely got through one round of chanting before the ghosts began to materialize. They arrived all together, their bluish-green forms drifting in the surf. Tamara, Colin, and Jesse—for the last time. Orange light still flickered around the spirits' edges, but there were no longer sand dollars over their eyes.

Nick let out a soft whimper at the sight of his brother. Mina put a calming hand on his shoulder. After what he'd done to help them both, a little comfort felt like the least she could do.

"Are you ready?" she asked the ghosts. They nodded.

Mina waded into the surf, Evelyn beside her. She reached forward and touched Colin's hand. The moment their fingers brushed, he started to disintegrate, blue light spilling out onto the waves. On her left, she saw Tamara's spirit was doing the same. Soon only Jesse was left, staring right at Nick.

"Go ahead," Mina said gently, turning. "You can say goodbye."

She and Evelyn stepped back, and Nick stepped forward. He was weeping openly now, sniffling; the words he spoke were soft and choked, too low for Mina to hear over the surf. She was grateful for that. This moment belonged to Nick and Jesse alone.

"Okay," he said finally, his voice cracking. "I'm ready."

He stepped back. Mina and Evelyn stepped forward. Together, they reached for Jesse's outstretched hands, and as he melted away into the surf, he did so with a smile.

When he was gone, the beach felt strangely empty. Nick excused himself quickly, explaining that he'd known this would be hard on him and he needed to process it privately.

The tide rose gently on the beach as she and Evelyn cleaned up, both of them still a little misty-eyed. The moon was new tonight, and the dark, peaceful sky felt like an ending and a beginning all at once.

"It's done now," Evelyn said after the candles had been put away. "Is it weird that I keep bracing myself for whatever happens next?"

"I don't think so," Mina said. "I've been doing the same."

There would be more ghosts. Maybe more demons, too. The line between life and death would ebb and flow like the tides, changing in ways that demanded adaptation. But she had Evelyn now. She had the cliffs and the beach, the stars winking down onto Sand Dollar Cove, the moon that, although invisible, still felt as if it were watching them from its impossibly high perch in the sky.

"Wait," Mina said, turning to Evelyn. "Before we go home, there's something I want to do."

She'd already kicked off her shoes, but now she shrugged out of her thin cardigan and tossed it on the sand. Her ruffled shorts and tank top would get salt on them, but that didn't really matter. Mina knew this could be dangerous. Most of the debris had been cleared from the water, but there was still a chance it could hurt her. And there might be hostile spirits waiting for her beneath the waves.

But there would always be danger. And Mina was done succumbing to fear.

She waded into the surf, pulse pounding in time with the crashing waves. And then she dove beneath the water, salt stinging her eyes, the Sound cool and refreshing against her skin. When she came back up, Evelyn was laughing so hard she was doubled over.

"You always surprise me," she managed to choke out, untying her flannel. "Now wait up."

Mina's wrist glowed beneath the water as Evelyn waded in, a tiny blue lantern, but she heard no voices in her head besides her own.

The ocean in her mind stirred to life again. For so long, Mina had dreaded this sensation, but now she welcomed the surge of emotion. She would no longer be afraid to immerse herself in it.

And she wouldn't sink. She wouldn't drown.

She would swim.

Acknowledgments

The Drowning Summer feels like a book carved straight from my heart in more ways than I can count, and over the last five years, I've done my best to write Evelyn and Mina the story they deserve. But so many others have championed this book along its road to publication, and all of them deserve my gratitude.

Kelly Sonnack, my agent—thank you for being a constant champion throughout my career. This book has been on quite the journey, but you've provided unfailing support for me and this project at every step. I'm so grateful to be your client.

Deirdre Jones, my editor—thank you for all your help with bringing Evelyn, Mina, and Cliffside Bay to life. Your sharp insights and suggestions have been instrumental in making *The Drowning Summer* the book I've always dreamed it would be.

Thanks as well to the entire team at Little, Brown Books for Young Readers, including Hallie Tibbetts, Jen Graham, Erica Ferguson, Patricia Alvarado, Stefanie Hoffman, Shanese Mullins, Katie Boni, Savannah Kennelly, Christie Michel, Shawn Foster, Danielle Cantarella, Anna Herling, Celeste Gordon,

Katie Tucker, and Naomi Kennedy. Cliffside Bay and all its ghosts are in very good hands.

And a huge thank-you to Karina Granda, Patrick Hulse, and brilliant artist Carolina Rodríguez Fuenmayor for creating a book cover and jacket that suits *The Drowning Summer* perfectly.

Hannah Hill—you understood exactly what this story meant to me from the very beginning. Thank you so much for everything. I'll always cherish the time we spent working together.

Amanda—whether it's taking on the real world or polishing up a fictional one, there's no one I'd rather have at my side. Thank you for literally holding my hand through my darkest moments and figuratively holding my hand while I patched up my plot holes.

Rory—words are my job, but I fail to find the right ones for how much you mean to me or how much you helped me with this book. Evelyn and Mina wouldn't be the same without you, and neither would I.

Allison Saft and Akshaya Raman—thank you for reading versions of *TDS* that were decidedly unfinished and giving me the support and love I needed to make this book better. Sarah Hollowell—thank you for reading it *twice* and talking through everything.

To the rest of the Cult, including Kat Cho, Janella Angeles, Mara Fitzgerald, Axie Oh, Meg Kohlmann, Maddy Colis, Erin K. Bay, Tara Sim, Katy Rose Pool, Ashley Burdin, Claribel Ortega, Melody Simpson, Amanda Haas, and Alexis Castellanos—I'm so incredibly grateful to be part of our crew.

Thanks as well to Emma Theriault for the writing sprints, Rosiee Thor for the garden updates, Jenn Dugan for some very coordinated TV watching, and June Tan for the cat pictures. All of you kept me going through revisions.

A very special thank-you to my parents, to Poppy, to Aunt Sally and Uncle Louie and everyone else in my family who really *knows* Long Island, for answering my questions and telling me their stories. I'd also like to thank my siblings, who have kept me from sinking more times than I can count.

Nova—I'm sorry, no cats in this one. But I'm happy to negotiate on future projects. Trevor—whether the water is calm or stormy, whether the moon is new or full, whether the tide is high or low—I love you.

To the readers who've stuck with me from Four Paths to Ilvernath—I hope you enjoyed your visit to Cliffside Bay, ghosts and all.

And to my younger self, wading through the Sound with barnacle-scraped feet and hair coated in salt, full of feelings I didn't yet understand: I wrote this book for the ocean inside of you.